AS IT SEEMS

Jayne Conway

DEDICATION

I dedicate this book to the survivors.
You know who you are.

REWIND

"If I could but know his heart, everything
would become easy."
~Jane Austen

PROLOGUE

L ibby leans back against the heated leather seat, listening to the low hum of the radio while she sits in the warm cocoon of her car. *Should I stay or should I go?* The frigid November rain has been falling relentlessly since the previous morning and the heavy sheet obscures her surroundings. Littleton, Nantucket, Providence, Bayside, Boston? Squinting her eyes, she scans the parking lot for familiar signs but the buildings and cars are blurred, the colors running together; an Impressionist painting. It's beautiful. She could be anywhere; a different time, another place.

Lifting her digital camera from its case, she removes the lens cap and adjusts the focus to capture the watercolor created by the fat droplets of rain on her windshield. Click, click, click. She takes a dozen photographs and smiles to herself as she reviews them. *These are good. I may be able to use these. There's a new series here...*

She returns the camera to it's case and pulls the wool-lined raincoat close to her body, taking deep breaths in and out, deliberating whether to get out of the car. She's not afraid of braving the storm outside; it's the one raging in her head stopping her. *I'm safe here*, she thinks, leaning her head against the steering wheel. *Nothing can hurt me if I stay*. She arrived thirty minutes early and has been sitting in the parking lot for over ten. This is her opportunity to escape without being seen. He'll be here soon and the choice will be much more difficult to make once she sees him.

What am I doing? The past few times they got together were agonizing, both of them pretending to be fine, trying to pick up where they left off before that fateful day. It's impossible! If there's one thing she's learned over the past couple of years...*you can't go back.* There is no rewind button. One split second decision is all it takes to change the course of someone's life.

Everything is different now, their lives unrecognizable from the ones they were living just a few months ago. She's changed. He's changed. Holding onto the past can only cause her pain, and that, she does not need! She's created a good life for herself out of the wreckage. The kids are happy; her career is satisfying. Why would she deliberately put herself in emotional harms way?

Because I love him. Because I want what we had.

Knock! Knock! Knock! Libby jumps in her seat, her heart stopping in her chest. Someone is fiddling with the handle on the front passenger side door and she takes a moment before rolling down the window a crack, then breathes a giant sigh of relief when Ginger's face comes into view.

"Jesus, Libby! Let me in!" Ginger cries, her face wet from the rain, hair sticking to her face.

Libby unlocks the door, quickly clearing the camera case and random papers from the seat to make room for her friend.

"Oh my God!" Ginger says, climbing in. "It's crazy out there!"

She slams the door shut and Libby hands her the few napkins she finds in the console to dry her face.

"Well?" Ginger asks after a minute. "Are you coming in?"

Libby bites her lip and turns her face away, then shakes her head.

"No," she whispers.

"C'mon, Lib," Ginger pleads, resting her hand on Libby's. "Just one cup of coffee."

"I can't do this, Ging. I just can't..." her voice trails off.

Ginger leans her head back against the seat, her eyes closed.

"I can't force you, Lib," she murmurs. "I just wish things were different."

So do I, Ginger. So do I.

"I'll call you later," Ginger sighs and kisses Libby on the cheek. "Love you."

"Love you, too," Libby replies, relief flooding her body.

Ginger climbs out of the car, then races across the parking lot and into the coffee shop. Libby turns the wipers on to watch her go and a minute later, shifts the car into drive. Before she pulls away, she notices a man standing a few feet in front of her, noticeable because he's the only person not running for shelter. He's wearing a raincoat, the hood pulled up covering his hair and most of his face, but it's unmistakably him.

He raises his hand in greeting and she hesitates, then shakes her head slightly, and lifts hers in farewell. Their eyes lock for a long moment, then he nods and walks away.

PART ONE

ROMANCE

"Happiness in marriage is entirely a matter of chance."
~Jane Austen

CHAPTER ONE

S *hit!* Libby mutters as she zips Nate's lunchbox closed, smearing peanut butter across Batman's face in the process. *Shit, shit shit!* she whispers to herself, licking the peanut butter off her hands and using her sleeve to clean the vinyl lid as she checks the clock once again.

"Emma! Nate! Get a move on! The bus will be here soon."

The first day of school is a day she anticipates with pleasure for weeks, and prays she survives once it's here. The slower, though equally stressful pace of the past few months, is replaced with a frenetic energy, and the total upending of the summer schedule is complete by the time the school bus arrives at seven-thirty. It's a shock to the system, not just for her, but the children as well.

"Let's go! Let's go!" Libby shouts, shoving Nate's peanut butter free lunchbox into his bright orange backpack.

Emma waltzes into the kitchen, in no particular hurry, and grabs her brand-new, peer-approved backpack on her way to the kitchen door. Her daughter is tall for her age, coltish, with long, thick chestnut brown hair and almond shaped green eyes.

Over the summer, she went through a growth spurt and is self-conscious about her height, her first experience with feeling awkward in her skin. *Just wait, my darling! It doesn't get any easier!*

"Hey!" she cries before Emma reaches the door. "Where's my kiss?"

Libby knows she won't get one at the bus stop. Emma is too cool for public displays of affection these days and her request elicits her first eye roll of the day. *When did my daughter start to dislike me?* she wonders, the corners of her mouth turning down. Emma is starting fifth grade and Libby was hoping for a couple of more years without serious attitude. *Looks like I'm not going to get it!*

Libby points to her cheek and Emma rolls her eyes again, gives her a quick peck, then shrugs the plain purple backpack over her slim shoulders. Libby closes her eyes and shakes her head, remembering the fuss Emma made yesterday over using last year's perfectly good, rather expensive backpack.

"Mom! I can't use this one! It has a princess crown on it!" her daughter cried when she found it washed and ready for use in her room. "Princesses are out! Everyone will think I'm a baby."

"Emma, you picked out that eighty-dollar bag less than one year ago…" she replied, trying to keep her tone calm but firm. "I'm sure your friends won't think you're a baby because of this tiny embroidered crown above your initials."

Emma threw herself on the bed and buried her face in her pillow.

"You just don't understand!" her daughter sobbed.

Libby raised her eyes heavenward, debating whether to push the issue, then sighed with resignation. She learned to pick her battles with Emma long ago and this one wasn't worth it. It pains her to admit this, but her daughter is moody at best and Libby can only imagine the hell she and her husband are in for when Emma hits her teen years. There isn't enough Valium in the world to get her through the anticipated anguish of the next eight years.

Nate runs into the kitchen, his auburn hair sticking up in every direction, and Libby bites her lip to keep from laughing.

"Honey, did you brush your hair?" she asks.

Nate nods and gives her a gummy grin, the gap from his missing front teeth making Libby smile. Her son is a delightful ball of energy, affection, and mischief. So like his father.

"With an actual brush?" she asks.

He wiggles his fingers at Libby, "Nature's hairbrush, Mom!"

Libby runs her fingers through his hair, trying to tame his wavy mane, then kisses his forehead and holds him close. She can't believe her baby is starting first grade. Where has the time gone? The past ten years have been devoted to raising the children and helping her husband build his consulting business. This is the first year both children will be in school all day.

Subconsciously, Libby's been waiting for this very moment, but now that it's here, she can't remember why. She's fairly certain it had something to do with freedom to pursue her own interests, her own career. Unfortunately, she has no idea what she wants to be when she grows up. Next month, Libby turns forty and that qualifies as a grown up in anyone's book.

There are some perks to being an adult. Libby closes her eyes and smiles, her body tingling at the memory of Ted's early morning wakeup call. Her husband flew to Chicago this morning on business and will be gone for four days. She misses him terribly when he's gone but is used to his frequent trips.

"Baby?" he whispered into her ear.

Libby woke to Ted softly kissing her lips, her cheeks, her neck, his hands sliding up her nightgown and cupping her breasts. She moaned, half asleep, her arms finding him beside her. Ted had already shed his boxers and t-shirt and was working on removing her underwear before she was fully awake. She opened her eyes to his smiling face inches above hers.

"Good morning sunshine," he whispered, positioning himself between her legs.

"Good morning…" she sighed, finding her husband's mouth and wrapping her legs around him.

Libby has been married to Ted for twelve years and still finds him incredibly sexy. Some of her friends discuss the lack of sex in their marriages and how much of a chore it can be when they are intimate. *A chore?* She keeps her mouth shut on such occasions. What would she say? *Sorry, I don't get it. I can't get enough of my husband!* Their physical connection is what brought them together and the tie which binds them closely. She hopes their desire never fades.

When they met fourteen years earlier, Ted was a political consultant at a firm in Boston. She was a graphic designer working in the art department at an advertising agency in the Back Bay. Libby avoided networking events like the plague, truly despised them, and still does. The purpose of going is to make new business contacts, but they're really for people looking to hook up. It would be one thing if the men were single, but in her experience, the majority are married and looking for a little side action.

On this particular occasion, Libby caved to the pressure of her co-workers. She was going to be in Cambridge anyways and could stop at The Meat Market (as she not-so-affectionately dubbed these events) before heading to The Middle East, a nearby club. She'd been on a couple of dates with one of the musicians in the band playing that evening, and had plans to meet Geoff later on. The dichotomy of his life intrigued her; stock broker by day, drummer by night. An unusual combination.

Libby was twenty-six years old and figured her youth afforded her the luxury of being selective about the men she dated and could tell in the space of five minutes whether she wanted to know someone better. After the long hours she put in at work and the complete absence of a ticking maternal clock, she'd rather curl up on her couch with a cup of tea and a good book than make small talk with a stranger she had no interest in seeing again.

She was unwilling to settle for anything less than spectacular in the relationship department, would rather be alone than in a marriage void of all emotion like her parents before they split. For years, she watched them treat each other like roommates who happened to have children once upon a time. Libby wanted passion and excitement, to feel a genuine connection to another person, but after a series of dating fiascos, she started to wonder if such a connection existed. Was she fooling herself? Maybe this magical concept of love she'd read about was simply a fantasy concocted by hopeless romantics?

On that frosty, February night, Libby arrived at the networking event with her coworkers but quickly found herself sipping her gimlet alone at the bar, when she first laid eyes upon Ted. He's the kind of man who is hard to miss. At six feet four, two hundred and ten pounds, his size commands attention, but his personality *demands* it. He's one hundred percent Irish, with thick wavy auburn hair and smiling eyes. Born and bred in South Boston, he's a natural storyteller with a voice that penetrates the din of any crowded room.

He was holding court across the bar, surrounded by a crowd of men and women who were enthralled by whatever tale he was in the midst of telling, weaving yarns which captivated his audience and had them roaring with laughter. She kept her distance, nursing her drink, but she couldn't take her eyes off of him. Halfway through one of his stories he locked eyes with Libby and smiled. She doesn't know if she returned his smile, but her heart skipped a beat and she certainly kept looking.

When he finished his tale, Ted excused himself from the crowd and made his way over to the bar, leaning against the wood railing beside her. Libby felt her cheeks blazing with heat and stared into her drink, swirling the tiny black straw in circles.

"Hi. Ted Fitzgerald," he introduced himself, extending his hand toward her and grinned.

She looked into his brilliant emerald green eyes and gave him a tentative smile. He wasn't the best looking man in the room, but literally oozed confidence, something Libby had in short supply. Whenever she was in these settings, she opted to draw attention away from her appearance, dressing conservatively in an attempt to blend into the background.

She nodded and shook his hand, then took another sip of her drink, noticing the leggy blond who had sidled up beside him and the gorgeous brunette behind him, both clearly anxious to make their move.

He laughed, waiting for her to offer up her name, and realizing it wasn't forthcoming asked, "And you are...?"

The mob gravitated toward him, the empty spaces around them quickly filling in until a semi-circle was formed, five people deep. Ted didn't appear to notice the growing crowd encircling them, which meant he was either oblivious to his magnetism, or so used to the attention it didn't phase him. Either way, she found it unnerving. He's one of those rare species of men who appeals to both sexes; men want to be his friend and women want to sleep with him. Libby identified this quality in him immediately.

"Libby Taylor. Nice to meet you."

"You're not much of a talker are you, Libby?"

"Conversation seems to be your specialty." She glanced at him sideways and raised an eyebrow, "I'm willing to bet you could carry one on without my input at all."

Ted burst out laughing.

"I probably could, but where's the fun in that?"

"Maybe not for you, but it would be fun for me," Libby countered.

Ted gazed at her, one corner of his mouth turned up with amusement. She watched as his eyes brazenly moved up and down her body.

"Are you checking me out?" she asked, surprised by the ease of their flirtatious banter.

Again he chuckled and nodded.

"Yes, I am. Three words pop into my head. Smart. Sassy. Beautiful."

She took a sip of her drink, observing him over the brim of the glass, then placed it on the little square napkin in front of her.

"Ah, now there's a line," she sighed.

"I've got tons of them," he grinned.

Libby nodded, looking him over, "I'm sure you do."

Just then, the eavesdropping blond with the short skirt and the mile-long legs grasped Ted's arm, turning him toward her.

"Fitz! So great to see you again!" the blond gushed.

She leaned in and kissed his cheek. Ted smiled and introduced Libby to Siena.

"Pleased to meet you," Siena smiled, her eyes glued to Ted's face.

Libby sat on the stool, feeling extremely awkward, as Siena draped her arm around his waist and they discussed the campaign he was working on. Taking in Siena's appearance, the woman's blatant sexuality, Libby glanced down at her jeans and turtleneck sweater and shook her head. *What man with a pulse would choose a virtual burka over Siena's big boobs and backless dress?*

They're in different leagues, she acknowledged, sighing with disappointment. She'd never felt such a strong attraction to anyone before and it was unlikely she'd ever see him again, but she wasn't going to compete for his attention. When Siena pressed herself against Ted and whispered in his ear, Libby took that as her cue to exit.

Turning away from them, she checked her watch, then gathered her coat and bag, preparing to leave. But as she rose from her barstool, Ted placed his hand on the small of her back and leaned in close, startling her.

"You're not leaving yet!" he frowned.

"I'm afraid I am," she said, buttoning her coat and shrugging her bag over her shoulder.

He took her hand and whispered close to her ear, "Not without me."

Libby stared into his eyes and he leaned down and kissed her, his lips soft against hers. A delicious tingling spread throughout her body, flooding her with desire. A moment later she opened her eyes and slowly shook her head back and forth, a smile spreading across her face. *No, not without you.* Ted grabbed his coat and walked into the cool night air, Libby's hand in his.

The Middle East and the dichotomous drummer all but forgotten.

❄

"Mom. Mom!" Nate tugs at her shirt. She snaps out of her daydream and quickly turns to the clock. Shit! The bus!

"Okay, lunch boxes, backpacks," she ticks off the checklist in her head. "Everyone all set?"

Libby opens the kitchen door and waves them outside.

"Wait!" she shouts and grabs her camera off the counter. She can't forget first day of school pictures. "Stand in front of the bushes," she commands her children.

Emma rolls her eyes for the fourth or fifth time this morning, wrapping her arm around her little brother, plainly annoyed by this ritual. Nate grins broadly, his eyes squinting shut, oblivious to his sister's irritation. Libby quickly snaps a few photos, hoping one turns out decent, then follows them to the bus stop where a group of children and their parents have gathered.

As she approaches the corner, she hears a collective sigh of relief from the women, the entire group smiling as she walks closer.

"I'm sorry I'm late!" Libby apologizes. "We still have a few minutes."

Over the years she's become the neighborhood photographer, and everyone looks forward to her first and last day of school shots, posting them on Facebook as soon as they enter their inboxes. In a couple of hours, she'll find their happy, shining faces smiling back at her in her newsfeed. Holding the camera still, Libby snaps a few candid shots, then, one by one, the children pose for her before the bus arrives.

Photography has fascinated her since childhood. Through the viewfinder, Libby could find beauty in the ugliness of the city streets she called home. Her camera, a filter enabling her to see the world from a different perspective. For practical reasons, she majored in graphic arts in college, wanting to be employable once she earned her degree, but she minored in photography and her professors urged her to do more with her talent. But Libby is a realist when it comes to money, and photography was more of a passion than a profession in her mind.

Growing up, her parents scrimped pennies together every week to make ends meet. That's not how she wanted to live. From an early age, she longed for a sense of financial security, and worked hard to put herself through college. Now, she takes online photography classes and experiments with the latest technologies as they become available. It's a hobby, one that brings Libby and those around her pleasure.

The roar of the school bus engine as it makes its way around the corner drowns out the excited chatter of the children and parents. Libby takes a deep breath in and tilts her head to the sky, feeling the warmth of the sun on her face, and smiles. It's been six years since they moved to Garland Drive in Littleton, Rhode Island. Libby still can't believe she lives in this beautiful neighborhood, so removed from the tenement buildings of her childhood. The only neighborhoods she saw like this were on *The Brady Bunch* and reruns of *Leave it to Beaver*.

Living here is the embodiment of the American dream, and while it was something of an adjustment moving to this small, affluent suburb, Libby has made some close friends and built a life for herself and her family.

They live in the quintessential family-centered, upper middle class neighborhood in a picturesque town along Narragansett Bay. Her home is one of twenty Victorian gingerbread houses built in the first decade of the twentieth century, lovingly restored to its original glory by its previous owners. The houses are beautifully kept, the lawns manicured to perfection with not a blade of grass out of place.

Early each morning, the men filter out of their houses to commute to offices in Providence, Boston or beyond; doctors, lawyers, executives and entrepreneurs. And every weekday morning, September through June, the neighborhood mothers shepherd their children to the bus stop dressed in workout clothes, anxious for their precious bundles to be taken away on the mustard school busses so they can focus on self-improvement and managing their household responsibilities.

The only exception in this very traditional neighborhood is Truman and Caroline Whitaker. Caro, as she is known, is a high-powered attorney who works around the clock, yet somehow finds time to run the neighborhood association and look like she stepped out of the pages of Vogue. Her husband, Tru, works from home building and maintaining websites. Once his daughters are on the bus, he goes for a run and sometimes meets the ladies at the coffee shop. He is the primary caretaker of their children, the only dad at the bus stop each morning, and the sole father to attend PTA meetings. Strangely, he fits right in.

The school bus carrying the neighborhood children pulls away from the curb and each adult is temporarily released from parenting duties. Libby turns toward her neighbors, noting the guilt etched on many of their faces, and shakes her head. They've had this conversation before. Of course they love their children, of course they would do anything for them, but if they had to spend another second with them they'd lose their minds!

"Thank God they're gone!" Libby says what everyone else is thinking. "I'll have the pictures to you in an hour or so."

The mothers giggle and thank Libby in advance for the pictures before dispersing to their homes. No one goes to the gym on the first day of school. Today is supposed to be a day of rest and relaxation after the demands of the summer schedule, and while several of her neighbors have spa days planned, Libby has some catching up to do at home and the office.

"So, Lib, what is your plan for liberation day?" Truman asks as they walk toward their houses from the bus stop together.

"Pretty much the same thing I do in bondage, without having to listen to my children arguing or whining. Edit the pictures, laundry, grocery shopping, pick up their messes, run to the office and make dinner. Then split the atom and broker peace in the Middle East. You?"

"I've got to work on a website after my run, then dinner. But I'd be happy to call Abbas and Netanyahu to help you negotiate a peace deal."

Libby laughs and nods her head.

"That would be helpful. Is Caro around tonight?"

"No, she's out of town," Truman replies.

"Do you want to bring the girls over for dinner? I'll make the main course, you bring the salad and dessert? We can make it a first day of school celebratory dinner."

"Sounds like a plan," he smiles. "See you later then."

Truman waves and picks up his pace, beginning his daily run. He's training for the Boston Marathon this coming April and is following a regimented schedule. No rest and relaxation for him either.

Libby and Truman have become close friends over the years, and occasionally the subject of neighborhood gossip. Some people find it impossible to believe that a man and woman can be friends, but nonetheless it true. They're both married to workaholics and help each other out when needed. Neither of their spouses questions the nature of their friendship, and in the end, that's all that matters.

CHAPTER TWO

The house is eerily quiet without the children. Libby wanders from room to room, then heads to the kitchen and makes herself a cup of tea and toast, before bringing the camera into the study to download the pictures she took this morning. She sits at the desk and closes her eyes, going through her to do list for today. After lunch she needs to stop at the office and sort through the stack of papers she's sure have accumulated on her desk while she was away on vacation. There's always something to do at the offices of Fitzgerald and Associates.

The year Ted and Libby married, Ted started his own consulting firm and they had to move because of a non-compete agreement he had with his former employer. He couldn't operate a business in Massachusetts for five years, so, Ted and Libby packed up and left his beloved Boston to start a company in nearby Rhode Island.

When they first moved to Providence, it was just the two of them operating out of their home on the East Side. She spent her time answering the phones, writing and designing marketing materials, then campaign literature, and doing the accounts receivables and payables. She had no experience running a business, but learned quickly.

Ted was the 'talent', the agency front man responsible for networking and building their client base, and he was spectacularly successful at his job, taking on more clients than he could possibly manage himself. Within four months they had to hire another consultant and rent an office space downtown. By the end of their first year, three additional consultants were hired.

They celebrated their rapid expansion, but were in no way ready for it behind the scenes. Libby found herself taking on the additional responsibilities of human resources and payroll, burning the midnight oil alongside her husband, until she became pregnant with Emma.

Before they took their vows, Ted said he wanted them to have at least five children. He comes from a large family and wanted their kids to have the same camaraderie, the same sense of belonging. She envies Ted's relationship with his sister and brothers, it's one of the things that drew her to him. The Fitzgerald's are indeed their own tribe and when they're together, it's wonderful. Each gathering is a bacchanalia of sports, food, beer, and laughter. She loves being part of this raucous family, so completely opposite from her own.

Some girls dream of getting married and having babies; planning their weddings and picking baby names before they graduate high school. Not Libby. She may have thought about 'love' before she met Ted, but marriage wasn't a priority and having children rarely crossed her mind. Libby dreamt of financial security and passion, not babies.

Early on she understood how important having children was to Ted and had come to terms with the idea of having one, maybe even two kids down the road, but five? He couldn't be serious!

But Ted is used to getting what he wants and ruthlessly uses his gifts of persuasion and not-so-subtle coercion to achieve that end.

"Are you planning on carrying these five children in your body for nine months at a time?" she asked when he first expressed this wish to her.

"I would if I could Lib, but that ain't in the cards!" he laughed, rubbing her stomach in slow circles. "Come on baby, think of how much fun we can have making them…"

His hand made its way between her thighs, teasing her.

"We can have just as much fun practicing…" she said, her breath catching in her throat.

He smiled, and withdrew his hand, leaving her gasping, wanting more. Ted rolled onto his back, crossed his ankles, and placed his hands behind his head, a smile on his lips.

Undeterred, she climbed on top of him, her mouth twisted in a half smile, half frown.

"Is this your plan? To deny me an orgasm if you don't get your way?"

He nodded his head, smiling seductively. Libby reached down and removed her negligee. The room was dim, but the candle illuminated the smooth skin of her still taut and youthful body. Ted knows how to play dirty, but he met his match in Libby. He's the most sexual man she's ever met, a relentless flirt with a perpetual hard on. This was a game she knew she'd win.

"Oh well, guess I'll have to take care of myself."

Libby ran her hands along her breasts, one hand finding the spot he abandoned, and began to moan. She could feel him harden against her, and she moved off him, onto her back, pleasuring herself. Ted watched her, his eyes burning with desire, and before she climaxed, he rolled on top of her, pinning her arms above her head, poised for entry.

"Two children," Libby said, raising an eyebrow.

"Three," he laughed and shook his head.

"Deal," Libby nodded.

His mouth came down hard on hers and Libby wrapped her legs around him, pulling him close. She figured she could renegotiate those terms another day.

By the time their first anniversary rolled along, Libby was six weeks pregnant. She was twenty-nine, Ted had just turned thirty-three. They went to Block Island for a long weekend to celebrate the 'Trifecta' as Ted called it; their success in business, making a baby, and marital bliss. Not in that order, he assured her. And it was blissful, and busy, and stressful, all at the same time. It would have been overwhelming if not for Ted's confidence, his absolute belief in their success.

She's never met anyone with more drive than her husband. Ted had a similarly impoverished background, and Libby understood his desire to make more of himself, to rise above the circumstances of his birth. Whenever he works late or is away on business and she's feeling overwhelmed by the children or lonely at night, she reminds herself why he works so long and hard. He wants to give their family a better life.

When Libby was six months pregnant with Emma, she was forced to take a step back from the business when she awoke one morning, her underwear wet. Confused, she realized she was bleeding, not a lot, but enough. She grabbed Ted's arm and called out his name, waking him from a deep sleep. Crying, Libby pointed to the blood on the sheet. Equally panicked, but as always cool under pressure, her husband calmed her fears.

"I read in your book that spotting is fairly normal, baby. I'm going to call the doctor right now, okay? Do you think you can get dressed?"

She nodded and smiled through her tears. She didn't know he'd been reading the book on her nightstand. *What to Expect*

When You're Expecting is the Holy Grail for all first time mothers. Libby knew Ted wanted this baby, but he'd been so busy, she didn't think he was particularly interested in the actual pregnancy. But that wasn't the case after all. He's been keeping up with the changes in her body and the baby's growth all along.

The doctor put Libby on bed rest for two weeks and advised her to take it easy for the duration of her pregnancy. When she had to write out her job description, Ted was shocked by her list of responsibilities. They were forced to hire an accountant and HR manager to take over Libby's various duties at the firm.

"I'm so sorry! I had no idea how much you had taken on, babe," Ted held her hand and apologized. "Why didn't you tell me we needed to hire more people? You know I would've agreed."

She shrugged in response. She wasn't sure why she took on so much responsibility at the company. Maybe she wanted to make herself invaluable to him? He spends so much time at the office, maybe this was her way of staying connected to him?

"I wanted us to build something together," she whispered.

"Lib, we're having a baby," he sighed, wrapping his arms around her. "We're building a family together. Doesn't get more important than that."

So, Libby relinquished control over the daily operations of the company, and kept creating the marketing campaigns for the firm and their clients. She could do the majority of her work from home, but she likes to get dressed for the office, and escape 'house frau' mode. Keeping her toe in the pond gives her something to discuss with Ted that is unrelated to the kids or the house, and that's important to her.

✳

While Libby's editing the photos she'd taken at the bus stop earlier this morning, she hears the squeak of her front

31

door opening and smiles. Only one person would walk into her house without knocking; Ginger.

"Hello! Lib? Where are you?" her friend's voice echoes through the house.

"In the den!" Libby shouts from behind her desk. She has one more photo to edit and send and she'll be done.

"What are you doing?" Ginger asks, leaning over Libby's shoulder. "Ah, first day photos. You know, you really should charge these women."

Libby shakes her head and continues adjusting the exposure on the photo. Ginger is her closest female friend, a divorcée from the wealthiest part of town, and she believes Libby is being taken advantage of by her neighbors. 'People pay good money for photos like these!' Ginger has said on several occasions, encouraging Libby to open a studio.

"I enjoy doing it, Ging. I'd call it an even swap," Libby says, hitting the send button and spinning around in her chair. "Want some tea?"

"Today, I need industrial strength coffee," Ginger sighs dramatically. "Alex woke me up at the crack of dawn then drove me bonkers at drop off. I was seriously willing to swap him for another child. Those mothers must think I'm insane."

"What happened?" Libby frowns.

"Please, don't get me started! I came here to relax," Ginger groans. "Let's just say the 'wubby' was involved. I'm going to burn that damned blanket!"

Libby laughs and turns off her monitor, then heads to the kitchen to make coffee, Ginger close on her heels.

They met at story hour at the local bookstore shortly after she and Ted moved to the suburbs. Ginger was sitting on the carpet next to them with her son Alex, when Nate dozed off half way through *The Giving Tree*. Not wanting to disturb her sleeping child, Libby discreetly pulled a copy of her favorite book, *Sense and Sensibility*, from her bag and began to read. Ginger tapped her on the shoulder and giggled, holding up her well-worn copy of the same book, and a friendship was born.

"Are you Elinor or Marianne?" Ginger whispered.

"Umm…a little of both I think," Libby smiled.

"Ah, passionate and sensible," Ginger nodded. "Good combination! I'm afraid I'm more Marianne. Passionate and impulsive."

"Marianne comes to her senses in the end," Libby replied. "She marries Colonel Brandon."

"She does indeed!" Ginger smiled. "There's hope for me yet!"

Theirs is an unlikely friendship, having grown up on opposite sides of the proverbial tracks. While Libby's family lived in a three family home in Lowell, Massachusetts, Ginger grew up in Manhattan, the great-granddaughter of wealthy industrialists from the turn of the twentieth century. An heiress, she was raised in a very privileged world, consorting with families Libby had only read about in magazines and newspapers.

Ginger attended Brown University, and started her own business making all-natural, organic face and body lotions while still in school, long before it became fashionable. These days, she puts most of her energy into her charitable foundation, funding literacy programs for inner-city children around the country, having sold her company for several million dollars when she was just shy of thirty. Ginger still sits on the board of the company, collecting a handsome paycheck for attending monthly meetings.

Libby had no idea her friend came from such a pedigreed background and would be hard pressed to find a more down to earth person. It was quite by accident she found out the details of her friend's past. About a year after they met, Libby came across an article on the Internet about successful Brown alumni, and Ginger was the featured profile. Her friend was embarrassed by her discovery and feared it would change their relationship, it had ruined many for Ginger in the past. But her fears were unfounded. They are kindred spirits, and along with Truman, have become the best of friends.

"Hey there!" Truman calls out to them from his deck a little while later.

Truman cuts through their adjacent backyards to join Libby and Ginger on her patio. Freshly showered from his run, he sets his coffee mug on the wrought iron table and settles into a cushioned chair, then reaches for the book in front of Libby, *Under the Tuscan Sun*, and flicks through the pages.

"Have you finished it?" he asks, looking from Libby to Ginger, the corners of his mouth turning down.

"Three books ago," Ginger says. "I need to refresh my memory for next week's meeting."

Several years ago Libby formed a book club with Ginger and Truman. They named their club *Booklovers Anonymous* and Libby hosted their first meeting, calling them to order.

"Hello, I'm Libby Fitzgerald, and I'm a book addict. It's been three days since I last read a good book, and two days since I purchased one. The new Wally Lamb novel is coming out soon and I can't wait for my next fix. I'm going through withdrawal."

Nothing stays secret in their neighborhood for long, and once their neighbors caught wind, several women asked to join their reading group. At one point there were twelve people attending monthly meetings but their numbers dwindled quickly once the ladies realized they were expected to actually read the books, and not simply drink wine and socialize. The group is down to a manageable six members.

"I'm almost finished," Truman sighs, closing the book. "I have an idea for next month's book. How about a biography or some historical fiction? You're killing me with all of this women's lit."

"Not my fault!" Libby laughs. "You can blame our other esteemed members for the estrogen-laced reading. Whose turn is it to select the book for October?"

"Yours," Truman says, hopeful. "Please, Lib, I'm dying here!"

"Ah…the power." Libby smiles. "What do I get in return?"

"My eternal gratitude," he grins.

"Oh, all right," she sighs dramatically.

Libby turns to Ginger, who has been uncharacteristically quiet throughout their exchange, and finds her studying Truman's face.

"Ging?" Libby nudges her arm. "Any ideas?"

"You're so pretty, Truman," Ginger blurts out.

Libby covers her mouth to stifle her laughter as Truman's neck and cheeks turned bright crimson and he conceals his face with his hands.

"I'm sorry Tru, I didn't mean to make you uncomfortable, but really, you are beautiful. Lib, wouldn't you kill for his eyelashes?"

"Leave the man alone!" Libby swats Ginger with the book.

This isn't the first time Truman's looks have come up. He's an extremely handsome man, a 'trophy husband' Ginger has called him in private, and self-conscious about his appearance. His straight, light brown hair has a dusting of grey, giving his otherwise youthful appearance an air of maturity. He has full lips, dimples, a square jawline, and warm hazel eyes framed by long, thick eyelashes that curl up naturally.

"Don't worry, Tru," Ginger assures him. "I'm not hitting on you. You're more like a chick with a dick, too pretty and sensitive for my taste. You're a Ferrars and I like a Willoughby."

Truman shakes his head, the corner of his mouth twitching with amusement, "I think I'll take that as a compliment. Kinda, sorta. Edward Ferrars is the good guy in *Sense and Sensibility*, right?"

"Well, there are two good guys, but you're not as old as Colonel Brandon," Ginger replies. "But you're not as young as Edward Ferrars either. Who do you think he's more like?"

Libby shakes her head and smiles to herself. She loves her friends and is so grateful to have Ginger and Truman in her life. They've made her transition into suburbia much easier than she thought it'd be initially.

✳

Her first few months in Littleton were unsettling, and she was afraid they'd made a terrible mistake moving here. A group of ladies who organize the neighborhood association greeted an astonished Libby as she was unpacking boxes, wearing her husband's t-shirt and an old pair of leggings, shortly after the move. She opened her front door to find three impeccably dressed and groomed women, each bearing gifts. The blond in the center of the group smiled, taking in Libby's disheveled appearance.

"Hello! Welcome to Littleton! I'm Caroline Whitaker and this is Gemma Stanton and Greta Stein."

Stunned and incredibly self-conscious, Libby introduced herself.

"Hi, I'm Libby Fitzgerald. Nice to meet you."

"A little something for you." The ladies handed over their offerings.

"Thank you so much…"

Welcome wagons still exist? she wondered as she placed the tray of desserts, the gift bag containing hand-dipped beeswax candles, and the basket of violets on an end table. The welcoming committee walked into the entry of the house and couldn't hide their curiosity, peeking down the hallway and into the adjoining rooms.

The walls were freshly painted and the floors refinished before they moved in, but the house was a disaster, piles of boxes in every room, some half emptied with bubble wrap thrown about haphazardly. The children's bedrooms, the master suite and the den were the only habitable rooms since their move from Providence three days earlier.

"Would you like some tea?" Libby asked, praying they would decline. She wasn't prepared to entertain, and didn't want to give them a tour of the house in its current state.

"Oh, no!" Caroline smiled. "We don't want to bother you while you're unpacking. We just wanted to say hello and invite you to the neighborhood association cookout next weekend. Here's the information."

Libby didn't know it at the time, but the Memorial Day cookout is one of several annual events planned by the neighborhood association, including the Independence Day celebration, Labor Day cookout, Halloween party, Holiday Stroll, and Easter Egg Hunt. Everyone brings a side dish, salad or dessert, and the rest of the food is paid for by the dues each resident contributes yearly.

The street was blocked off and picnic tables covered with vinyl red and white-checkered tablecloths were arranged on the street. They organize a myriad of children's activities, including face-painting, a bean bag toss, hula hoop contest, and a bouncy castle, and the association hires an army of babysitters to run the activities and watch the children so the adults can relax and enjoy the day.

She remembers walking down the street from her house balancing a tray of cookies in one hand, carrying one-year old Nate in the other and five-year old Emma riding her scooter close on her heels. Right before she reached the dessert table, Emma bumped her scooter into Libby's back foot, nearly sending her sprawling onto the pavement. Fortunately, Truman was close by and steadied Libby and baby Nate, somehow rescuing the tray of cookies. She felt her ears grow hot with embarrassment, but she turned her eyes up to meet his and smiled in gratitude.

"Thank you so much!" she sputtered, securing Nate against her hip. "I'm Libby Fitzgerald. We moved in last week."

"I know," he smiled, shaking her hand. "I live in the house to the right of yours. I'm Tru Whitaker."

Whitaker? she thought. *As in Caroline Whitaker?* Cringing, she realized the leader of the neighborhood association lived right next door! How could she possibly live up to that standard?

Just then, Truman's daughters, Sadie and Bette, ran over to them.

"Daddy, we're going in the bouncy house," Bette announced, brimming with excitement.

Emma tugged on Libby's hand, her eyes pleading to go. Truman made the introductions between the girls and they all ran off together.

Libby eyes darted from neighbor to neighbor, house-to-house, not sure what she was supposed to do next. *I'm just a girl from Lowell.* She wasn't equipped to handle this social setting. All around them, women wore Lilly Pulitzer sundresses in shades of pink, turquoise and green. Some with pearls, most with diamonds, all perfectly coiffed and manicured. The men wore khaki shorts or Nantucket reds and polo shirts, brown deck shoes on their feet.

"The invite said 'cookout', didn't it?" she murmured, looking down at her clothes. Libby was wearing black leggings and a plain white t-shirt, black Converse sneakers on her feet. Her hair was pulled back in a ponytail, and her only accessory was the wedding band on her left hand.

Truman nodded his head with what appeared to be sympathy.

"I reserve my Grateful Dead t-shirts and jeans for out-of-town excursions these days," he whispered. "Makes it easier."

Libby looked into Truman's eyes, and sensed that this stranger somehow understood what she was feeling in a way her husband wouldn't appreciate. Moving to Littleton was only part of Ted's dream; *belonging* was equally important to him. He was very eager to embrace this new lifestyle, which meant she had to embrace it as well. The thought of socializing in this circle ignited every insecurity within Libby. *Am I good enough? Will they sense I'm different? Will I ever belong here?* she wondered as she stood beside Truman that sunny afternoon.

A few weeks after the move, Libby and Ted were lying in bed, and Ted wanted to know how she liked living in the suburbs. Libby paused before answering her husband's question, trying to find the words to convey how she was feeling without upsetting him. He had worked hard to provide a good life for their family. His pride was evident every time he pulled into their driveway, his eyes glowing with satisfaction as he walked through the front door every evening. She didn't want to ruin this for him with her insecurities.

Ted frowned, nudging her gently with his elbow and she stared at the ceiling, mulling over the right words.

"Well, I love the house, and the yard is perfect for the kids. Everyone here is really nice…"

"But…?" Ted squeezed her hand.

Libby sighed, and turned to him. She'd always been honest with her husband, but since their move, her silence on the subject was beginning to feel like a lie.

"I don't think I fit in here, Ted," she whispered, her eyes filling with tears.

"Baby, why do you say that?" he asked, his brow furrowing.

"These women…they grew up in this world. They're so pretty, perky and proper. They dress different and talk different and want different things. I don't want to embarrass you."

"Libby, you could never embarrass me," he kissed her softly. "Listen to me sweetheart. I love you just as you are. If it's the clothes making you feel uncomfortable, go shopping. Buy whatever you want. You'd look adorable in one of those bright pink dresses," he teased.

"I wouldn't be caught dead in one of those dresses. But I don't want to stick out like a sore thumb either," she paused for a moment, burying her head in his chest. "I don't know…I feel like I'm in a time warp. Everyone here is playing a role straight out of the fifties. The women are wives and mothers and the men are providers. There's a *Twilight Zone* element to this, don't you think?"

"I think it's different from the city, but really, how different is it from how we grew up? My mom stayed home, my dad worked. No matter how broke we were, that's just the way it was."

She shrugged, thinking about her own experiences as a child. Her mother was home when Libby was young, but divorce spread through her urban neighborhood like a virulent virus when Libby was in high school and all of the ex-wives had to find work, her mother included.

"Baby, please give this place a chance. It's a great town with nice people. Look at the big picture. We're giving our kids the kind of life we could only dream of. Don't you want that for them? We can be very happy here, it's just an adjustment. Promise me you'll try."

"I'm sorry. I promise I'll try."

And Libby has tried. Six years later, she's woven herself into the fabric of Littleton life, at least on the surface. She joins the women at the gym and coffee shop, helps organize the neighborhood association activities, attends dinner parties and charity events, sits on the board of the PTA and is an active member of the country club, taking up tennis a few years back.

Her life is full and it's only in rare moments of reflection, she feels like a fraud; dressing and acting the role of a wealthy suburban housewife and mother. But those days are fewer and farther between. *Is it possible*, she wonders, *that by pretending to be someone I'm not for so many years, I've managed to become that person?* The fact that she questions the transformation suggests it's incomplete. She hasn't decided if that's a good or a bad thing.

CHAPTER THREE

R enata, the receptionist at Fitzgerald and Associates, greets Libby with a smile as she pushes open the thick glass door to their office suite.

"Hi Libby! I didn't know you were coming in today."

"I have some catching up to do! I won't be here too long."

The company recently moved into a larger space in a renovated mill building on the outskirts of downtown. The exterior walls are exposed brick, the original wooden beams crisscross the ceiling, the floors were stripped and refinished in their natural chestnut hue, and the windows are huge, letting in tons of sunlight.

Libby was in charge of renovating the space and she's pleased with how it turned out. The reception area is open, but warm and welcoming, with Renata's sturdy antique wooden desk front and center, sitting on a large faded oriental rug in shades of red, orange and brown. There are two soft, dark brown leather chairs, with a rustic wooden chest between them holding various magazines, a small loveseat reupholstered in a burlap-colored fabric, and an old iron coat rack.

The large conference room is located off the reception area, and ten offices, a kitchen, a smaller, private conference room and the 'war room' with a wall of televisions set to different cable news channels was built within the cavernous space under her direction. Ted's office is the largest, and Libby's smaller office is next to his.

She walks down the hallway, poking her head into the associate's offices, checking in on everyone. She likes to know what's going on in their lives, and with their families. Ted's assistant, Felice, recently resigned, and Libby is surprised to find a young woman in her early twenties sitting at the desk outside his office.

"Hello?" Libby greets her, a question in her voice.

The girl stands, straightening her short black skirt, and extends her hand.

"Hi. I'm Heather, Mr. Fitzgerald's new assistant."

Libby raises an eyebrow, shaking Heather's hand.

"Hello, Heather, I'm Libby, Ted's wife."

"I know," Heather laughs nervously, "I've seen your picture in his office. Nice to meet you."

Libby looks into Heather's big brown eyes, an uneasy feeling settling in her stomach, and forces a smile.

"Nice to meet you too. I'll just be in there." She points to her office, turns, and then stops. "I'm sorry, Heather, I had no idea Ted hired anyone. When did you start?"

"Oh, umm... two weeks ago."

Libby nods, and heads back toward her office, closing the door behind her.

Ted hired an assistant? Libby has always been part of the hiring committee, for all employees. *Why didn't he tell me?* She sits in her swivel chair, looking out the window at the city skyline. She took the kids to Ginger's house on Nantucket for the last two weeks of August before school started, as she does every year. But apparently Heather had already been hired before she and the kids went on vacation.

Frowning, she picks up the phone and hits Ted's number on speed dial. He called her when his plane landed in Chicago three hours earlier and said he'd be in meetings all day. Sure enough, the phone rings but goes to voicemail.

"Ted, it's me…" she pauses. "Never mind, I'll talk to you later."

Libby ends the call and takes a deep breath, sifting through the paperwork piled on her desk.

❋

"Kids! It's time to eat!" Libby calls out, trying to round up the children jumping on the trampoline in her backyard while Truman sets the table on her patio. They are a well-oiled machine, Libby and Truman, and pick up where the other leaves off; chopping vegetables, marinating meat, washing and drying dishes, managing the children. They've been doing this together for so long, it's become second nature.

Sadie, Truman's eldest, is reading a book on the lounge chair.

"Sadie, will you please help?" he asks impatiently. "Can't you see we're trying to have dinner?"

She sighs dramatically, rising from the chair.

"What do you need me to do, Dad?"

"How about bringing out the salad and the pitcher of lemonade?"

"Fine," Sadie huffs and stomps into Libby's house.

Truman stares after her, his brow furrowing, his expression, forlorn.

"It'll pass," Libby rests her hand on his arm, "I'm sure I was much worse at her age, and look at me now? A model citizen."

"I hope you're right," he sighs.

Libby follows Sadie into the house. They've always had a close relationship. With Caroline's frequent absences she's become a surrogate mother to Truman's children.

"Hey, Sadie, how about taking it easy on your dad?"

Libby picks up the tray piled high with a dozen ears of corn and the bowl of green beans. Sadie shrugs holding the salad bowl, her eyes downcast, shoulders hunched. Libby frowns. Something isn't right.

"What's the matter, sweetie?"

"Nothin'," Sadie lifts her hazel eyes, her mouth drawn.

"Sade, you know you can tell me anything."

"I got my period today," the tall, skinny teenager whispers and looks down at her sneakers.

Libby's eyes grow wide and she wraps her arm around Sadie's childlike shoulders.

"How do you feel?"

"I'm okay."

"Did you tell your dad?" Libby asks, remembering Caro is out of town.

"No!" Sadie's face contorts with horror and exclaims, "I got it afterschool and found some pads in my mother's bathroom!"

Sadie's emphasis of the word 'mother' is laced with resentment.

"Sadie, your mom would be here if she could, you know that, right?"

"Yeah, right," Sadie smirks. "She cares more about her job than us."

"Honey, that's not true," Libby replies, shaking her head.

"Whatever," Sadie says and walks to the French doors that lead to the patio carrying the salad and lemonade.

Libby sits on a stool, her heart aching. *Poor thing.*

"Everything okay?" Truman pokes his head into the kitchen and Libby motions with her hand for him to join her.

"What's up?" he asks, his eyes concerned.

"Your daughter got her period today," she says in a hushed voice.

"What?" Tru's mouth drops open, his eyes filling with absolute terror.

"And she's upset Caro isn't around to help her through this."

"Holy shit…" Truman whispers, running his hands through his hair and takes a seat beside Libby. "Help me! I have absolutely no clue what to do!"

"Well…" Libby squeezes his hand and stands, picking up the trays of food, "The first thing we're going to do is feed the troops, then I'll sit and have a talk with her. You should call Caro after dinner and tell her."

"What?" Truman asks, in what appears to be a state of shock.

"Call your wife! She should talk to Sadie."

❋

Their bed feels heavenly tonight, Libby sighs as she relaxes against the pillows. It was a very long day. She stares at the bedroom ceiling, holding Ted's pillow to her, and breathes in deeply. The pillow smells like her husband, a combination of soap, shaving cream, shampoo, and…*Ted*. The unique mix of pheromones which drew her to him.

She closes her eyes taking another deep breath into his pillow until the ringing of the cell phone beside the bed snaps Libby out of her aroma-induced trance. Reaching for it, she sees it's Ted, and sits up. "Hi sweetheart."

"Hey babe! What's happening on the home front?" She can hear a lot of background noise, music and voices.

"Where are you?" Libby winces, "It's so loud, I can hardly hear you!"

"A restaurant. I wanted to check in before you fell asleep. How was the kids first day of school?"

She wants to ask him about his new assistant, and find out why she was left out of the interview process, but something tells her to wait.

"Good. They like their new teachers."

"I'm glad they had a good first day," Ted shouts over the din. "Well, babe, they're waiting for me. I'd better go. I love you."

"Okay. I love you too," she says. "Be good."

"Kiss the kids for me," he chuckles. "Bye."

She reclines in bed and stares at her phone. *Be good?* She's never said those words to him. Libby's never been suspicious of her husband's actions before. He's a charismatic man. Women throw themselves at him constantly, even in front of her! She can only imagine what they do to tempt him when she isn't there. But she's never doubted his fidelity. *Is that what I'm doing now? Doubting him?* She bites her lip, frowning. He works so hard, and their sex life is fulfilling, when would he have the time?

His new assistant's face, Heather, flashes in her head. Libby checked Heather's file before she left the office today. She just turned twenty-two, is a recent graduate of Boston University, and lives in an apartment in Providence. Ted is forty-three years old. He wouldn't be so foolish. Libby turns onto her side and hugs his pillow to her. No, he wouldn't risk everything for a piece of ass.

♂

Thank God for Libby, Truman thinks as he climbs into bed. She handled Sadie's 'situation' better than he ever could. He just left his eldest daughter's bedroom, having spent the past hour sitting beside her while she slept, wondering where the time has gone. His little girl is a woman now. Well, not quite a woman, but capable of womanly things, like getting her period.

Truman lies back against his pillows and sighs. She's thirteen, not a child anymore. He got off the phone with Caroline a little while ago, but he wasn't able to talk to her. She was on her way out to a dinner meeting and is unaware their daughter reached a physical milestone today. And that pisses him off.

This is when Truman resents his wife's job most, moments like this. They have two daughters. She should be here for them! While the girls were small, he could handle whatever problems they brought to him. Teasing, arguments with friends, even crushes on boys, he could deal with those issues. *Menstruation? Sex?* No. He's not equipped to advise his daughters on tampons, pads, cramps, birth control pills...*Oh God*, Truman groans, feels sick just thinking about his girls becoming sexually active. *They're my babies!*

He sighs, picking up a family photograph from his nightstand. It was taken two years ago for their Christmas card and because of his wife's crazy schedule, he had to reschedule this photo shoot three times. It's a rare shot of the whole family. He has thousands of pictures of the girls, and Sadie taught him how to take 'selfies' of the three of them, but Caro is conspicuously absent from photographs except on holidays and birthdays.

How did I end up raising the girls virtually alone? This is not what he signed up for, being a stay-at-home dad. He didn't always work out of the house, but when Caro's career took off, it was a matter of simple mathematics. At the time, she made three times the money he did, probably five times as much now. Someone needed to be home for the children, and since neither of them wanted a stranger raising the girls, he got the job by default. Truman cut back his workload and turned the study on the first floor into an office.

Their lives would've been considerably more modest if he were the primary breadwinner. They wouldn't live in this beautiful home, in this fancy neighborhood. The girls wouldn't be taking horseback riding or sailing lessons. In that scenario, he would have been the parent trying to make it up to the girls on weekends, and he's glad he doesn't have to do that. He tries not to hold it against his wife for being absent from the girls lives the majority of the time… but it's hard. *It's very, very hard.*

His relationship with Caroline is a partnership at this point. Their marriage began its steady downward slide when Caro made partner in her law firm four years ago. They make love one, maybe two times a year, usually on their anniversary or birthdays if they've had enough to drink; the kind of gift you give out of a sense of obligation, putting no thought into it, like roses on Valentines Day.

About a year after her promotion, they went to counseling at his request. It became evident after a few sessions that Caroline wasn't willing to compromise her work in any way for the sake of their marriage. Her rejection left a gaping hole in his heart and he ached inside for months.

For another year, he slept beside her, wondering what he did wrong and tried to figure out how he could fix them. Then Caroline did something she couldn't undo, changing the way he's looked at her since.

One evening, Truman was walking down the hallway to tuck the girls in when he overheard his wife talking to Sadie, and what he overheard stopped him in his tracks.

"Sadie," Caroline was saying. "No one likes a chubby girl. You need to lose weight.'

Truman sprinted into Sadie's room and found his daughter in tears. Sadie was eleven and had gained a few pounds before a growth spurt, as most kids do, but she was in no way overweight. Enraged, he escorted Caroline out of the room and thought his head was going to explode!

"How could you say that to an eleven-year-old girl?" he demanded. "What the fuck is wrong with you?"

"I'm just being honest with her Truman! She's getting pudgy and I don't want her to struggle with her weight and get made fun of. Girls are mean!" she replied.

"So are mothers, apparently!" he hissed. "There's nothing wrong with Sadie's weight or her eating habits. Not that you'd know, since you're never here. Do you want her to develop an eating disorder? Jesus Christ, Caro! She's such a sensitive girl. Do you know what you just did?"

"I would never hurt my child, Truman. I want what's best for her. She's turning into the weird girl, so dark and brooding."

"She's going to be who she is, Caroline. That might not be who you want her to be…but it's who she is! Do you understand?" He threw his hands up in frustration. "She's eleven! If she wants to read and paint and hang out with other kids who read and paint that's her choice, not yours."

"What kind of life is that? Don't you want her to have a lot of friends and some fun for a change? Why would you encourage her to be different? To stand alone?"

He stared at Caroline, dumbstruck. In that moment, Truman realized what's broken between them could never be fixed. They are very different people with different priorities and there's nothing he could do to change that. Caro wants Sadie to be popular, to dress like the other girls, to fit in above all else. All Truman wants is his daughter to be happy.

"Don't ever let me hear you criticize her weight again, either of the girls. I mean it, Caroline. You crossed the line."

That was it for him. The final straw. He slept in the guest room that night and never went back to the master suite. Sadie refused to eat anything but lettuce and apples for days, she wanted so much to please her mother. Any thought of leaving Caroline evaporated in an instant. Who else would protect the girls from their mother's careless words and unrealistic expectations if not him?

He'll be in his early fifties by the time Bette is out of high school and sometimes the thought is unbearable. Moments like today, his daughter getting her first period, make him feel like the years are flying by, but whenever he takes the time to reflect on his situation, the next eight years seem to stretch on interminably.

He doesn't think anyone suspects how shitty his marriage actually is. Certainly the guys he plays basketball with on Saturday afternoons have no clue. None of the men discuss their marriages, though several comment on their extra-curricular sex lives. He knows their wives and wants to shake them. *Open your eyes, ladies! Your husband has sex with anything that moves!* But he keeps his mouth shut, it's not his place.

Truman misses sex. He misses the feeling of wanting another person, and longs for the anticipation, the desire he felt when everything was new and exciting. He used to be a very passionate person. When he and Caroline first met, they couldn't get enough of one another. Now, he runs. He runs to the point of exhaustion so that when he does go to bed, he doesn't have the energy to feel sorry for himself. He can fall into a deep sleep and start the routine all over again in the morning.

✳

He's running through the woods, a thick mist covering the ground. He keeps tripping, but picks himself up and continues. For miles and miles, he runs, never seeing more than a few inches ahead of him. Finally, when his lungs are on fire, he collapses to his knees and a voice whispers, "Who looks outside, dreams. Who looks inside, awakens."

Truman wakes with a start and rolls onto his back, trying to focus his eyes. He's damp with sweat and his head's pounding. *What the hell?* It takes him a moment to realize the voice he heard was his mothers and that it was just a dream. *Great, now my mother is haunting my dreams, quoting Jung!* He rolls onto his stomach and closes his eyes. *Who looks inside, awakens...* What is the dream telling him? *That I'm dead inside?* Tears fill his eyes as he considers the message. His heart aches in his chest and he feels the walls closing in on him. *I want to feel alive!*

"Daddy. Daddy, wake up!" Bette jumps onto his bed in her pajamas.

"Bette, sweetheart, stop jumping. Please." He wipes his eyes and reaches out for his cell phone, holding it out to her. "What time is it baby?"

She cuddles up beside him, "Late."

Truman sits up, and squints at the phone. Holy shit! He forgot to set the alarm last night. They have fifteen minutes until the bus arrives.

"Bette get dressed. Is Sadie up?" She nods and runs to her room. "Sade!" he shouts down the hallway. "Get ready and come downstairs for breakfast. You have five minutes!"

Missing the bus wouldn't be the worst thing in the world, but he likes to stick to a routine as much as possible. Truman tries to shake the heavy fog of his dream off as he considers his day. The website he's been working on is going live and he found a few glitches in the code yesterday. This is a huge client and if they're happy, other big companies will seek him out. Caroline may make the big money, but he makes a good living himself.

Grabbing his wallet off the bureau, he takes out two five-dollar bills. *Hot lunch it is!* Throwing on sweatpants and a t-shirt, he runs down the stairs to find his eldest daughter fully dressed, hair brushed, eating a bowl of cereal.

"Morning," Sadie says, flipping through a magazine.

"Why didn't you wake me up, sweetheart?" he asks, slipping on his flip flops.

"I tried," she shrugs. "You were out of it."

"Sorry, I forgot to set the alarm." Truman walks around the counter and kisses the top of Sadie's head.

Bette runs down the stairs and slides into the kitchen, taking her seat at the counter, and pours way too much cereal into her bowl. Truman smiles at his youngest child, so full of energy, and grabs the brush, running it through Bette's blond curls while she eats. One day soon she isn't going to let him brush her hair. Libby's daughter, Emma, is the same age and already sprinting into tween-hood. Thankfully, Bette is lagging behind. That's a race he'd be thrilled to see her finish last.

He turns toward the clock.

"Okay, my beautiful, brilliant girls, time to brush your teeth and head out!"

They are the last to the bus stop, and Truman sighs with relief as they join the group on the corner. The foggy feeling is lingering but he smiles when he spots Libby talking to Greta, a member of their book club.

"Morning, Tru," Greta greets him. "We were just discussing our next meeting. Since the book was set in Italy, I thought I'd do an Italian theme for our meeting. Italian food, drink, music. What do you think?"

"Sounds great," he nods, smiling. "Let me know what to bring."

"No need. I'll take care of everything."

The book club meets the second Wednesday of every month, and Greta is hosting the September meeting, which means it will be over the top. Greta loves opening up her lavish home to neighbors and holds dinner parties regularly. She's one of Caroline's groupies, one of several women in the neighborhood who look to Caro for social cues and guidance. His wife may not be home much, but she still manages to run the neighborhood association and uphold the illusion of being an active participant in their daughters' lives.

The bus arrives and once the kids are on their way and the crowd disperses, Truman takes Libby's arm.

"I can't thank you enough for last night. I honestly don't know what I would've done if you weren't there for Sadie."

"No problem, Tru," she pats his arm. "Did she talk to Caro?"

Truman shakes his head, the corners of his mouth turning down.

"Nope. Caro was too busy to chat last night."

He's fighting back his anger, but it's obvious he's pissed off. He and Libby have discussed on more than one occasion their irritation with their spouses, how they work too much and parent too little. He supposes that's something every stay-home parent has in common. But Libby adores her husband and her irritation is always short lived, whereas Truman's only seems to build, growing a little bit every day.

"Are you okay?" Libby asks, her brows drawn together.

"I'm fine," he smiles and laughs, trying to shrug it off. "You know how it is."

"That, I do." Libby stops in her tracks and grabs Truman's arm. "Oh my God, I think I'm going to be sick."

She sprints toward her house, and worried, he follows her. Closing her front door behind him, he hears her retching in the guest bathroom on the first floor and grimaces. Truman grabs a clean dishtowel from the kitchen and runs it under cold water, then waits in the living room until she finishes. A few minutes later, Libby stumbles out of the bathroom and collapses on the couch. Kneeling on the rug beside her, he places the cool towel on her forehead.

"Would you like some water?" he asks.

She nods, and he returns a moment later with a glass, and props her head up while she takes a small sip.

"Thank you, Tru," she says and lies back against the pillows.

"How are you feeling?"

"Like I've been hit by a truck. I hope it's not a stomach bug," she groans. "They've been back in school one day for Christ's sake!"

"Do you want me to stay with you for a bit?" he asks.

"No, no. Go for your run. I'll be fine."

He rises and studies her face. She doesn't look fine. Libby's face is ghostly white, her eyes glassy. He drapes a blanket around her, then leans down and rests his palm on her forehead.

"You don't feel feverish, but take it easy, okay? I'll be back in a bit to check up on you."

"Yes, mother," Libby smiles up at him, then turns onto her side and closes her eyes.

Truman sits on the ottoman and tucks her in, then brushes the hair away from her face. She opens one eye and a corner of her mouth turns up.

"You take good care of me, Truman," she murmurs, her eyes closing again.

"You'd do the same for me," he says with absolute certainty.

She's proven that time and again over the years. Last winter, Bette came home from school with the chicken pox and before he knew it, all four kids had it...as did Truman. At first he thought the itching sensation was pure paranoia, but Libby spotted a pock on his neck when she came over with a pot of soup for dinner.

"I can't have chicken pox," he said, scratching his neck. "Isn't that a childhood disease?"

"Truman, anyone can get it, regardless of age," she sighed. "Did you have it when you were a kid?"

"I have no idea. I don't remember..." his voice trailed off.

"That's it. Strip," she ordered him.

Truman removed his shirt and Libby inspected him for more marks, and sure enough, he was covered. She sent him to bed, brought her kids over and set up the air mattresses in the finished basement for the children to recuperate, watch movies, and play games, while he rested upstairs.

She was a trooper, spending the entire week playing nursemaid to Truman and the kids, dabbing each of them with calamine lotion, swatting their hands away from their faces (he was the worst offender), cooking and caring for the lot of them. She never complained, just did what had to be done, mothering his children when he couldn't.

It's a relief to know Libby's there for him and the girls. The arrangement they have is far from traditional, but it works. He needs her in his life, far more than he needs Caroline, and so do his daughters.

Grabbing a bucket from beneath the sink in case she gets sick again, Truman kneels down beside Libby, rubs her back and sighs. She's already asleep, her breathing deep and even. She looks so young and vulnerable curled up on the couch, the blanket tucked beneath her chin, and a surge of emotion floods him.

"You deserve to be taken care of, Lib," he whispers, then leans down to kiss her, and catches himself.

What the hell am I doing?

Quickly, he rises, then turns on his heels and practically sprints to the door. Once outside he leans against the huge maple tree between their two houses and takes a deep breath in. *Who looks inside, awakens...*His heart pounds against his chest. Awakens to what? That damned dream is messing with his head. He's never had the impulse to kiss Libby before. She's his best friend in the world.

Protective. I feel protective of her, that's all, he mutters to himself, *she's like a sister to me.* Feeling a bit better, he walks over to his house and changes into his running clothes. A good, long run will straighten him out.

CHAPTER FOUR

L ibby has been sick for days. It's Friday and this stomach bug has lingered since she first fell ill on Tuesday. It only took the kids one day back in the school incubator for the germ-fest to begin! The kids haven't gotten it, which is a blessed miracle in her eyes, and for that she's thankful. The nausea comes in waves throughout the day and it takes everything in her to get the kids out the door in the morning.

Truman has been checking in on her while Ted is away, bringing her chicken soup and crackers, and driving the kids to practice. She's exhausted between running to the office and trying to hold down the fort at home. Fortunately, she doesn't have to go it alone in times like these. Truman has always been there for her and the kids and she'd be lost without him. In many ways Libby needs Truman more than she needs Ted, not that she'd ever admit that to her husband! The two men in her life couldn't be more different, her husband inhabiting the spotlight, her friend avoiding it.

Later that evening, Ted arrives home from Chicago in the middle of a Fitzgerald-Whitaker family dinner. Libby, Truman and the children are sitting on the patio finishing their meal when her husband sweeps into the backyard, making his presence known, the air around them shifting.

"Daddy!" Nate shouts as Ted walks onto the flagstone patio and runs into his father's arms. Ted scoops him up and squeezes him tight. *Two peas in a pod*, she thinks, *both little boys at heart*. Her own heart pounds hard inside her chest at the sight of him. It always does when he's been gone for a few days. Though he's not home much during the week, she misses having him in bed beside her at night, misses waking up in his arms each morning. But she's used to his insane schedule and the frequency of his business trips. Doesn't mean she likes it, but she accepts his absences as the norm. It makes their time together even more special.

"Well, hello everyone!" Ted smiles and kisses the top of Emma's head, then rounds the table to greet her. Libby rises to her feet and walks into her husband's embrace, her body sighing into his.

"Hey, baby…" he whispers, holding her close. "It's so good to see you."

She looks up into Ted's eyes and smiles, her heart swelling with emotion. She's so in love with him, after all of these years. Most couples she knows are more companions than lovers at this stage in the game, but Libby and Ted never got past the honeymoon stage, and the chemistry that first attracted them to one another is intact. Maybe it's because of his schedule they're able to maintain these feelings?

Ted holds her against him and she closes her eyes, feeling safe and adored in his embrace.

"Hi Tru, kiddos, how's everyone doing?" Ted asks a moment later.

"Good." Truman rises to shake his hand. "Good to see you, Ted. Here, take my seat. I'm just about done."

"Thanks, man. Caro should be home soon. I bumped into her at the airport," Ted says, sitting in Truman's vacated seat.

Sadie's face clouds over, but Bette jumps out of her chair and runs next door to see if her mother has returned home. Libby raises an eyebrow. Apparently, Caroline has yet to have a conversation with her daughter about her entry into womanhood. Libby squeezes her shoulder and heads into the kitchen to grab Ted a beer, while Truman fires up the grill to make more burgers.

"Medium-rare, thanks Tru." Ted sits back in his chair, beer in hand and sighs, "It's so good to be home!"

❈

Once the children are in bed, Libby slips on Ted's favorite negligee and unpacks his bags while he's in the shower, sorting through his dirty clothes. This pile for the dry cleaners, the rest into the hamper. Ted is notorious for leaving money, credit cards, and other vital items in his suits, so she goes through every pocket before sending them off to the cleaners.

As usual, she amasses a pile of loose change, receipts from dinners (need those for tax write-offs) and business cards he collected on his trip. She grabs his dress shirts and checks them for collar stays and frowns when she catches the distinct whiff of ladies' perfume. Holding the shirt to her face, her stomach turns over. *Chanel?* Yes...Ted once gave her a bottle of Chanel No. 5. Libby doesn't like perfume in general, but this scent is particularly offensive to her.

Why does his shirt stink to high heaven of Chanel?

Libby sits cross-legged on the floor holding the shirt, her thoughts racing, and grabs his briefcase, searching for his folder of receipts. He's not the most organized person, but he usually manages to get the hotel, car service, and flight receipts into the folder she created for that purpose. She takes out the hotel bill, looking for evidence of...what? *Room service for two? Champagne?*

Escort fees? Scouring the list of charges, she doesn't see anything unusual, and takes a deep breath in, relief flooding her body. What has gotten into her lately? First the new assistant, now perfume...It doesn't mean anything. Maybe he sat next to a woman on the plane drenched in Chanel?

"What are you doing down there?" Ted walks into the bedroom, a towel around his waist, his hair slicked back from his shower.

"Just sorting through your laundry." She grabs the pile of restaurant receipts she found in his pockets and sticks them into the folder. "When are you going to learn, my dear? Receipts, all receipts go in the folder!"

"I know, I know," he nods sheepishly and pulls her to her feet. "What would I ever do without you?" Ted wraps his arms around her and nuzzles her neck.

"Let's hope you never find out!" she laughs.

"I see you're wearing my favorite nightie..." His hands wander up and down her body, lifting the silken negligee over her head.

"Not anymore I'm not..."

♂

Caroline joined them in the backyard shortly after Ted's arrival this evening. Bette dragged her into the backyard of the Fitzgerald house moments after Truman fired up the grill. He couldn't help but compare their frosty reunion with the warmth of Libby and Ted's moments before. Truman raised the metal spatula in the air in greeting, pretending to be busy making burgers. No hugs, no kisses, no lustful glances each other's way. Caro kissed the top of Sadie's head, smiled stiffly toward him and took a seat at the table, chatting with Ted while he and Libby served them, then played a game of badminton with the children.

62

Right now, his wife is in Sadie's room, having a long overdue talk with their daughter. After he helped Libby with the cleanup, the two families went their separate ways and Truman pulled Caro aside as soon as they stepped into the house. She was furious with him for not sharing this news earlier in the week, and he had to bite his tongue to keep from lashing out at her. *I tried to tell you, Caroline! You're always too busy to talk!*

"You're unbelievable, Truman! Honestly!" she said before storming out of the kitchen and following Sadie to her bedroom. *What was I supposed to do?* He unloaded the dishwasher, loudly stacking the dishes in the cupboards, flinging the silverware in the drawer. He learned long ago he can't force her to leave a business meeting or excuse herself from dinner with colleagues or clients! *Why bother trying?*

Tonight, he feels very alone and in desperate need of a drink. He made sure Bette took a shower and tucked her into bed, then headed to his bedroom with a bottle of scotch. Pouring some of the amber liquid into his glass, he knocks it back in one swig, then takes a seat in the leather chair beside his bed and picks up the book on his nightstand. He tries to read a few lines to get his mind off of *life* but that's not happening tonight.

Unable to focus, he flings the book onto his bed, pours himself another drink, then walks over to the window and stares at the moon. It's been a strange week. Ever since he had that dream, he's been fighting off the instinct to run away, resisting the urge to escape this life and his marriage. It's not the first time he's felt that urge, but it's never been more powerful.

More disturbing is the shift in his feelings toward Libby. His thoughts have been decidedly less than pure. Last night he had a very vivid dream about her and woke with a start, fully expecting to find Libby beside him in bed. He could hardly look her in the eye at the bus stop this morning.

During his run earlier he tried to sort through his feelings and thinks he's figured it out. He's lonely and Libby is the most constant female presence in his life. He cares for her and is so grateful his daughters have a mother figure to turn to. He believes the combination of loneliness, sex deprivation and gratitude have mutated into desire for Libby in his mind.

He can handle this, Truman reassures himself. He just needs to redirect this pent up energy and frustration. Libby is his best friend, his neighbor, and he needs her, so it doesn't matter if he's developed a bit of a crush, nothing can ever come of it. He's trying hard to squash these feelings and behave as he always has around her, and so far, he's done a pretty good job.

Tonight was tough, though. When Ted walked onto the patio he felt his ears turn red with shame, so guilty for having indulged in sexual thoughts about the man's wife. On top of the guilt, he was jealous! Those two are so dewy-eyed around one another. He felt like he was intruding on a very intimate moment. He'd give almost anything to have someone feel that way about him again.

Maybe it's time to have a talk with Caroline. Some people have open marriages and it's worked for them. He can't be fantasizing about Libby, and his hand just isn't cutting it these days. He needs physical contact with another human being.

Caroline knocks on his door, then walks into his bedroom while he's nursing his third...possibly fourth drink. She changed out of her grey suit into a short, sleeveless, white cotton nightgown. With her face washed clean of makeup and her blond hair pulled back in a ponytail, she looks the same as when he first met her over twenty years ago.

"Truman, I'm sorry I snapped at you earlier. That had nothing to do with you."

He nods his head absently, distracted by her long, lean legs, the outline of her breasts visible through her nightgown. His wife's a very beautiful woman, she's always been stunning. Bette resembles her, while Sadie looks more like him.

"How's Sadie?" he asks, pouring himself another drink. He's definitely drunk now.

Caroline sits on the side of his bed and sighs, shaking her head back and forth.

"She's angry. She wishes Libby was her mother, not me."

Ouch. That had to hurt. He sits beside her and wraps his arm around her shoulder, then Caro buries her face into his chest and starts to cry, clinging to his t-shirt.

"I don't know what I'm doing anymore, Tru," she whispers.

When she lifts her face to his moments later, he brushes away her tears, then she surprises him and presses her lips against his, her arms winding around his back, pulling him close. He's not sure how it happened, but in the blink of an eye they're naked, Caroline on top of him, riding him like she hasn't in years. Closing his eyes, he imagines Libby above him, his hands on her breasts, his mouth on hers, and stops himself from crying out her name as Caroline collapses beside him, her breathing ragged.

Libby? Jesus Christ, this has to stop! He squeezes his eyes shut, trying to wipe her from his thoughts, and turns on his side to study his wife. Running his fingers along her body, he notices a small bruise on the side of her neck, another on her left breast. *Hickies?* He didn't give them to her, that's for sure. Sitting up, the room begins to spin, so he lies back down beside her.

"Caro. I think it's time we had a talk."

"Hmmm? About what?" she murmurs.

Truman points to the two hickies and smiles. Caroline looks down at her breast, her eyes flying wide open and her hands rising to her neck and chest, covering the marks someone else made on her body. He's so glad he's drunk for this conversation!

"I'm not going to ask who gave you those, Caroline. Honestly, I don't care. Thank you for the guilt fuck, it was great, but there's no need to feel guilty anymore."

"Truman…" she sits up and pulls her nightgown over her head. "What are you saying?"

"I'm saying you're free to have sex with whomever you want. You live your life and I'll live mine. And when the girls are grown, we'll go our separate ways. But for the girls' sake, please be discreet."

"Are you sleeping with someone else?" she asks, her eyes bright with curiosity.

"No," he says, shaking his head. "But it's time I did."

♀

Jesus, Mary and Joseph! When is this bug going to work its way out of me? Libby heaves into the bowl again, then lies back against the tile, a damp facecloth pressed to her mouth. She needs to get ready to take the kids to their soccer games but can't move without wanting to vomit.

Ted appears in the doorway to their bathroom in his boxers, his hair disheveled, rubbing the sleep from his eyes.

"Lib? Are you okay?" he asks.

She shakes her head wearily back and forth.

"I've had a stomach bug since the kids started school."

"You seemed fine last night."

"It doesn't last all day. It comes in waves, but it's worse in the morning. Can you bring the kids to their games, please? I can't get up."

Ted frowns and sits beside her on the bathroom floor, his brows drawn together.

"You feel worse in the morning? Libby...do you think you're pregnant?" he asks, his eyes growing wide.

Pregnant? She feels panic building in her chest. No...I can't be pregnant! I'm almost forty years old for God's sake! Closing her eyes, she tries desperately to remember the last time she had her period. Not last month on Nantucket...the Fourth of July? *Oh dear God. The Fourth of July!* That's over two months ago! A wave of nausea washes over her again and she clutches the bowl, emptying her stomach.

When she's finished, Ted helps Libby back to bed, tucking the blankets around her, then sits down on the edge of the mattress and smiles.

"Libby. When was your last period?" he asks, taking her hand in his.

"The beginning of July?" she whispers.

Ted leans down and hugs her to him, but she's lost all feeling in her body. She's completely numb. He's always wanted them to have another child but it never happened and she was secretly relieved. Now, the thought of doing this for a third time is making her physically ill. She's done with infants and diapers, potty training, childproofing, breastfeeding, and sleepless nights. *Done!* No more maternity clothes, stretch marks, swollen ankles, cravings, sciatica, or waddling. *I'm too old for this!*

"Baby, I'm so excited," he says and jumps from the bed, clasping his hands together.

Her face is frozen in shock. She can't speak or move.

"Libby, are you okay?" he asks, and sits back down beside her.

Still immobile, she shifts her eyes toward him. He wants them to have a baby! She looks up at the ceiling again and feels faint. This can't be happening. She thought she was finished. Having a baby would mean another five years of intense childrearing and she can't do it. She doesn't want to do it!

Libby loves her children…but she struggles with parenthood. Being a mother is the hardest thing she's ever done, and raising Emma has been particularly trying. For four years before Nate was born, she was home with her daughter full-time and felt like a failure every single day, blaming herself for Emma's colic and temper tantrums. Surely if she'd been a more patient and loving mother, her daughter would have been a happier child?

When she found out she was pregnant with Nate, she never told Ted how frightened she was, afraid she'd be incapable of caring for another child. She was barely managing with one! After Nate was born, Libby suffered from post-partum depression and found it difficult to get out of bed in the morning. She had little interest in the baby, and couldn't bear Emma's neediness. Overwhelmed with her responsibilities, Libby believed it wasn't a matter of whether she would screw up her children, it was a question of how badly? Her goal was minimum damage. She's sure this anxiety added to her depression after Nate's birth.

Fortunately, the older Emma and Nate get the easier parenting has become in some ways. She's able to communicate with them, find out what's hurting and figure out how she can fix it. Babies are a mystery. When she's exhausted her bag of tricks, fed, burped, changed, and snuggled them, and they won't stop crying? She has no clue what to do! She can't do this again, she just can't!

"Lib, you're scaring me. Blink once if you're okay, twice if I should take you to a hospital."

She blinks once, then turns onto her side and bursts into tears. Ted lies down beside her and wraps his arm around her waist.

"Hey there," he murmurs into her ear. "This is wonderful, Libby! We always wanted three kids!"

"No, Ted, we didn't, you did," she snaps.

"I wanted five kids, remember? We agreed on three," he counters, an edge to his voice.

"I can't do that again, Ted," she turns toward him, resting her palm against his cheek, her eyes pleading with him to understand. "I just don't have it in me. We have two great kids. We're in our forties. We're done."

He looks into her eyes, his face pained.

"What are you saying, Lib? You want to get rid of our child?" he asks.

Her eyes open wide and her chin trembles. Ted's face has turned red, his eyes narrowing into slits. She's seen her husband this angry before, but never directed toward her. It's frightening to be on the receiving end of his glare.

"Our hypothetical child, Ted," she swallows hard, then continues, "We don't even know if I'm pregnant."

He jumps out of bed and throws on a pair of jeans and a t-shirt, then slips on his shoes and grabs his wallet and keys.

"I'll be right back," he mutters, and storms out of their bedroom.

Her thoughts are racing, her heart beating hard against her ribs. *He's going to buy a pregnancy test!* How did she not realize this sooner? If she had half a brain, she would have put two and two together, and had time to process this before she spoke to Ted. If she spoke to him about it at all! She's never kept any secrets from her husband, but she knows how he feels about having a big family. And he may be liberal in his politics, but with his Catholic upbringing, he's conservative in his beliefs about abortion. *This is a nightmare!*

Noticing the time, she climbs out of bed and slips into her robe, then pads down the hallway to wake the children. Pregnant or not, life goes on. The kids need to eat breakfast and get ready for their soccer games, and it's best they aren't here when she takes the pregnancy test. Her breasts are tender, her abdomen bloated. She was so busy with life she missed all of the signs. The test is going to be positive, she's sure of it, and she's absolutely certain of something else. She doesn't want to have another child.

On autopilot, Libby gets the kids ready and pours their cereal before walking outside to the Whitaker house. Still in her robe, she knocks on the door and Caroline answers, which takes her by surprise. Caroline always sleeps in on Saturdays, making her grand appearance at the soccer field twenty minutes before the end of the game, looking impossibly put together and sophisticated.

"Hi Caro. Sorry to bother you. I was hoping Tru could bring the kids to their games today."

"I'll be taking the kids today, and of course Nate and Emma can come with us. No problem. Is everything okay, Libby?"

Libby nods her head, then looks away, tears filling her eyes.

"Yup. Everything's fine. I'll send them over shortly."

Ted pulls his BMW into the driveway, and climbs out of the car carrying a CVS bag, his face grim.

"Good morning, Ted," Caro waves and smiles.

"Morning, Caro. Lib, I need to talk to you," he says, then heads inside the house with his purchase.

Caroline frowns and stares after Ted, and Libby turns to follow him, her stomach churning.

"Thank you," she calls out before shutting the kitchen door behind her.

✳

The kids will be out of the house for at least three hours. Once they're gone, Libby and Ted head upstairs to their bedroom and her husband empties the contents of the CVS bag onto the bed. He purchased three boxes of tests, two tests to a box. She sits on the mattress and stares at the assortment. *It only takes one stick, Ted!*

"I don't want to do this," she whispers.

Ted sighs and lies down on the bed.

"Come here, baby," he says, his voice returning to its normal, loving tone.

She lowers herself down beside him but is at a loss for words. He kisses the top of her head, and neither of them speaks for several minutes.

"Look, Libby, I understand you're nervous, and I know you're the one who would have to carry the baby, but I'm not going to lie to you, I'm ecstatic. We make beautiful babies. I'd love to have another child with you! And you wouldn't have to do it alone. I'll pitch in and take some of the night shifts…"

"No…" she whispers, closing her eyes. "This is about so much more than having a baby."

"Libby…" he shakes his head and she grabs his hand.

"Ted, please listen to me. I'm turning forty in a few weeks. If I'm pregnant, and we have this child, we'll be in our sixties by the time he or she is out of college! And what about the increased possibility of birth defects? Women my age have a much higher chance of having children with problems. Could you handle that? I know I can't. Don't you want to relax and enjoy our twilight years? You promised we'd travel the world once the kids are grown. I'd like to be young enough to enjoy it!"

Ted kisses her hand and leans back against the pillows, then takes a deep breath in and sighs.

"Let's just take the test," he says. "There's no point in having this conversation if you're not pregnant."

✳

Who is this person? Libby stares into the bathroom mirror and doesn't recognize her own reflection; her eyes are sunken in, her cheeks hollow. *I'm a ghost.* She raises her hand to her face (yes, it's really me) and covers her mouth to keep from crying out. *Please God, no!* In shock, she looks down at the pregnancy tests again. It took ten seconds for both tests to reveal a plus sign in the little window. Ten seconds. She didn't even have the opportunity to flush the toilet before the plus signs appeared. Her husband is waiting for her on the other side of the door and she knows how he feels. Now they have to have the discussion, and it could get ugly.

Leaving the sticks on the sink, she slowly opens the bathroom door and Ted turns to her expectantly. She opens her mouth to speak, then panics and walks straight out of their bedroom, down the stairs, and into the backyard, with Ted calling out after her. She walks to the corner of their property and stands in front of a giant oak tree, rests her hands on the rough bark, and fights the urge to scream at the top of her lungs.

Moments later, Ted is behind her, his arms around her waist, one hand resting on her abdomen.

"Baby, it's okay. Everything is going to be fine. We can do this, I promise."

He promises? He promises! She can't turn around, can't bear to look at his face. The only way this is going to be fine is if she doesn't have this baby, and in her heart she knows he'll never allow that. Never. There won't be a discussion. She'll cry, he'll placate, then he'll issue a directive, and if she wants to keep the peace, she'll obey. He's a good man...but don't get in the way of what he wants. And right now, he wants this baby.

"Ted...Please don't make me do this," she whispers.

"This isn't about you, Libby." Ted drops his hands and turns her around to face him. "Can't you see that? This isn't about you! What's gotten into you? You're being so selfish."

She shakes her head, teeming with anger.

"Fuck you, Ted! I'm the one who has to carry this child. I'm the one who'll be up all night feeding it till my nipples bleed. I'm the one who will care for it while you're off doing God knows what. This is all about me! There's no 'we' in this scenario!"

"Doing 'God knows what?' Libby, what the hell are you talking about?"

"Heather. I'm talking about your new assistant, Heather! I'm talking about the woman I heard call out your name on the telephone the other night. I'm talking about Chanel No.5 and all of your late nights working and schmoozing at network events!"

Ted looks down at his feet and shakes his head.

"Libby, I'm going to chalk this up to pregnancy hormones. You're talking nonsense."

He turns and walks toward the house, his head down, hands in his pockets.

No, no, no, no, no! He's not walking away from this! She runs after him and grabs his arm.

"Who's Heather? Why did you hire her without talking to me?" she asks.

"I didn't want to bother you with it, you had enough on your plate. You were leaving for Nantucket, shuttling the kids back and forth to camp...A friend of mine recommended her when he found out Felice left. Heather just finished school and moved back to Rhode Island and was looking for a job. What's the big deal? Barry said she's a real go-getter and I needed the help. Do I need to continue? I don't understand where this is coming from, Libby."

She covers her face with her hands, lowers herself to the ground and cries. She's never questioned him before, not his love for her, or his faithfulness. Maybe he's right? Maybe these are pregnancy hormones talking? *I'm pregnant. What am I going to do?* She sobs into her hands, and Ted sits beside her, holding her while she cries.

Eventually she quiets down, and looks up to find Truman standing on his deck, his face pained with concern. Their eyes lock and she wipes away her tears, her chin trembling. Ted helps her rise unsteadily to her feet and together, they walk back to the house. But she's not the same person who walked out of it twenty minutes earlier. She's going to have this baby for her husband and the resentment is growing, a tumor inside her, getting larger by the second.

CHAPTER FIVE

C lutching a glass of wine, Libby and the other book club members gather in Greta's living room for the pre-meeting mingle. She's been here a little over half an hour, wandering around her neighbor's house in the perpetual daze she's been in since discovering her pregnancy four days earlier. She wasn't going to come tonight, has been avoiding everyone while she absorbs this new reality. But this evening, Ted practically pushed her out the door, encouraging her to share their "good news" with friends, hoping that a little social interaction will snap her out of this funk.

She hasn't told a soul she's pregnant. Not Truman, not Ginger, no one. Ginger has been out of town, which made it easier, but Truman saw her crying on the lawn Saturday with Ted. He knows something's wrong and she can't keep this a secret forever. She stayed in bed all day Sunday, but Monday morning at the bus stop he asked what was wrong, and Libby lied. She said they had an argument about the kids, no big deal. Truman stared into her eyes for a long moment, his brows drawn together. He doesn't believe her, but she's not ready to talk about this.

Nor has she managed to make a doctor's appointment and Ted said he'll make it himself if she doesn't call the doctor tomorrow. She has, however, driven by Planned Parenthood a dozen times, sometimes parking in front and chewing on her fingernails while watching the women enter and exit the building. How easy would it be to walk inside and ask for the magic pill? She could tell Ted she miscarried, he'd never have to know. But how could she go forward in a relationship polluted with her lies? She'd be ripping the foundation of their marriage out from under them. And if Ted ever did find out, he'd leave her, and she wouldn't blame him. That's an unforgiveable lie.

But how different is it from what he's asking her to do? He wants her to live a lie, pretend to be happy about this baby when she's not. He's forcing her to sacrifice the next five years of her life! Ted's life won't change no matter how many promises he's made to do more this time around. She can count on two hands the number of times he changed Emma and Nate's diapers, and the man can sleep through an earthquake. There's no way he'll be getting up for early morning feedings. Nothing will be different this time, she's not an idiot.

She can't stand to be around him right now. Anger and resentment have twisted her insides into knots. She's never felt this way about Ted, has never been so angry she fantasizes about smothering him with a pillow while he sleeps. They've had arguments in the past, but nothing close to this; forgetting to pick up milk on his way home from the office, not calling to let her know he's working late, leaving wet towels on the bathroom floor, receipts in pockets, taking business calls in the middle of family dinners. Little things, forgivable things. Misdemeanors.

76

What he's asking her to do now feels more like a crime. He's hijacking her body, stealing years of her life, robbing her of her legal right to choose.

"Libby, I know you're not all right," Truman whispers, joining her at the window.

She takes a sip of wine and stares out the picture window, staying mute.

"Why won't you tell me what's wrong?" he asks.

"I can't Tru. I just can't talk about it yet," she says, her eyes filling with tears.

Truman wraps an arm around her shoulders and gives her a squeeze.

"I'm worried about you, Lib. When you're ready to talk, I'm here. Okay?"

She nods her head and wipes her face, then turns to Truman and takes his hand in hers, thankful for his friendship and understanding.

Just then, Ginger joins them at the window with a couple of friends she invited to the meeting. Libby's never met them, but one women has been living in Italy on and off for over a decade and Ginger thought she'd spice up the conversation. The other woman is a friend from college she recently became reacquainted with via social media. Libby was looking forward to meeting them both but is not feeling up for conversation tonight. She takes a deep breath in, wanting to make a somewhat normal impression on Ginger's friends.

"Hey, there!" Ginger kisses them each on the cheek. "I'd like you to meet my college roommate, Ellie Kennedy...I mean Perkins. I'm not used to your married name!" she laughs. "And this is Ellie's sister-in-law, Julia," she introduces them. "Ladies, these are my dear friends, Libby and Truman."

"It's nice to meet you both," Libby shakes their hands. "Ginger's told me a lot about you."

"Oh dear God," Ellie cries. "I can only imagine! We got into all sorts of trouble in college, didn't we Ging?"

"That's for sure! Do you remember when…"

Libby's mind wanders as they reminisce about the old days and she takes another sip, finishing off her wine. Staring into her empty glass, it dawns on her that she shouldn't be drinking…*but I'm going to.* Having a couple glasses of wine may be the only way she'll get through this evening. As if reading her mind, Truman reappears by her side and hands her a fresh glass, and she closes her eyes for a moment. She needs to pull it together and make it through the next couple of hours. The last thing she wants is to be the subject of neighborhood gossip.

♂

The book discussion is under way, but Truman is having difficulty focusing on the conversation. He finished the book earlier today and found himself drawn into the story near the end. He could identify with the main character's plight; starting over once your marriage disintegrates. Longing for love and family, and feeling like it'll never happen, until you wake up one day and realize it's been in front of you all along. He stares at Libby sitting across the room. She's a part of his family, just like the neighbors in *Under the Tuscan Sun* became part of Frances' family.

Something is very wrong with Libby. Saturday morning, while he was standing at the kitchen sink, he overheard Libby shouting at Ted in the yard. He couldn't make out what was said, but he'd never seen her so distraught. She won't talk to him and it's driving him nuts! He cares about her. Forget his recent lust-filled fantasies, he just wants his friend to be all right.

She's been very quiet this evening, distracted. *Delicate.* That's not a word he'd normally associate with Libby. She's tall, athletic, strong and capable. And pretty. Not 'scream in your face, drop dead gorgeous' like his wife, but a natural, wholesome beauty. The girl next door with bright blue eyes and a smattering of freckles on her nose.

Tonight, her shoulder-length chestnut brown hair is pulled away from her face with a tortoise shell headband, and she's wearing a loose-fitted ivory tunic, but despite her summer tan, she looks washed out, exhausted. It's her eyes, he realizes. Normally, they're bright and alive with curiosity. Tonight they're glazed over and empty.

He tries to focus on the discussion, but his efforts are in vain. Ginger's friend, Julia, is discussing her family's life in Italy, and everyone is listening intently to her stories, leaning in and laughing. Everyone except Libby. *And me.*

Taking a deep breath in, Truman draws his attention to the assortment of women sitting around the room and shakes his head. *How did I get here?* He's living the life of a middle-aged suburban housewife, mingling with other housewives. How will he ever meet someone if these are the only people he socializes with? He needs to make some serious changes.

Where to begin? He hasn't been on the market in twenty years! It's not like he can ask his friends for referrals. He could place an ad in the paper. Do people still do that? He grimaces at the thought. Too seedy. A dating website? What would he say? 'Married man in open relationship seeks woman for no-strings-attached sex? Must be STD free?' He closes his eyes and takes a deep breath in. *I sound like a pervert.*

Since he discovered Caroline's infidelity the other night, he's felt a burden lifted. After four years trapped in a sexual wasteland, he's free to do as he pleases. If he thought Ginger could keep a secret from Libby, he'd consider confiding in her, ask if she knows any single women who could handle the complexities of his situation. Except to complain about Caro's long hours, he has never discussed the status of his marriage with either Ginger or Libby. He was embarrassed to admit his wife lost interest in him years ago, even to his best friends.

Just then, he and Ginger lock eyes and she walks the perimeter of the room toward him.

"Truman," Ginger whispers, taking a seat beside him. "Are you okay? You haven't said a word all evening."

"I'm not the only one," he says.

Ginger's brow furrows and she scans the living room.

"Libby? She said she's not feeling well."

He raises an eyebrow and shrugs.

"Is everything all right at home? Anything going on between you and Caro?" she asks.

Truman smiles, then begins to laugh, slapping his hand over his mouth. The women seated near them turn and scowl, their faces disapproving, but he can't help it, he can't stop laughing.

"Excuse me," he whispers and walks through the house to the patio, then takes a seat on a lounge chair and closes his eyes.

Ginger joins him outside and plops down beside him, her arms folded across her chest.

"What's gotten into you?"

"Ging, I wouldn't know where to begin. I'm sorry...I'm not myself tonight. I should just go home."

"Tru, I asked how things are between you and your wife and you burst out laughing. That's a pretty clear indication things are not okay. Talk to me. Are you having problems with Caro?"

He shrugs his shoulders, then shakes his head slowly side to side.

"Nothing's ever as it seems, is it Ginger? You know that better than anyone. Everything looks fine on the surface, but who knows what goes on behind closed doors?" he asks, thinking of his own marriage, and Libby and Ted. If he hadn't seen them in the yard he would never guess they were having problems.

"Very true. So you've hit a rough patch...or is it more serious? You know, if you can't talk to your friends, who can you talk to?"

Before he can respond, Libby opens the door and joins them on the patio, her eyes downcast.

"I'm really not feeling well. I'm heading home."

"Oh no!" Ginger cries. "I wanted you to join us for drinks after the meeting!"

"Sorry," Libby says. "I need to lie down. Another time."

"I'll walk you home," Truman says, rising from the lounge chair.

She squeezes his hand and shakes her head.

"No need. I'll see you tomorrow."

Libby kisses them both on the cheek, then walks through the backyards separating Greta's house from hers, Truman watching her until she is safely home.

"You really care about her, don't you?" Ginger asks, tilting her head in the direction of Libby's house.

He looks down at his feet and clears his throat.

"She's my best friend," he says, meeting Ginger's gaze.

She studies him, her eyes narrowing, and he feels his neck growing hot, his ears turning red. Truman smiles and kisses her on the cheek.

"Goodnight, Ginger." he says, then follows Libby's path home.

✳

She's going to talk to me tonight, whether she wants to or not! Truman thinks as he washes the dishes, watching Libby from the kitchen window. They finished dinner with the kids a little while ago and he told her to relax while he cleaned up. She's curled up on a lounge chair in his backyard, staring into the fire pit, wrapped in one of his sweatshirts. Caroline is out tonight and Ted is working late, so it's just the two of them. And four children. But Sadie's in her room, and the other kids are in his basement watching a movie. He dries his hands on a dishtowel and pours two glasses of wine, then sets his jaw and heads outside, determined to get to the bottom of what's troubling her.

Libby looks up from the fire when he hands her the glass of wine and smiles, then sits back against the blue and white cushioned chair. Together, they sit in silence for several minutes, each sipping their wine. When Libby finishes her glass she takes a deep breath in and sighs.

"I'm pregnant," she says, her voice no more than a whisper.

Truman coughs behind his hand. *Did she say pregnant?* He leans forward in his seat, and takes her hand in his.

"And this isn't good news?" he asks, shaking his head.

"Not for me. But, Ted? That's a different story."

He sits back in his chair and looks up at the sky. The stars are bright, and there's a chill in the air. It will be fall before long. Another baby! Good God!

"What're you going to do, Lib?"

"Have the baby, of course!" she snorts. "That's what Ted wants after all! And what Ted wants, Ted gets!"

He's never heard Libby speak of her husband with such contempt and has no idea what to say. The first thought that pops into his head is, *Who cares what Ted wants?* How would he have felt if Caroline had come home pregnant with Bette and said she wanted to have an abortion? He wouldn't have been happy. But Caro was thirty-one at the time, he was thirty-two, not forty! He doubts his reaction would be the same if she came home today with that announcement, even if they had a solid relationship.

"Libby…I'm so sorry," he whispers.

She snaps her head in his direction, her eyes narrowing.

"You don't think I'm selfish for not wanting this baby?"

"No, of course not. You thought you were done. I get that. How far along are you?" he asks, noting this is the third glass of wine she's consumed this evening. And the other night at book club she had at least that much. She's never been much of a drinker, two glasses (usually) her limit.

"I'm not sure. At least eight weeks, probably ten. I haven't been to the doctor yet. I'll know more next week. Ted made an appointment with my OB for Tuesday."

Again, he notes the anger in her voice.

"Libby…Ted can't make you do this, you know."

"My marriage would be over, Tru. He'd never forgive me if I got rid of it."

"Will you ever forgive him for making you keep it?" he asks, his voice soft.

Their eyes lock for a long moment, then she bursts into tears. Covering her face with her hands, she folds over and rests her head on her knees, her body trembling with emotion. He kneels down beside her and rubs her back, his heart breaking for Libby and the position she's in. It's not like Ted's going to pick up the slack when this baby is born! This is Libby's burden to bear.

Ted's not one of Truman's favorite people. They get along fine when he's around, but something about him doesn't sit right with Truman. It's Ted's arrogance, his sense of entitlement. He takes his family for granted, takes Libby for granted, and she's different when he's around; quieter, more guarded. Truman enjoys Libby most when she's not around her husband; when she's totally relaxed and in his eyes, most herself.

But in all the time he's known her, she's been happy in her marriage and deeply in love with Ted, and her husband seems to return those feelings. Truman can see it in both of their eyes, particularly when Ted comes home from a trip. He's been envious of their relationship for years and has wished he and Caro felt a fraction of what Libby and Ted feel for one another. Love like theirs can't be faked and as Libby's friend, that's all that matters to Truman, her happiness. He doesn't have to like the guy. He just has to be nice in Ted's presence.

Once Libby's sobs subside, she sits back and curls up on the chair, pulling her knees to her chest. She looks so tiny in his sweatshirt, and again the word 'delicate' pops into his head. Not just physically delicate...mentally fragile.

"Libby, if you're going to do this, if you've made up your mind to keep the baby...you should probably talk to someone. You need to make peace with this decision or it'll eat you up inside. Have you thought about seeing a therapist?"

Libby frowns and shakes her head.

"Have you ever been to one?" she asks, her eyes curious.

He nods his head. Not alone, but he has with Caroline.

"Did it help?"

He looks into his friend's eyes and shakes his head, smiling.

"Not really!" he chuckles.

Libby raises an eyebrow, then bursts out laughing and he joins her, the two of them in tears when Caroline joins them in the backyard moments later.

"What's so funny?" she asks, sending them into another fit of laughter.

A few minutes pass before Ted walks into the backyard and the laughter subsides. Truman forces himself to keep a smile on his face and Libby wipes away her tears and stashes the wine glass under the lounge chair, her face transforming into an emotionless mask. She stares into the fire pit again and Ted walks up behind her and massages her shoulders.

"Hello, everyone. Did I miss the party?"

Truman rises and shakes Ted's hand, just as he would any other day.

"Can I get you a beer?" he asks.

"No thanks, Tru," Ted says. "Just came to collect my family."

CHAPTER SIX

L ibby sits in the elegantly appointed waiting room, chewing on what's left of her fingernails. She thought she'd kicked the habit years ago, but it reared its ugly head again once she discovered her pregnancy. She sits back on the love seat and looks around the small sitting area, taking in the antique maps hanging on the wall across from her, the faded Oriental rug and the plush armchairs. The diploma framed beside the door says Brown Medical School. Everything in the room screams quality, taste, money. *Probably old money...*

This is her first visit to Dr. Bradford, the therapist Ginger recommended to her. The past two months have been...difficult. The morning sickness was short-lived, but her anger mutated into an oppressive sadness as the reality of the situation hit her square between the eyes. She's hardly left the house, or her bed for that matter. All she wants to do is sleep this pregnancy away and be left in peace.

Libby never goes into the office anymore and Ted turned over most of her responsibilities to his assistant, Heather, who majored in marketing and was only too eager to take over Libby's projects. "She's excited to apply what she learned in college in the real world," Ted said. "But we need you Libby. Please come back," he pleaded with her the first month she was gone.

Then Ted went silent on the topic.

Initially, Ted was attentive, trying to coax away her sadness and fuel the flames of their excitement, but her depression has put a damper on the pregnancy for the whole family. When Libby and Ted finally sat the children down to share the news, her husband did all the talking. The kids were excited, Nate more so than Emma. Her son hooped and hollered, running around the room before throwing his arms around her. He's hoping for a baby brother; Emma doesn't have a preference. Libby tried to feign happiness but barely managed a smile. She's found it impossible to fake enthusiasm, even for the sake of her children.

Ted explained to the children that sometimes pregnant women feel sick and that's what's happened to Mommy. Having a baby is hard on the body, so everyone needs to help her out until she feels better. *If I ever feel better.* Every morning, Nate runs into her bedroom, hoping this is the day she's back to normal, and it breaks her heart to see his disappointment when she shakes her head. *Not today, Nate.*

Nina, a young Cape Verdean woman who has been babysitting for the Fitzgerald's since Nate was born, has been taking care of the children for her after school every day. The sitter meets Nate and Emma at the bus stop, and Truman helps shuttle them to practices and lessons. Then Nina comes back to the house and does the laundry, cleans up after the kids, prepares dinner, and makes sure their homework is done. Nina doesn't ask questions, just quietly goes about the business of raising Libby's children while she stays holed up in her bedroom.

The only parental duties she's responsible for these days are tucking them into bed and getting the kids out the door for school in the morning. As soon as they're on the bus, she goes home and crawls under the covers, exhausted, too tired to care what the neighbors are saying about her disheveled appearance and now obvious pregnancy.

Her marriage is strained in a way it's never been before. A fog has infiltrated the corners of her mind, rendering her virtually speechless in his presence. Ted has tried to reach her, but she can't string the words together to express her feelings. Over the past few weeks, he's taken to working even longer hours than he normally does. Ted crawls into bed after midnight most evenings when he believes she's asleep, but she's not sleeping. She knows exactly what time he's coming home.

Once the rhythm of his breathing steadies, she sneaks out of bed and wanders the house, then takes a walk outside, desperate for a little fresh air. It's almost Thanksgiving and the air is crisp, little puffs of smoke appearing with each breath. The neighborhood takes on an otherworldly quality in the early hours of morning, the moon casting mysterious shadows over most of the landscape.

She brings her camera with her on these excursions and attempts to capture the mystical quality of her surroundings. Once again, the lens has become a filter between herself and the world, distracting her from reality. Little critters join her roaming the streets, and the tiny creature in her belly has begun to flutter and kick, confiscating her body, reminding her that time is running out. This brief period of relative freedom will be over in a few short months.

❋

"Mrs. Fitzgerald," an elegantly clad woman in her mid-to-late forties opens the door to the adjoining office and greets

Libby, firmly shaking her hand. "Please, come with me. May I get you some water or maybe tea?" she asks.

"No, thank you," Libby says, gathering her coat and purse and follows the doctor into the connecting room.

Dr. Bradford takes a seat in an armchair in front of the fireplace and motions for Libby to sit on the loveseat across from her. Libby sinks down into the comfortable cushions and resists the urge to close her eyes. It's only eleven o'clock in the morning, but she's usually in some state of semi-unconsciousness at this time of day.

"So, Libby, what brings you here today?" the doctor asks.

"I was hoping you could prescribe something for depression," Libby says, getting straight to the point. She'd like to be in and out of here in ten minutes.

The doctor studies her for a moment, her eyes narrowing slightly.

"I'm not in the habit of writing prescriptions without understanding the underlying cause of my patient's depression."

She doesn't want to talk. If she actually understood what she was feeling, she'd talk to her friends or her husband. She doesn't need a doctor for that. All she wants is the prescription. Libby sighs, resting her head back against the couch and looks around the office. The doctor has a collection of terrariums with a variety of plants by the window. African violets, cacti…she tries to remember the names of the other flowers.

If her friends hadn't pushed the issue, she wouldn't be here at all. Ginger and Truman have been checking in with her often and in her uniform of sweat pants, t-shirt, and cardigan, she occasionally sits with them in the living room while they discuss world events, books and town news, trying to draw her out of her shell. She rarely contributes anything to the conversation and refuses to discuss her pregnancy.

When Libby suffered from post-partum depression after Nate was born, she took anti-depressants for a few months and they worked wonders. So, when Ginger handed her Dr. Bradford's card last week, she agreed to make an appointment, hoping the drugs will make things better again.

This fog feels different from her post-partum depression; it's thicker, denser, harder to navigate. Everything is slipping away, her husband, the children, her work. Every morning she tells herself today will be different. *Today I will accomplish something.* Take a shower, empty the dishwasher, make the kids beds. Anything! But the effort required to perform even the simplest tasks seem monumental, impossible in her current state of mind.

When Ginger called to check on her this morning, Libby cried into the phone, unable to muster the energy to take a shower. So her friend came over and got her ready for this appointment. Ginger helped her bathe, then wrapped her in a terrycloth robe. Libby sat on the bench in front of the dressing table while Ginger dried and styled her hair, applied a little blush and lipstick, helped her get dressed, then hand-delivered her to the doctor's office in Providence.

"The underlying cause of my depression?" Libby asks. "I'm forty years old and almost five months pregnant. Wouldn't that depress you?"

"Not necessarily, Libby. Let's take a step back. You're unhappy about this pregnancy. Why did you decide to have the baby?"

Libby crosses her arms over her chest, resting them on her small bump and frowns. This isn't going to be as easy as she thought.

"Multiple choice," the doctor continues. "Did you decide to keep the baby for A) Religious reasons? B) Moral reasons? or C) Against your will?"

Staring into the fireplace, Libby mutters, "C."

"Your husband?" the doctor asks.

She nods her head, her teeth clenched, brow furrowed.

"At the risk of sounding too 'shrinkish', how does that make you feel?" the doctor smiles, waiting for a response. "Libby, I can't make you talk, but I won't write you a prescription unless you do."

"I hate him!" she shouts, startling herself. "I hate this baby! I hate feeling like this! I want to be a mother to the two children I already have. I want to love my husband again." Libby begins to cry, "I want my life back...I just want to go back..." she sobs into her hands.

"Go back to what point in time exactly?" Dr. Bradford asks gently, handing her a tissue.

The question confuses her, halting the flow of tears. *Back to what time?* Images from her life before Ted come to mind, when she had her own career aspirations, her own money. When she was her own person, not pushed and pulled in a million directions trying to please everyone around her. She should say, she wants to go back six months and not get pregnant. But she wants to go further back. Much further back.

"There are no right or wrong answers here, Libby," the doctor says.

"I want my life to be my own again. I want to pursue my own dreams. I'd like the opportunity to figure out what they are! I don't even remember anymore. For the past twelve years it's been all about Ted's dreams. This is the first year both of my children are in school all day. I thought I was finally free," she says and winces as the words tumble from her lips.

"Free of what?"

"Responsibility," Libby murmurs.

"You're a wife and mother. Responsibility comes with the territory. Before you found out you were pregnant, were you happy in your marriage?"

"Yes," she replies, and to her relief, genuinely means it.

"Was there any room for improvement?"

"Isn't there always, doctor?" she raises an eyebrow.

"Of course. Anything specific?"

"I wish Ted were more involved in our daily lives. He works very long hours at the firm, and travels for business often. It's like he's a visitor, swooping in and out of our lives..." her voice trails off, considering how little time Ted actually spends at home. These past few weekends he's spent more time with the kids than he ever has...because he's been forced to by her depression.

"Which puts the full responsibility of running the household and raising the children in your hands."

Libby stares at the doctor, the knot of resentment in the pit of her stomach tightening.

"And now he's adding another huge responsibility to your already considerable list of responsibilities," the doctor pauses. "Why didn't you just say no?"

She shakes her head back and forth, her feelings of resentment transforming into disgust, but not toward her husband. She's disgusted with herself for turning into the type of woman she used to mock, the kind of woman who would allow a man to control her life. She wasn't always like this, was she? She remembers being independent and ambitious...before she met Ted.

"You could have refused, Libby...why didn't you?"

"Because he wouldn't let me," she murmurs, looking down at her hands. "And I didn't want to lose him."

✳

Prescription in hand, Libby meets Ginger outside in the parking lot and climbs into her friends Mercedes SUV, a fire burning in her stomach. *He wouldn't let me! But I let him control me. This is my fault. And I'm the only one who can make this better.* She feels more focused than she has in months.

"Ginger, please drop me at the office."

"What? Wait! What happened in there?"

"I need to talk to Ted."

Ginger drives across town to Ted's office building and pulls into a space in the lot. She was quiet the entire ride over, but her thoughts are racing. She's not even sure what she wants to say to her husband, but feels the need to see him. *I'm sorry I let you control my life? I love you but I don't like you very much right now. I've turned into a pathetic, needy woman and that ends now?*

"Do you want me to come in with you? Or wait here?" Ginger asks.

"I don't know how long I'll be. Ted will drive me home. Thank you, Ginger," she says and kisses her friend on the cheek before opening the door and stepping onto the pavement.

Pushing through the doors at Fitzgerald & Associates, Libby realizes how much she misses interacting with others on a professional level. She never imagined she'd be designing campaign materials for politicians and lobbying groups when she began her career in advertising. This type of work doesn't exactly lend itself to creative expression. Design a logo, come up with a slogan, create a 'brand identity' for the candidate or cause. She can do it in her sleep.

It's time for something new, and she has a lot of thinking to do, needs to understand what she wants for herself and figure out how she can incorporate those goals into the life she and Ted have built, baby and all. Having another child felt like a death sentence to her, but it's not. It's just a setback. She can do this. With Ted's help, she can juggle her many responsibilities. And Nina's help…and Truman's help…and Ginger's… It takes a village to raise a child.

"Libby!" Renata rises from the reception desk and gives her a tentative hug. "It's been so long! How are you feeling?"

"Better, thanks. Is he in a meeting?"

Renata's eyes dart around the office, then she picks up the phone and buzzes Ted's office. Libby holds up her hand and walks down the hallway to the office suite where she finds Ted's door closed, the blinds shut. That's odd. Usually, Ted keeps his door and blinds wide open. He wants to see the hustle and bustle of the firm for himself. Several associates greet her, their eyes downcast, and brush past her while she stands in front of his door. What is going on here?

Ted opens the door smiling, his face flushed.

"Sweetheart! What a pleasant surprise," he says, kissing her cheek and maneuvering her back down the hallway toward the reception area. "Let's go to lunch! I was just about to grab something at the deli across the street, but we could find a nicer place."

Frowning, Libby wrenches her arm free from his grasp and stands her ground. A wave of exhaustion washes over her and she leans against the wall.

"Ted, I just arrived. What's the rush?" she asks.

"I'm sorry, baby," he says, pulling on his coat. "I have a meeting at one, which gives me…" he checks his watch, "Not much time to eat."

She hasn't shown her face in the office in two months, he hasn't seen her in anything but sweats and pajamas in all that time, they've hardly spoken a word to each other…*and he wants to grab a quick bite?* Libby turns around and walks back down the hallway, enters his office and lowers herself onto the loveseat, her arms folded across her chest. She fights to keep her eyes open as her body sinks into the soft cushions, then snaps her head up and picks up the pillow beside her. *Chanel No.5?* Yes. It smells like that horrid perfume.

A moment later, Ted sits beside her and shifts uncomfortably in his seat. She studies his profile as he settles in, her eyes narrowing with suspicion. *Who was in this office before she arrived? Why are his blinds closed?* Something's going on but she's not up to dealing with anything other than the issue she came here to discuss. She needs to reserve the little strength she has for this conversation.

"Ted, I want to talk to you."

He turns his head toward her, and she catches a fleeting expression cross his face, that of a naughty schoolboy about to be punished.

"What about?" he asks, then settles back against the cushions, adopting an air of bravado. She raises an eyebrow, thinking, that's the Ted I know. Confident. Cocky.

"You need to ask? Ted, we've hardly spoken in months."

"Are you all right?" he asks, his eyes immediately dropping to her stomach.

"I went to a doctor today. A psychiatrist…" her voice tapers off. *What do I want to say?* "I've been so angry with you about this baby. Angry and depressed."

Ted turns away from her and stares out the window, the muscles in his jaw clenching.

"But today I realized it's not your fault. No one can make me do anything. I made the choice to have this baby, then I made you pay for my decision. I can't go on like this. It's not fair to the kids, and I know it's not fair to you. I'm sorry I've been pushing you away."

Ted turns to her, his eyes filling with tears, then grasps her hand and pulls her closer to him.

"We're having another baby. Good lord, Ted. A baby!" she says and leans forward, rubbing her hands over her eyes. "I'm scared shitless and I can't do it alone. I need to know we're a team. Promise me we'll do this together."

Ted wraps his arms around her, holding her tight.

"Oh, baby..." he murmurs into her hair. "I promise we'll do it together. I've missed you so much. I thought I'd lost you."

She winds her arms around his broad chest and blinks back tears. Her resentment hasn't magically vanished over the space of the past two hours, but her thoughts are a little clearer now. The lines of communication had completely broken down, in large part because of her. Ted tried to get through to her...she just needed time, and Dr. Bradford to help open her eyes.

A moment later, the door flies open and Heather enters the office. Startled, Libby lifts her head from Ted's chest and their eyes meet, Heather's wide with shock. She releases her hold on Ted, and he wipes his eyes, then turns around and quickly rises.

"Heather, what do you need?" he asks, his voice strained.

The girl stands immobile, her eyes on Libby, then snaps herself out of her daze and hands Ted the folder she was carrying.

"Sorry, just wanted to get these mockups to you before your meeting. Hello, Mrs. Fitzgerald," Heather mumbles, then turns on her three-inch heels and leaves.

Ted tosses the folder on his desk, holds his hands out to Libby, and pulls her off the couch and into his embrace.

"Libby, I love you. I'm so glad you're back."

"I love you too," she whispers, locking eyes with Heather. The young woman has taken up residence beside her desk outside of Ted's office, her face red, her eyes filled with anger.

Ted...what did you do? She closes her eyes and tries to block out all thought. He wouldn't...he couldn't. She's so young. They haven't had sex in almost two months and Ted's a very sexual man. *But Heather?* She shakes her head, trying to eradicate the thought. Libby's physically and mentally unable to go there, to entertain the possibilities associated with Heather's glare. What's done is done. She can't make the past two months disappear. It's time to concentrate on getting better and prepare for this baby who'll be here before long.

CHAPTER SEVEN

D*ating sucks.* And trying to date anyone under these circumstances sucks that much more. Was this ever fun? Truman can't remember the last time he went on an actual date before he met Caroline. He went to his share of parties in college and had plenty of 'hook-ups' back in the day. But he was a kid. Nineteen, twenty years old! Going to the movies and making out in the back row of the theater was his idea of a good time back then. Parking his VW bus on the beach and skinny-dipping in the moonlight was as adventurous as he got.

That actually sounds pretty good to him right now. Whatever happened to that VW bus? His parents still live in Vermont, eternal hippies who moved there from Minnesota back in the sixties to live on a commune when he and his sister were babies. They moved off the farm a few years later when his dad began teaching English at the local middle school and his mother opened a general store selling her jams, jellies, and other locally produced goods. Truman was six when they moved to town, but he remembers running around naked with the other kids in the summer and the smell of marijuana takes him back to those early days instantly.

JAYNE CONWAY

He inherited the VW bus from his parents when he left home to study oceanography at the University of Rhode Island. A summer vacation to Cape Cod when he was ten years old sparked a life long fascination with the ocean and the world that exists below the surface. Below the surface. So much goes on below the surface of every living thing. It's the same with people. He's drawn to hidden depths, feels the desire to uncover them while fearing what he'll find. It's a quest for understanding in a world that doesn't make sense.

After graduation, his plan was to move to Woods Hole on the Cape and work at the Oceanographic Institute, but when he met Caroline senior year, everything changed. She was the most beautiful girl he had ever laid eyes on…and she chose him. He didn't understand why at first. He was by no means the big man on campus, but he was one of the better looking ones according to his friends. That was apparently enough for her, though it took him a while to come to terms with this simple fact. He's never been comfortable being the pretty boy and wanted to believe women were attracted to him for more than his looks.

They met taking a math class, a pre-requisite they both needed in order to graduate, and he sat in the row behind her in the lecture hall. Every time she turned around to pass him a paper his breath caught in his throat. He felt ridiculous, knew better than to judge a book by its cover, but couldn't help but admire the beauty of her 'cover'. He didn't say a word to her for weeks, not until she asked him to help her study for the mid-term exam.

Later that night, they met in the library and it took less than one hour for them to find their way to her bedroom at the sorority house. That was it. He was twenty-two years old and completely captivated by Caroline, spending every free moment in her arms, blissfully unaware he was falling victim to the very thing he loathed in others; surface admiration…or adoration in this case.

When she decided to attend law school at Roger Williams University, she asked him to make the move with her and he didn't hesitate. Truman would have followed Caro to the ends of the earth in those days. So, he stayed in Rhode Island and they rented a small place in downtown Bristol, living in their three-room apartment until she finished law school.

Those were some of the happiest days of his life. He bartended down the road at Murphy's Pub and took classes in computer engineering once Caroline convinced him computers were the wave of the future. She was right. Computers are here to stay and he's always been able to find work. His Connecticut-bred, Gold Coast girlfriend managed to convince his hippy Vermont heart to follow the money and succumb to capitalist greed.

Looking back, he sees himself for the pathetic puppy dog he was, being trained to fit the lifestyle Caroline was accustomed to, but it wasn't a comfortable fit. When they married and moved to Littleton shortly after, the first thing they did was join the yacht club. It made sense to him. They have a boat and he loves to sail. He didn't realize there would be social obligations attached to the membership. Caroline was in her element, hobnobbing with Littleton's finest, but he found himself wandering down the dock and retreating to their boat during these events more often than not.

Gone were his evenings bartending at Murphy's Pub and the camaraderie he had found amongst the patrons and co-workers. This move ushered in the era of desk jobs, suits, and a closet full of khakis and polo shirts. If it weren't for his children, and Libby and Ginger, he doesn't think he would've made it this long in Littleton, especially since his marriage fell apart. At least before then, he had his wife to hold onto when he was grasping for a life preserver. Those days are long gone.

His parents were disappointed when he abandoned his dreams for Caroline's, though they've mellowed out about his choices since the girls were born. But every time they come to visit him in Littleton, their disapproval is written clearly across their faces. Every manicured lawn, flat-screen television, stainless steel appliance, Land Rover, iPad, tennis lesson, and visit to the yacht club elicits a groan or eye roll from them. "What did we do wrong?" is their common refrain. As if wealth is something to be ashamed of! It was never his goal to be wealthy but he's not ashamed of having money, even if his wife earns the vast majority of it.

They've never warmed to Caroline, but they adore their granddaughters and have pleaded with him on more than one occasion to move back home so they can be a bigger part of the girls' lives. Every summer, he brings his daughters to Vermont for a month and his parents do their best to undo the 'damage' done by their lives of privilege. They insist the girls remain technology free, help out with chores and give back to the community. The girls love staying with his parents and those weeks up in Vermont rejuvenate his spirit as well.

While Libby was in the throes of depression, Truman spent a lot of time with Ginger and decided to confide in her about his situation with Caroline, swearing her to secrecy, especially from Libby. She was shocked to learn his marriage had devolved to the state it's in and urged him to get a divorce, to cut the cord entirely. Once Ginger realized that wasn't likely to happen, she tried to fix him up with a few women, all divorced, all successful and attractive, all…exactly like his wife.

It's been a disaster. He could've had sex with these women, they made that very clear, but the last thing he wanted to do was have sex with someone who reminds him of Caroline.

Ginger's latest scheme to find him a woman involved joining Facebook. He doesn't understand the correlation between Facebook and dating. If he wanted to stay in touch with people from his past, he would have done so in some other way. Like the telephone, or the US Postal Service, even email! But he agreed to set up his profile to placate her. So far, a bunch of old friends from high school and college have reached out to him, but he hasn't interacted with anyone other than to say hello.

"Tru, you don't understand! Facebook is chock full of unhappily married people putting out feelers, hoping to find a reason to leave their spouses! It's a dating site for all intents and purposes. That's how I met all the men I've dated over the past three years! Guys I went to college with who are separated or newly divorced. There's a whole other world out there in cyberspace. People do and say things they'd never have the guts to in person. It's a perfect breeding ground for immoral behavior!"

"Immoral behavior?" he asks, raising an eyebrow.

"You know what I mean! Maybe you'll meet someone and fall in love, someone who'll make you want to leave Caro."

"You really don't get it, do you? I'm not separated like the men you've dated. I'm not leaving my wife. She's not leaving me. We just live our own lives."

"They don't all start off separated, Tru. Don't be so naïve! The average man needs a fallback plan. A lot of women do too. Don't you want to fall in love again?" she asks.

"That's what my fifties are for," he responds with a sigh.

"Then you'll be too old to get it up! I don't know what to tell you Tru," she throws up her hands in exasperation. "Hire a hooker. Save the money you would spend on dinner and a show, and just hand it to a prostitute. There are some high end call girls, disease free and everything!"

"I'm not quite there," he grimaces.

"Wait a second…" she says, her face lighting up. "How could I forget Ashley Madison?"

"Who's Ashley Madison?" he asks.

The name is vaguely familiar, but he can't place her. Is she a mom at the school?

"Not 'who', Truman…'what'. Let me look it up," she says, grabbing her iPad.

Ginger types in the name, waits a moment, then bursts out laughing.

"What?" he asks, mystified.

"Hold on…" she raises her hand and continues giggling as she skims the page. "Okay, Tru, this is exactly what you're looking for." Ginger clears her throat, then reads from the website. "Ashley Madison is the online personals and dating destination for casual encounters, married dating, discreet encounters and extramarital affairs."

His eyes grow wide as she reads. He doesn't know what to say. That such a website exists is sad. Sadder still? He now remembers where he's heard the name; on the basketball court and at the yacht club. A whole lot of married Littleton men have gone out with 'Ashley Madison.'

Whenever the men discuss their extracurricular sexual activities Truman heads in the opposite direction. It's better he doesn't know the details so he's not tempted to tell their wives at book club (in two cases) or the coffee shop (in three additional cases).

"Oh my God…" he whispers, shaking his head. That's five men in his neighborhood alone! One quarter of all the men on his street! Unreal!

"What? It sounds perfect for you. You are married, Truman. How do you expect to meet women who are looking for the same thing? Uncomplicated sex."

"That's not all I want, Ging. Friendship and sex would be nice. A friend with benefits," he sighs and runs his fingers through his hair.

"God, I wish I were attracted to you," she laments, and Truman bursts out laughing. "I mean...wouldn't that be easy? We're already friends, and you're a good-looking guy. But it'd be like kissing my brother."

"Agreed," he says, smiling. "Speaking of friends, Libby's doing much better since she started visiting the doctor, don't you think?"

Ginger raises an eyebrow, a corner of her mouth turning down.

"What?" he asks, his heart skipping a beat. "Is she okay? Is the baby all right?"

"Yeah, yeah. They're fine. I took Libby to her OB appointment yesterday. It's Ted. I don't like the rumors I'm hearing about him and I don't know what to do about it. I don't want to upset Libby; she's still in a fragile state of mind."

Rumors?

"What are you talking about Ginger? What have you heard?"

"This stays here, right?"

He rolls his eyes. Does she even have to ask?

"I've become friendly with one of the consultants at Ted's firm. I met Mark at a fundraiser and we've gone out a few times, but he has no idea how close I am to Libby, and last week he made a comment about Ted sleeping around, specifically with a woman in his office."

Truman's brow furrows, a knot forming in his stomach.

"So I asked him, casually, what he knew and he said everyone knows Ted has a mistress."

Truman remains mute for a minute, staring into space, then closes his eyes, dizzy with anger.

"I'm going to fucking kill him," he says through clenched teeth. "He gets her pregnant, guilts her into keeping the baby, then cheats on her? I'm going to castrate him...then kill him."

Ginger rests her hand on his arm, "Tru, I have no proof. People make up stuff all the time, but the way Mark said it...I believed him. Ted's always been a huge flirt, but they seem so happy. At least until she found out she was pregnant..." her voice trails off. "Maybe she knows? Maybe she's in a situation similar to yours and doesn't want anyone to know? Look how long it took you to tell me? I mean, I knew you and Caro weren't exactly soul mates, but I had no clue, none whatsoever, how bad things had gotten."

"You're grasping at straws Ginger. I'm a guy, we keep stuff to ourselves. It's in our genetic makeup. She'd tell you something like that."

Truman rises and paces around his living room. It's Christmas next week and it looks like Santa's workshop blew up in here. He always lets the girls do the decorating and there's garland and ornaments hanging from every surface. Pausing in front of the fireplace, he shakes his head, then slams his fist onto the mantle, causing one of the wise men to fall to the floor and shatter. If Ted's screwing around, Libby doesn't know anything.

"We need to find out if it's true," he says.

"Is it really our place, Truman?"

"Did you really just ask me that? She's our best friend, Ginger! Wouldn't you want to know?"

"That is what happened to me, remember? My ex-husband was having an affair with his secretary, how cliché! Sometimes I wish I'd never found out." Ginger looks down at her hands, touching the finger her wedding band used to reside. "I thought we were happy, Tru. I was happy."

"But you were living a lie, Ginger. If your husband was happy in your marriage, he wouldn't have felt the need to cheat. I'm telling you happily married men don't sleep around."

"You really are naïve," she snorts. "Not all men are like you, Truman. Some men screw around just because they can. It has nothing to do with the state of their marriage."

"So we're going to do nothing? Pretend we haven't heard these rumors?" he pauses. "I can't do it, Ginger. I won't sit by and watch him destroy her. If it's proof we need, I'll follow him myself."

"Tru Whitaker, private eye?" Ginger laughs. "And if you come up empty?"

"I hope I come up empty! I don't want her to get hurt. I don't think she'd recover from something like this."

"You don't give women enough credit, my friend. She'd recover…we all do."

♀

"What about this one?" Libby asks Ginger. They're at Nordstrom shopping for a dress for the company Christmas party tomorrow night. It's being held later this year than usual, just one of the many things that fell through the cracks while she was out of the office.

"Uh huh, that's nice," Ginger answers, looking down at her cell phone.

"Did you even see it?" Libby asks, shoving the red material under her friend's nose.

"I'm sorry. Just got a text…" her voice tapers off and she shakes her head. "Sorry!" she says, snapping her head up and shoving the phone into her purse, her face strained.

"What's going on? Is it Jasper? Is he bailing on taking Alex over the holiday again?"

Ginger's ex-husband is a piece of work. Jasper remarried within a year of their divorce and has two small children with his second wife. He hardly sees Alex at all, backing out of his visitation at the last minute on a regular basis. The poor boy is so hurt by his father's indifference.

"No, as of today The Turd's still picking him up on the twenty-third. We shall see! I haven't even told Alex about the visit, just in case it doesn't happen."

"So who sent you a text? You seemed upset."

"Oh...one of the directors from my foundation. It's nothing."

Libby raises an eyebrow, getting the distinct impression her friend is keeping something from her, but she knows not to push. Ginger only shares what she's ready to share. She's one of the most private people she's ever met, and the most stubborn. Her friend is calm and cool under the most difficult of circumstances, but when she's ready to talk...watch out! All hell can potentially break loose!

Shortly after Libby and Ginger met, they went to see a play in the city and headed to a restaurant for drinks and appetizers afterwards. While at the bar, a man began flirting with Ginger, and aware she was newly single, Libby let them be. She quietly drank her cocktail, ate some shrimp, and watched the news on the television above the bar.

She was about to text Ted to come pick her up, when Ginger threw what was left of her drink in the man's face and went on to rail against this stranger, who turned out to be married, about the sanctity of wedding vows and the meaning of monogamy and committing to one person for life. Libby stood by and watched her calm, cool friend unravelling before her eyes.

That's the night she learned Ginger's husband had cheated on her, and was marrying the 'slutty secretary' as soon as their divorce was final. When Ginger found out about her husband's affair, she wanted to work through their issues, but Jasper wasn't interested in staying. He'd found a younger, bouncier version of Ginger and wasn't turning back.

Her friend was thirty-eight years old at the time, beautiful, a millionaire in her own right, and her forty-year old husband left her for his twenty-five-year-old assistant. Ginger described herself as angry, confused and humiliated, and was happy to know how successful she'd been at concealing those feelings.

At the time, she admired Ginger for keeping it together on the surface. But, as Libby's learned the past few months, hiding feelings, especially from the people you love is a dangerous business. Unexpressed, they're a cancer to the body and mind, eating away at the healthy cells and positive thoughts until nothing is left but malignancy and bitterness. Those first two months after she found out she was pregnant, she felt like she was dying inside a little bit every day.

She couldn't hide her depression from anyone, and for the first time since they moved to Littleton, she wasn't concerned with what anyone thought, didn't have the energy to plaster a smile on her face and fake it for them at the bus stop. At the time, she considered it a major accomplishment to have gotten out of bed at all!

Why do people pretend their lives are perfect? What's the goal? To make other people jealous? Lately she's given the topic a considerable amount of thought. No one's life is perfect, no matter how wonderful it may seem to others. There are degrees of happiness, and the roller coaster called life goes up and down, twisting side to side, jerking people back to reality at the slightest hint of perfection. Everyone suffers trials and tribulations; to pretend otherwise is a waste of energy. She sees that now.

"How about this one?" Ginger asks, holding up an empire-waist black velvet dress made of some stretchy material.

Armed with a half dozen dresses, Libby steps into the dressing room with her selections and begins the ordeal of trying each one on. Shopping for clothes while pregnant is horrible. Women either look fat, or like they've swallowed a bowling ball, distorting even the slimmest figure. She's six months pregnant, and even though she's been gaining weight at a much slower rate than her doctor would prefer, she's carrying it all up front. There's no hiding this belly, that's for sure, so she might as well emphasize it.

The dress Ginger selected has a low, pleated neckline and long bell sleeves. It clings to her figure and accentuates her long neck and now full breasts. She's not naturally endowed with a large chest, but they're pretty impressive while she's pregnant, and Ted is enjoying the changes in her body. Over the past month, they resumed their sex life and her husband has been very attentive, more so now than he has been in quite a while. Maybe they needed a little break?

Inspecting herself in the three-way mirror, she admires her reflection. The dress is flattering and she feels sexy, despite her giant belly, and that's something she hasn't felt in months! Yesterday she went to the salon and had her color touched up for the first time in her life. She didn't mind the few grey hairs that'd sprouted along her hairline over the past year, but a grey-haired pregnant woman? *Nope. Not happening.* She splurged and had a manicure and pedicure as well and almost feels like herself again.

The meds have definitely kicked in, though she's kept that bit of information from Ted. He'd disapprove of her taking anything while pregnant, but her obstetrician agrees it's safe. And this was her decision to make, not her husbands. She's learning the difference. Maybe she would've pulled herself out of her depression without the aid of medication, but she wasn't going to take that chance.

Visiting Dr. Bradford has been helpful in so many ways. She's been sorting through her feelings and although she's still struggling to fully accept the baby, Libby doesn't feel hopeless anymore. Her life doesn't have to revolve around this child all day, every day. Nina has already agreed to work full-time for them once the baby is born and that's a huge relief. She'll have time to figure out what she wants to do with her life and pursue those goals.

Ready to make her grand appearance, Libby opens the door to the dressing room to model the dress for Ginger, but finds her furiously texting on her phone, her face pinched. She waits, hands on hips, tapping her toe impatiently.

"What do you think?" Libby asks.

Her friend holds up one hand and mutters, "Just a sec," and continues texting with the other. "What the fuck?" Ginger blurts out a moment later, her eyes opening wide, then holds the phone to her chest before shoving it back into her bag.

"What's the matter?" Libby asks, sitting beside her on the bench.

Ginger seems to be in some sort of shock, then turns to her, her face ghostly white.

"Jesus, Ging, are you okay?"

"Can I come to the Christmas party tomorrow night?" Ginger asks.

"Of course you can. What the hell is going on with you?"

"You just never know, do you?" Ginger whispers, looking down at her hands folded in her lap. "Please, don't ask...I can't discuss this with anyone right now."

Those are the magic words. Libby knows it's pointless to push the issue, but something is very wrong. And why does Ginger want to come to the company Christmas party? She's never asked to come before, but she has been dating one of their associates. She's surprised Mark didn't ask Ginger himself. Then again, they don't seem to be very serious, just another one of Ginger's flings. Taking a deep breath in, Libby resigns herself to the fact that Ginger will keep her in the dark until she's ready to share what's happening.

✳

Once she leaves the mall, Libby heads to the office. She's been scrambling to pull this Christmas party together. There's so much to do before tomorrow night and she needs to finish tying up loose ends; confirm the band, arrange a time for the centerpieces to be delivered, wrap the employee gifts.

She's back to going into the office a couple afternoons a week. At first she felt a bit out of place, like she was somehow usurping Heather's role. She can feel the resentment directed toward her every time she steps foot near the young woman (who definitely doesn't wear Chanel No.5). No one said this situation was permanent, that Libby was never coming back.

Over the course of those two months, Heather was lead to believe she has the ability to plan and execute major marketing campaigns straight out of college. For some unknown reason, Ted felt it was his responsibility to help Heather grow into a role she's completely unsuited for, far outside her ability and talent. Looks like her husband didn't think she was coming back to the office either!

Now, Heather has to run everything by Libby, and the girl doesn't like it one bit. An ambitious bitch has replaced the demure young woman she met back in September, and Libby has no patience for her. If she doesn't like the arrangement, she can leave! Until they find someone capable to fill Libby's shoes, Heather is going to have to deal with her. Libby has been actively searching for her own replacement and has several interviews set up with qualified candidates after the holidays. Her position should be filled by the end of January.

Last week, Libby interrupted a meeting between Heather and Ted and when she walked around the desk to grab a folder, she saw boards spread out on her husband's desk, the campaign ideas she'd shot down the day before. Slowly, she turned toward Heather, and found herself on the receiving end of the nastiest, most defiant glare. This is not how you treat the boss. And when it comes to marketing, Libby is definitely the boss. The young woman either has a crush on her husband or is angling for Libby's job. Either way, she's out of line.

Libby rested her hand on Ted's shoulder and squeezed it, their signal for a moment alone. He looked up, his eyes questioning, and she raised an eyebrow, her lips drawn together in a tight line. Ted rose and took Libby's hand.

"Excuse us, Heather. We need a moment."

Heather shot her another nasty look for good measure and reached for the boards.

"No," Libby said, resting her hands on the desk. "Leave those please."

Heather looked up at Ted with her big doe eyes, a silent plea for assistance, but Ted shook his head and Heather left the office pouting.

"What's the matter, baby?" Ted asked as the door closed behind the young woman.

Libby walked to the window and closed the blinds, then turned toward him.

"Ted, I want that girl gone."

"What?" he asked. "Why?"

Libby picked up the boards from Ted's desk and held them up, one by one.

"I told her these were unacceptable yesterday, and here she is today, thinking she can go over my head. There is no over my head! Why doesn't she understand that?"

"Honey, she had a little taste of power while you were gone and it's an adjustment to be answerable to you now. I'll talk to her. She needs to understand you're in charge of marketing."

"Let's tell her now. I'm sick and tired of her attitude. Someone has planted the idea in her head that she's good at this, and she's not."

"This is a delicate situation, Libby…" his voice trailed off.

"Really? How so? She's an insubordinate employee. If you won't talk to her, then I'll fire her myself. I don't need this stress right now. I have enough going on."

He remained silent for a moment, then nodded his head and hit the intercom on his phone, summoning Heather back into the office. Ted pulled a chair behind his desk and they sat together as Heather entered the office, taking a seat across from them.

"Heather…" Ted began. "I know you're used to coming directly to me with your ideas, but Libby's in charge of marketing, and what she says goes." He held up the boards and said, "You can't come to me with these anymore. Libby has final say, and if she doesn't think they're ready, then they're not."

As Ted spoke, she watched Heather's neck turn pink with splotches of bright red, the color working its way to her face. By the time Ted finished his little speech, Heather's ears were blazing red, her eyes filling with tears.

"I'm willing to work with you Heather," Libby interjected. "But not with your attitude. If it doesn't change, you're done here. I'm sorry if that sounds harsh, but this is the real world and you either play by the rules, or you leave. It's that simple."

Heather's eyes grew wide and she kept turning to Ted, as if he would come to her defense, but he remained silent, looking down at the calendar, fiddling with the pens on his desk. A moment later he cleared his throat.

"You can learn a lot from Libby," he said, then rose. "So, we're all on the same page now? Libby's in charge…okay?"

Heather nodded and left the room without a word. Libby closed the door behind her, then turned toward Ted.

"What the fuck was that?" she asked leaning against the door. "Were you asking her permission?"

"Don't you think you were a bit rough on her? Jesus, Libby! 'You either change or you're out of here?'" he mimicked. "She's just a kid for Christ's sake! This is her first job out of college!" He sat back in his chair and ran his fingers through his hair.

"No, Ted, I don't think I was rough enough on her. She's been a total bitch to me since I came back. I get that she liked the freedom she had when I was gone, but you've created a monster. Why are you treating her with kid gloves? She's an employee, like any other employee. She needs to know her place."

"I've never heard you speak so harshly toward an employee before," he said. "Toward anyone for that matter!"

"I've never had any reason to! Whose side are you on here?"

Ted closed his eyes and sighed, then reached for her, resting his forehead against hers.

"Yours, of course," he sighed. "Just take it easy on her, okay?"

Since that day, Heather's been respectful, but limits her interaction with Libby to the bare minimum. Honestly, she doesn't care if the young woman is comfortable around her or not. Maybe that is bitchy of her, but something about that girl

115

doesn't sit right with her. She's trying to stake her claim on territory that doesn't belong to her.

CHAPTER EIGHT

T oday, Libby arranged a catered luncheon for the staff and everyone is gathered in the large conference room eating and laughing when she walks in, taking the empty seat offered to her beside Ted by one of the associates. The deli provided quite a spread and she's starving after her shopping excursion. Eyeing the chicken salad sandwich, she touches Ted's arm.

"Sorry I'm late," she whispers in his ear and kisses his cheek. "I was buying a dress for the Christmas party."

He smiles into her eyes and brushes the hair away from her face, then leans in and kisses her full on the mouth, his hands in her hair. For a moment she forgets where she is and returns his passionate kiss, until everyone around the table begins to applaud. Startled, she feels the heat rushing to her cheeks and bites her lip before making eye contact with the group assembled. The associates are whooping it up, cheering them on, and she laughs through her embarrassment.

"Come with me baby," he whispers and helps her up. "Excuse us. I need a word with my wife."

"Is that what they're calling it these days?" someone shouts as they leave the room.

Ted takes her hand and leads her down the hallway into the small conference room. As soon as the door closes behind them, he presses her back against the wall, his mouth on hers, his hands wandering beneath her sweater. Closing the blinds, he locks the door, then quickly removes his tie, kicks off his shoes, and impatiently removes her sweater.

"Ted, what's gotten into you?" she murmurs.

He stops, his eyes meeting hers and they are filled with such longing... Ted kisses her in response, his tongue finding hers, and desire surges through her body. She hasn't felt this urgency, this physical need to feel him inside of her, in months. Unhooking her bra, his mouth finds a hard peak, and she moans with pleasure, goose bumps rising all over her body.

Ted lifts her onto the conference table and hastily removes her skirt and tights, slides her panties down and kneels before her, his mouth resting between her legs. The table is cold against her skin, but her breath catches in her throat and the heat floods her body while his lips and tongue work their magic. Her back arches and her limbs tremble as he brings her to the brink once...twice. A guttural moan escapes her lips, and Ted rises, knowing she's about to climax.

He shifts her hips to meet his then slides inside of her, his head tilting back...eyes closing and he's still for a moment, his breathing heavy. She feels herself pulsing around him, waiting for him, wanting him desperately. She sits up, praying the table can handle her weight, then wraps her legs around him, pulling him deeper inside. His mouth comes down hard on hers and she's dizzy with desire, their arms clasped around each other, their bodies slick with sweat.

Ted looks into her eyes, his own filled with longing and whispers "I love you, baby" then begins to move inside her, his hips grinding against her and she meets him with each thrust.

"Oh God, Libby. Yes…" he murmurs and she throws her head back, crying out as she's swept away on a wave of ecstasy.

Their breathing uneven, Ted holds her against him, trembling, his face buried in her neck. A moment later, he takes her head in his hands and she tries to focus her eyes, but she's still lost in another world. She blinks and the room comes into focus, Ted's face inches from hers.

They haven't had sex in the office since…she doesn't remember when. Months. This used to be a regular occurrence. She'd be at her desk and he'd come and whisk her away in the middle of the workday, find an available room, or take her to their car in broad daylight. Ted's drawn to risky scenarios, the higher the probability of getting caught in the act, the more exciting the encounter. She can't count the number of public places they've had sex over the years.

Ted pushes aside the chairs and helps her move to the carpet, and they lie beneath the conference table, his arms holding her close.

"God, I've missed that," he whispers. "Do you have any idea how much I love you? How incredibly sexy you are? Do you?" he asks, his voice cracking.

She turns toward him, her brows drawn together. His emerald eyes are bright with tears, and she rests her palm on his cheek.

"Ted, what's the matter?"

He shakes his head back and forth and wipes his eyes.

"Nothing's the matter, baby. When you walked into the conference room earlier, I realized how lucky I am to have you. I don't want to lose you, Libby." He kisses her again, then rests his head on her chest. "I'd never want to hurt you or the kids. You know that, right?"

She nods her head, her throat closing in on her. *What is he trying to say?*

"I did something stupid, baby."

She sits up and whacks her head on the conference room table, then lies back down, groaning. *Please don't tell me this,* she thinks, her head throbbing. She's been suspicious of his relationship with Heather since the day she met the girl, and by the look on her husband's face, she's about to get confirmation.

"Honey, are you okay?" he asks.

"What did you do, Ted?" she whispers.

"I'm sorry. I shouldn't have said anything here."

"Too late. Finish what you started." Her voice is harsh, but between the pain in her head and the fear in her heart she has no patience to spare.

"When we were having problems...I slept with someone."

"Heather?" she asks, bracing herself for his answer.

"No! No one you know..." he pauses, then turns his head away. "It happened once."

She lies back, staring at the underside of the table, taking deep breaths in and out. *How do I process this information?* Part of her is thankful he's not having an affair with his very young assistant, as she suspected. Now she doesn't know whether to be furious he had a one-night stand or relieved it was only one night.

"Why are you telling me this?" she asks, closing her eyes. She never would have known.

"I feel awful, baby. I'm so sorry...you wouldn't talk to me, that's no excuse, I know it was wrong. I just couldn't keep it from you any longer."

A one-night stand? Before she met Ted she didn't believe in monogamy. It didn't seem realistic for one person to satisfy every sexual need over the course of a lifetime. Especially men, they're wired differently than women. But now? Ted is her husband. The father of her children. It may not be a realistic expectation, but he doesn't have the right to have sex with anyone else. That's not in the marital contract.

Crawling out from beneath the table, she grabs her clothes, and hastily pulls them on, then takes a seat at the table, and runs her hands along the smooth finish. Fifteen minutes ago she was on top of this table, making love with her husband. That's what the giant clock on the brick wall indicates. Just fifteen minutes…The baby kicks an organ, causing her to wince with pain, and she shifts in the chair, trying to get comfortable.

Fully clothed, Ted sits beside her and her eyes meet his for the first time since he shared this news.

"Say something, Libby. Call me an asshole, slap me across the face. Just talk to me, please!"

"Do you feel better now?" she asks, her voice soft. "That's what this was all about, right? Clearing your conscience?"

He blankly stares at her, and the anger begins to fester within her.

"You weren't thinking about me when you told me that."

"Are you saying you'd rather not know?" he asks, incredulous.

The baby does a somersault and she sits back and closes her eyes, her hands coming to rest on her abdomen. *That's exactly what she's saying.* This is information she could have done without. *What am I going to do?*

Her mind is blank for several minutes, then she sits up. She knows in her heart she's not going to leave him over a one-night stand. An affair? Yes. One night? One stupid, insignificant night with some stranger? No. *But he doesn't know that…*

"I want you home for dinner every night," she says. "No working on weekends unless you bring it home with you, and you can forget about business trips for the time being."

He nods his head, contrite. These demands have less to do with his one-night stand than her needs and the needs of her family. If she has to use this information as leverage to get what she wants from him, so be it.

"I want you to be a bigger part of our lives, Ted. I'll forgive you in time for this…'fuck up' seems appropriate. But I won't forgive you if you aren't there for us. Do you understand?"

He rests his head in his hands for a moment, then turns to her with tears in his eyes.

"I thought you'd leave me," he whispers and takes her hand in his.

"I meant it when I said for better or worse," she sighs. "It'd better not get any worse."

Ted takes her face in his hands and gently kisses her, then nods his head in agreement.

Libby doesn't feel blameless in this. She virtually disappeared for over two months. She wasn't there for him. It's not exactly the same thing. She had no control over her depression, while he chose to have sex with someone else. But sometimes good people do bad things, she rationalizes. It could have been a lot worse.

♂

Everyone is distracted this morning as they sit at the coffee shop. Ginger keeps checking her phone, Libby is staring out the window, sipping her decaf, and he's exhausted, trying to keep his eyes open. Truman almost wishes Ginger never mentioned Ted's possible infidelity to him. He's been tossing and turning for the past few nights, not sure what, if anything, he should do with the information. Ginger's right…it's not his place. But he cares about Libby and watched her suffer from severe depression for over two months. He doesn't want to see her get hurt again. Ignorance truly is bliss.

"What would you do if you found out Caro had a one-night stand?" Libby asks him a few minutes later.

Ginger coughs, spitting a mouthful of coffee onto the table, and Truman's eyes open wide. Libby is staring at him, waiting for his response and he feels his ears growing hot.

"What would I do?" he asks, trying to sound nonchalant. Ginger raises an eyebrow as she mops up her mess. He shrugs his shoulders. "Probably nothing," he answers truthfully.

"Really?" she asks, her eyes narrowing.

"One night? One time? No," he answers, trying to remember how he would have felt before their relationship disintegrated. He would have been upset, but he wouldn't have left her.

"What about you Ginger? If Jasper had slept with the slutty secretary one time and confessed to you, what would you have done?"

"This is a very odd line of questioning, Libby," she says. "Has something happened?"

Libby stares out the window for a moment, then shakes her head.

"Just curious," she says.

"Bullshit, Libby Fitzgerald," Ginger sputters.

Libby opened up the can of worms and Ginger's not going to let her shut the lid. Sitting on the edge of his seat, he waits for Libby to respond.

"Ted had one…when I was depressed," she mutters, her eyes downcast.

"How did you find out?" he asks. "Are you okay?"

"I'm fine, really. He told me yesterday. Said he felt horrible and couldn't keep it a secret from me anymore."

They sit in silence for a moment and Libby tears a napkin into little pieces, forming a pile in front of her.

"Out of nowhere, Ted says he had a one-night stand?" Ginger asks, dubious.

Libby nods and all three of them sit quietly, lost in their own thoughts. There's no need to follow Ted now! He spilled the beans himself. *But…why?* It's so out of character. He can't imagine Ted offering up this information voluntarily. Something isn't adding up.

"Libby, I don't want to overstep, but who was she?" he asks.

"He said I didn't know her," she whispers. "I thought he might have been having an affair with his twenty-two-year-old assistant."

"Why didn't you tell us?" Ginger asks, taking Libby's hand in hers.

Libby shrugs.

"I didn't want it to be true. I thought if I said the words out loud, somehow it would be," she sits back against the chair, her hands coming to rest on her belly.

"What made you think he was sleeping with his assistant?" Ginger persists.

"Nothing specific. He's protective of her in some ways I suppose. But mainly, it's Heather. The way she behaves around him…and me. She's out to get something from Ted. I just assumed it was sex. Maybe I'm wrong. Maybe she just wants power and is maneuvering to get it once I find my replacement. We set her straight last week."

"Fire Lolita's ass!" Ginger raises her voice. "Don't put up with that shit!"

"Trust me, I've brought it up. But she's Ted's assistant…it's not up to me."

Truman's certain of one thing as he sits across from Libby at the coffee shop; Ted told Libby about a minor indiscretion to cover his ass for something huge. Maybe there's something to Libby's suspicions about Ted and Heather? Her husband is definitely up to something.

As soon as they go their separate ways, before he's even pulled out of his parking space at the coffee shop, his phone rings.

"He's fucking lying, Tru!" Ginger shouts.

"How do you know?" he asks, holding the phone away from his ear.

"Mark sent me a picture of Ted making out with someone yesterday while I was at the mall with Libby! He was out in broad fucking daylight, near the office from what I could tell. And the picture was time-stamped from last week, not over a month ago! I couldn't make out any details about the woman except she's blonde."

Truman's sick inside. He was right. Ted is lying to Libby... but what is he hiding?

"Why would Mark send you a picture like that?" he asks, resting his head against the steering wheel. "I mean...why would he even take a picture of Ted with another woman?"

"Maybe he wants to blackmail Ted? Or maybe he realized how close I am to Libby and wants her to know she's married to a shit! I don't know! I've been trying to pry information out of him without being obvious and while we were texting back and forth, he made a comment about Ted and the other woman. I said I didn't believe him, just to see what he'd say. I did not expect to receive a photograph of Ted with his tongue stuck down someone's throat just seconds later! I almost shit my pants. I was in the dressing room with Libby!"

"Jesus...why didn't you tell me yesterday?"

"I think I was in a state of shock. And you're over there acting crazy, talking about killing Ted and spying on him! I needed time to process this. I'm going to their company Christmas party tonight. I want to see for myself who this Lolita is, and if I catch the vibe between those two, I'll put her in her fucking place. Then you can castrate Ted and kill him or whatever you have planned."

✳

All evening he's been sitting in front of the Christmas tree, waiting for a message from Ginger. Caroline hasn't been feeling well and came home early again tonight. That's five nights in a row. Since she's here, he assigned her the task of wrapping the girls' gifts. Each one is labeled, and she should be able to manage this one Christmas related responsibility. He did all of the shopping as usual.

Around eleven-thirty, as he's about to doze off, his phone beeps. It's a text from Ginger: **Too much to type. Let's meet tomorrow. Go to sleep.**

Go to sleep? Now? Not a chance! What does that mean, 'too much to type'? What the hell happened at that party?

He types: **Did you talk to Lolita?**

Ginger responds a few minutes later: **Better. Ted. Libby's home. Driving Ted back as promised. He's drunk and he's talking.**

She's getting information directly from Ted? He'll never sleep now. He wanders around the first floor, then looks out the dining room window and notices Libby's bedroom light is on. Considering the circumstances, she was holding it together today. He's been checking in on her and she'd been a little sad, but managing. He's worried she'll slide into another bout of depression. He had never seen her in such a state before and it scared him.

Truman picks up his phone and texts her: **Still up?**

A few minutes later Libby walks out onto her patio and motions for him to join her. Grabbing his coat, he opens his back door and meets her outside. A light snow is falling, the first of the season, and Libby holds her hands out, catching snowflakes. Her cheeks are pink from the cold and she's wearing a long flannel nightgown under her down jacket.

"I love the first snowfall," she says, her eyes bright.

"You okay?" he asks.

She sits on the stone bench in her garden and takes a deep breath in, then pats the spot beside her. He sits down and she leans into him, resting her head on his shoulder. Truman's heart swells in his chest, overflowing with love and concern for her, then wraps his arm around her shoulders.

"Everything's going to be all right, Libby," he whispers, pressing his lips to her forehead.

She looks up at him with her big blue eyes and smiles weakly, then kisses him lightly on the lips and holds onto him, her arms winding around his back, pulling him close. They've hugged hundreds of times, but this is different. She just found out her husband had sex with someone else, and she's seeking comfort, affirmation that someone cares. So that's what he does. He sits in the snow, holding her close, his heart aching…knowing deep down…the worst is yet to come.

Ginger pulls her Mercedes into the driveway and a moment later, Ted stumbles out of the car. In all of these years he's never seen Ted drunk. Libby rises from the bench and walks toward the driveway and his eyes meet Ginger's. They're brimming with anger, but she puts on a show of being concerned for Ted and Truman helps her bring him into the house, depositing him on the sofa. Libby stands over her husband and shakes her head.

"He can sleep here. Tru, can you help me with his coat and shoes?"

"I'll do it, Lib. Go to bed, we've got this."

Libby nods and climbs the stairs to her bedroom. Ted attempts to sit up on the couch, but slides back against the cushions.

"Tru, what're you doing here? We swapping wives?" Ted asks, then laughs.

"Yeah, Ted, that's exactly what we're doing," he mutters, yanking off his coat.

"Caro...she's a fine lookin' woman. Be careful there..." Ted slurs and closes his eyes. Truman stands over Libby's husband, wondering what the hell he's talking about. "I got the best wife in the world," Ted continues. "She forgives me, ya know. She forgives...don't deserve her."

He's got that fucking right! Truman removes Ted's shoes and steps back, taking in the sloppy sight of the man he's grown to loathe. Ginger tugs his sleeve and they leave Ted sprawled out on the couch, locking the front door behind them.

"How did he get so trashed?" he asks once they're sitting in Ginger's car.

"He was half-way there when I arrived at the party. Libby was tired so she took Ted's car home around nine, and I promised her I'd bring him home. I just sat back and watched him at the bar, drinking one shot after another. He wasn't himself, very quiet and distracted. You know him, always putting on a show, entertaining the crowd...but not tonight. When he was completely shitfaced, I sat beside him at the bar and told him I know about the other woman, then asked if he makes it a habit. I'm pretty sure he thought I was propositioning him at first, which opened the door, but he wanted to talk, Tru."

"What did he tell you?"

"In his words, women just fall into his lap and he resisted them for years because he loves Libby." She shakes her head and frowns. "He said the other women mean nothing to him, it's just sex. Like that somehow makes it better! At that point I didn't know whether to pity him or smack him. It was pathetic. I knew this was an opportunity to get the truth and he was on a roll, so I kept my mouth shut. He wants to stop, at least that's what he said."

Truman holds his head in his hands. Libby can't ever know this. Not all of it. Maybe it's best she believes he just had a one-night stand...

"Once everyone left and it was just the two of us, he got really sloppy. He said he broke things off with 'CeeCee' last week, and is committed to his wife and kids. He said he couldn't live without Libby and he won't let 'that woman' destroy his family. He'd never leave Libby for 'her'."

"Wait. Who's CeeCee?"

"The hell if I know! I asked but he waved me off. He wasn't making much sense at that point," her voice trails off and she rests her head back against her seat. "Do you think he's a sex addict, Truman?"

"No, I think he's a narcissistic pig," he mutters. "CeeCee is obviously someone he's been seeing regularly, if he had to break things off with her. What about Lolita? Did he mention her?"

"His assistant? She was there with her boyfriend. I didn't get the vibe between them, though there's something off with that girl."

"Then why does Mark think Ted's sleeping with her?"

Ginger shakes her head, "I don't know. Mark never said it was his assistant, he just said someone at the office. After Libby made that comment about Heather, I just assumed it was her. Anything's possible at this point. Oh! And she's a brunette, not a blond. The woman in the picture was not Ted's assistant."

"Let me see the picture," he says.

Ginger digs in her bag for her phone, then finds the message and holds it out for him. The picture was taken from a distance, but the woman definitely has blond hair...and wait a minute...Truman squints his eyes, zooming in on the photograph. She's wearing a coat exactly like Caroline's.

I bumped into Ted at the airport... I had dinner with an old friend... I'm working late tonight... Be careful there...

His head is swimming. *Caroline and Ted?* Caroline wouldn't have an affair with his best friend's husband...their neighbor for Christ's sake! *Would she?*

"What's the matter, Tru? You look like you're going to be sick."

He drops the phone in Ginger's bag and lowers the window for some fresh air. Caroline wasn't feeling well tonight. She hasn't been feeling well all week. *CeeCee...Caroline Christianson*, his wife's maiden name. She's not feeling well because Ted broke things off with her. Truman rests his head in his hands. *Oh, Caro, what have you done? And how long have you been doing it?*

"We can't tell Libby any of this now, it would kill her," he whispers. "Especially in her condition. And don't give me this bullshit about all women surviving betrayal. Your ex-husband slept with one woman, and married her once you were divorced. He wasn't a serial offender. How would you feel if you knew he slept with several women over the course of your marriage?"

"I don't know what's right anymore," she sighs.

"She's six months pregnant, Ginger. She doesn't need to know anything right now. When the baby is born we'll figure something out."

✳

Once Ginger leaves, Truman heads back to the house, his heart heavy. He drags his feet up the stairs, but instead of going to his bedroom, he walks down the hallway to Caroline's and listens. The television is on low, and the light filters into the hall from under her door. He knocks, then without waiting for her to answer, walks in to find her on the floor, wrapping gifts, her eyes puffy and bloodshot from crying, her nose red and raw, surrounded by used tissues.

If he weren't so angry with her, he'd feel bad. She's suffering right now...and she deserves it. He takes a seat on her chaise lounge and watches as she struggles to compose herself.

"How long have you been having an affair with Ted?" he asks, calmly.

Caroline stops wrapping the box, her lips parting, her eyes opening wide.

"Caro, just tell me," he says, his voice soft.

Her eyes fill with tears and she grabs a tissue, blowing her nose and tossing it into the pile.

"Almost four years," she says, her chin trembling.

Truman's heart stops beating in his chest and he closes his eyes. *Oh my God.* He nods his head with understanding. That's when she began to pull away from him. That's when their marriage began to disintegrate a little bit every day to the point of oblivion.

"You're in love with him?" he asks, swallowing hard.

She nods her head and bursts into tears, covering her face with her hands.

After a minute, he says, "Caro...you're such a fool. Did you think you were the only one?"

Her brows draw together in confusion and he laughs. His wife has no clue what Ted's been up to these past four years.

"Oh, you didn't know about the other women? Just his pregnant wife who happens to live next door?" he asks, his voice laced with bitterness. "Let me guess. You asked him to leave Libby and he broke it off?"

She raises her eyes to meet his, guilt tattooed across her face. *You've got to be fucking kidding me*! After all they've been through to keep it together for the girls, the sacrifices he believed they were both making. But they weren't in it together after all. Turns out Truman was doing all of the sacrificing. Caroline was getting exactly what she wanted and was ready to walk away from them, and break up two families in the process!

"Sorry to spoil the fantasy, CeeCee, but you mean nothing to him. Ted doesn't love you. He loves his wife. You're just one of many women he's used along the way. You don't get a happily ever after."

He's being cruel, but he doesn't care. *Four years!* He can't tell Libby she's married to an adulterous asshole, but this is the next best thing. Breaking the news to his wife, who also happens to be in love with Ted, feels pretty fucking good. He was so confused when Caroline began her disappearing act, so hurt, but eventually he accepted the situation, assuming it was the pressure of work pulling them apart. And part of him felt that she was disappointed in him somehow. By staying home and focusing on the children he wasn't as masculine, and therefore undesirable.

Maybe it was a little of everything, but he never suspected another man was involved for so long. When he discovered her hickies in September, he naïvely believed it was the first time she'd been with another man. But it wasn't, she was fucking their neighbor for years! Now he fully understands what was behind her withdrawal, and Truman wants to hurt her as much as she hurt him.

"You could've fucked anyone and you chose my best friend's husband? Do you have any sense of decency? How could you do that to Libby? To me? To our family?" he shouts. He needs to rein it in or he might do something he'll regret.

"I hope it was worth it, Caro," he rises and walks to the door, leaving her sobbing on the floor. "I'm taking the girls to Vermont for Christmas. I'm done pretending. This is over."

CHAPTER NINE

The past two months have been very strange. Truman and Caroline are getting divorced and Caro moved out over the holidays under the cover of darkness, one suitcase at a time. The Queen of Garland Drive abdicated her throne, slinking away with zero fanfare, leaving her 'subjects' shocked and confused. The neighborhood women have talked of nothing else since the New Year, wondering why Caroline would leave Truman and her children. What could possibly be so horrible she'd walk away from her life in Littleton? Caroline had it all!

Libby wasn't terribly surprised by their split. She could tell Truman was lonely, could see the sadness in his eyes. He never brought it up and she hoped he'd talk to her when he was ready. But he never said a word until he came back from Vermont after New Year's and made the official announcement, then filed for divorce the next day. *What was the final straw for him? What pushed him to make a complete break from Caroline?* She doesn't know and he won't say.

Truman has been distant with Libby since his separation. At first she thought he was depressed. Who wouldn't be getting divorced after fifteen years of marriage? But he seems angry more than anything. She wants to help him through this tough time, but he won't let her in. Over the past few weeks, she's come to understand that she depends on Truman's emotional support as much as his help with the kids. The baby is due in six weeks and she still has mixed feelings about having it. In the past she would have discussed her fears with him, but now she can't and she misses her best friend.

He and Ginger have grown closer over the past few months and that hasn't sat well with her either. She feels left out of their circle for the first time and is actually jealous of Ginger's relationship with Truman. As tight as the three of them have become over the years, Libby's always had a closer connection with Truman. They've been raising their children together, how could they not create a tight bond?

Maybe he feels more connected to Ginger because she's divorced? Maybe he feels she understands what he's going through in a way Libby can't? That makes sense in a way, but doesn't make her miss him any less. Ginger's been a bit off as well. She can't pinpoint what's different, but her friends are keeping something from her and it's making her crazy!

Or maybe it's the pregnancy hormones making her a little paranoid? That's what Dr. Bradford has suggested in not so many words. She's been visiting the psychiatrist weekly and has been working through her hurt feelings about Ted's one-night stand. She still keeps him on a tight leash, showing up at the office unexpectedly, insisting he's home for dinner. He's kept his word and is home every weekend, attending games and taking them on daytrips.

They've had more time together as a family in the past two months than the past five years. Their family unit is closer than ever before. Maybe this one-night stand and the possibility of losing everything was exactly what Ted needed to stop taking them for granted?

Her husband being around more has contributed to the changed dynamic with Truman. Tru said he doesn't want to intrude on their family time, that it's important for them to work on their relationship without his family hanging around. He's probably right, but she misses their big dual-family dinner gatherings. That was the norm for years, big loud noisy dinners, all four children talking over one another. Now, mealtime is decidedly tame. It's taking some getting used to, the four of them together without the Whitakers. Libby's traded in one family unit for another, unfamiliar one. How strange to think her actual family, just Ted and her children, is the unfamiliar one.

Caroline keeps the girls on weekends. At first, Truman seemed lost without them, but he started dating and is out most nights now. Libby was shocked how quickly he got back into the dating game, barely pausing for breath between announcing his separation and going out with other women. Some men can't be alone…she just didn't think Truman was one of them. But, he's a good-looking man in his prime, and divorced women in their thirties and forties are a dime a dozen, according to an article she read in the *Providence Journal* last week. Truman has his pick.

Ginger said he and Caroline had been living separate lives for some time, so it's not surprising he's running a bit wild right now. Ginger believes this phase will pass, she went through the same thing when she and Jasper first separated. She needed to know she was still desirable to others, that there were other fish in the sea. There are plenty of fish, according to Ginger, the problem is the good ones get caught almost immediately, and what's left…no one wants. They're too damaged, too weird, or too ugly.

❋

Tonight, Libby made roast chicken and asparagus and from the den, the aroma fills her nostrils, her mouth watering. The bird is almost done. Heading into the kitchen, she coughs, choking on the smoke beginning to fill the room. *What the hell?* She runs to the stove and turns everything off. The burner under the pan with the oil ready to sauté the asparagus was turned on, she must have bumped the knob with her stomach a few minutes ago. *Shit! I need to be more careful!*

She grabs a potholder and removes the pan from the stove, then reaches across the sink and opens the window to let out the smoke, taking deep breaths of the cold night air. Ted should be home soon, he texted her a half hour ago to let her know he's on his way.

As soon as the thought crosses her mind, she hears his voice through the window, coming from the yard. *The snow is two feet deep in the backyard, what is he doing out there?* It's dark out and the lights are on in the kitchen, so she can't see him, but she hears a woman's voice. *Is that Caro?*

"I don't care what time. Come to my place when she's asleep," Caroline says.

Libby's body turns cold, her breath catching in her throat. The room starts to spin and she grabs the counter to steady herself, lowering her head so they can't see her.

"CeeCee, I told you. It's over. What don't you understand? I can't do this anymore."

"I'll make it worth your while," Caroline says, followed by silence.

Unsteady on her feet, Libby makes her way into the darkened dining room and opens the curtain. The moonlight reflects off the snow, throwing a spotlight on her husband and Caroline in the throws of a passionate kiss. Libby stands paralyzed in front of the window and watches as Ted lifts Caro up against a tree, her legs wrapped around him, arms around his neck. She's immobile as he raises her former neighbor's skirt, rips off her nylons and drops his pants in the snow.

Her husband is having sex with Caroline thirty feet in front of her and she's completely numb, unable to move or speak. It's as if she's watching a film…but somehow she's part of it. The yard is a movie set, the dining room the setting for the next scene.

An intense pain grips her stomach, jolting her back and away from the window. Libby groans, sliding to the floor. *Oh my God!* The pain ripping through her is unbearable. *Am I going into labor? Not now, please God, not now!*

Libby crawls across the room and is hit with another sharp pain as she enters the living room. *I need my phone!* Grasping the side table, she tries to rise and catches sight of a picture of her family. It's the one she used on the Christmas card this year, all four of them smiling on the beach in Nantucket. She reaches for it, knocking it to the floor, and the glass smashes, distorting their smiling faces. Libby collapses, clutching the frame in her hand, and sobs.

Broken. The picture, her family, their lives.

Ted opens the front door a moment later and sets his briefcase and coat down. Another pain stabs her, slicing open her insides and shredding her heart. *It's too soon! This can't be happening!* She cries out and is writhing in agony when her husband enters the living room.

"Libby!" Ted kneels beside her, his eyes wild with panic. "Oh, Jesus…" he mutters, reaching for his cell phone. "Sweetheart, I'm here. I'm calling 911."

She swats at him with the picture frame, wants to scratch his eyes out, but the pain is too intense. Every time she moves the stabbing pain gets worse. *Get away from me, Ted!* The voice inside her is screaming. *Get the fuck out of my house!* Ted is on the phone and the next thing she knows, Truman is kneeling beside her, wiping away her tears.

"It's going to be okay, Libby. The ambulance is on its way," he whispers. "I'll stay with the kids while you and Ted are at the hospital."

She shakes her head back and forth, "No Ted. I don't want Ted."

Come with me, Truman. Please. I don't want my husband with me!

"Libby," Ted takes her hand. "Baby, I'm right here."

"Get away from me!" she screams, and Ted's jaw drops. "I saw you..." she whispers through her tears. "I saw you with her..."

Ted sits back against the wall, his face turning white.

"Truman, come with me. Please..." She hears the sirens from the ambulance wailing. "Please," she pleads.

"Okay, Libby," he says. "I'll come with you."

"The hell you will!" Ted shouts.

"Mommy!" Nate cries, his eyes filled with tears. "What's wrong?"

Both of her children are standing over her crying. *It's okay, babies...it's okay...* She tries to reach out for them, but another pain shoots through her. Everything is happening too fast. Ted and Truman are arguing and when the doorbell rings a moment later, Emma runs to answer it.

Before Libby knows it she's being lifted onto a stretcher and carried away from her home...from life as she knows it. She closes her eyes as the paramedics work on her and hears Truman's voice from a distance, answering their questions as the ambulance drives away.

♂

Libby's been admitted into the hospital and is in a private room now, resting. Truman's afraid to leave her side and sits beside her, clasping her hand tightly in his. *What did she see that caused her to go into early labor?* Ted met them in the emergency room at Woman & Infants Hospital within the hour, after they'd stabilized Libby and given her medication to stop her premature contractions. At the sight of her husband, Libby became so agitated, the nurse asked him to leave, then put something in her IV to make her sleep.

He received Ted's panicked phone call right after Caroline picked up the girls and ran right over. *Did they meet up in the driveway? Were they kissing?* He can't ask Libby, wouldn't risk upsetting her again, but he plans on asking Ted the next time he sees him. They almost came to blows over who would ride in the ambulance with her as the paramedics arrived, but in the end, Truman convinced Ted to call Nina and follow them to the hospital.

Once Libby's sound asleep, Ted enters the room and stands off to the side, tears in his eyes. *You should be crying you piece of shit.* Truman can't stand the sight of the man. Since he found out about his affair with Caro two months earlier, he's kept his interactions with Ted to the bare minimum, keeping his mouth shut for Libby's sake only.

"What did she see, Ted?" he asks, keeping his eyes on Libby.

Ted remains silent.

"What were you doing with Caroline?" he persists.

"It doesn't matter," Ted mutters, shuffling his feet. "Look, I'm sorry Tru. About everything. It was a mistake."

"A mistake? You fucked my wife for four years and that's all you've got?"

"What do you want me to say, Truman?"

He shakes his head. Something more than a simple apology would be nice! Maybe admit he's a total fuckup? That he ruined not only Truman's family, but his own because he couldn't keep it in his pants? An acknowledgement of the damage he's caused at a minimum. But to characterize a four-year affair as a mistake? Not good enough.

"Did you ever love Caro?" he asks, genuinely curious.

"No. I've never loved anyone but Libby," he says, his voice thick with emotion.

"Why'd you do it? Really? You have everything, Ted. A wife who adores you, two great kids, another baby on the way, a successful business. Why would you risk everything?"

Ted takes a seat across from him, careful not to get too close to Libby and spots the broken frame, the picture of his family on the tray beside her bed. He picks it up and holds it against his chest, covering his eyes with his hand, his shoulders shaking.

"I don't know," Ted says a few minutes later. He grabs a tissue and wipes his face, then continues. "Every day was the same. Everything was good, but there were no highs, no lows. When I imagined fifty more years of the same thing, day in and day out, I couldn't stand the thought. One day, excitement found me…and things got out of control. I've never stopped loving my wife, that's the truth, Truman. And I never meant to hurt anyone."

"So, you were bored?" he asks, his eyes narrowing. "Because your life was too good?"

Ted sighs, resting his head in his hands.

"I guess," Ted says, his voice cracking.

"Skydiving would've probably done the trick," Truman mutters. "God, you're an idiot."

"She's never going to forgive me, is she?" Ted whispers, looking down at the family photograph again.

"Would you? You're lucky she doesn't know about the other women," he says.

Ted's head snaps up, his eyes narrowing.

"What are you talking about?"

"You don't remember? The night of the Christmas party...you told Ginger everything. How did you think I found out about you and Caro?"

"I figured Caro told you. I don't remember talking to Ginger at the party," he pauses. "So...you two know everything and haven't told Libby?"

Truman nods.

"Why?" Ted asks, visibly confused.

"Look at her, Ted. Your pregnant wife is in the hospital. This is why."

♀

Early the next morning, Libby awakens to find a nurse checking her blood pressure, adjusting the cuff on her arm, and Truman asleep in the chair beside her. Her body is leaden, her head foggy. It takes a few minutes to bring her eyes into focus, for the memory of the previous night to flood her consciousness. The young woman smiles at her, oddly perky for this godforsaken hour, and removes the blood pressure cuff, then checks the IV bag.

"It's okay, sweetie," the nurse whispers. "Your pressure is good and the baby is doing well."

"I want to sleep," she murmurs.

"Close your eyes, Mrs. Fitzgerald. It's still early."

Libby checks the clock mounted on the wall across from her. Five o'clock. The picture she smashed last night, the one of her family is laying on the tray beside her and she picks it up, studying each of their smiling faces. Emma was throwing a fit not ten minutes before this was taken. Ted had to be torn away from his cell phone and she was irritated with him. Nate wanted to go in the water and whined until moments before the photographer they hired took this shot.

It's an illusion, their happiness. Fake. And she bought it. She believed the fantasy of the happy family in this photograph. Closing her eyes, she sees the truth, Ted pressing Caro against the tree, thrusting inside of her, and she takes the picture out of its frame then tears it into tiny pieces, watching the fragments of her delusion float to the ground.

Drugs. I need drugs.

She grabs Truman's arm and shakes it. He rubs his eyes, sits up in the chair and smiles before his eyes fill with concern.

"Should I call for the nurse?" he asks.

"I don't want to think. I just want to sleep," she says, panic rising, clutching her heart.

"Libby…take a deep breath. Don't work yourself up, please. Think of the baby."

She looks down at her huge belly, anger surging through her. Grabbing her stomach, she wishes she could make this baby disappear. *I never wanted this baby!*

"Get me the drugs, Tru! I can't take this," she sobs. "Please! I want to sleep. I need the drugs!"

Truman buzzes the nurse's station and a few minutes later the same nurse enters the room.

"She needs a sedative," Truman says.

The nurse checks her chart, then shakes her head.

"I'm sorry, Mr. Fitzgerald, but she's not supposed to have any more medication. It's not good for the baby."

Please! I need to sleep! Her breathing is shallow and she's having trouble catching her breath. Grabbing Truman's arm, she starts to hyperventilate and he leans over her, trying to calm her down, but she can't hear him.

"Neither is this!" he shouts at the nurse. "Give her the fucking sedative!"

The nurse runs from the room and a moment later the doctor on call enters the room.

"What's the problem, Mrs. Fitzgerald?" the doctor asks, but she can't speak, so he turns to Truman.

"Doctor," Truman says calmly. "She is due in six weeks and last night she found out her husband is having an affair."

The doctor frowns and turns to her, his face concerned. *Yes, pity me, please. Take pity on me and give me the meds!*

"I'm very worried about her. She's had depressive episodes in the past and right now she just wants to sleep. Please give her something, she's been through enough."

"I'll have the nurse administer a mild sedative, but we need to contact her doctors. Does she have a psychiatrist?"

"Yes, Dr. Anne Bradford on Waterman in Providence."

After the doctor leaves, the nurse inserts a needle into her IV, and she relaxes a little, waiting for the medication to kick in and sweet oblivion to return. *Oh Truman, thank you, thank you!* Truman brushes the hair away from her face with his fingertips, and she clasps his other hand, gripping it tightly. He made Ted go away, he made them give her the drugs and she's grateful.

Feeling the meds enter her bloodstream, she takes a deep breath in and it dawns on her she's not the only one hurting. Truman was also betrayed. He must have known. This explains why he's been so distant. He didn't want her to know the truth. How has he been keeping it together? She can't bear the pain, but he's been fully functioning all this time. She has no idea how long Ted and Caroline were having an affair, but Truman is just as much a victim here as she is.

"Thank you for staying with me," she says.

"I'm not going anywhere," Truman smiles.

"You knew?" she asks.

He nods his head, his face sad.

"I'm so sorry," she says, tears filling her eyes.

"There's nothing for you to be sorry about, Lib. They're the ones who should be sorry."

"I saw them in the backyard," she whispers, closing her eyes. "She was against the tree. He was..." she sobs into her hands. "They were.... I saw everything."

"Oh my God..." Truman murmurs. "Oh, Libby."

She moves to one side of the bed, making room for him and he climbs in, wrapping his arms around her. She rests her head on his chest and cries until the drugs kick in and she fades away.

♂

"What the hell?" Ted squeezes Truman's arm, waking him with a start. He fell asleep with Libby in his arms. She's still sleeping, her head on his chest, pinning him down. Is Ted seriously jealous? *Ted can sleep with my wife for years, but I can't comfort his when she finds out?* This guy is too much.

"Shut up Ted," he hisses. "Don't you dare wake her."

He struggles to get out of the small hospital bed without disturbing Libby, then grabs Ted's arm and leads him into the hallway.

"You had sex with Caro in your backyard? What the fuck is wrong with you?"

Ted's face goes completely white, his eyes growing wide.

"Yeah, she saw the whole thing, Ted. Had my wife up against the tree, did you? While your wife watched."

Truman pushes Ted against the wall and grabs his sweater, aching to take a swing at him. He's almost as tall, but Ted has thirty pounds on him, easy. Ted shoves him away and they stand toe-to-toe, hatred spilling from Truman's eyes. He wants to pulverize this man, make him feel the pain he's caused everyone else. Before he has the chance, Ginger arrives, carrying a bouquet of daisies.

"Whoa! That's enough you two," she says, inserting herself between them. "Ted, why don't you take a walk and cool off."

Ted looks down at the tiled floor, then nods and walks away. Ginger raises an eyebrow at Truman and laughs.

"Really? A hospital brawl? What were you thinking?"

"I wasn't thinking. I just want to kill that prick. You want to know why Libby's in here? She saw Ted and Caro having sex in her backyard."

"I'm sorry, what?" Ginger asks, her brows drawn together in confusion.

"You heard me right. In the snow, twenty degrees outside, just a few yards away from her. She saw everything." He sits down on the bench outside of Libby's room. "She just wants to sleep, Ging. She's in so much pain…" he blinks back his tears. "What're we going to do? She's devastated."

Ginger sits down beside him, the flowers falling to the floor. She's speechless, her eyes glazed over. They sit in silence for several minutes until Ted reappears in the hallway, and the color comes back to Ginger's face until it's glowing red with rage. Slowly, Ginger rises and faces off with Ted.

"You listen to me," she says, pointing her finger in his face. "You're going to leave this hospital, go home, pack up your shit, and find someplace to stay. And unless she asks for you, you're not coming back here."

"She's my wife, Ginger. You can't make me do anything. I have power of attorney."

"Not for long you don't. I'll have a lawyer here within the hour to draw up a new document. No one has declared her incompetent. She can change it at any time." Ginger picks up her phone and hits a button. "Mr. Caldwell, please," she says into the phone. "It's Ginger Stafford. Yes, that Stafford. Thank you." She taps her toe for a moment. "John, meet me at Woman & Infants Hospital. Now. Thank you."

She hangs up and raises an eyebrow at Ted. Truman bites his lip, trying to stifle his laughter. Ginger just called the most powerful attorney in the state, hell, in New England, and he's on his way here. Ted stares at them in an apparent state of shock.

"Fuck you, Ginger," Ted finally snarls, then turns to leave. "She's still my wife, and they're my children. Don't forget it."

♀

The doctors decided to keep Libby in the hospital for observation for a few days out of concern for the baby and she's so relieved. She's not ready to go home. From a distance, she can hear everything that's going on, but she doesn't have the energy to speak or move. Dr. Bradford has been discussing medication options with her obstetrician and the possibility of delivering the baby via C-section, sooner rather than later.

She doesn't care what they do. Whatever meds they're giving her are wonderful. She's in a daze, a pleasant, perpetual daze and she never wants it to end. But she can't escape forever, as much as she'd like to.

Ted's sister, Maureen, stopped in to visit the day after she was admitted into the hospital, and was horrified to find her so heavily medicated. Maureen gave birth to six children without painkillers, before or after the delivery, and sees it as a sign of weakness in others when they do.

They were extremely close when Libby and Ted lived in Boston but have grown apart the past few years. Since their father's death, Maureen has taken over her mother's family responsibilities, hosting holidays at her house and keeping the brothers in line. She's tough and her life has been far from easy, but Libby admires her ability to make the most of the hand she's been dealt.

She's genuinely concerned for Libby and the baby, but it didn't take long for the true motives behind her visit to surface. Maureen was there on Ted's behalf, there was no doubt in

Libby's mind. Ted confessed what happened to his sister, and since he's not allowed to visit her, he sent Maureen in for damage control. Fortunately, the medication made it impossible to react to what Maureen was saying, but it couldn't stop her from absorbing her words.

"Lib, you know I love my little brother. What he did was wrong. He knows it. I know it. No one is disputing that fact. I gave him a tongue lashing the likes of which he's never heard before and the little shit deserved it. But Lib…Ted loves you more than anything. He'll do whatever it takes to prove to you how much. Give him a chance, sweetheart. He's devastated."

She turned away from the sound of his sister's voice. Ted doesn't know the meaning of the word devastated. *This is what devastation looks like, Maureen!* He's just sorry he was caught!

"Listen to me, Lib," Maureen grabbed her hand. "He's a guy, sweetie. They aren't too bright! They think with their pricks and the big brain and little brain have minds of their own. But look at you! You're about to have another baby! Is this really the time to make such a huge decision? Wait it out, Libby. He's human and he's sorry. You two can work through this, I promise. Don't break up your family. Don't do this to the kids."

Libby looked into Maureen's eyes and shook her head.

"I didn't," she whispered, her voice scratchy. "He did."

"I know, I know. What he did was so wrong," she paused and sat back in her chair, looking out the hospital window. "Our dad did the same thing…did you know that? My mother tossed him out a few times, but always let him come back home. She knew my father loved her, no matter what direction his pecker led him. My mom could've saved us a lot of heartache if she'd just ridden out the storm instead of reacting to her feelings. In the end, she loved the old bastard, flaws and all, and he loved her. Women are so much stronger than men, Lib. It's our job to keep it together, to work through the rough patches."

Libby didn't know about Ralph's infidelity, but he was always an incorrigible flirt. Ted is so much like him. *How did Doris do it?* How was she able to move past Ralph's infidelity? While Ted's father was alive, Doris' life revolved around her husband...but since his death, Libby has noted on more than one occasion how much happier she seems. There's a lightness in Doris that wasn't present before. She travels and plays bingo and goes with friends to dinner theater. Her life is her own for the first time in fifty years and she's making the most of it.

While she was ruminating on this information, Truman entered the hospital room and Libby turned to him, her eyes silently pleading for help. She couldn't listen to anymore of Maureen's rationalizations. He raised an eyebrow and nodded, then mobilized into action.

"Maureen, nice to see you," he said, shaking her hand. They'd met a few times over the years.

"Tru, how are ya'?" Maureen asked, rising from her chair, eyeing him suspiciously.

"Fine, thanks," he replied. "Lib, the kids made you something," he said, inching closer to the bed. "Excuse me, Maureen." He then took the seat Maureen had been occupying.

"This is from Nate..." he said, winking at her. "Look at his drawing..."

Truman proceeded to show her the cards the children had made her, reading their messages, commenting on the artwork, then arranging them on her nightstand, near the flowers Ginger had brought with her earlier. *Nice work, Tru!* she thought. He effectively froze Maureen out. Ted's sister stood near the foot of her bed while Truman was talking, her brows drawn together.

"I'll be back, Libby," she finally said. "Take it easy, Tru."

Libby closed her eyes when Maureen walked out of the room then smiled into Truman's eyes.

"Thank you," she whispered.

The doctors are going to release her tomorrow unless she can convince them otherwise. What will she do when she goes home? She has to tell the children their father is moving out and she's petrified. She's afraid of being a single parent. Ted might not be around much, but he was her backup. Emma's causing grief? *Watch it, or I'll call your father.* That was usually enough to get her daughter to tow the line. What now? *How will I raise the children without their father?*

"Libby, please listen to me," Ginger cries, clutching her arm. She's visited Libby every day this week. "They're talking about committing you to a psych hospital if you don't snap out of this. Then Ted will take this baby and your kids away from you! Sweetie, please focus on my words!"

I hear you, Ginger, she thinks. A few more days in the hospital? That sounds pleasant. She could sleep in peace and avoid reality a little longer.

"Libby, I have the best lawyers working for you, but none of that matters if you keep behaving like this. They think you're crazy, Lib! Do you understand? You'll never see Emma or Nate again. Libby. Your children won't have a mother."

What is she talking about? Crazy? I'm not crazy...just tired.

Ginger starts to cry and Truman enters the room and hugs her to him, glancing Libby's way. She frowns and motions with her finger for Truman to come over to her bed. She hasn't spoken since the day Maureen visited. Libby's been lost inside her own head, paralyzed by fear, floating in and out of consciousness.

"Why is she crying?" Libby whispers, her voice scratchy and hoarse.

Truman grabs her hands, his eyes filling with tears. *Why is everyone crying?*

"She wants you back. I want you back. We're worried about you," he says, taking a seat beside her in bed.

"Not crazy, Tru. Tired," she says, closing her eyes.

"I know you're not crazy, Libby."

"They can't take my kids away, can they?"

"No, Lib. If you sit up and start talking, they can't. Can you do that for Emma and Nate?"

She nods her head. *She'd do anything for her kids. Anything.*

"Help me up, Tru."

He helps adjust her in bed and uses the remote control to elevate it slightly.

"How's that?" he asks.

"A little more," she says and Truman smiles, working the remote again. "That's good."

Ginger takes a seat beside her and holds her hand, and Truman holds a cup of ice water in front of her, bringing the straw to her lips. Dr. Bradford walks in just then and stops in her tracks, her face lighting up.

"Well, look at you!" she exclaims. "This is good! How're you feeling today?"

"Foggy. Tired," she replies.

"That's to be expected. You've had quite a shock to your system. Truman, Ginger, can I have a few minutes alone with Libby?"

They leave the room, and Dr. Bradford takes a seat.

"Let's get you better and out of here," she says with a smile.

CHAPTER TEN

Ted has been staying at the office and using the shower at the gym next door since she was discharged from the hospital two weeks ago. Every night he comes over to tuck the kids into bed and Libby stays in her room, Ginger or Truman standing guard outside her door. He's at the house for an hour or so, then leaves. Last weekend he took the kids to stay at Maureen's in Boston. This weekend he's taking the kids skiing since he doesn't have a place to live yet. They're leaving Friday after school and will be back Sunday night. He's tried to contact her, but she ignores his phone calls and only returns texts related to the children. She's not ready to speak to him, unsure of what she wants to say.

The kids are frightened. Nate has been sneaking into her bedroom. She wakes up in the middle of the night to use the bathroom and finds him curled up beside her. Even Emma is tiptoeing around her, afraid to get too close. She knows something horrible has happened but hasn't asked any questions and spends as much time as possible out of the house. Her already emotionally fragile pre-teen daughter has withdrawn into her shell and Libby's simply not able to help her at this time.

The doctors have decided it's best she has a C-section, so she's scheduled to go in for surgery in a couple of weeks, a week before her due date. She doesn't know how she's going to handle raising this child and prays she doesn't resent him or her. It's not the baby's fault she never wanted another child and was too weak to stand her ground. It's not the baby's fault her marriage fell apart.

She's since learned Ted's affair with Caroline had been going on for years. Libby was living a lie for years and didn't know it. She didn't fall apart when she found out as Truman feared, a sort of numbness has settled in and though she's functional, she's an emotion-free zone. Nothing upsets her, or brings her joy. She feels nothing but emptiness.

Whether it's the meds or her, she doesn't know, and right now, she doesn't care. All she can do is focus on keeping it together for the sake of her children. There's no way she's going to let Ted take them away from her. He's never been a hands-on parent. Ted doesn't know the names of their doctors and teachers. She's the one who schedules their appointments and schleps them to activities. She sits by their bed when they're sick, not Ted! She'll get through this and get back to the business of raising her children.

The divorce paperwork has been filed. Ginger hired the best divorce attorney in the Northeast who can practice law in Rhode Island, and has been handling all of the paperwork for her. Libby just has to do is sign at the X and her friend takes care of the rest.

"You'll get everything, Libby, I'll make damned sure of that. The house, half the assets including the business, huge child support payments, and a pile of alimony. He'll be paying all of your bills, health coverage, car payments, you name it...forever by the time I'm through with him."

"I don't want his business...I don't want this house."

"Then he can buy you out of the business and you can sell the house. We'll build you a nice little nest egg. We've already frozen his assets and accounts. He can't move any money around without our knowledge."

"Ginger, I appreciate everything you're doing...but I don't want to talk about it anymore."

"Of course not, I'm sorry Lib. I just want to make sure you and the children are taken care of, even if the dirt bag drops dead of a heart attack, God willing."

She's grateful to Ginger for all she's done, but Libby wants to slow the process down, just a bit. She's so hurt by Ted, by what he did, but she can't help wondering what she did wrong. It takes two for a marriage to fail, and that's what an affair indicates, right? Failure? What's lacking in her? She thought their relationship was strong, passionate and fulfilling. Why did he stray? What did Caroline give him that she couldn't? She wants the answers to these questions before she moves forward with legal proceedings.

❋

Later that afternoon, after Ginger is gone, Truman arrives to bring Libby to her doctor appointment. Ginger had a big meeting this afternoon and was going to cancel it to be her chauffeur, but Truman volunteered to take her, as he has on a couple of other occasions. Her doctor is very worried about the baby. Libby has been losing weight instead of gaining as she should be, and they are doing an amniocentesis today to see if the baby's lungs have matured enough to move up the delivery date. The doctor is aware of her stressful situation and thinks it would be better for the baby to be outside her womb at this point. Libby couldn't agree more. The baby should never have been inside her womb and its time for check out.

Truman has been her rock, her port in the storm. One would think his presence would be a constant reminder of

Caroline and Ted, but that's not the case. His presence soothes her in a way no one else's does. He doesn't pressure her to talk, he never mentions the affair. He makes sure everything in her house is running smoothly, that the children are where they're supposed to be when they're supposed to be there. While the kids are at school, he reads to her, brings her tea and her favorite foods, but doesn't push her to eat anything. She can simply relax.

She's been waiting for close to an hour lying on a cot in a hospital gown, feeling vulnerable and exposed. Normally, she would have Truman or Ginger wait outside the office, but this visit is in the hospital and she asked him to stay with her. She's never had an amniocentesis test before so she read up on the procedure before her appointment. The idea of a huge needle being inserted into her abdomen and the amniotic sac is freaking her out!

Finally, a doctor and nurse enter the room and prepare her for the test, rubbing iodine on her stomach and jelly for the ultrasound. Her blood pressure is through the roof according to the monitor beside her and the nurse frowns.

"Relax Mrs. Fitzgerald. This is a very common procedure. Just close your eyes and lie still and it will be over before you know it."

She nods, trying to take deep breaths in and out. Truman sits beside her and holds her hand.

"I'm here, Libby. Everything is going to be okay. Just look at me."

She focuses on his hazel eyes and winces as the needle is inserted. He squeezes her hand and smiles.

"Excuse me, doctor," the nurse says with urgency.

Libby turns toward the nurse and notices the fluid being extracted is tinged with strands of pink. She's mesmerized by the pink fluid swirling inside the giant syringe and holds her breath as she stares. Pink is not a good sign. Her book said it's supposed to be clear, not pink!

"Mrs. Fitzgerald…I hope you don't have any plans for today because it looks like you're having your baby."

"I'm sorry? What?" Truman asks.

"Why?" she asks, her heart pounding against her ribcage.

Careful what you wish for! She wanted the baby out, now she's petrified. She thought she had at least another week. No…Ted is on his way to New Hampshire with the children. She doesn't have her hospital bag with her clothes, or her toothpaste, deodorant, hairbrush. Stupid, insignificant things occupy her mind to distract her from the fear gripping her heart, the imminent arrival of the baby she's afraid to meet, the child Libby's afraid she won't love.

"It seems we've nicked the baby with the needle, that's the blood you see in the amniotic fluid, and we need to get him out soon." The doctor turns to the nurse. "Go book the OR." And she scurries from the room.

"What do you mean you 'nicked the baby'?" Truman snaps. "What does that mean? Did you hurt him?"

He? Him? Why is everyone referring to the baby as a boy? She didn't want to know, though she supposes it doesn't matter now. She'd know soon enough.

The doctor explains that he's sure everything is fine, but the environment in her womb can no longer support the baby. *No longer?* She's surprised it ever could! When she was pregnant with Emma and Nate she wanted to protect them. They were loved from the moment they were conceived despite her fears of being an inadequate mother. The emotions surrounding this baby since the moment she found out about his existence ranged from disgust, to hate, to indifference. Not love. Not peace.

What if all of the negativity she's felt, the distress and horror of the past few months have hurt the baby somehow? What if he comes out angry and bitter, hating her from the start? She closes her eyes and takes a few deep breaths in and out. There's nothing she can do about the past, all she can do is shower this child with love when he's born, try to make it up to him by being the best mother she can possibly be. *Can I fake it for eighteen years? Will I have to?* Or will the love come naturally once he's born?

"Jesus Christ," Truman mumbles under his breath and runs his fingers through his hair.

The doctor leaves the room and Truman's eyes are full of concern and a hint of fear.

"Looks like you're having a baby! Do you want me to call Ted?"

"No, I don't want him here, not until the baby is born," she says, a feeling of calm washing over her. This will all be over soon. "Can you call Ginger and ask her to bring my bag? She packed it and knows where everything is."

"Of course," he says reaching for his phone.

"Truman…" she pauses and grabs his hand. "I don't want to be alone in there. I know this is a lot to ask, but will you come into the operating room with me?"

He sets his phone down, his lips parting and remains mute.

"You don't have to, Tru," she whispers. "I'll be okay."

"Libby, of course I'll come with you. I'll be right by your side."

♂

Getting scrubbed in and slipping on the paper gown and cap for the delivery, Truman has a strong sense of déjà vu. Caroline had C-sections for both of their girls and he knows exactly what to expect. The bright glaring lights, the sterile environment, a team of nurses, an anesthesiologist and doctors. So many doctors. He can tell Libby's unnerved by her surroundings, the IV in her arm, the monitors attached to her body. She delivered her other two children naturally, with candles lit and music playing. This is a totally different experience, still miraculous, but lacking the magical, personal touches of her previous deliveries.

As he stands behind the curtain, holding Libby's hand, he explains what's happening as they give her a spinal block, make the incision, and assures her the tugging sensation she feels is normal. He doesn't tell her they're basically removing her organs and putting them on trays to make room for removing the baby, or how many layers they have to cut through to reach him. He made the mistake of looking over the curtain when Sadie was delivered and almost vomited on the spot. It looked like an autopsy being performed or some biology experiment gone horribly wrong.

A few minutes later, he hears the baby's cry and Libby's eyes grow wide.

"Is that it?" she asks. "He's here?"

Truman nods and watches with tears in his eyes as the nurse carries the baby to the scale and cleans him up.

"You have a beautiful baby boy!" The nurse swaddles him and carries Libby's child over to him. "Would you like to hold your son?" she asks Truman.

He turns to Libby and raises an eyebrow and she smiles, both taking a moment to absorb the improbability of this situation. There's no point correcting the nurse. Everyone in the room believes he is Libby's husband.

"Go ahead, Tru," Libby says. "I want to see him."

As the baby's placed in his arms, Truman's overcome with emotion. What an extraordinary gift to be present the moment a new life is brought into the world. *But what a world to be brought into,* he thinks. Truman holds the baby close to Libby. She's hooked up to all kinds of machines, and the doctors are still working on her. She couldn't hold the baby if she wanted to. Looking at her son, the corners of her mouth turn up and her eyes are bright with tears.

"He's beautiful," she whispers, then her eyelids flutter and her mouth goes slack.

"Libby? Libby?" his voice becomes increasingly panicked. "Excuse me. Nurse! Someone!" he shouts. "She's unconscious!"

"Get the dad out of the room," he hears one of the doctors' shout. A nurse rushes over to him and takes the baby from his arms.

"Mr. Fitzgerald, I'll bring your son to the nursery. Please follow me."

"What's happening to her?" he asks. He's lightheaded, his heart racing. "What's going on?" he yells, but no one will answer him.

He's escorted to a private waiting room off the operating room and rips off his scrubs, his throat closing in on him. *Dear God, please let her be okay.* He sits in a chair and rests his head in his hands. *Don't let anything happen to her, please.* Truman finds himself pleading with a god he's not sure he believes in.

Ten excruciating minutes later a doctor comes into the room, his eyes downcast.

"Mr. Fitzgerald…" he pauses. "Your wife has lost a lot of blood. We've managed to stop the hemorrhaging, but she's still unconscious."

"But she's going to be okay?" he asks, not recognizing the sound as his own voice.

"We're doing everything we can for her. We'll keep you updated," he says, then leaves him alone in the room.

Truman can't feel his body. She's unconscious…that means she's in a coma. He stands immobile for what feels like an eternity, then jumps when his phone rings. He pulls it out of his pocket and looks down at the screen. Ginger.

"Truman? Hello?"

"Yeah. I'm here."

"Where are you? I just pulled into the parking garage." She sounds so excited.

"I have no idea," he replies.

"Truman, what's wrong?" she asks, her voice rising in pitch.

"She's in a coma, Ging," he whispers. "I'm in a room outside the OR."

She's silent for a moment then says, "I'll find you."

＊

"We have to call Ted. But we can't tell him anything's wrong, just that they had to deliver the baby today because of the amnio. We don't want him driving in a panic with the kids in the car. It already ten…the kids are probably asleep. Should I wait till morning? And I'll call Nina and see if she can meet them here, outside the hospital. I'll tell him that because of the operation they won't allow the children in the room, he won't know the difference. I don't want him to show up with them hoping for a visit. But what time should I tell her to arrive? I need to talk to Ted."

Ginger is on a roll, rambling and thinking through all of the scenarios out loud, taking care of business, as is her way. He's still in shock. The doctor came in after Ginger arrived and explained what happened in some detail, but he couldn't follow along. He was listening for the magic words that would make this all better. He was waiting for the doctor to say she'll be fine, but he never did.

The next twenty-four hours are critical, he caught that part, and if she doesn't come out of the coma by then, they will reevaluate.

Before the doctor left, he asked if Libby had a living will. *A living will?*

"Does she want extraordinary measures to be taken to prolong her life…if it comes to that?"

"Are you talking about life support?" Truman asked, his voice hoarse.

"Yes. Have you had that discussion with your wife?"

Truman turned to Ginger for help, but she had turned an unnatural shade of white, and remained silent.

"You do everything you can to save her life. Everything," Truman demanded.

Ginger went home around midnight, but Truman insisted on staying. The girls are with Caroline and he wants to be here when Libby wakes up from her long nap. *That's all this is, a nap,* he tells himself. She's had a rough few months and needs her rest.

Libby was moved to a private room, hooked to monitors and an IV. She's dreadfully pale though they've given her several transfusions. She's had no difficulty breathing on her own, a nurse reassured him, so unless something catastrophic happens, like an aneurism, stroke, or blood clot (is that all?) she should wake up on her own soon. He leans forward in his chair and rubs his hands over his eyes. *This can't be happening.*

"Don't worry, Mr. Fitzgerald, I've seen this happen many times before. I'm not supposed to say this, but I think she's gonna be fine."

In the wee hours of morning, a nurse brings the baby into the room for Truman to feed him a bottle. Holding him in his arms, he can't believe how small the boy is, weighing six pounds, little more than a bag of sugar. His daughters were both over eight pounds, and he's tiny in comparison. But he's feisty! He doesn't want to be swaddled and fights against the fabric. The boy is happy to be out of his confined quarters, wanting to stretch his limbs and take in the sights. His bright blue eyes are alert for a newborn and he's got one hell of a grip, clutching Truman's finger tight.

"Hey baby boy," he whispers, his heart filling with love for Libby's son. "Your mommy will be so happy to meet you. She's just resting."

A little after seven in the morning, Ted enters the room while Truman's rocking the baby. He doesn't look happy to find Truman by his wife's side, but smiles when his eyes rest on the baby, then Libby. Truman rises from the rocking chair and Ted takes his seat, then he reluctantly places the baby into his father's arms. Ted takes Libby's hand in his and kisses it, leaning close to her and whispers her name.

"She can't hear you," Truman says.

"What do you mean?" Ted seems puzzled, a natural reaction.

When Ginger finally got in touch with him, all she said was Libby had the baby and was resting.

"I'll get a doctor." Truman turns to leave, but Ted stops him.

"Tru, what's going on?" Ted turns to Libby and shakes her arm. "Libby? Sweetheart?"

He takes the baby from Ted's arms and places him in the bassinet, then motions for him to come out in the hallway.

"There were some complications with the operation. Libby's in a coma," Truman says, his eyes cold. "She's been unconscious for over twelve hours."

Ted stares at him, his eyes wide with shock, then he watches as Libby's husband sinks to the floor and turns to him, helpless.

"You did this to her, Ted," he says. "This is all your fault. Look at her lying there. Are you happy now?"

Ted buries his face in his hands and lets out an animalistic noise, something between a groan and a howl. Several nurses peek their faces out from behind their station while Ted sobs. Truman stands over him watching until the baby's cry draws him back into Libby's room. Just as he's about to pick him up, Ted is by his side.

"Stay away, Tru," he says, his voice ragged. "This is my son."

"Who was here when he was born, Ted? Who has been by your wife's side for weeks? Me, not you."

Ted grabs his shirt and shoves him away from the bassinet.

"Ted..." Libby whispers. "Stop it."

Truman cries out in relief and rushes to her side and Ted takes hold of Libby's hand.

"I don't want this anger around the baby. From either of you." She withdraws her hand from Teds. "You're here for the baby, not me. I'm not ready to talk to you, Ted."

She attempts to sit up in bed, then gives up and holds out her arms for the baby. Ted places him in her arms, then takes a step back, visibly stung by Libby's words.

"I want to call him George, after my father," she says looking down at her son with a smile. Then she turns to Ted, daring him to challenge her. Ted nods his head and backs away, taking a seat near the foot of her bed. Libby squeezes Truman's hand and smiles, "Thank you."

PART TWO

DISILLUSIONMENT

"It is better to know as little as possible…
the defects of the person with whom you
are to pass your life."
~ Jane Austen

CHAPTER ELEVEN

George was born six weeks ago and Libby spent the first week in the hospital, recovering from surgery. Since she's been home, he and Ginger have helped out as much as possible, which in his case meant taking Nate and Emma to practices, lessons and rehearsals. Ginger has been bringing over meals, and Nina is working full-time, helping with the baby and around the house. Truman was worried Libby wouldn't be able to bond with George, but to his relief, she's very affectionate with her newborn son.

It's her other two children he's worried about. Nate's become very clingy and sensitive and Bette has taken him under her wing, It's sweet (and reassuring) to watch her adopt the role of nurturer, trying to comfort and protect him. Bette may look like Caroline, but she doesn't act like her. Thank God.

Truman's heard some disturbing stories about Emma lately. According to Bette, she's taken up with a new group of girls, has been sneaking makeup to school and 'acting weird' around the boys. Emma's become one of the 'mean girls', picking on other kids and forming an exclusive clique. Libby's daughter has always been a bit of a drama queen, but these new developments are disturbing and Libby should be made aware of the situation at some point.

Ted's been around. A lot. And the sight of him still makes Truman sick. Libby's husband comes over every night to tuck the kids into bed, just as he's done since he got caught with his pants down, but Libby's called off the guards. She doesn't want anyone there while Ted is at the house, wanting the baby to be 'surrounded by peace'.

This Zen approach to parenting is a bit surprising given the circumstances. Since Libby awoke from her blessedly short coma, she's been oddly tranquil and together, as though the past few months never happened. He wondered at first if she'd experienced memory loss? Some form of amnesia? But she hasn't. Libby remembers everything, she's just choosing not to focus on it. It's hard to believe she experienced two bouts of severe depression this year, given her present demeanor. She's like the Libby who existed *before*, but even calmer.

That's how Truman refers to life now. There's *before* he found out about Ted and Caroline, and *after*, life since that day.

For so long he thought it would be better for the girls if he didn't upset the rhythm of their lives, to maintain the image of an intact nuclear family, especially in this town. Change is not welcome here, and people's attitudes toward him have already shifted.

Their book club has been unofficially dissolved. Libby hasn't been to a meeting since September, and they held their last meeting before the holidays. Since the New Year, and the announcement of his separation, the other three members of their group, Sarah, Greta and Anabelle, have been steering clear of him, averting their eyes whenever he's around.

Having lived here for more than a decade, he gets it. The ladies believe divorce is contagious. If it can happen to him, it can happen to them, so the goal it to stay away from the source of the disease with the hope they stay immune. Or maybe they blame him for Caroline's disappearance? She was their ringleader after all. Whatever is the cause, he doesn't care what other people think about his new circumstances. He knows who his real friends are, he just hopes his pariah status doesn't rub off on the girls. He doesn't want them to suffer because of his decision, to be excluded from activities.

No one wants to put their children through the emotional upheaval of a divorce, but kids are resilient. Far more damaging was the example he was setting for his daughters by staying in an unhappy marriage. During one of his long runs, it dawned on him that his relationship with Caroline was the example the girls will emulate when forming their future relationships. The thought literally stopped him in his tracks. He'd never want them to believe sleeping in separate bedrooms and showing no affection is normal, or that work is more important than family.

The girls are spending far more time with their mother now than they ever have, which keeps him up at night. Bette is adjusting and seems happy, but he's very concerned about Sadie. God only knows what Caroline has been saying to her. He's warned Caro repeatedly to watch her step, but since January, his daughter has shut down completely.

He's had Sadie in counseling for a few months and her therapist has encouraged her to express her feelings through art, writing and music. She hasn't shared anything with him yet, but he's hopeful she'll come out of her shell. He misses Sadie's smile.

✳

Truman almost passed out the first time he found Ted's car in Libby's driveway at six o'clock on a Saturday morning. He woke early for his morning run, saw the BMW, and had to steady himself against the tree, holding onto it for several moments as he contemplated what would possess Libby to allow Ted back in the house. George was one month old and Libby had been home for all of three weeks before Ted managed to weasel his way back home.

As Truman was running that morning, all sorts of scenarios went through his head, none of them good. Ted's a master manipulator. *That fucker isn't just a manipulator,* he thought, *Ted's a frigging magician if he's managed to convince Libby to take him back.* Pounding the pavement, Truman did the calculations. Libby discovered Ted and Caro's affair seven weeks ago. Not even two months have passed! That's less than two weeks' banishment for every year of his affair. That isn't right! Shouldn't the punishment fit the crime? A life in exile seems appropriate for four years of clandestine carnal relations with your neighbor. Not seven weeks! *She can't be this naïve, she just can't!*

When he saw her outside later that afternoon, he had to ask, trying hard to conceal his anger.

"It's none of my business, Lib, but please," he hesitated, feeling the heat rising to his cheeks. "Please tell me what the hell Ted was doing at your house this morning."

So much for concealing his anger! Libby rested her hand on his arm.

"It's not what you think," she explained. "Ted will be sleeping in the guest room on weekends until George is sleeping through the night. I'm exhausted."

"Why didn't you ask me to take the baby a couple of nights a week?" he asked.

Libby was visibly taken aback by his suggestion.

"It never occurred to me to ask you. That would be a huge imposition, not just on you, but the girls as well."

"I would have done it in a heartbeat, Lib" he sighed. "I'd love to have George over. Why don't you tell Ted you don't need him?"

170

Libby took a deep breath and looked at the ground.

"Truman, thank you for offering. You are a true friend. But, this isn't just about Ted helping me out. I'm giving them an opportunity to bond. That's important. He's George's father."

Truman closed his eyes and shook his head. That was the worst thing she had ever said to him. He may have had nothing to do with George's conception, but he thinks of George as his own, which he realizes is absurd, but true nonetheless. Being present for George's birth created a bond between them and he loves that child.

"I'm sorry, Truman. This arrangement is temporary, and if Ted steps over the line, he's out."

Out? He thought Ted was already out! Where exactly is this imaginary line, Libby? He was aching to ask the question, but stopped himself. Asking would be crossing a different kind of line. They're friends. She doesn't owe him an explanation for her decisions.

That thought didn't sit well with him either. They're not just friends. They've been through hell together and he's been there for her through it all. She owes him clarification on this sensitive issue. Inviting Ted back home, even on a temporary basis, effects Truman too.

He was so frustrated when he left her that afternoon. Doesn't she realize what's she's done? She gave Ted an in. That's what Ted was hoping for, and now he's got it. The nightly visits to the kids weren't enough to sway Libby, so he stepped up his game.

Ted's never hidden his true motivations. He wants to make things work with Libby, and to Truman's dismay, she's giving him the opportunity to do it. Ted can't come out of this with his life intact. He just can't! What about the laws of karma?

Truman can't live next door to that man again. He couldn't bear to watch them play happy family, couldn't stand to witness her suffering when Ted betrays her again. He doesn't doubt Ted loves his wife, but he loves himself more. The man is a classic narcissist. He will cheat again, it's part of his nature. The excitement, the thrill of sneaking around, the possibility of getting caught only fueled Ted and Caroline's desire for one another. They took bigger and bigger risks as time went on, he sees it so clearly now and wonders how he could have been so blind, for so long?

They were begging to get caught, hardly bothering to conceal their relationship. Conferences in the same cities, coming home within minutes of one another at the oddest hours. He can't count the number of times he found them alone in his own backyard, or how they'd always go down to the basement together during cookouts and dinners to find 'the perfect bottle of wine.' *They were the wine aficionados after all!* They were flaunting their infidelity, doing it right under their noses, and he and Libby were so distracted raising their children they didn't see it.

That doesn't feel good. He'd already been turned into something he didn't recognize before he found out about Caroline and Ted. His sense of self worth only sank lower upon that discovery. Now, he feels humiliated as well as emasculated.

Dating other women has helped rebuild some of his confidence. The day he filed his divorce papers, Ginger helped him set up a profile on a dating website and she was right, there are a whole lot of fish in this vast ocean of divorcées. His inbox has been inundated since the night he set up his account. It was overwhelming in the beginning. There are a lot of lonely, and shockingly aggressive women out there! Ginger was part of the selection committee, quickly weeding out the nut jobs, but he got the hang of it after a while.

Truman's had more sex in the past four months than he's had in the past five years. It feels good in the moment (really, really good) and he thought sex would be enough, but afterwards, he just wants to go home. He never believed he was the kind of guy who would run out the door as soon as he has an orgasm, but he doesn't want to wake up beside a woman he hardly knows or make breakfast with a stranger. He doesn't want to do intimate things like take a shower or brush his teeth in front of them.

He's made excuses so far, claiming he has a babysitter at home with the girls and has to get back, and he should feel bad for lying. But what's worse? Saying 'Hey, it's okay for me to stick my dick inside of you, but cuddling? Not a chance.' Or a little white lie? Ginger agrees, in this case, honesty is not the best policy.

✳

His relationship with Libby has been strained since their conversation about Ted's weekend sleepovers three weeks earlier. She hurt his feelings. She didn't take Truman into consideration when she allowed Ted home on the weekends. After all they've been through, how could she not? The man was fucking his wife for years! He wants to know what Libby's thinking, what her plans are with Ted. Whenever he's with her, it's the elephant in the room. Does she sense the shift?

"Are you jealous?" Ginger asks one afternoon as they're leaving Libby's house.

"Of what?" he asks, confused.

"Ted," Ginger replies, eyebrow raised.

"No! I just don't understand how she can let him in the house. Ted makes me sick and I can hardly stand the sight of Caro."

"Tru, you'd fallen out of love with Caro long ago," Ginger explains. "Libby was still in love with her husband when she discovered his infidelity. She's wondering what she did wrong. That's what I did. But here's where the situation differs…Ted still loves her, while Jasper was done with me. And let's not forget they just had a baby. Libby's hormones are all out of whack. But instead of making her nuts, they're calming her down. That won't last forever!"

They just had a baby…that stung.

"So you think she'll end up taking him back?" he asks, his eyes downcast.

"She's never said as much, but I wouldn't be surprised if that's what happens. Did you know the vast majority of couples stay married in the wake of an affair? I just read an interesting article. In it, the doctor used a set of statistics claiming seventy-five percent of couples survive infidelity."

"Is that true?" he asks.

That doesn't seem possible! He would never have taken Caro back if he found out about her affair four years ago. Never! All he'd ever think about was someone else touching her, wondering if the other guy was superior to him in some way. Did he make more money (in Ted's case, yes), was he more attractive (hmmm…in this one area, his looks work in his favor), was he a better lover (he doesn't want the answer to that one, but he'd still think about it!).

"That's what I read. It also said about half of those couples will do only that…survive. The other half 'embark on a process of growth and self-exploration.'"

"I don't fucking believe it," he mutters.

Is that what's happening? They're going to explore their relationship and miraculously come out stronger? He's maddened by the thought! What else does Ted have to do to convince Libby he's a selfish pig? How can she forget the image of Caroline up against a tree and her husband's pants in the snow? He didn't witness it, but the vision is still burned in his brain!

"You are jealous. Holy shit!" Ginger declares.

He feels his ears turning red, the heat spreading from his neck to his cheeks.

"Don't be ridiculous. I just don't want to see her get hurt again. And for Christ's sake Ginger, I don't want to live next door to that man. I think that's understandable, don't you? Jesus, you have an active imagination," he says, sounding unconvincing to his own ears.

"Look at you blushing like a schoolboy!" she laughs. "You're in love with Libby, aren't you?" Ginger pauses for a beat, then her eyes grow wide. "Oh my God! You are in love with her! It all makes sense now."

"I love Libby. I am not 'in love' with her. Grow up Ginger."

He walks into his house and shuts the door behind him, leaning up against it and taking deep breaths in and out. I'm not in love with Libby. He shakes his head, trying to clear his mind of this unwanted thought.

Taking a seat in the den, he stares out the window. It's April, the week before the Boston Marathon, and the leaves are blooming on the trees and bushes outside his house. The windows are open in the den and the sweet scent of cherry blossoms waft into the room, reminding him of the passage of time.

The years are flying by at warp speed and he's not getting any younger. He wants love in his life. It's rare to meet someone you feel a connection with, he's realizing just how rare now that he's re-entered the dating world. He's always felt a connection to Libby, from the moment they met, but even more so now.

He closes his eyes and his heart sinks with the realization. *I am in love with her.* He wasn't always, but somewhere along the way his feelings transformed from friendship...to more. He first became aware of the not-so-subtle shift back in September and tried unsuccessfully to bury the unwelcome emotion. What's he going to do? He's in love with a married woman, his best friend.

Now what?

CHAPTER TWELVE

B oundaries. It's all about setting boundaries with Ted. The man has brass balls, using their children to insert himself into her life. When Libby first came home from the hospital, she denied Ted's request to continue the nightly visits with the kids. The first night he didn't show up, Nate and Emma called him to ask why he wasn't there and Ted didn't hesitate to point the finger at Libby.

They cried and begged her to let them see their father and she felt awful. Hadn't she put them through enough this year? She didn't see any way to prevent yet another major disruption in the children's lives, so she agreed. He's welcome to visit the kids here as long as he leaves her alone.

For the two hours Ted's in the house, she retreats into her room, runs errands, or does chores. She has to figure out her next moves and thinking about the future is particularly difficult in the sleep deprived state she's been in since George's birth.

Once the kids are in bed, Ted heads back to the studio apartment he's renting in the city. When he informed her of his living situation, she raised an eyebrow and told him he should have gotten a larger place. He said if he believed it was over between them, he would have. He's not giving up on them.

She stared at him, speechless. How could he possibly believe she'd take him back? He betrayed her during the most vulnerable period in her life. She'd just turned forty and was about to have a baby! She felt unattractive and old and he'd been having an affair with lithe, gorgeous Caroline right under her nose for years! Not months…years! How could she ever forgive him for such a massive betrayal of trust?

Maureen has stopped by several times to plead Ted's case, and she recruited Ted's brothers in the Fitzgerald full frontal attack. She's been inundated with phone calls, texts and emails from his siblings, all delivering the same message. *Family is family. Forgive and move on.*

Libby's had enough. She finally told her sister-in-law if the sole purpose for her visits are to convince Libby to take Ted back, she isn't welcome in her home. That did not go over well with Ted's strong-willed sister. Maureen's attitude shifted quickly from blatant manipulation to downright anger.

"I can't believe how fucking selfish you're being Libby," she hissed. "You're not thinking of the kids. You're only thinking of yourself!"

She stormed out of the house and Libby hasn't heard from her in over a week. Thank God.

The one person in Ted's family who's been noticeably quiet on the matter is Ted's mother. Doris came to visit Libby at the hospital, and again the other day. On both occasions, she focused all of her attention on George and the kids, never mentioning the situation between Libby and Ted. When she kissed Libby farewell, her parting words were, "I'm here if you ever need me. No matter what you decide."

When Ted first suggested they attend marriage counseling, she shot him down point blank. As the days turned into weeks, she finally agreed to go for one simple reason; Libby wants answers. Why did he feel the need to have an affair when everything was so good between them? *Why?* What did she miss? What could she have possibly done different? *What's wrong with me?* That's all she wants, answers to these basic questions before she moves forward with the divorce.

Libby and Ted had their first counseling session three weeks ago. Sitting across from the doctor, she kept her composure, answered whatever questions she was asked, then sat back for forty minutes and listened to Ted discuss her depression and withdrawal from him, her desire to abort the child initially and how horrible he felt knowing she didn't want his baby.

She sat there, checking her cuticles, thinking about making an appointment for a manicure, and calling her stylist for a cut and color. *Maybe Steven can squeeze me in next week?* She thought about Truman stopping by every day to see the baby, the corners of her mouth turning up. He's very attached to George. She can see it in his eyes whenever he's around the baby. He comes over every morning while the kids are in school for his 'morning fix', and spends up to an hour in the nursery rocking the baby and feeding him a bottle while Libby showers.

Truman's upset about Ted spending the weekends at home and he has a right to be. It wasn't fair for her to make that decision without talking to him and she's sorry for causing him more pain. She'll never be able to repay him for what he's done for her, for simply being there in her time of need. She hopes Truman understands how much he means to her, to her family. *He is family* and she'd do anything for him.

At the session drew to a close, the doctor turned to her.

"Libby, you've been very quiet this evening. Do you have anything you want to say to Ted?" he asked, pulling her away from her thoughts of Truman.

Hmmm…do I have anything to say to Ted? She chuckled to herself. Oh, she has lots she wants to say to her husband, but none of it constructive.

"I want to know why you had an affair with our neighbor for four years," she said, her face deliberately hard, inscrutable.

The doctor's eyes flew open, his mouth dropping as he turned to Ted. Her husband turned pink and closed his eyes for a moment. *Forgot to mention that, eh Ted?* Why does he think she came to this session? To listen to him make up a bunch of bullshit excuses for a one-night stand? By diverting attention away from his affair, did he think she would miraculously forget about it?

"Ted, do you have an answer for your wife?"

He shook his head back and forth, chewing on his bottom lip.

"Not a good one," he finally said.

"Unfortunately…we are out of time today, but I would like to pick up here at our next session, that is, if you agree to come back," the doctor said, looking directly at Libby.

"Sure," she said. "I'll come until I have my answers."

They walked to the parking lot together in silence and when they reached her car, Ted turned to her and grabbed her hands, looking deep into her eyes, as if trying to read her mind. She emptied her head of all thought, all feeling as her eyes met his.

"Do you hate me?" he asked, his eyes bright with tears.

"No," she replied. "I think you're pathetic, selfish, and weak. And cruel, Ted, very cruel."

"I never meant to hurt anyone, least of all you. I love you with my whole heart, Libby, and if I could take back what I did, I would."

"So Caro was just a piece of ass? She must have been something else to keep you coming back for more all those years. Are there diamonds between her thighs? Was she that good in bed?"

Ted looked down at the pavement and sighed.

"Don't do this, Libby."

"What else am I supposed to do? You broke us, Ted. You broke our family. For what? There has to be a reason."

"It had nothing to do with you, baby," he reached out to caress her cheek and she slapped it away.

"Don't call me 'baby'. I'm not your baby anymore," she hissed, her anger finally rising to the surface. "Tell me why you did it Ted! And don't say it had nothing to do with me. When you feel the need to fuck someone else for almost one third of our entire marriage, it has to do with me! There had to be something missing in our relationship. Some hole you needed to fill. In what way did I fail you, Ted?"

"Libby, listen to me. You never failed me, ever. There's nothing lacking in you or our relationship… It was me, Libby. I felt old and started taking everything for granted. When my father died, I was stuck in a rut. The years were slipping by and I was feeling old…"

She held up her hand, putting a stop to his rambling. *When his father died five years ago?*

"Are you saying you had an affair because you feared death?" *Am I Olympia Dukakis in Moonstruck?* "Okay, Cosmo, I want you to know 'no matter what you do, you're still gonna die.' Are you going to tell me that you woke up one day and realized your life was built on nothing?"

"This isn't a joke," he snapped. "You want to talk about it? Fine, let's talk, but don't start with the sarcasm. You know that gets us nowhere quick. I'm trying to explain what happened."

"Fuck you. You don't get to tell me how to handle this or what tone I'm allowed to use. What makes you think I'm trying to get us anywhere? You think I'm here because I want to work things out with you? Ha! Not a chance. I'm here because I want the truth. I want to know how we got here. I want to know why you never told me you were unhappy in our marriage," she said, her voice cracking. "I thought we were happy."

Goddammit, I swore I wouldn't cry in front of him! But it was too late, the tears rolled down her cheeks against her will.

"I thought you loved me," she whispered, covering her face with her hands and leaned against the car. "I would've done anything for you. I had another baby for you…and you…you…" She couldn't breathe, was choking on her tears when Ted wrapped his arms around her, stroking her hair and her back.

"I'll never be able to express how deeply I regret what I've done to you and our marriage, or apologize enough for how much I've hurt you," he murmured into her hair. "I don't expect you to believe me, but it'll never happen again. I don't want to lose you, Libby. You and the kids are my life."

"You're right," she wiped away her tears and backed away from him. "I don't believe you."

She climbed into her Volvo SUV and drove away.

✳

The following week, the doctor began the session by asking Libby to share 'her side of the story.' Without sentiment, she filled him in on the events Ted conveniently left out the previous week. Not just about the affair and her pregnancy, but the many years he's been a passive, mostly absent part of their family's life. The vacations they've never taken because of his work schedule, the games and performances he missed because 'something suddenly came up', the parent-teacher conferences he didn't attend. It wasn't until her husband was faced with losing everything that he made a concerted effort to participate in their lives, and she resents it. *Too little, too late.*

"You're worried about your life slipping away, Ted? The years passing by too quickly?" she asked. "Then why didn't you slow down and appreciate what was right in front of you?"

Her husband sat and listened, his brows drawn together, perplexed, as if it was the first time he'd ever heard these words uttered from her lips. Maybe she had never been so blunt, had never delivered this message without dressing it in loving kindness, but this isn't news. If this is the first time he's actually listened to her complaints, they have even bigger issues to address.

He didn't have any answers for her that week, or the week after. Ted has the gift of the gab, and that's what he does as he sits on the loveseat (there has to be a better name for it!) beside her each week…gabs. Trying to win over the marriage counselor with anecdotes, punctuated with the occasional insight into his psyche. *Ted must think this PhD is an idiot.*

Dr. Stein is no fool. Libby watches him while Ted goes on and on. He smiles benignly, taking notes, but it's his eyes that give him away. They narrow just a hair whenever Ted diverts the conversation, and she glances at her watch whenever this happens. The doctor allows Ted to drift off for precisely two minutes (his eyes never leave Ted's face, how does he know it's been two minutes?), then deftly brings him back around to the purpose of these visits. Their marriage. Or lack thereof.

What has become clear to Libby throughout these sessions is where her husband's priorities lie. At the top of the list? Money. He shared his rags to riches story, his humble beginnings and the grand manner in which they now live. He's proud of his family, and his ability to provide a good life for them with a big house, nice cars, enough money to enable Libby to stay home and raise the children. He's giving them a better life. Isn't that worth some sacrifice on both of their parts?

She studied his face as he spoke. Financial security has always been a priority for her as well...but is it worth the sacrifice? What difference does it make if they have a big house if he's never there to enjoy it? Is having a fat bank account more important than spending time together as a family? All the money in the world can't make up for his absence from the children's lives. Doesn't he see that?

Next on Ted's list of priorities? Self gratification. He's proud of the business he's built with his own talent. He enjoys the admiration of others, the attention and respect showered upon him in the political and business communities. She raised an eyebrow at that comment. Why this need to be the best and win the admiration of others? There can only be one reason. He needs it to feed his ego.

But nothing, Ted claims, is more important to him than his family. He would have moved to Washington, DC years ago, where the real action is, if not for his family in Boston and most importantly, for her and the kids.

"I think it's important for children to have a place to call home," Ted explained. "They've lived in Littleton since they were babies. I wouldn't want to take them away from their home."

He was thinking about us? Bullshit. Libby knew how ambitious he was when she met him. She would've moved wherever he needed to be. She doesn't have any family in the area. Her parents are both gone, her brother lives across the country. *This doesn't have anything to do with us.* From the night she met him, she understood there would always be a woman waiting in the wings, offering...tempting him with a taste of forbidden fruit. She was dumb enough to believe he'd never take a bite.

"Libby, do you want to respond to Ted's comment?" Dr. Stein asked.

"I think it was more convenient for him to keep his family separate from his extra-curricular activities," she replied, arms folded across her chest.

Ted's body sagged against the sofa and he ran his fingers through his hair, a sign of frustration, tinged with defeat.

"Is there any truth to that, Ted?" the doctor asked.

"No…I don't know," he whispered.

"I want you to think about that this week." The doctor checked his watch and grabbed his appointment book. "We're out of time for today, but that's where I'd like to pick up next week."

✳

Never in her wildest dreams did she believe she'd be in the position she finds herself in now. *Divorcée.* The word itself makes her want to cry. Libby was thirteen years old when her parents divorced and she vowed if she ever had children, she'd never put them through the heartbreak. When she married Ted and made the decision to have children with him, her commitment to their family was absolute and for life.

To be in this situation now is unreal. She took for better or worse seriously, but there comes a point when 'for worse' is simply unbearable.

Libby's not stupid. She understands exactly what Ted's doing. *He's trying to wear me down.* He thinks if he can prove to her he's changed, she'll forget the sight of him having sex with Caroline. That's never going to happen, Ted! What he did was unconscionable, unforgiveable. The legal proceedings may be on hold, but the end game is the same. Before that happens, however, she has a few things to work out.

Libby's been wracking her brains, trying to figure out a way to make this okay for her kids. She doesn't want them to live out of a suitcase like she did. There has to be a way to prevent that from happening. Maybe if they buy houses next door to one another? Or find a house with an in-law apartment for Ted? Condos in the same building?

All of these scenarios are possibilities. Each one would involve moving. Would they stay in Littleton? Or move back to Providence? Would she consider moving to Washington, DC if Ted felt it necessary? These aren't small matters. These are big, life altering decisions and she must consider every one of them carefully.

Before she proposes anything to Ted, she needs to do her homework. Whatever they decide, it has to be in the best interest of the children.

Libby has attempted to open up a dialogue with her daughter on a few occasions. Emma's old enough to grasp what's happening, but the few times Libby's brought it up, she changed the subject. Her daughter's living in denial and that's a place Libby knows well. If they don't talk about it, it's not real to her.

Nate, on the other hand, thinks she and Ted just had a really bad fight and eventually his parents will kiss and make up. *Ah, the naïveté of youth!*

"When are you going to say sorry and sleep in your room?" he asked Ted one night before bed.

Libby had just entered the bedroom to kiss her son goodnight and held her breath.

"I have apologized, buddy, but sometimes that's not enough," Ted said, making eye contact with her. "Sometimes people don't make up for a long time."

At least he didn't lie. She wanted to add that sometimes people don't ever make up.

CHAPTER THIRTEEN

The neighbors don't know which side is up at this point. All anyone can do is speculate, which probably makes matters worse. People's imaginations are far more vivid than reality...though in this case, maybe not. Their curiosity and confusion is palpable each morning at the bus stop and Libby has come to dread the daily march into the lion's den. Those five to ten minutes standing on the corner are torture. The women 'ooh and aah' over George for a few minutes, then the conversation dies out and Libby finds herself on the periphery of the group with Truman. Two outsiders.

Last week, Greta and Sarah came to visit Libby bearing gifts. After Libby made tea, they sat together in the living room while Libby opened their presents for the baby; a powder blue layette embroidered with George's initials from Greta, and a silver baby rattle and stuffed elephant from Sarah.

"Thank you. They're beautiful," Libby smiled, setting the gifts aside.

"We've been meaning to come sooner," Sarah sighed, "But you know how it is with the kids."

Libby nodded, taking a sip of her tea.

"So, Libby…" Greta's voice trailed off, a crease forming between her brows. "How are you?"

"I'm fine. Tired as you can imagine. George is waking up every three hours or so at night and it's exhausting."

Greta and Sarah exchanged looks, then Greta set her teacup on the coaster and leaned forward in her chair.

"Of course. And this situation must make it worse."

"Situation?" Libby asked, playing dumb.

"With Ted…" Greta sighed, shaking her head.

Sarah nodded, her eyes sympathetic. Libby looked from Greta to Sarah, her eyes narrowing.

"Not that it's any of your business…" she paused, then rose to her feet. "You know what? Let's just leave it at that." Libby walked to the front door. "Thank you for the gifts, but it's my nap time. You know how precious sleep is at this stage."

The ladies followed her to the door and Greta rested her hand on Libby's shoulder.

"Take care, Libby."

Closing the door behind the women she considered friends for so many years, she was seething. Greta didn't come out of concern for Libby; she was fishing for information. Sitting across from them, Libby realized Greta's the new Queen Bee, the face of the neighborhood association. Sarah's just the lapdog, following her master. If Libby had shared anything about her situation with either of them, it would have been spread around the neighborhood in record time.

Poor Libby, her husband leaves her when she has a baby. How awful. Well, fuck them! I don't need their pity. And she certainly doesn't need anyone nosing around in her business.

Her neighbors are waiting for her to crumble. It would make them feel better about their own lives. *At least we aren't Libby, poor thing.* They'll be waiting a long time. She's not going to fall apart because her husband is a philandering asshole.

Libby's tired of faking it for her neighbors. Over the years, she convinced herself and everyone else she belonged in quaint, suburban Littleton, that she fit in. But she doesn't and she doesn't want to anymore. She doesn't know where she belongs, but definitely not here.

The older she gets, the more she realizes nothing is as it seems. It's all an illusion, the lives of her neighbors, the lives her friends have created for themselves on social media. Her own life, for that matter! Carefully crafted personas bearing little resemblance to their actual lives or the inner workings of their minds. How many of them are bored out of their skulls sitting at their kids' soccer and lacrosse games? Shuttling them to dance class, sailing lessons, tutoring sessions?

They'll eventually grow weary of the endless stream of soul-sucking, meaningless activities they engage in to impress or outdo one another. Or maybe they won't? Maybe they can cure the tedium of their lives with a few drinks and a pharmaceutical cocktail of Prozac and Valium? Who is she to judge? *Whatever gets you through the day, ladies.*

Libby's taken to fastidiously studying those happy family shots on social media, searching for the truth in the tilt of a head, the gleam in their eyes, the downward turn of someone's mouth. If you look closely enough, the lies begin to reveal themselves. A raised eyebrow, a slight sneer, a glimmer of contempt directed at the person taking the photograph, boredom, a fake smile repeated in picture after picture. She's spent hours studying other families' photos, dissecting their facial expressions until a more honest image emerges. They'd be horrified to learn she's dismantling their meticulously cultivated façades.

She's guilty of the same trickery, sharing the happy moments, excluding the monotony and frustration of real life from her news feed. No one posts pictures of their kids when they're throwing a tantrum or slamming a door in your face. Nobody was there to snap a photograph of her face when she found out she was pregnant with George, or the horror she experienced while she watched her husband screwing her neighbor.

They see the cover photo of a picture perfect family taken on Sconset Beach in Nantucket last summer before her life crumbled before her eyes. A photograph of baby George, round and jolly, his beautiful blue eyes smiling into the camera, not crying for his two AM feeding, not as the cause of so much personal despair in the months leading up to his birth.

It's become an obsession. Once she was through with her 'friends' on Facebook, she became fixated on her own family photographs. Searching for clues, signals of distress. She sits on the rug, surrounded by thousands of pictures in her bedroom, her laptop propped up beside her, and studies Ted's body language, his facial expressions. She's cross-sectioned the planes and angles of his face to compare each photograph.

Every nuance suggests he loves her and adores his children. He looks happy and engaged in virtually every shot. What is she missing? The only possible explanation is she's too close to the situation and can't objectively study a subject so close to her heart.

Flipping through the stacks that never made their way into albums, she found several photographs of Ted and Caroline together, her stomach clenching as she pours over every detail. It's all right there, plain as day, and she turned a blind eye. Caroline leaning into Ted, her hand on his arm, her adoring smile, eyes bright and excited whenever she looks at him. And her husband, face relaxed and…*satisfied*, is the only word that comes to mind. Smiling like a Cheshire cat. No guilt…not one ounce of remorse or shame. Contentment, that's all she sees, an entitled man who has everything he wants, everything he believes he deserves.

On the flip side, the tension between Tru and Caro virtually assaults her, leaping out of the few pictures she's found of her neighbors together. Their bodies subtly turned away from one another, his brows drawn together, Caroline's demeanor, dismissive. Libby missed that too. She was living in a fantasy world, completely oblivious to the drama and intrigue swirling around her, ignorant of the 'behind the scenes' in the lives of the people closest to her.

And she feels like an idiot.

Now that her eyes are open, she can't close them, though part of her wishes she was still in the dark. Being clueless required no effort at all. Being aware, she can either pretend to be happy or live her truth. She doesn't have it in her to fake it, to continue living a lie. She's exhausted.

She hadn't picked up her camera in months, but once she did, her hobby took on a new, not entirely healthy spin. Libby's become obsessed with taking pictures of people at unexpected moments, wielding her camera like a loaded weapon, ready to shoot unsuspecting victims.

She zooms in on the details, up close and personal. Her neighbors unloading bags of groceries from the car, picking at a scab while waiting for the kids at the bus stop, their eyes as they walk out of Starbucks clutching their morning caffeine fix.

Libby's a stalker with truth her only prey. She's trying to make sense of the world around her, of the life she's been living for the past fifteen years. And since Ted doesn't have any satisfactory answers as to why he was unfaithful, she will try to uncover truth wherever she can find it.

✳

Through her sessions with Dr. Bradford, Libby has come to realize how much Ted's preferences overshadowed her own wants and needs. Libby put her husband ahead of herself, everyone and everything for fifteen years. How could she let that happen?

"When do you think you lost your sense of self?" Dr. Bradford asked during a recent session.

"Don't you mean, when did I turn into a concubine?" Libby muttered. "My only goal to please and serve Ted?"

"Libby, you are far too hard on yourself. Marriage is about compromise and it sounds to me like you've done most of the compromising in your relationship. Was it that way from the beginning?"

She stared out the window at the budding trees, remembering their early years together as a whirlwind of passion and excitement. Her life revolved around Ted from the start. She made it a priority to keep him happy.

"Yeah..." she whispered. "Right from the beginning."

"You know what my next question is going to be..." Dr. Bradford paused, folding her hands in her lap. "Why do you think that is? Why did you surrender yourself to him so readily?"

Libby shifted in her seat watching the birds outside the office window.

"He was my Willoughby..."

"Your Willoughby?" Dr. Bradford asked, her brows drawn together. "The character from *Sense and Sensibility*?"

Libby smiled and nodded. It sounded ridiculous coming from her therapist's mouth, but Ginger would've understood.

"Are you supposed to be Marianne?" she asked, jotting notes down on her pad.

"Not exactly, but he brought out the Marianne in me. Before I met him, I was all Elinor. Practical and responsible. I had to be. I put myself through college and didn't have time for fun. And when my parents died..." Libby paused, her eyes filling with tears. She shrugged and grabbed a tissue. "I was on my own."

"Until your Willoughby came along and swept you off your feet," the doctor added.

"Yes. He swept me off my feet. Ted was everything I thought I wanted in a man. Charismatic, handsome, romantic, intelligent, sexy and strong. He was also ambitious and family-oriented, two things I desperately needed at the time. He took care of me. He could protect me. I wasn't alone anymore."

"Willoughby's selfishness almost destroys Marianne. Her love for him almost kills her."

"Trust me, Doctor, I've noticed the similarities. Maybe that's why Ted was attracted to Caroline? I was too weak for him."

"Weak?" Dr. Bradford's brow furrowed. "That's the absolute last word I would use to describe you, Libby. You're an incredibly strong woman. You've been through hell, and you're still standing."

"Then why? I want to know why he did this! I need to know why he had an affair!" she cried.

"Libby. Would it really make you feel better to know Ted preferred her strength over your passivity? Or that she was better in bed?" her doctor asked, raising an eyebrow. "Would it help you to know he was more attracted to Caroline's beauty than your own?"

Her heart screamed, 'YES!', her head whispered, 'no.'

"Knowing the answers won't help you move forward. Focusing on the questions is what keeps you mired in the past. You need to ask yourself what you want for yourself and your children. Do you want to continue down this path of self-doubt or get back to being you?"

"When you put it that way…" Libby sighed.

"The Elinor in you will help you through this difficult period," Dr. Bradford smiled, reassuringly. "Embrace her."

CHAPTER FOURTEEN

G inger's offered Libby the use of her house on Nantucket for the entire summer. She sold her house in the downtown district this past fall and bought another home on the other side of the island, in Siasconset, right next to Libby's favorite beach. She's only seen pictures, but it's a gorgeous turn of last century, three thousand square foot, 'summer cottage'.

The interior needed a complete overhaul, and over the winter it's undergone major renovations, but the majority of the work is complete. Ginger's contractor is now working on the guesthouse, and should be finishing up sometime in July. It will be peaceful, despite the occasional hammering. Her friend has to travel a lot so the house would otherwise be empty. "You'd be doing me a favor!" she exclaimed.

Ginger didn't have to work too hard to convince her! Two solid months on Nantucket, just steps from the beach? She's counting the days until she leaves. It will be such a relief to get away from Littleton for a while and she can't wait to get away from Ted.

When she shared her summer vacation plan, Ted balked, saying he couldn't be away from the baby for two whole months. She told him he could visit on weekends but he'll have to stay in the unfinished guest cottage. He agreed to that plan. *As if he had a choice.* She loves calling the shots for a change. This newfound sense of power, self-determination…freedom, is heady.

The school year will be over in less than two months, and she's sending the kids to sleep-away camp in Vermont for six weeks; all of July and half of August. In the past, she was against the idea, believed her children were too young to be separated from her for so long. This year? It'll be good for them to get away from the drama she's trying so hard to protect them from. It will be good for her to have some alone time with George as well.

Last year Emma begged to go away to camp and threw a temper tantrum when Libby and Ted refused to send her. This year she wants to go to the camp her new friends are attending in the Catskills. Earlier today, Emma came home from school with a brochure for Camp Birchwood and Libby's mind was open to the idea of switching camps, until she flipped through the pages of the brochure and saw the associated fees. She doesn't care how much money they have, twelve thousand dollars for six weeks in the woods is obscene.

Is Wolfgang Puck preparing dinner every night? Are the sheets one thousand thread count Egyptian cotton? Are facials and massages included? They're kids! Sleeping in log cabins and swimming in a lake!

"Never going to happen, my dear," Libby laughed, dropping the brochure on the counter.

"Mom, this is the camp I'm going to. If you won't let me, I'll run away!" Emma threatened.

"I'll help you pack your bags, Emma Jane, because there's no way you're going to that camp," Libby replied. "Unless you're paying for it. Do you have twelve thousand dollars?"

"Mother! All of my friends are going to Camp Birchwood! How can you do this to me?"

"You'll make new friends, Emma, I have no doubt," Libby sighed.

"Daddy will let me go," her daughter challenged, arms folded across her chest.

"Guess what, Em? There's a new sheriff in town. What I say, goes, and I say no. So you can beg Daddy all you want, but I'm calling the shots. Do you understand me?"

"I hate you! You're the worst mother in the world!" Emma shouted. "You don't care about anyone but yourself. Why don't you go to bed, Mom? Maybe sleep for a few more months and leave me alone."

Libby felt the heat rise to her cheeks, a vein pulsing in her neck, as her arm rose involuntarily into the air. She's never wanted to slap her daughter as badly as she did in that moment but caught herself, clasping her hands tightly together.

"Go to your room, now," Libby whispered, lowering her face inches from Emma's. "And don't come out until I say so."

Emma stepped back, her eyes wide with fear, then ran to her room and slammed the door.

Libby took a seat at the counter, her body trembling with a combination of rage and shame. *Go take a nap, Mom.* She slept through most of the year and convinced herself the children hadn't felt her absence. Truman, Ginger and Nina were around to pick up the slack, but that doesn't change the fact that while Libby was trapped inside her head, the world kept turning. Her children were effected and it seems what little respect Emma had for her disappeared while she was sleeping. Libby didn't think she could feel worse than she already did, but she was wrong. *I'm a horrible mother!*

While Ted tucks the kids into bed, Libby sits in the nursery feeding George, wondering how she can make up for lost time with Emma and Nate. She can't change the past, so what's the best way to move forward with them? She's deep in thought when Ted joins her in the nursery, camp brochure in hand. She eyes him and the pamphlet warily as he leans against the changing table.

"Emma wants to go to this camp instead of the one in Vermont. All of her friends are going there and I think it'd be good for her to be with people she knows this summer. What do you think?" he asks.

Libby sighs, considering her daughter's manipulations and blatant disrespect. There's no way she can back down on this one. Emma will believe she can get away with murder if she caves.

"She already asked me, and the answer is no."

"Don't you think we should discuss this type of decision, Libby? They're my kids too."

"You were never part of those decisions before, why start now?" she asks.

Ted's eyes darken, perceptively narrowing as he folds his arms across his chest.

"Look at page four, Ted. What does it say there?" she continues.

"Twelve thousand dollars. So? We can afford that."

She stares at him, mouth agape, her eyes growing wide. Did she hear him right?

"I'd rather donate the money to charity," Libby scoffs. "That's not who we are, Ted. That's not who I want our children to become."

"What do you mean?"

"It's a camp for privileged brats, Ted. Not to mention a waste of money! Two thousand dollars per week, per child? That's more than our monthly mortgage payment. That's enough to send one of them to private school for an entire year! My answer is no, and that's final."

Ted's anger is simmering just beneath the surface. She knows that look. He's being cut out of the decision making process and he doesn't like it. It's the same look he gave her last September when she said she wanted an abortion. *Too damned bad, Ted!* The glare doesn't have the same effect anymore. *Marianne is gone.*

He pulls out the ottoman and sits down beside her, bowing his head, his shoulders sagging.

"Is this how it's going to be, Libby? Is this how you're going to make me pay, by stripping me of my right to collaborate and decide how to raise our kids?"

"Do you think this has anything to do with you? Are you that self-absorbed?" she counters. "I don't want our children growing up in that environment, Ted. It's hard enough here in Littleton, trying to keep them from becoming spoiled brats. You grew up in Southie for Christ's sake! I grew up in Lowell! I'd rather send her to the Y camp in town and make her volunteer at a homeless shelter than send her to that over-priced camp with those entitled children."

He runs his fingers through his hair, then clasps his hands together, tilting his head up.

"And if I disagree with you?" he asks, his eyes meeting hers.

"Then you're not the person I thought you were," she states emphatically, then shakes her head and smirks. How absurd! *The person I thought he was? Was he ever the person I thought he was?*

"You're right, Libby. That's not who we are."

She raises an eyebrow, wondering if he's saying that to appease her, or if he genuinely means it. Does it even matter? She sets the empty bottle on the nightstand, done feeding

George, then tosses a cloth over her shoulder and repositions the baby, his soft head nestled in the curve of her neck. Patting his back, she feels a surge of love flow through her body, the anger she felt during their exchange evaporating as she holds her baby close, breathing in the sweetness of his skin.

Now that George is here, she can't imagine life without him. Somehow, his presence has cushioned the blow of Ted's affair. Whenever she's feeling down, she picks up her infant son and he soothes her, finding it impossible to remain upset with her baby in her arms.

"You used to look at me like that," Ted whispers, his eyes glossy with tears.

She closes her eyes and nods, holding George close to her.

"I'd give anything to see you look at me that way again."

She swallows hard, resisting the urge to cry and Ted kneels beside her, resting his head against the ottoman, one hand brushing against her ankle. His back trembles and he buries his face in his arms and cries.

She stares at her big, strong husband, crumpled up, crying at her feet and tries to muster up the anger she felt just moments before, but can't. She doesn't know what she's feeling as she rests her hand on his head, her fingers combing through his thick hair, comforting him.

A few minutes later, he lifts his face to her, his eyes bloodshot, the creases on his forehead and around his mouth creating deep grooves in his skin, resembling scars. She pulls a clean cloth from the basket beside the rocker and wipes away his tears. Then, rising, she settles George in his crib and returns to the rocking chair, staring straight ahead.

Moments later their eyes meet and she can't look away...can't do anything but sit immobile in the chair, trying to read his mind and extract the answers she's been seeking. But all she sees is grief and loss. Without thinking, she runs her fingers over his wrinkles, noticing the grey hair sprinkled along his hairline. When did that happen? He's never had grey hair before. He's getting older. Is it possible he's getting wiser? Does he truly regret his actions? *Did he ever really love me?*

Ted wraps his arms around her, his head pressed against her chest and holds her tight, and she consoles him as she would one of her children if they were sad.

"I'm ready to tell you the truth," he whispers.

Libby's heart stops beating in her chest. *Come on heart, start pumping!* This is the moment she's been waiting for. Maybe Dr. Bradford's right? Maybe it's best she doesn't know? She releases her hold on him and sits back in the chair, then studies his face and slowly nods her head. It's now or never.

"Sit with me?" Ted pats the space next to him on the rug and she lowers herself down beside him, shaking. "May I hold your hand?" he asks.

Again, she nods, and holds her breath, thinking how odd it sounds, her husband asking for permission to hold her hand. She hasn't allowed him to touch her in over two months, hasn't been in the same room with him for more than ten minutes. This is by far the longest conversation they've had since she saw him in the backyard with Caroline.

Ted laces his fingers through hers, and bows his head, taking a deep breath in and out.

"Libby, do you promise you'll hear me out? That you'll listen before you react?"

"Yes, I promise," she replies, her voice hoarse, her breathing shallow.

"I have loved you from the night I met you and that love has never wavered, Libby. Not once in all these years. No matter what my actions, I never did anything because I felt less for you. Please understand what I'm saying. Not for one second of one day have I loved anyone but you," he turns to her, his eyes pleading for her to understand, to believe him.

She nods, her eyes wide, her body trembling.

"It wasn't just Caro and the one-night stand in November," he pauses and glances at her from the corner of his eye. Her stomach flips, her body turning cold. "I've had a few one-night stands. The first time it happened was just after my father died. I was out of town, got drunk and had sex with a woman I met at a bar."

She swallows hard, fighting back the tears. *Please God, no.*

"When I came home I felt awful, could hardly look at you...I was afraid of what that night meant for our relationship and wondered if we'd lost something along the way. But the moment I looked into your eyes I knew my feelings for you hadn't changed. I still loved you completely. I still loved our life together. Having sex with another woman didn't change that."

She closes her eyes, resting her head against the changing table, her heart aching in her chest.

"The next time it happened...maybe six months later, I knew it probably wouldn't be the last. In my mind, having sex with other women was in no way related to my feelings for you. I thought I could have the best of both worlds. A beautiful wife and family I adored, and fun while I was out of town. I thought it was harmless and rationalized, it was just sex. But I was being selfish," he pauses. "Those women meant nothing to me, Libby."

George stirs in his crib and whimpers, echoing Libby's feelings exactly. She rises unsteadily to her feet, in the midst of an outer body experience. Floating, she watches the scene from above. Standing over George, she soothes him and places the pacifier back into his mouth, but can't feel her limbs.

She turns to Ted, her eyes wide. She wants to know everything. *The truth, the whole truth, and nothing but the truth, so help you God.* He's on trial and she's the judge and jury. Ted's afraid...she's never seen this sort of fear in his eyes before. Swallowing hard, she assumes the same position she was in before George cried, her hand resting in his.

"What happened with Caro?" she whispers.

Ted takes a deep breath in, shifts toward her and clasps both hands around hers.

"Caro...Caroline was a mistake. What started as a flirtation spiraled out of control. It was the rush I fell for, Libby, not her, the kind of rush you only experience when something is forbidden. There was nothing wrong with our sex life, baby. The sex with her wasn't better...it was just different. It was the fear factor. The fear of getting caught somehow made it more exciting, and I was addicted to that high. That's the only reason the affair lasted as long as it did."

She closes her eyes and nods her head. He's a forty-four-year-old 'teenager' looking to get high. Willing to ruin his life, risk everything, to get stoned. How pathetic.

"Looking back, I see how insane the whole thing was. The risks we took were ridiculous. I wasn't in love with her, sweetheart. I never once said those words to her. For me, it was just sex."

She looks down at her free hand, and stares at her wedding band. She never took it off, even when she filed the divorce papers. Tucked away in the very back of her mind she thought she could somehow fix this...fix them. Twisting the ring on her finger she realizes, some things can't be fixed.

"Over the past year...things shifted," he continues. "Caro said she'd fallen in love with me and started showing up at the office when you weren't there, booking flights to whatever city I happened to be traveling to. I pulled away from her, tried to set boundaries, but she ignored them. That day you came to see me, the first time you went to the psychiatrist...she was there."

She remembers that day, how he steered her down the hallway, away from his office. *Chanel No. 5*. Caro wears that perfume. She must have snuck out while he distracted her. I'm such a fool. Everyone knew, the associates, Renata. She bows her head in humiliation, feeling the heat rising, her ears growing hot.

"Shortly after that, she said she wanted to divorce Tru, wanted me to leave you. That's when I ended it. The day of the luncheon, before the Christmas party...she threatened to tell you the truth. She was so upset, I thought she actually might. If you were going to find out, baby, I wanted it to be from me. But when I tried to tell you, I couldn't get it out, so I told you about the woman in DC. I was so afraid of losing you."

He turns to her, wiping away his tears.

"I promised myself it wouldn't happen again and for months I steered clear of Caro. Our relationship was getting stronger, I felt more connected to you and the kids than ever before. Then I bumped into her the night you saw us and...there's no excuse for what I did. It was selfish and cruel...I missed the rush. I never meant to hurt you, Libby. I never meant to hurt anyone. You're the only woman I've ever loved and that love is stronger now than it's ever been."

They sit in silence for several minutes. *He loves me. They meant nothing to him. Caro means nothing to him. He loves me...*on and on those words swirl around in her head. *They mean nothing...*

Finally, she speaks.

"I believe you, Ted," she says, clearing her throat. "If it's forgiveness you're seeking I can't give it to you...but I believe you."

It was just sex...they mean nothing...he loves me.

"Thank you for telling me," she says, rising to her feet.

He looks up at her, his face ravaged, and she wishes she had her camera to capture the raw expression on his face.

Devastation. Despair. Loss. *I know exactly how you feel.* Standing there, she sees herself in his eyes and sinks to the ground beside him.

Ted gathers her in his arms, their lips coming together, quickly, forcefully, Libby seeking to obliterate the excruciating pain the only way she knows how, in the sweet oblivion of his arms.

She wants him…she wants to hurt him.

He removes her shirt and she bites his lip, can taste the blood, but can't stop herself. She wants more. Pulling off his t-shirt, she longs to feel his skin against hers…she wants to punish him. Libby claws her nails into his back and he cries out in pain, but never stops tasting her mouth, her neck, her breasts.

"I'm so sorry, baby," he whispers again and again. "So sorry."

He tugs off her yoga pants and looks into her eyes with tenderness. *Don't do that!* She slaps his face then pulls him down against her body, yanking his hair, bringing tears to his eyes. She wants him to feel pain…she wants to feel him inside her.

Make the pain go away, please, Ted. Make it go away!

She reaches for him and he slides his hands beneath her hips, sinking his fingers into her. I shouldn't do this! Swirling in a whirlpool of passion, pain, bliss and anger, Libby bites his shoulder, breaking the skin.

I hate him…I love him.

Their eyes meet and his emerald eyes are glistening, filled with love as he slides into her, her body dissolving into his, betraying her head, falling victim to her heart. She can't stop the flow of tears as she meets him thrust for thrust, her nails piercing his skin, her legs wrapped around his pulling him closer and deeper until they both cry out in pleasure and pain.

Agony and ecstasy. Love and hate.

These emotions swamp her, tearing at her insides as she lies beside him, catching her breath. He couldn't take away her pain. Even in the throws of passion, it was there. Ted presses his body along her side, kisses her shoulder and wipes away her tears. Her husband looks so relieved...so joyous. *You have nothing to be happy about, Ted!* Does he think this means she forgives him?

Hate...love...the other women mean nothing...he loves me...they mean everything.

She turns away from him and swallows hard, pushing back the tears.

The other women mean everything.

"You know this means nothing, right?" she says, an edge to her voice. She turns to face him, her eyes meeting his. "It was just sex."

Ted's face folds. Where there was hope just seconds before, there is now despair. *Good. I want you to writhe in agony, just as I did.* She collects her clothes, slips on her underwear and shirt and leaves him in a state of shock, vulnerable and naked on the nursery floor. Again, she longs for her camera, wanting to capture his pain, raw and intense, in stark contrast to the pastel rug with the alphabet border, the stuffed elephant sitting just inches from his hand.

At last...the truth. Ugly and twisted, red and blotchy. Truth.

She pauses, snapping a mental image for the album locked inside her head, and looks directly into his eyes.

"You can sleep in the guest room tonight. Watch the baby," she says, and crosses the hallway to her room, turning the lock on the door.

CHAPTER FIFTEEN

T ruman is taking the girls to Vermont to visit his parents for the month of July, and Caroline's parents are taking them to Martha's Vineyard for the month of August, with Caroline visiting on weekends. That's the 'equitable arrangement' they've worked out in their surprisingly smooth divorce. Apparently, Caro does have a conscience, and it's dictating the terms of their settlement. She's been generous and nothing has to change for the girls, but he doesn't see himself staying in Littleton for long. This isn't where he sees himself now that he's free.

What does freedom look like for him? He's still the primary caregiver of two young girls, that doesn't allow for much freedom. But he's free of his loveless marriage. He's free from a life of celibacy. What else does he want to release? He wants to free himself from this life of conformity and the judgment of his neighbors. Most of all, he wants to free himself of the torture he endures nightly, when Ted pulls his car into the driveway. To free himself from watching the woman he loves walk back into the arms of her deceitful husband.

He's seriously considering moving back to Vermont. He can do his work from anywhere, but it's time for a career change as well. *Maybe teaching?* He could help adults learn useful skills in computer science and web development. Community classes, maybe even volunteer to help women in need develop a skill that could lift them out of poverty? He could make a difference. He's never enjoyed working with computers, but has a sneaking suspicion he'd love helping others learn to do what has become second nature to him over the past fifteen years.

His parents live outside Burlington. There are several colleges up north within a forty-minute drive of their farm. His mother would be beside herself with joy, has always wanted her granddaughters close, to help raise them, and save them from a life of privilege. And his sister lives in Middlebury, Vermont with her husband and two boys. Family is important. The family he unknowingly created with Libby is dissolving before his eyes and he misses that connection. In Vermont they'd be surrounded by his blood relatives. It wouldn't be the same...but better than no family at all.

The Boston Marathon is this coming Monday, and Libby's bringing the kids (minus George) to the race so they can watch him cross the finish line. This race symbolizes the end of a long journey for him, the end of a life that never suited him. Pounding the pavement has kept him sane and given him perspective and insight into issues he's ignored for far too long. Whether he stays in Rhode Island or moves to Vermont, life is about to change for them all.

The day before the race, Libby prepares a celebratory dinner at his house. The weather has been beautiful all week, so they decided to eat outside on his deck. She made a carb-laden pre-race meal and for the first time in almost a month, they're sitting around the table together, Libby and her children, Truman and his girls. Ginger and Alex have stopped by for dessert; they can't go to the race tomorrow but wanted to wish him luck.

He looks around the table at each smiling, happy face and is filled with longing for simpler times, when this was the norm, not the exception. It's been a wonderful night. Bittersweet. He misses their dinners together. He misses Libby and their grown up interaction, conversation and camaraderie, preparing meals together, wrangling the children as a team. His heart aches in his chest. *I miss my family.*

Some nights, he peers out his window, into Libby's living room and watches Ted roaming about the house, their family intact. Together! And he can't believe his eyes. It's literally a shock to his system every time he sees Ted's car parked in the driveway, his smug face through the curtains of her house. He's staked his claim, digging in for the uphill battle he's wagering to win back Libby's heart.

Ginger was right. *I am jealous.* It physically pains him to imagine Libby in Ted's arms, forging ahead into a future which doesn't include him.

But tonight? He won't allow his thoughts to go there. Tonight he is surrounded by friends and family, love and laughter. The conversation flows freely, the kids refraining from bickering for once, maybe sensing this is a treat, not something they can take for granted anymore. Everyone is excited to go to Boston tomorrow for the race.

"You can really run that far?" Nate asks, his voice tinged with awe.

"I sure hope so," he laughs. "I've been practicing for a long time."

"I can't wait to see you cross the finish line!" Bette exclaims.

He can't wait either! And he's so happy his children will be there to see him achieve this goal, a true milestone in his life.

"Hi everyone." Truman hears Ted's voice behind him, sending shockwaves through his body.

He freezes in his chair and holds his breath while the kids call out to him, inviting Ted to join them for some pie. *The fucker just couldn't stay away.* Libby quickly rises and squeezes Truman's shoulder sympathetically.

"Daddy has his own pie in the house," she says, stepping off the deck. "I'll be right back." Libby leads Ted back to their yard, and Truman turns around, his eyes wide with disbelief. *The nerve of that guy! Wandering over here as if nothing ever happened!* He turns to Ginger and she raises an eyebrow, shaking her head back and forth.

"Truman…why can't my daddy have dinner with us anymore?" Nate asks, his eyes sad.

Oh, Jesus. He forces a smile but can't find the words to explain to this seven-year-old boy why his father is no longer welcome here. He turns to Ginger for help.

"Don't be silly, Nate," Ginger says. "Your daddy has to work, you know that."

Nate's not buying it, Truman can see it in his eyes.

"Is it because Daddy was kissing Caro?" he asks.

"What are you talking about?" Sadie hisses, followed by a cacophony of children's voices in various levels of disagreement, confusion and disgust.

"Dad would never kiss Caro!" Emma shouts.

"But I saw them!" Nate cries.

Everyone at the table freezes, their mouths hanging open. Truman rests his head in his hands, anticipating the nuclear fallout of Nate's revelation. This is going to get ugly unless he can control the situation, but his mind is completely blank and he begins to panic. Again, his eyes implore Ginger to come to the rescue. She rises and walks around the table to Truman, and kisses him on the mouth, just a moment longer than a peck.

"There! See? Grownups kiss each other all the time," Ginger says unconvincingly. "Now let's have some more pie."

Sadie raises an eyebrow, her face visibly transforming with the dawn of understanding.

"Holy shit," his almost fourteen-year-old daughter whispers. "Now I get it…" her voice trails off.

"Sadie Elizabeth Whitaker!" he bellows. "Language!"

She turns toward him dazed.

"Excuse us," he says, and grabs his daughter's arm, ushering her into the kitchen.

Once they're away from prying ears, his face softens, his heart aching for his daughter. They sit on the stools at the counter and he kisses her forehead. Sadie has figured it out. He can try to sugarcoat it, but she's old enough to know… If she wants the truth, he'll tell her.

"Ted and Mom were having an affair?" she asks.

Truman nods his head.

"Is that why you're getting a divorce?"

"No, sweetheart, that's not why," he wraps his arm around her shoulders. "We fell out of love a long time ago. Finding out about Mom and Ted is what tipped the scales, but our divorce was a long time coming."

"Does Libby know?"

Again, Truman nods and together they sit in silence.

"Is that why she was in the hospital for so long?" she asks, her voice no more than a whisper. "Is that when she found out?"

"Yes, sweetie. She saw them…kissing, and was very upset. But she's fine now. Everything's fine. You can't tell the other children. Not your sister, not Nate and Emma. No one."

"I hate him. I wish he would leave us alone. Then everything would go back to normal."

His daughter said a mouthful there! Ted and Caro were hardly present before. Now Caro is gone, and if Ted would leave, things would return to their version of normal. Libby opens the French doors and enters the kitchen, her eyes darting between them.

"How's everyone doing in here?" she asks, her voice soft.

Sadie turns to her and bursts into tears, wrapping her arms around Libby's waist.

"There, there, Sade..." she soothes his daughter. "It's okay sweetheart." Libby kisses the top of Sadie's head and holds her tight.

"I'm so sorry, Libby," Sadie says. "I hate her! I hate my mom for what she did!"

"Hey, you have nothing to be sorry about. You haven't done anything wrong. Listen Sadie, sometimes good people do bad things. Your mom wasn't trying to hurt me. I'm angry with her, I'm not going to lie, but she's your mom, and she loves you very much. She made a mistake. We all make mistakes. That doesn't make your mother a bad person."

Truman listens closely as Libby rationalizes Caroline's behavior to his daughter, inserting Ted's name whenever she mentions Caro. *Ted* made a mistake. *Ted* wasn't trying to hurt her. *Ted* is a good person who did a bad thing. *Ted* loves her. She's angry with *Ted*...but she'll get over it. Yes, he understands now, has the confirmation he's been seeking. Libby may not know it, but she's going to give Ted another chance. He can't do this anymore. He can't watch her make the biggest mistake of her life.

♀

As soon as they walk home, Libby guides Nate into his bedroom to discuss what he saw between Ted and Caro and when he saw it. Her son watched them kissing from his bedroom window last summer, just before school started and she breathed a sigh of relief. *Last September...not this week...not last month.* Over eight months ago. She didn't think she'd care, but was relieved to know Ted hadn't lied to her again. How much more can she take?

"It was a big kiss, Mommy. Like the kind Daddy used to give you," Nate says, his face scrunched up in confusion. "It wasn't like how Ginger kissed Truman at all. It made me sad, Mommy."

"I know this is confusing, sweetheart." Libby's eyes fill with tears and she holds Nate to her. "When you're older you'll understand it better. I don't want you to worry about it anymore."

"I love you, Mommy," Nate murmurs against her chest.

"I love you too, sweetheart. Get ready for bed, okay?"

Closing the door behind her, Libby paces back and forth along the hallway. Ted is batting zero for two tonight. First, he crashes Truman's marathon dinner, now this. They had a hideous fight earlier this evening. Libby was furious with him for showing up at Truman's and instead of being apologetic, he was dismissive.

"What were you thinking?" she shouted. "You can't go to Truman's house!"

"I got here a little early and wanted to see the kids. What's the big deal?" he asked.

"The big deal? The big deal is you were having an affair with his wife!" she replied.

"He needs to get over it," Ted muttered, turning away from her.

Shocked by the flippancy of his remark, she stood frozen in place for a moment, not quite believing her ears. *He needs to get over it?* Libby grabbed his arm and with all the force she possessed, slapped him across the face.

213

Stunned, Ted stepped back, holding his hand to his cheek.

"Truman doesn't need to get over it, and neither do I!" she screamed.

"I'm sorry," he murmured, then retreated to the guest room.

She stood immobile for several minutes, as surprised as Ted by the violence of her reaction, the sheer force behind the blow. She's never physically lashed out at anyone before this week. Now? She has to rein it in and resist the strong impulse to slap or kick Ted whenever she sees him. Anger is a vice gripping her heart, trying to squeeze out what little love remains.

Libby refuses to discuss his confession or the incident that followed with Ted. She refuses to discuss much of anything with him since the other night. The experience utterly confused her. Love, hate, passion, pain. She thought knowing the truth about Ted and Caro would be cathartic, would help her move on. It's done just the opposite.

She spent an extra hour with Dr. Bradford this week, trying to figure out what she wants to do now that she knows what really happened between them. She believes Ted loves her. She believes the other women meant nothing to him. She believes a man can have sex with someone else and still love his wife. She even believes he never loved Caro.

It's 'the high' that stops her in her tracks, his need to find excitement outside of their bedroom.

All of these years she believed their sex life was incredibly passionate and fulfilling, but he needed more. The night she saw him having sex with Caroline against a tree, he did it because he "missed the rush." He may love her, but she'll never be enough for him. Can she be with a man she doesn't trust? She wants to forget what he told her, to erase that night in the nursery from her memory, but it's always there. She's paralyzed with indecision, unsure of what to do with this new reality.

Without knocking, she swings the guest room door open to find Ted sitting up in bed, hugging George to him, his eyes closed. It's a beautiful sight. Another photo worthy moment. If she weren't so upset she'd run back to her room, grab the camera and snap a shot, but she's fuming. Nate saw his father making out with Caroline. What about the other children? What have they witnessed through their windows over the years?

Standing at the foot of the bed, she doesn't feel any confusion. She wants to hit Ted again, harder this time. She wants to kick him out of the house and never let him back in.

"I hope you're happy," she whispers, not wanting to wake the baby.

"Libby, what's wrong now?" he asks, sighing with resignation.

"Our son asked if the reason you can't have dinner with Truman and the girls had to do with you kissing Caro in the backyard last summer. He announced it in front of the children."

Ted's mouth drops, his brows drawing together.

"How does that feel, Ted? Your daughter...your son...the girls next door...Alex...they all know what you did. How's that for a rush? Are you feeling the 'high' now?"

Ted rubs his hand over his eyes, gently lays George in his bassinet, then turns onto his side and cries. She stands over him, her lip curled in a sneer. She's so sick of his tears. When did he become such a big crybaby?

"Do you ever think about the example you're setting for our children? Would you want someone to do this to Emma? Our sons to do this to their wives? Or would you pat them on the back and say, 'Good job, son! That's the way we treat women in this family'?"

Ted can't speak, just shakes his head back and forth, his hands over his eyes, his body shuddering with grief. She watches him for several minutes, but when he reaches out for her, his eyes pleading with Libby to come to him, to soothe him, to forgive him, her heart is closed for business.

"Poor Fitz," she snarls, then turns and walks out of the room.

CHAPTER SIXTEEN

The crowds are roaring on Boylston Street in Boston as they stand near the finish line, waiting for Truman to pass. It's Patriots' Day in Massachusetts, a state holiday to commemorate the battles of Lexington and Concord that kicked off the Revolutionary War. Everyone has the day off, and by the looks of it, the whole city of Boston is lined up along the marathon route to cheer the runners along. The streets are packed with spectators and they're waiting about half a city block from the finish line, holding up signs that read, *Go Daddy! Go Truman! We love you! You did it!* Lots of hugs and kisses, hearts and balloons.

"Where is Daddy?" Bette asks for the hundredth time in the past half hour.

Truman should be finishing up the race soon. It's just after two-thirty and he said he'd be finished by three o'clock.

"Soon, Bette, soon. Be patient," she says.

It's been a really long day. They got up at the crack of dawn to drive to Boston, got stuck in two hours of traffic once they hit the city, and finally made it to Boylston Street around noon, just in time for the kids to complain about their grumbling tummies (though they ate snacks the entire ride to

Boston). Every restaurant in the area was packed, so they grabbed pretzels, hotdogs and lemonade from a street vendor and found a place to watch near the corner of Exeter and Boylston. She's glad they're here for Truman, but she's ready to call it a day!

"There he is!" Bette shouts, waving her sign ecstatically. "Daddy! Daddy!"

The children jump up and down, shouting his name and Libby smiles, snapping pictures of him, exhausted but victorious, as he makes his way the final two blocks of the race. Through the zoomed in lens of her camera, she watches as Truman throws his hands up crossing the finish line, and then a thunderous boom knocks her to the ground, and she lands sprawled across a fallen barricade.

What just happened? Libby's ears are ringing, her vision blurred. She tries to get her bearings and can just make out the fuzzy outlines of people scattering in every direction...and smoke. The air around her is acrid, hardly breathable. *The children!* "Nate! Emma!" she calls out for them. "Sadie! Bette!" She screams their names but all she hears is the ringing in her ears.

Panicked, she grabs a signpost and pulls herself up, trying to focus, when another loud blast sends her reeling into the street. *My babies! Where are the children?* She cries, calling out their names for what feels like an eternity, then feels several arms being flung around her. She touches their heads, can make out the outlines of Bette and Sadie, then Nate...where's Emma?

"Emma!" she screams. "Emma Fitzgerald!"

The children are sobbing, clinging to her. Her vision begins to clear and she is horrified by the carnage around her. People are bleeding, arms and legs severed. Bombs! Those loud noises she heard were bombs! *Oh my God. Where's my daughter? Where's Truman?*

"Emma! Truman!" she screams, standing in the middle of Boylston Street with three children clinging to her for dear life, as paramedics and spectators rush past carrying the injured toward the first aid tent near the finish line.

"Mommy!" she hears Emma's voice and her legs almost give out beneath her. Frantically she searches the crowd for her daughter.

"Mommy!" she hears Emma's voice again, but can't place which direction it's coming from.

"Libby! Over there!" Sadie cries.

Her daughter is lying on the sidewalk, bleeding. *But alive... she's alive.* Libby and the children run to Emma, and she kisses her daughter's face, then searches for the source of the blood. She has a gash on her arm, another on her leg, and her face is scraped where her head hit the pavement.

"Baby, you're going to be fine. You have a few cuts. We're going to get you some help," she says, trying to keep her voice calm and soothing.

As soon as she turns for help, Truman is kneeling beside her and Libby is giddy with relief. *He's okay. We're all okay.* Truman holds the girls to him, then checks Emma's cuts.

"They're not too deep, do you have a scarf or something..."

"Here," Sadie hands them the shirt she had tied around her waist, and Truman tears it in half, wrapping the material around Emma's wounds. Then he lifts Emma off the ground and carries her toward the first aid tent.

Off duty doctors and nurses from all over have made their way to the finish line and are working on the injured runners and spectators, while ambulances arrive to take the more seriously wounded to the area hospitals. There, they're treated for superficial wounds, while Emma receives stitches.

"I thought you were dead," Truman whispers into her ear as a nurse stitches Emma up. She turns to him and he embraces her, holding her close. "All of you. I thought you were all gone." She can feel his body shaking while she clings to him. "I never would've forgiven myself if anything had happened to you or the kids," he says, kissing her temple.

"I'd be lost without you, Tru," she says and bursts into tears. He is her rock. Without Truman, she's adrift.

"I love you, Libby," he says.

She smiles and opens her mouth to return the sentiment, but looking into his hazel eyes, she understands what he's really saying. He's *in love* with her. Her eyes grow wide and her lips part, startled by this revelation. Before she can say anything, he leans in and kisses her, softly, quickly, then holds her to him, his other arm, wrapped around the children.

A moment later, her phone rings, a high-pitched bell tone Nate selected for her, and she winces, searching for it in her purse, then pats herself down, discovers her camera is still hanging from her neck, and finds the shrieking phone in the back pocket of her jeans.

It's Ted. She's missed seven calls, but didn't hear the phone ringing with all the commotion. Even now, sirens are squealing, people screaming out in pain.

"Libby? Libby are you there?" Ted's voice is panicked.

"I'm here, Ted. Everyone is okay. Emma is getting a few stitches on her arm and leg, but she's fine, we're all fine."

"Oh, thank God! I couldn't get in touch with you...you weren't answering. I was watching the race on TV and saw the explosions," he pauses. She can tell he's been crying. "I didn't know what to do. I'm in my car now, driving toward Boston."

"We're fine, Ted. There's no need to come, you'll never get through."

"I don't care!" he cries. "I have to see my children. I want to be with you."

Mentally and physically exhausted, Libby sighs into the phone, the little remaining adrenaline draining from her body.

"We're at the first aid tent at the finish line. When you're in the city, call me. I'll let you know where we are."

She hangs up the phone and watches Truman interacting with the kids. *He's in love with me?* She doesn't know what to think or feel about that. She loves him dearly. She needs him desperately. Her life has been a disaster this year and he has stood by her every step of the way. Those few minutes she thought he might be dead she could feel her heart breaking in her chest. Actual, physical pain. How would she ever survive without him?

Libby's been drawn to Truman from the day they met, but she felt the same way with Ginger. Some people are meant to be in your life and the connection is simply there. It's a chemical reaction, a sort of energy drawing you to particular people. It's not always romantic in nature, these connections, it's simply nature's way of letting you know, *Yes, this person is supposed to be here. This person is meant to be a part of your life.*

Is Libby attracted to Truman? Absolutely…who wouldn't be? He's extremely handsome, but she's never thought of him as anything more than a friend. Her best friend. Why? Because she was married. He was married. *And our spouses were sleeping together.* Her musings are interrupted by the nurse working on her daughter.

"Miss Emma here is all set. The stitches will dissolve, just make sure the wounds are clean and new bandages applied regularly."

"Thank you…" Libby says, but the nurse has already turned to the patient in the next cot.

"We need to get the children out of here," she whispers in Truman's ear. "There's too much blood...too much... everything." Her senses are in overload. She can't imagine how the kids are processing these events. It's been a terrifying experience. "Let's find a hotel."

Together, they walk toward Exeter Street, holding the children close, instructing them to keep their eyes down, not wanting them to see the injured people still being treated in the street, the pools of blood and the sight of the buildings blown open by the two blasts.

They were standing just a few yards away from the bomb when it exploded. Five yards closer to the finish line and they would've been seriously injured...or dead. If Truman was five seconds slower, he would've been injured in the explosion. The magnitude of what they experienced hits her as they turn the corner, walking away from the crime scene.

Truman steers them to the first hotel they find away from the blast sight. The desk clerk is preoccupied with the news playing video of the blasts in slow motion over and over.

"Excuse me. We need a room," Truman calls out, and the young woman turns, her eyes glazed over. She takes in their disheveled appearance, Truman's running attire with his number still affixed to his shirt, the dried blood on their clothes, a crease forming between her brows.

"You were there..." she says, her voice trailing off.

The children are staring at the television, transfixed. She looks up, about to tell them to stop watching, when she notices the runner crossing the finish line on screen is Truman. She searches the crowd and watches in shock as she and the children are thrown to the ground moments later, a fireball erupting just a few feet away from them. She watches herself being thrown into the air, and landing in the street on her side, the kids disappearing into the mass of bodies tumbling down onto the sidewalk.

She turns toward Truman and he's staring at the screen, his mouth gaping open. Libby touches her left hip, and sure enough it's sore from the fall. *This actually happened.* Watching it on repeat, her throat closes in on her. *We're lucky to be alive.*

"We only have one room left..." the girl says.

Libby doesn't hear the rest, just nods and hands the clerk her wallet. Nate and Emma bury their faces into her chest, and Truman's children encircle him, their arms wrapped around each other. Libby and Truman's eyes meet over their heads and his are overflowing with love and naked desire.

She's overwhelmed with sheer emotion, and for the first time, Libby sees Truman in a different light. He's more than a friend, he always has been. *He loves me.* Her lips part and she's overcome by the strongest desire to kiss him, to feel his arms around her. Slowly, Truman nods, understanding. He wants the same thing.

Once she finishes checking them in, they all squeeze into the elevator, Libby and Truman's shoulders touching, their pinkies brushing up against each other. She can feel the heat radiating from his body, and her breathing grows shallow as she considers what could happen...if she lets it.

What am I doing? This is Truman! Truman! My dearest friend! But what she's feeling right now doesn't feel like friendship, it feels sexual and intimate. She turns away for a moment and frowns. It feels like confusion piled on top of more confusion.

The last available room turned out to be the presidential suite. The suite is huge with a living area and two bedrooms; one with a king sized mattress, the other with two queen size beds. Plenty of room for all of them. In the living room, the bellboy points out that the couch also turns into a bed, then leaves them standing, huddled together in the living room.

The children need distraction, they need rest, and water and dinner. She tries to shake herself out of this lustful daze and concentrate on being a mother to their children. Her daughter was injured in a bomb blast, for heaven's sake, and all she can think about are Truman's lips.

"Let's order some food," she says, her voice hoarse.

Libby walks over to the desk, grabbing the heavy leather binder filled with visitor's information, descriptions of hotel amenities and services, and assorted menus, then dials for room service and orders two large pizzas, feeling Truman's eyes upon her the entire time. Hanging up the phone, she bites her lip and turns toward him. All that stands between them are four frightened children...and a wedding band. *I'm separated*, she rationalizes. *I'm not married. Not really.*

"I need to take a shower," Truman says. "Kids, let's pick a movie." He turns on the huge television, and lets the children make their selection. "I'll be in there," he says, and points to the bedroom. Moments later she hears the shower running.

Their kids are exhausted, and make room for one another on one of the two couches, not wanting the space they normally fight for. All four of them snuggle up together on the cushions, and she throws a blanket over them, kissing the tops of their heads.

"I'll be right back," she says, and follows Truman into the bedroom, closing the door behind her. She leans against it for a moment, noticing he left the bathroom door open a crack. If she walks into that room, there's no going back. Nothing will ever be the same between them. *Be sensible, Libby! What would Elinor do?* She closes her eyes, then turns the lock on the door and walks into the bathroom. *Not this. Elinor would never do this.*

The room is steamy, the mirror fogged over. Truman steps out of the shower and wraps a towel around his waist, but keeps the water running. She takes in his lean, muscular runner's body, so unlike her husbands. She's seen his bare chest hundreds of times, swimming in the ocean and in their pool. Her eyes linger, studying his face, his torso, the light dusting of hair on his chest, following the faint line down his abdomen to the white towel covering his growing erection.

Her breath catches in her throat as their eyes meet and before she has the chance to think, they're in each other's arms, coming together for a long, slow, sensuous kiss. His lips are soft against hers, his tongue exploring her mouth as they touch and taste one another for the first time.

Her body tingles with pleasure and anticipation. His fingers are in her hair, then cupping her face, tender and loving. She doesn't want him to ever stop. Truman presses her body against the bathroom wall and she runs her fingertips along his chest, down to his waist and pulls him closer, her body molded against his. He doesn't attempt to remove her clothing or his towel, and she's content with his slow exploration of her mouth and face, her neck and ears.

Goose bumps rise all over her body. *Is this what Ted was talking about?* she wonders, then banishes the thought. Her husband doesn't belong in this room, in this beautiful moment. This doesn't feel dirty and wrong. This is nothing like his meaningless encounters over the years. This is Truman, sweet, sensual, breathtaking, devoted, Tru.

"Mommy?" Nate's muffled voice brings their exploration to an abrupt halt. He knocks on the bedroom door and tries to turn the knob. "Mommy? Someone's at the door."

The pizza! Room service said it would take forty-five minutes to an hour. Has it been that long? The time passed too quickly...she wants more time. She wants more of Truman.

"Okay, sweetheart, tell Sadie to let them in," she calls out, her mouth meeting Truman's again. They have to stop, but she doesn't want to. Truman buries his face in her neck, then looks up and traces his fingers along the side of her face. Libby kisses his fingertips, filled with desire.

"Mommy!" Nate calls out again. "They need you to sign it."

She closes her eyes and groans.

"I'll be right out," she says, trying to sound cheerful.

Libby pulls away from Truman reluctantly. He nods, leaning against the doorframe, adjusting his towel. *My God, he's a beautiful man.* She's always thought so, but right now, he literally takes her breath away. Libby runs her fingers through her hair and straightens her clothes.

Unlocking the door, she turns to Truman, her closest friend and confidant...and smiles.

CHAPTER SEVENTEEN

What is Libby thinking? What are they doing? What does she want from me? It's been over six weeks since the Boston Marathon and he's never been more confused in his life. After the bombings, they stayed the night in the hotel. The children fell asleep on the couch after they ate pizza, and he and Libby carried them to their bedrooms. She took the king sized bed for her, Nate and Emma, and he took the room with the two queens for himself, and the girls.

Once the kids were in bed, they sat on the couch making out like two lovesick teenagers. He couldn't believe what was happening. His heart was bursting with joy, and he wanted her, God, how he wanted her! But knowing the situation she's in, he didn't try to take it any further than kissing. And that was enough for him. To be able to hold her, touch her, taste her. He had almost lost her, and there she was, beside him, returning his kisses, smiling and sighing with pleasure. It was enough.

During the race, he'd been thinking about what needed to be done in order to put the house on the market; what had to be fixed, or painted, making a to-do list in his head. When Caro first moved out he'd spoken to a real estate agent and she was excited about the property. They live in a highly desirable neighborhood, and houses seldom come on the market. At the time, Maggie Rose, realtor extraordinaire, came by for a tour and was eager to move forward with the listing, but he held off, said he'd call her when he was ready.

That morning in Boston, he was ready.

As he neared the finish line, he saw the kids with their signs, Libby waving and snapping pictures and got all choked up, thinking, *there's my family*...and he's about to break it up, split it in two. But this time, it would hurt. This wouldn't be easy. Caro moving out was a blip, a slight adjustment, his heart was completely intact. Leaving Libby, Nate, Emma and George? *Heartbreaking.* That was the word floating through his head when he crossed the finish line, that was the word stuck in his head when he heard the explosion and turned to see a burst of fire and smoke where his family had been just moments before.

"NO!" he screamed, his eyes wide with horror. "No!" he cried as he ran toward them, but was stopped by security guards. Then he heard the second blast and froze. *Heartbreaking. My heart is breaking...* He pushed his way past the guards and ran into the chaos while others were trying to escape. He called their names, trying to find them, but the smoke was burning his eyes and throat. He saw a little boy lying on the sidewalk, his family standing over him screaming. *Heartbroken. My heart is breaking for his parents.* He saw dozens of other people reaching for limbs that had been torn off in the explosions. *My heart is breaking for them.*

Where is my family? Please, let them be all right.

He stopped, was spinning in circles searching the faces around him, and had begun to hyperventilate, when he saw Libby surrounded by the children, kneeling on the sidewalk. He burst into tears and sprinted toward them, throwing himself down beside her, holding anyone he could reach, then saw the fear in Emma's eyes, the blood streaming from her injuries. He didn't think, he just acted, tearing Sadie's shirt, wrapping her wounds, then carried her to the first aid station.

Standing beside Libby while Emma was stitched up, he was overwhelmed with emotion. He thought they were dead. He couldn't live without them. Any of them. He loves her children as much as his own. That's when he knew he couldn't leave her. He couldn't leave Littleton.

"I'd be lost without you Tru," she said.

And he couldn't hold it in any longer.

"I love you, Libby."

Saying the words, he felt a rush of relief. It's out there, she knows. What will be, will be. He could see the confusion in her eyes, startled by his admission, but he didn't care. *I'd be lost without you too.* Standing in the lobby of the hotel, watching their nightmare unfold and repeat itself again and again, something shifted in her and he saw the love and desire he felt reflected in her eyes.

Perhaps watching their near death experience, thinking about what might have happened, opened her heart to him? He doesn't know. But something changed. Along with love and desire, he saw fear and confusion. He felt the electricity flowing between them in the elevator, and she came to him while he showered. He didn't know if she would…and that would have been okay too. But she did come to him, and touching her face, kissing her lips, he was intoxicated, drunk on love.

Then, around ten o'clock, Ted arrived in Boston. Libby answered the phone, her face resigned. Dread and fear filled her eyes.

"He's here," she whispered. "What do I do?"

"He can sleep on the couch. I'll go to my room," he kissed her again and she clung to him, then nodded and he left her to greet her husband.

The following morning, Truman woke early, and the couch was made up, but Ted wasn't in it. Confused, he paused for a moment, then inhaled sharply. *He's in bed with Libby and the kids.* The bedroom door wasn't closed completely, and he couldn't stop himself. He peeked in the room and watched Libby, Nate, Emma, and Ted, in that order, sleeping. His heart ached in his chest. She wouldn't have invited Ted to join them. Ted snuck in there in the middle of the night, and...he couldn't blame him. He probably would have done the same thing if he'd been in Ted's shoes. But it hurt. Seeing them together in that bed was a kick in the stomach.

Ted's an intruder, a wedge between Truman and Libby. Is she through with him? Will she finally divorce him? That morning in Boston, he felt sure she would end her marriage at last.

Six weeks later...Ted's still here.

Every night after dinner, and all weekend long, her husband is very much a part of their lives. An unwelcome invader who swoops in and forces Truman back home, away from Libby and the children. He can't go on like this much longer. He wants to be a bigger part of her life. He wants their family intact. As long as Ted's around, he and Libby can't move forward.

One evening, two weeks after the marathon, they were sitting in his backyard, enjoying the unseasonably mild weather while Ted tucked the kids into bed. They were relaxing and looking up at the stars, but when he held her hand to his lips, she jumped, snatching it away from him and sat up in her chair.

"Tru! The neighbors! And Ted's right next door!" she said, her eyes wide with panic.

"I understand that, Libby. But you're separated and my divorce is almost final. What difference does it make?"

"I don't want anyone to know about us," she whispered and sat back against the chair, closing her eyes. "Not yet."

"I'm not comfortable sneaking around, Libby," he replied, his brow furrowed. "That's what they did for years, but we don't have to. We aren't like them."

She turned to him and smiled, but he saw fear in her eyes.

"Right now...this is ours, Truman. Just you and me. I'm not ready to share what we have with others. Can't we keep this to ourselves for a little while longer?"

"What are you afraid of, Lib?" he asked.

"As soon as other people find out, there will be questions and accusations. They'll turn this into something ugly. Ted and Caroline...the neighbors."

"I don't care what they think."

"I care what the children think," she replied. "Once the rumor mill starts, they'll be effected."

"Libby, our families have been the subject of gossip for months. The children have already been effected. We can't protect them from everything. All we can do is cushion the blow."

They clasped hands and she nodded, her eyes sad. Libby rested her head on his shoulder and he kissed the top of her head, so wrapped up in their own world, they didn't hear Ted approach.

"Well...isn't this cozy?" Ted asked as he entered Truman's yard. His eyes darted between them, his mouth set in a grim line.

Libby sat up and pulled her hand away from his.

"Ted, you're not welcome in my yard," he said firmly, rising to his feet.

"What's going on here?" he demanded.

"That's none of your fucking business," Truman snapped.

Libby stood between them and shook her head.

"Enough, please," she said and turned to Ted. "Are you done tucking them in?"

Ted's eyes narrowed as he attempted to figure out what was happening between them.

"Yeah," he finally answered. "Lib, can I talk to you?"

She paused for a moment, then nodded.

"Goodnight, Tru. See you tomorrow."

✳

Ted's weaving a web around Libby, ensnaring her in his trap of lies. The man has persistence and patience. When Ted wants something, he'll do whatever it takes to get it, no matter how bad the odds or how long it takes. He keeps his target in sight and laser sharp focus on his goal. How did he manage to make his way through the front door? Truman has given that a lot of thought, and it's now clear to him.

Ted figured out Libby's weakness...*the children.*

It's not exactly a mystery. She will do anything for them and that's where Ted has the advantage over him. Truman may have raised them, but they are Ted's kids at the end of the day, and the bastard's tactic is working. He's using Nate, Emma and George to get what he wants from Libby. *Time.*

Last weekend, Ted recruited the children to persuade her to go on a 'family outing' to the Mystic Aquarium. The girls were with Caro and he had nothing to do but wait for their return, watching the hours pass slowly. *Is today the day he convinces her to take him back?* he wondered, holding his breath until they came home later that night. Truman watched from his window as Ted carried a sleeping Nate into the house, with Libby, George and Emma following behind him.

He felt awful as he took a seat by the window, but a few minutes later she sent him a text message. **Long day...I miss** you. XO. Truman breathed a sigh of relief. Ted didn't manage to win her over that day.

He feels helpless, teetering on a delicate balance. If he pushes too hard, he's afraid she'll run from him. If he remains silent, she may get sucked into Ted's trap. Is it his job to open Libby's eyes? She could easily dismiss his concern as jealousy, after all Truman is invested in the outcome. *But Ginger's not.* Libby may listen to Ginger. Unfortunately, their friend has been in Europe for weeks, but she's returning tomorrow. Maybe she can help Libby see reason?

What am I doing? It's a question he asks himself daily, but he always comes up with the same answer. Truman made a choice that day in Boston. He chose Libby. He knew he was taking a chance, understood there was a slim possibility she might decide to stay with Ted, even after all he's put her through, and Truman decided to stay. But how long can he live like this?

He never thought he'd be in this position. *The other man.* Truman and Libby are doing the sneaking around now. The secrecy is what makes it feel like they're having an affair, in all aspects but one; they haven't had sex. When they came back from Boston, Libby asked to wait until her situation with Ted was resolved, not wanting them to be compared to Ted and Caro in any way. He understood...for about three weeks, then realized it was impossible to compare their relationship with Ted and Caro's. They love and respect one another, and it's because Truman loves Libby, he has respected her wishes.

She's fooling herself though, making rationalizations to appease her conscience. Physically, what they've done is hardly different. He wants to lay beside her in bed, feel her naked body against his. Now, he feels like a teenager waiting for Libby's parents to come home, in this case, not wanting to get caught by the kids, or Ted. Stolen moments. He thought that was better than nothing. Now? He's not so sure.

These days are numbered. School is out next week. Libby is going to Nantucket in less than two weeks and he's heading to Vermont with the girls. He doesn't want to be away from her all summer, especially knowing Ted will be visiting Nantucket on weekends, but she needs this time to figure things out. All he can do is pray she follows her heart home to him.

❋

Ginger is finally back from her trip and he stopped by her house for coffee this morning. Truman's been dying to talk to her about his relationship with Libby, but isn't quite sure how to bring it up. They've deliberately kept her in the dark while she was traveling, but agreed to tell her upon her return. How could they keep this a secret from their best friend?

"What is going on with you?" Ginger asks, a brow rising. "You're acting so weird."

He's been sitting with her laptop, going through the photographs of her trip, remaining largely mute as she shares the stories accompanying each picture. Ginger is the person Truman turns to when he needs insight into Libby and he trusts her with his secrets. Today, he needs her take on this situation. She's usually right…and that's what worries him.

He places the laptop on the coffee table, then turns to her and sits forward in his chair, but when he opens his mouth, nothing comes out.

"Tru! You're making me nervous! Is anything wrong?" Ginger insists.

"No! I don't know…it's just…" his voice trails off and he looks down at his hands.

"Is it Libby?" she asks "Did something happen?"

Is she a frigging mind reader? Truman bites his bottom lip, shifting his eyes away from Ginger, then nods. A moment later he glances her way and raises an eyebrow.

Ginger's eyes grow wide with shock.

"Are you serious?" she cries, her face lighting up. "Jesus! I'm gone a few weeks and miss all the good stuff! What happened?"

He decides to dive right in, telling her what happened at the hotel after the marathon, and what's happened since. For over fifteen minutes he talks uninterrupted while Ginger sits silently in her chair, her face telling its own story.

When he's finished, she sits back in her armchair and stares out the window, her face clouding over.

"I don't want to see you get hurt, Tru," she finally says.

His heart sinks in his chest.

"You think I'm going to get hurt?" he whispers.

She shrugs and shakes her head.

"I don't know. It's like you two are in a holding pattern of Libby's making. What is she doing? I don't doubt her feelings for you, Truman, what I question are her feelings for Ted. Why hasn't she continued with divorce proceedings? It doesn't make any sense unless she thinks there's a chance they could work things out…As you said yourself, she'd do anything for her children. That could be enough to keep her in a shitty marriage, despite the love you feel for one another."

He tilts his head back against the couch and sighs. Ginger is the mirror of truth; the good, the bad and the ugly.

"And, Tru, why are you going along with this situation?" she asks. "What if after all this, she chooses Ted? Are you going to be okay with that?" she pauses. "Would you be able to live next door knowing she's going to bed with Ted every night?"

He closes his eyes, his stomach flipping at the mere suggestion she'd chose Ted.

"You'd be in the same position you've been in for years, Truman," Ginger continued. "She'd continue to be your surrogate wife and you'd be in another sexless marriage for all intents and purposes. And Ted would be the man who 'tore you apart', just like he did with Caro."

Ouch! He never thought about it that way. Is he simply repeating a pattern? He sits with that one for a few minutes. No, the love he feels for Libby is real. It just so happens she's married to the man who helped break up his marriage. That's a coincidence.

"Tru, I don't want to discourage this relationship. If you two end up together, I'll throw the fucking wedding. I'd be overjoyed for you both. But the sooner you know where you stand the better. You and Libby are my best friends and I'm telling you, what she's doing isn't fair to you. It's not right. Don't let anyone string you along, you deserve better than that. You need to be up front with her. You have to tell her to choose. And Truman, if she chooses Ted? Don't stick around. As much as I'd miss you, don't stay."

♀

She's worried. Truman sent her a text message saying he wasn't feeling well and asked if the girls could come for dinner. Why would he feel the need to ask? They've been having dinner together every weeknight since the marathon, eating early so they're finished when Ted arrives to spend time with the children before bed.

Weekends are tough with Ted around so much, and he's suspicious of any time she spends with Truman. Whenever she disappears from the house, he manages to find a way to draw her back home. It's frustrating, not only for her, but for Truman as well.

Something must be wrong. He usually stops by for lunch while the kids are in school, or sends her sweet text messages to let her know he's thinking about her. Today, nothing. Maybe she's overreacting? He could have been busy working on a project all day. He does work from home after all! And he was fine this morning when he visited George. Not to mention the divine hour they spent in each others arms when she got out of the shower… It's his silence since then that has her senses on high alert.

This is ridiculous. If she wants to know if something is wrong, she simply needs to walk next door.

Libby finds Emma sitting at the kitchen counter, doing her homework.

"Sweetheart," she says and kisses Emma's forehead. "I'll be back in a few minutes."

Emma looks up from her assignment, smiles and nods. "Okay, Mom. Love you."

Libby watches her for a few moments, her heart swelling in her chest.

"I love you too," she whispers.

They've come a long way in the six weeks since the marathon. Libby has watched in wonder as Emma transformed, virtually overnight, from a spoiled little girl into a somewhat mature young woman. The bombing had a profound effect on all of them, but particularly Emma. Witnessing firsthand what other people lost that day, knowing how close she came to losing her own life, has given her daughter a deep appreciation for what she has. That doesn't mean the drama queen has disappeared entirely, but Emma's overall attitude is one of gratitude versus entitlement.

Libby grabs the baby monitor and heads next door.

"Tru?" she calls out.

"Hi Libby," Bette runs into the kitchen and wraps her arms around her waist.

"Hi pumpkin pie. Where's your dad?"

"Upstairs. Resting."

"I'm going to check on him," she says, heading toward the staircase. She pops her head in Sadie's room. "Hey Sade, could you take your sister to my house? Dinner will be ready soon. And can you listen for George?"

Libby waits for the door to close behind the girls before entering Truman's bedroom. She knocks quietly then enters his room, closing the door behind her. Truman is lying in bed, his arm thrown across his eyes. *Migraine?*

She climbs into bed beside him and wraps her arm around his waist, and her heart flutters, warmth spreading from her stomach throughout her body. She doesn't know how they've refrained from having sex this long. It's been an exercise in restraint. She feels as long as they don't have sex, she isn't doing anything wrong. No matter how she tries to rationalize it, she's still married.

Libby kisses Truman's cheek, and he wraps his arm around her.

"How are you feeling?" she asks, pressing her palm to his forehead. He's not feverish.

"I don't know, Libby..." he sighs. "We need to talk."

The hairs on her arm stand on end. Those are ominous words. Her parents started the conversation about their divorce that way, 'Children, we need to talk'. Her mother used those words when her father was killed in a car crash. 'Libby, Charlie, we need to talk.' And when her mother was dying from cancer, 'Sweetheart, we need to talk.' *We need to talk* is never about anything good. She sits up, her heart pounding.

"About what?" she asks, swallowing hard.

Libby, you idiot! You know what!

Truman pulls her back down beside him, holding her tight, then turns onto his side facing her, so she does the same. Taking her hand in his, he looks deep into her eyes.

"Do you love me, Libby?" he asks, his voice soft.

"I do," she murmurs. "Very much."

"It's time, Lib. You need to make a decision. Me or Ted? It's been months and I can't do this anymore. I don't want to sneak around or hide my feelings for you. I don't care what the neighbors think, and believe me, the last thing I care about is hurting Ted or Caro's feelings. I love you. I want you. I want our family…but not like this."

Our family…Libby smiles. When she thinks about Truman and the girls, those are the exact words she uses. *We are a family.* Even before the marathon she felt that way, but those bonds have grown stronger since that day. She didn't know he felt the same. She touches his face, sees the sadness in his eyes and wants to take it away. He should never be sad another day in his life.

She kisses him softly, her heart swelling with emotion. She wants to say the words to him. *I love you Truman. I choose you.* The words are on the tip of her tongue, but she can't get them out. She feels a weight pressing on her chest, the same weight she feels every time she attempts to ask Ted for a divorce. Lying here beside this wonderful man, she tries to make sense of her feelings.

She loves Truman. It's a different type of love than she's ever known, one that's grown out of friendship over time. There's passion and longing, but so much more. Respect. Trust. Comfort. Partnership. It's a solid and grounded relationship. *This is 'Elinor and Edward' love*, she thinks, smiling to herself.

She doesn't know how she feels about Ted. He's the father of her children and she'll always love him, despite his past actions. They'll always be connected, but other feelings have taken place of the intense, all consuming love she once felt for him. Anger. Resentment. Bitterness. Pain.

Why have I allowed Ted to become such a big part of my life? He wasn't around a fraction of this amount in the past. Ted is trying so hard to make this work, and she's given him absolutely nothing to work with. Yet he persists, swearing he'll never give up on their marriage. The further she pushes him away, the harder he tries, and his persistence is confusing.

Why would he try so hard if he didn't love her? If he didn't regret his actions? He has the freedom to do whatever he wants now. Go, please! *But what he wants is me. What he wants is our family.* As much as the children love Truman and the girls, they want their father home more.

It's time to go back to Dr. Bradford. Skipping therapy since the marathon was not a good idea. Libby didn't want to confess her behavior to her doctor. She feels like a hypocrite, doing the very thing she condemned Ted for; sneaking around, having what is technically an affair. It's not a rush she's after, it's the warmth of Tru's embrace, the comfort and security of the life they've built together.

That's the real irony. Ted's been screwing other women for years, but she's a bigamist. Which is worse? She has two husbands, each fulfilling different needs over the years. She had Ted for passion and financial security, and Truman for everything else. If she's honest with herself, it's Truman she has come to love and trust, Truman she can depend upon. When something happens in her life, it's Truman she wants to tell, his company she looks forward to. And since the marathon, it's Truman she wants to wake up next to, Truman who stirs desire within her.

"Truman, I love you. I really do. Please, just give me a little more time to sort things out with Ted. One month? Visit me on Nantucket in one month? I promise you, I'll have a plan."

CHAPTER EIGHTEEN

T he night before Libby is set to leave for Nantucket, she has dinner at Truman's house with George and the girls. Ted is a guest speaker at a two-day conference in Connecticut, so he won't be stopping home to see the baby tonight, which is a relief after the intensity and drama of the past week. The sooner she leaves for Nantucket and gets away from Ted, the better.

Last weekend, Libby and Ted drove Emma and Nate to their summer camp in Vermont. George was home with Nina, and after they dropped off the kids, had a five-hour drive home, alone in the car. The first hour, she pretended to nap, then the car came to a stop. Ted pulled over at a rest stop with a beautiful view of the Green Mountains and a meandering stream close by.

"Libby, what are we doing?" he asked, gripping the steering wheel so tight, his knuckles turned white. "I love you so much, and I'm trying to be the husband you deserve. But you're giving me nothing, baby. I'm invisible to you. You haven't touched me since that night in April... You won't look at me most of the time. You refuse to come to marriage counseling and treat me like a stranger. Talk to me, Libby, please. This is killing me."

She stared out the car window at the stream. A lovely scene for such an ugly conversation. *I want a divorce Ted...I want to be with Truman...* She wanted to say the words so badly, she could taste them, feel them rolling off her tongue, but the weight bearing down on her chest forced the air from her lungs.

She looked down at her wedding band and a voice in her head whispered, *Fifteen years, Libby. For better or worse. You swore you'd never do this to your children. He loves you. What more does he have to do to prove it to you?*

But I'm not in love with him anymore! A voice echoed in her head, loud and clear. She covered her face with her hands and cried. *If I don't love him why can't I say those four little words? I want a divorce.*

"I can't breathe," she whispered and started to panic. She literally couldn't catch her breath and felt she was suffocating. She flung the car door open and ran down to the stream, taking deep breaths of mountain air, splashing cool water on her face. Then, she laid down in the grass and stared up at the clouds, reminding herself to breathe in...breathe out...breathe in...and out...

Ted sat beside her, running his fingers through her hair and along her cheek.

"If you don't love me, Libby, you have to tell me," he said, his voice deep, thick with emotion. "If you want out, I have to know."

It was her opportunity to end their relationship. He made it easy for her, all she had to do was nod her head. Libby looked into his eyes, cloudy and pained, and her heart was bursting in her chest. *I want a divorce!* How could she say those words to him? His anguish was clearly written across his face, deep and gut wrenching. She could feel his pain, felt it wrapping around her, soaking through her skin, seeping into her bones…and she was back on the living room floor, pain shooting through her, her heart breaking. *Just say it! Tell him how you really feel!*

Sobbing into her hands, she realized she couldn't do it. She couldn't say the words that would change their lives forever. She wasn't ready.

"I don't know what I feel!" she cried.

Libby closed her eyes, covered her ears, and shut everything out. Ted lifted her into his arms, cradling her, trying to soothe her, and wiped away her tears. She was a child in his arms and held onto him, clinging to the frayed threads of her old life, their marriage…him. Afraid to let it all go, and create a new one.

✳

After they put the kids to bed, Truman joins her outside in front of the fire pit. Together, they lay side by side on a lounge chair, wrapped in a blanket. His arms hold her close as she nestles against his body. It's a chilly evening for the end of June, but she's warm in his arms.

She's kept her distance from him outdoors, not wanting to add fuel to the fire of the neighborhood rumor mill. Tonight? She doesn't care. It's their last night together before she leaves in the morning for Nantucket. In two weeks, he'll come visit her…and she has a decision to make.

"You've been quiet tonight," he whispers, turning her face toward him. "Are you okay?"

She nods and smiles, curling up against his side. Truman pulls the blanket over them, holding her close and she's so comfortable, so tired, she feels herself nodding off.

"I'm going to miss you, Tru…" she whispers sleepily.

"I'm going to miss you too," he says with a sigh.

Libby didn't tell Truman what happened on the drive back from Vermont, how she clung to Ted like a baby, crying in his arms. She didn't tell him they made love in the grass by the stream and it was bittersweet. She hasn't told him that for the past three nights Ted has slept beside her in their bed, holding her close...almost as if he knows what's coming, that if he lets go...she'll disappear.

Ted is trying to hold onto their life together, and every day she drifts a little further away. She's letting go of the anger that's consumed her for months and trying her best to put the past behind her. It's time for a fresh start. A new beginning. And it scares her to death.

The future keeps her up at night. If Truman weren't in the picture...what would she do? Dr. Bradford posed that question to her this week and it caused her to step back and try to assess her situation from a different perspective. Would she be willing to walk away from her marriage without giving Ted another chance if Truman didn't exist, if he was never part of the equation?

She was shocked how quickly the answer came to her. *Probably not.* If she didn't know Truman she would probably stay with Ted, stick it out for the sake of the children and see what happens. Before she discovered Ted's affair, if anyone asked her what she'd do if her husband was unfaithful, she wouldn't have hesitated. She would have said she'd leave him, no questions asked.

It's not that simple. No one in a relationship wants to hear this basic truth. *Until it happens to you, it's impossible to know how you'll react.*

"So, if I'm understanding you correctly, Libby, without Truman's love and support you'd stay with Ted? You'd give your marriage another chance?"

She grew irritated with Dr. Bradford. *Truman is part of the equation.* Evaluating this situation without considering him is absurd! She's in love with him! He's her best friend. To suggest Truman is a crutch? That just pissed her off.

"This isn't a mathematical equation," Libby snapped. "Future minus Truman does not automatically equal Ted. Not anymore. Ted may have turned a new leaf, but he stripped away the most valuable asset we had. Trust. Is that something we can get back?"

Dr. Bradford nodded. "Over time, yes, it's possible. I've seen it happen many times."

She left her appointment feeling aggravated. She knows how she feels. The voice in her head by the stream was loud and clear. She's not in love with Ted anymore. Then what's stopping her from taking the final step? Why can't she say those four little words and end their marriage? *I want a divorce.*

It's the children.

Leaving her appointment, she had a bit more clarity. She has to decide what's more important to her in the grand scheme of things. What she wants (the selfish choice) or what's best for her children? *Could they be the same thing?* That's what she needs to figure out. Not which man she's in love with…she already knows the answer…but which life would be better for her children.

She'd give anything for a crystal ball, one that could show the outcome of two different scenarios. To be George Bailey in *It's a Wonderful Life*, getting a glimpse of an alternate future so she can appreciate the life she has…or let it go.

✳

Opening her eyes, she finds Truman's sound asleep, his face relaxed, his beautiful, full lips parted. *He looks like a little boy right now,* she thinks and smiles. She touches his face and leans in to kiss him then freezes.

Standing a few feet away from her, across the fire pit, is Ted. She takes a deep breath in and sits up, their eyes locking. *Oh my God.* How long has he been standing there? Truman stirs beside her and frowns.

"What's the matter, Lib?" he asks, rubbing the sleep from his eyes.

She can't speak, just stares at Ted, her heart pounding hard against her chest, threatening to burst through her ribcage and explode. Truman follows the direction of her eyes and sits up beside her with a start, his arm wrapping protectively around her waist. *Jesus Christ.* This is not how she wanted Ted to find out.

"Are we even now, Tru?" Ted asks, his eyes cold...hard.

"Ted..." she rises and walks toward him, but his eyes are fixed on Truman. "Let's go home," she says, and touches his arm, but he flicks her hand away. She has to get control of this situation. Ted has a murderous gleam in his eye. He's a big man, and strong. She doesn't want to know how strong.

"Ted!" she snaps. "We aren't doing this here...now. Truman hasn't done anything wrong. It's me you're angry with, and I have to say, you're really in no position to judge." He turns to her, his mouth set in a grim line. She shakes her head. "You have no right to judge either of us."

He takes a deep breath in, and exhales loudly, his shoulders sagging. Shaking his head, he turns and walks toward their house, and she breathes a sigh of relief, her knees almost buckling beneath her.

"You can't go back there, Libby," Truman says, clasping her hand.

"I have to, Tru. He's hurting right now."

"I don't give a shit if he's hurting. I'm more afraid of him hurting you."

"He would never..." she says, then kisses him lightly and follows Ted to the house, not quite believing her own words. *The look in his eyes?* Who knows what he's capable of right now? But if she stays, who knows what he might do to Truman? She can't take that chance.

She enters through the back door and the house is dark. *Where is he?* Quietly she searches for him, room by room and finds him sitting in George's nursery, rocking in the chair and staring straight ahead. She pulls the ottoman out and sits in front of him, resting her hands on his knees.

"How long have you been sleeping with him?" he asks, keeping his gaze fixed on the crib. George is sleeping peacefully, unaware of his parents' anguish.

"Ted...I've never slept with Truman."

He turns to her, his brow furrowed with confusion.

"But...I saw you...I saw the way you looked at him."

"We've never had sex, Ted."

His body sags with relief and he leans forward and grabs her hands, his eyes sad.

"But I do love him," she whispers, tears blinding her.

Ted groans and sits back against the rocker.

"You're in love with him?" he asks.

Libby nods her head, feeling the pressure build in her chest again. *Breathe, Libby...this is fear.* Fear of change...fear of taking the final plunge into the unknown.

"You don't love me anymore..." he chokes back a sob, pressing his palms against his eyes.

"I love you Ted. You're the father of my children. But I don't trust you and I don't think I ever will. How can we move forward without this fundamental ingredient?" She takes his hand in hers. "It's impossible. I can't do it."

"Please don't do this now, baby...please. I've changed, Libby, you know I have. Look at me, baby." She looks up into his brilliant green eyes, her heart breaking. "You and the children mean everything to me. I was a fool for so many years, but not anymore. I don't care about the business...I don't care about the money. Only you and our family. Don't throw away our family, Libby. Not when we're finally on the right path. Don't do this to our children."

She leans forward, resting her head in his lap, and he runs his fingers through her hair. *Don't throw away our family...our family...But what about the rest of my family? Truman, the girls...they're my family too.*

"Baby, I'm begging you. I know I don't deserve it, but please give me one year to prove this isn't a phase. Just one more year to rebuild our relationship and gain your trust. Please, Libby. If you still want me to leave next summer...I'll go. But not now, baby, don't do this now," he murmurs into her hair.

I don't know what to do...what's best for the children? What's best for me?

She looks into his eyes, studies the face she's loved for so many years...and crumbles. How can she say no? One year of her life to see if her marriage can be salvaged, to possibly save her children from enduring the pain of a divorce? She nods her head, swallowing hard. She can do that. She can do that for her children.

He kneels down and gathers her in his arms, holding her tight and she clings to him, her body trembling, wracked with tears. Doing this, she's sacrificing the man she's grown to love, her closest friend. Truman won't wait a year for her...she wouldn't want him to. *Truman...I'm so sorry...I love you...I miss you already...*

♂

Truman sits in front of the fire pit, staring into the flames. Libby forgot the baby monitor beside the lounge chair and he saw everything on the little screen…heard everything. He feels empty. *She's gone…she made her decision.* He shuts it off and throws sand on the fire, then turns and walks into his house.

He looks around and shakes his head. This life is gone. He's leaving it all behind. If Caroline won't agree to him moving the girls out of state, he's still leaving this town. She bought a condo in Providence…he'll move across the bay. Somewhere he'll never have to see Libby and Ted. He finds a piece of paper and writes a note, leaving it beneath the baby monitor for Libby to find.

Chapter Nineteen

T he waves crash to shore, and Libby leans back against her beach chair, watching the tide come in. She loves the sound of the ocean, finds it melodic and soothing. She's been on Nantucket for a week and the beach is where she feels most tranquil. Her whole body aches, as if it's been pummeled from head to toe, and she's exhausted. But she can't blame George this time. It's her conscience keeping her up, tossing and turning all night, every night.

She hurt Truman. *How is he feeling? What is he thinking? Does he hate me?*

She hasn't tried to reach Truman since she left Littleton last week. She's picked up the phone dozens of times to call him, longing to hear his voice, but it would be a selfish act, completely unfair to him. There's only one thing left to say. *I'm sorry. I'm so sorry, Truman.* She owes him that at the very least, but not over the phone. She has to apologize to him in person. He hasn't tried to contact her either…not that she expected him to after reading his note. But his silence hurts more than she can say.

Once she agreed to stay another year with Ted, to try and make their marriage work, she walked over to Truman's house, her heart aching as she entered his yard. It felt like a death march, with every step a little piece of her was dying. She had to tell him what had been decided and was trying to find the words. She expected him to be waiting for her in the backyard, but he wasn't there…the fire was out.

Heading toward the back door, she noticed the baby monitor sitting on the lounge chair they had occupied an hour earlier, and gasped with dismay. She had it turned on under the lounge chair while she was relaxing with Truman so she could listen for George. *He heard everything…he saw everything.*

She picked up the note he left for her, afraid to read it, and sat down, clutching the paper in her hands, then laid down on the lounge chair staring up at the stars. Pulling her knees into her chest, she curled into a ball and whimpered, trying to hold back her tears and block out the pain of losing him. Finally, she un-crumpled the note and read it.

Goodbye, Libby…I love you.

Her heart splintered into a million pieces, a piece of glass shattering as it hit the ground. *No…*she moaned…*no, no, no…* Libby rocked back and forth on the lounge chair, holding the paper to her chest, the pain unbearable. She doesn't know how long she laid there, but eventually, Ted came and lifted her into his arms and carried her back home. All night, she cried in his arms, mourning the loss of another man.

Libby left for Nantucket the following morning, numb and exhausted. Ted kept George with him for the week, arranging for Nina to help him while she's away and she's grateful. She needed this time and space to grieve. She's spent the entire week alternating between coming to terms with her decision and distracting herself by reading books, walking down to the beach, and taking photographs of her favorite subject; unsuspecting people.

Parents running along the shore with their kids, some happy, others annoyed. The boy who cried when a seagull snatched his sandwich from his hands. The teenage couple sitting on a blanket near sunset, awkward and nervous. A young mother rolling her eyes in exasperation while her children threw sand at one another. She knows the truth about her husband now, but that hasn't dampened her desire to uncover truth wherever she is.

She doesn't go anywhere without her camera. It helps. Focusing on the lives of other people, she finds relief from the profound sadness of losing Truman. *My other husband.* She's determined not to sink into depression again, but feels its tentacles trying to tighten its grip around her every day. Two severe episodes in one year is more than enough. She can't do it again.

Every day she takes her anti-depressants, two little white pills fighting the good fight, helping her ward off the darkness creeping toward her. She wouldn't think of weaning herself off them now, but one day this will pass. This sadness can't last forever.

Despite Dr. Bradford's assurance that trust can be rebuilt, she has a hard time accepting her pronouncement as truth. *Skeptical,* would be an understatement. She's no closer to trusting her husband now than she was five months ago, but if she's always looking behind her, she won't be able to move forward in any capacity.

She's married to an addict. Ted admitted he's addicted to the high of forbidden encounters. The next time he has the opportunity, will the need for a fix be stronger than his desire to keep his family together?

Do people really change? If they want to badly enough…she supposes they can.

How badly does she want to make her marriage work for her children's sake? Enough to give up Truman. It's almost more than she can bear. But as much as she doesn't want her sacrifice to be in vain, she won't live a lie. She will not pretend to feel something she doesn't.

It's going to take a lot more than the presence of love for their marriage to survive. It's going to take work. *A lot of work.*

The act of falling in love is accidental, fueled entirely by emotions. Anyone can fall in love. But there's a huge difference between falling in love, and building a relationship. She fell in love with Ted long before they built any sort of relationship. Her decision to marry him wasn't based on reason or logic, it was based on feelings and the possibility of the life they might build together. Sex has been at the core of their relationship from the start. But it can't be anymore.

They didn't walk into marriage blind. They were together for over two years before they got married and discussed the big three: family, money, and religion. Big picture talks, not what creating a life together would entail or how they would achieve balance in their lives. Libby wouldn't have known to ask what have turned out to be essential questions.

How do we plan on balancing the demands of family and work?
Should we equitably share household and parental responsibilities?
Will you be present in the daily life of your family?

She didn't know he would end up working almost every weekend and miss most of their lives, that he'd travel without her regularly for business, leaving her to raise their children alone. Money was Ted's solution to these problems whenever they did arise. Lawn needs to be mowed? Get a landscaper. Need help with the kids? Hire a sitter. Want help cleaning the house? Find a maid.

The majority of her complaints had financial solutions in his eyes. *But what about teamwork?* She had no idea how important this issue would become in their marriage; didn't realize how serious an issue it had become until their lives began to unravel.

When Ted confessed to a 'one-night stand' back in December, she used his guilt as leverage to get him to come home for dinner and spend quality time with their children. Essentially, she used what she thought was an isolated act of infidelity to bribe her husband to be present in their lives. That was far more important to her than him having sex with another woman.

Over the past week she's come to realize her relationship with Ted was built almost entirely on emotion. Without a solid foundation, what do they really have? A house of cards ready to fall apart at the faintest hint of a breeze. Building a meaningful relationship is purpose-driven and in their relationship, purpose has been an afterthought. If they're going to make this work, that needs to change.

With Truman, she fell in love with a man she was already in a relationship with. They had done the hard work and built a solid foundation of mutual respect and trust. What made their connection so special was that it was already filled with purpose.

However much unintended, it was in building their relationship, they grew to love one another. Falling in love was the icing on the cake. If the circumstances had been different...if she and Truman hadn't experienced the trauma of their spouses' affair, George's birth, and the bombing together, would that spark have ignited? She doesn't know. Maybe? Maybe not.

But it did happen. Their emotions did ignite. They did fall in love. Now it's over, and she feels that loss in the core of her being...can't imagine living next door to him once summer is over.

Ted arranged for his belongings to be moved back into their home this week while she's been away. When they return from Nantucket, her husband will be living with them again, with the man she loves living mere feet away. Her stomach twists in knots at the thought and she's considered the possibility of moving, but it doesn't make sense financially, not when the survival of their marriage is in question. Better to wait until next summer to make a major move.

Now, she needs to focus on her marriage. Her mind is as open as it's going to get for the time being. Ted will be arriving with George this afternoon for the first of many weekends together.

Her only request is that they concentrate on building a solid foundation. She doesn't want to divert attention away from the goal by having sex. Knowing Ted, he will try to use sex to strengthen the bonds of their relationship, creating a false sense of intimacy because he probably doesn't know the difference. But until she feels they've made some progress, sex is off limits.

❋

A few days into her vacation, Ginger finally called to check in with her. Libby was a little upset it took her so long to reach out. Not that she was in the mood to talk, but for those few days she felt like she'd lost both of her best friends, as if Ginger were taking sides by not checking up on her sooner, despite the fact Libby's staying in her house!

She stared at the phone screen, deliberating whether to answer, but picked up on the fourth ring, curiosity and concern getting the best of her.

"How are you, sweetie?" Ginger asked, her voice sympathetic.

"How is he, Ginger? Is he all right? Have you seen him?" she asked, the words tumbling from her lips. Tears filled her eyes and she swallowed hard, waiting for her friend's words of reassurance.

"Libby, he's fine. He left for Vermont today with the girls," she replied.

Fine? She wants him to be fine…but really? She took a deep breath in and wiped her tears.

"Good. I'm glad he's okay…" she whispered, her voice trailing off.

"Libby, are you fucking high? He's a mess. He didn't want me to tell you, but you should know the truth. You crushed that man."

Ginger was pissed, as she should be. Her friend has been wronged and Libby's the one who hurt him. *Why do I feel relief?* She doesn't want Truman to be crushed. She doesn't want him to hurt at all. If she's honest with herself, she doesn't want him to be fine without her either. *Shame on me!*

"What was I supposed to do Ginger? What would you have done if Jasper begged you to give him one year to try and make things work? Just one year! We're talking about my family! I have to do what's best for my children and right now I don't know what that is. So I'm giving my marriage another shot. If there's any chance we can be happy together, we owe it to our children to try."

"I get it," she sighed. "It just sucks in every possible way. You two are my best friends and I feel completely shitty for you both. And selfishly, I'll miss us, all three of us together. I feel like my friends are getting divorced and I'll need a visitation schedule," she paused. "Why couldn't you two stay out of love for Christ's sake?" she cried.

"It took me completely by surprise," she whispered.

"I saw it coming. You two are so close. I'd forget sometimes you're married to Ted. You and Truman work so well together, taking care of one another, helping each other out with the kids, family dinners...everything really..."

"Stop! Please, Ginger. I can't do this," she cried into her hands. "This is killing me! I miss him so much..."

"I'm sorry, Libby. That was totally insensitive. I know you're hurting, too" she said. "Are you sure you want to do this with Ted?"

"No. I'm not sure. But I'm going to do it for my kids."

"Well, I think you're making a mistake, Libby. What you have with Truman is pretty rare, but if your mind is made up, I respect your decision," she paused. "Sweetie...you know Truman won't wait for you, right?"

"I know. I just want him to know..." Libby sighed. *How much I love him? How much I miss him? How sorry I am?* "Never mind..."

"Okay, Lib...A few house details before I go. Ariana, my cleaning lady, comes by every day to touch up the rooms, wash dishes, make beds, etc. I'm sure you've already met her. So relax, don't do a thing. I have groceries delivered twice a week, so put your orders in on Mondays, which is today, and Thursdays, the number's on the fridge. The contractor, his name is Will, he'll be in and out with his guys for the next few weeks, but only in the guesthouse, so feel free to...I don't know...walk around in your skivvies if you'd like. Oh! I have a girl lined up to watch George, Monday through Friday. Just a few hours a day. Her name is Cadence, and she's a sweetheart. If you need her on weekends, just ask. How about eleven in the morning until three? Noon to four? Give you a few free hours to get into trouble. She'll start this Monday. Does that work?"

"Ginger...this is too much. I can buy my own groceries. I don't need a maid to come everyday. Or a babysitter...really."

"Yes, you do need this. You've had a horrible year, and you deserve this break. What good is having money if you can't spend it on the people you love? Besides, if you weren't there, I'd be doing this for some ungrateful relative. I'd much rather spend it on you."

"Thank you, Ginger..."

"No need. Okay, gotta run. Call me if you need anything. Talk soon. Love you."

❋

A little after four o'clock, Libby hears the crunch of tires as Ted's BMW pulls into Ginger's gravel driveway and she takes a deep breath in, blinking back the tears that spring instantly to her eyes. *I can do this*, she thinks, steeling herself for their reunion.

From the window, she watches Ted struggle to get George out of the car seat and smiles. He's not used to this. Even when Emma and Nate were little, car seats confounded the man. She's enjoying watching him trying to maneuver the various buckles and belts in an effort to release the baby.

Opening the front door, she walks toward them and George's face lights up when he sees Libby, causing her heart to melt. It's been wonderful having this week to herself, restorative and relaxing, but she's missed her little boy.

He's such a good baby, so calm and pleasant. For the past few weeks he's been sleeping peacefully through the night. Eight solid hours, bless his heart. To her relief, her fears about the tumultuous months he spent in her womb turning him into the spawn of the devil were completely unfounded.

"Hello sweetheart," she says, holding her arms out for him. George gurgles and smiles and she holds him to her. "I've missed you baby boy! I hope you and Daddy had fun this week," she says, turning toward her husband.

Ted is standing a few feet away, a bit nervous and unsure how he should greet her. She walks toward him, then stands on her tiptoes and kisses Ted's cheek. "How'd it go?" she asks, taking hold of his arm and leading him into the house.

"We had a great time, didn't we little man?" Ted says and stops in his tracks as soon as they cross the threshold into Ginger's house. His mouth hangs open for a moment, his eyes taking in their surroundings. "Holy shit," he whispers. "This is her new house?"

Libby smiles. She had much the same reaction when she walked in, and she'd already seen the photographs! Ted is walking in blind. Ginger's twenty-room 'cottage' sits near a cliff on Baxter Road in the village of Siasconset, and walking through the entry, her visitors are met with the most stunning views of the Atlantic Ocean. Resting on a slight incline along with its proximity to the bluffs, the house gives the impression it's floating on air, directly above the ocean. It's breathtaking… and momentarily disconcerting.

"So this is how the one-percent lives…" he smiles and walks around the great room, giant windows gracing every wall. Ginger had a decorator furnish the house and every piece she selected is in perfect taste, oozing luxury and comfort.

For the first hour or so, Ted unloads the car and helps her set up George's paraphernalia; baby monitors, vibrating bouncy seat (God's gift to mothers), swing, bottles, formula. It's amazing how much stuff a baby needs!

"Did you pack the kitchen sink?" she asks as she empties the last of the bags.

"Shit, I knew I forgot something," he sighs dramatically, then laughs.

Ted's laugh! She'd forgotten how much she loves his laugh. She walks over to him and wraps her arms around his waist, resting her head against him, and feels his heart beating hard against his chest. He kisses the top of her head and holds her close.

"I wasn't sure this was allowed," he whispers.

"Hugging is allowed," she murmurs and closes her eyes.

Focus on the positive, she thinks. It feels good to be in his arms. The image of him with Caro against the tree flashes in her head for a split second, but she pushes it away, trying to banish it from her mind, and is relieved it doesn't have the same effect it used to. It no longer makes her want to lash out at him. Now it's a momentary ache, a few seconds of sadness, then acceptance...and she takes a moment to remind herself Caroline didn't mean anything to Ted. Libby can't say the same about Truman.

She takes a deep breath in and sighs then turns her face up toward him. His eyes are searching hers for clues, next steps.

"Let's go to the living room," she says.

George is asleep in his crib and she pauses there for a moment, taking in his chubby arms and legs, his sweet smile. The thought of having a child at her age was horrifying, and the experience nearly killed her, but this time, Ted's obstinance was a blessing in disguise.

She takes his hand and leads him to one of the couches overlooking the ocean, and they sit for a moment in silence. It's time to set the ground rules and some of the goals she's thought of this week. Ted doesn't like to be dictated to and he likes ultimatums even less. She's been dreading this conversation, but it's time he understands what she needs from him.

"Ted...if we're going to do this we have to put the past behind us. I want you to know I'm trying very hard to do that. Don't give me a reason to stop."

He nods his head, his eyes wide and sincere.

"We need to decide what we want our life together to look like, and work our asses off to make it happen. Set clear expectations, discuss the non-negotiables...everything. This isn't going to be easy. You know that, right?" she asks.

Again, he nods.

"But if we can strengthen our relationship a little bit every day...who knows? Maybe we can create something meaningful, something that will stand the test of time. That's my goal for us. If by next summer, it's clear that's not going to happen... well...then we'll have to let go and move on."

"You were ready to leave me, weren't you," he asks, his voice soft.

She slowly nods her head up and down.

"If you're in love with Truman, why did you agree to stay with me for another year?"

"The children," she says without hesitation. "And I do love you, Ted. But this is going to be hard and we need to be prepared. This isn't about rekindling passion. We need to create something that's going to last."

"Libby, I will do whatever it takes. When I say I love you with my whole heart, I mean it. But you have to promise me...whatever you had with Truman is over."

She looks out at the ocean, trying to hold her tears at bay.

"It's over," she whispers.

CHAPTER TWENTY

H er days and weeks on Nantucket have settled into a pleasant routine. During the week, Libby spends her mornings with the baby, taking walks around the island, then Cadence comes at noon and she has the afternoon to herself. She has the freedom to relax on the beach, take a bike ride, or simply sit on Ginger's beautiful porch overlooking the ocean and read a book. She's gone through a stack already and has been binge reading different authors. Nathaniel Philbrick, a Nantucket resident, was the latest.

Whenever she finishes one novel, she bikes the eight miles into town and visits Mitchell's Book Corner, spends an hour or so perusing the titles, then makes her selection and walks down to the café for lunch.

She's become a little obsessed with Ginger's contractor and his family. Every afternoon, Will's wife, Julia, brings him lunch, sometimes with their other children, but oftentimes alone. The first week Libby was on the island, Will asked if she minded them having picnic lunches on the lawn, and she shook her head, smiling. "Please, help yourself! Anytime." A view this spectacular shouldn't be for her eyes only.

Three weeks later, their family has become a familiar sight. Will's son works with him most days. The young man is the spitting image of his father, their resemblance, remarkable. She thought she was seeing double the first time she laid eyes on Liam, then realized he was a younger version of Will. Almost as tall as his father, he has wavy blond hair, handsome features and the same sea blue eyes.

He's a nice boy, polite, and will be entering his junior year of high school this fall. Emma is sure to develop a crush on him if they're still working on the guesthouse in August!

Their daughter, Mae, is a spitfire, loaded with energy. She runs and dances around the lawn, always laughing. Her curly brown hair and big brown eyes are so like her mothers. She's about the same age as Emma but so different in demeanor.

And their little boy, Joe, is a little younger than Nate, a perfect combination of his parents, with big blue eyes and wavy brown hair.

A picture perfect family. So loving and delightful, she figures something hideous must be lurking beneath the surface. So she watches them interact, trying to uncover clues.

Warmth and love radiates between Will and his wife, the way they look at each other, in their every gesture. They appear genuinely happy, and that's not something she's witnessed since she began her study of people a few months back. She's seen it between mother and child, father and child, yes, but married couples? It's sad really, but when she thinks about it, she's hard pressed to come up with one example. Until now.

She started snapping pictures of their family from inside the house at first, then discreetly from the porch, but as the days wore on, she got a little bolder, walking around the yard, explaining to them she's an amateur photographer taking photos of the garden and the ocean. She furtively clicks a few shots of their family whenever she's turning her attention from one object to another; a ladybug, *the family*, the ocean, *the family*, the garden, *the family*. Click, click, click.

At night she studies the photographs, looking for signs of unhappiness, boredom, anything signaling distress and she's come up empty. *What's their secret?* Libby wonders.

She mentioned them to Dr. Bradford during their weekly Skype session earlier today and could see the concern in her doctor's eyes.

"Libby, I'm not sure this is healthy. Do you believe you're going to find the key to marital bliss by studying other peoples' marriages? You and Ted are going to have to figure out what works for the two of you. Every marriage is different. What works for the contractor's family might not work for you and Ted, even if you were to uncover their secret to happiness."

Damn this woman for being so logical! It's infuriating!

The doctor continued. "And Libby, I guarantee they've gone through their own set of problems, everyone does. What you're seeing in that family is more than likely the result of years of struggle as they figured out how to build a solid relationship. Perhaps they've gone through the hard times and are on the other side? That's the joy you see, the love and warmth. But you and Ted won't get to the other side unless you do the work."

She has a point, Libby thought to herself, grudgingly.

"And if you and Ted get there, your version of 'happy' won't look the same as the family you're studying. I don't think this deadline is a good idea. What you're attempting to do, rebuild your relationship from scratch with a whole new set of roles, rules, and goals...I don't know if that can be done on such a tight schedule. You're putting undue pressure on Ted, and yourself."

Maybe she's right, but having a timeframe helps Libby with perspective and frees her from feeling trapped. If things aren't progressing in a year, Ted knows what's going to happen. There may be tears and a little drama, but they'll be prepared. Maybe a few months from now, it won't seem as important, but right now? She's clinging to it.

✳

Every Friday, Ted arrives on the island on the five o'clock ferry and Libby and George drive into town to pick him up. Over the course of the weekend, their days are devoted to family time, and every night they discuss their marriage goals; what they're doing to achieve them and what they can do to help each other out. It's been intense…but she's hopeful.

Their time together hasn't been entirely dedicated to their version of couples counseling. They've made time for fun as well. Dinner at her favorite restaurant on the island, movies at the new theater, walks on the beach. Some nights they stay in playing cards, or one of the many board games they found in the den.

Last weekend they were up until two in the morning playing *Monopoly*. They laughed, and teased each other, built hotels, tried to negotiate deals when the cash was running low. It's the most fun they'd had together in years.

And she's discovered something new and surprising about Ted over the past few weeks. The man can cook! In fifteen years he's never done anything more than heat up leftovers in the microwave and stick meat on the grill. Over the past three weekends, he's made pancakes from scratch, frittata, biscuits and gravy. His hidden talent isn't confined to breakfast foods. He makes a killer shrimp scampi and chicken cordon bleu, tonight, a pot roast.

"Ted, this is unbelievable! When did you learn to cook?" she asks, taking another bite of roast.

"I learned from my mother. She said every man needs to know how to cook, do laundry, mop a floor and iron clothes.

I've been pulling out her old recipes and trying them at home. I find it relaxing. Don't worry, the kitchen isn't a complete disaster!"

She stares at him, wide-eyed with shock. *Cook? Iron? Clean? Laundry?* She can picture Doris saying those things, but Ted doing them? *Never.*

"Why are you staring at me like that?" he laughs.

She almost shoots a zinger at him, something along the lines of *'would've been nice if you'd made the effort before now,'* but stops herself. She loves this new piece of information. She loves that he's making the effort to cook. She enjoys her time with him in the kitchen, helping him chop and dice, and cleaning up together.

A zinger would taint this moment, and she recognizes, *this is a building block.* This is something they can work with. A first step.

"I just never knew you were so talented in the kitchen," she finally replies, and reaches for his hand. "And this means a lot to me. Thank you, Ted."

He kisses her hand and smiles, looking into her eyes, and her heart swells as she blinks back tears. They've stuck to the 'rules.' Ted's been sleeping in one of the many guest rooms and they haven't had sex.

She recognizes that look in his eye, can feel the warmth spreading from her stomach throughout her body, an automatic reaction. She's Pavlov's dog salivating in response to the bell. She thinks of Truman, guilt creeping up her spine, and closes her eyes. *One year, Libby.*

It's been months since she made love with her husband. She doesn't count the angry sex in the nursery when he confessed, or the goodbye sex by the stream. Neither of those experiences was joyful. If she has sex with him tonight will it spoil the progress they've made? *Will our relationship be all about sex again?* There's only one way to find out.

"Come with me," she says, leading him to her bedroom.

He was gentle, the urgency and intensity that has consumed them in the past replaced by a languorous, appreciative exploration of one another's bodies. He caressed every inch of her, and she luxuriated in his touch, the glow of love emanating from his eyes, and allowed his tenderness to touch her heart.

They made slow, passionate love, bringing each other such pleasure, so different from any of their sexual interactions in the past. It brought them both to tears. For maybe the first time, they experienced the coming together of two hearts...not just bodies.

Afterward, lying in Ted's arms, she realized that for those few hours, they were alone in the room. She was able to leave Truman and Caroline, and the faceless women out of their bed and felt profound relief knowing it was possible. There will be times like this when it's just the two of them, learning to love one another again.

❄

The first time she saw Julia, the contractor's wife, Libby thought she looked familiar but couldn't place her. She could see the faint glimmer of recognition in Julia's eyes as well. This morning, sitting at the General Store with George, Julia crosses the street, walking toward them and waves.

"Hi Libby. I was just at your place. Will forgot something this morning. Mind if I join you?"

"No, of course not. Pull up a seat."

"I know we've met before," Julia says, settling in. "I've been wracking my brain and I think I've got it. Last year I went to a book club meeting with my sister-in-law, Ellie. You were there with your husband, weren't you?" she asks.

"I was in a book club..." she pauses. *Ellie...Julia...* Ginger's friends. "Wait! You're the woman from Italy!"

"I knew it! It's been bugging me for weeks," Julia laughs. "You weren't feeling well, if I remember correctly, and your husband took you home."

Libby looks down at her hands. That was right after she found out she was pregnant. Julia's talking about Truman. *She thinks Truman is my husband.* He's been in her thoughts every day since they parted. She's been on the island for a month already. In two weeks Nate and Emma join them and Ted took the last two weeks of August off to spend time together as a family. The summer is passing much too quickly and she'll be back in Littleton before she knows it. Her heart sinks at the thought.

Ted doesn't want her to have anything to do with Truman, and she understands where he's coming from. But she misses him so much. His warmth, his kindness, his support and understanding. She misses his friendship most of all. Regardless, Truman might not want anything to do with her, and the gravity of the situation is a weight bearing down on her chest.

"That's right," she murmurs, peering at George in the carriage. "I wasn't feeling well that night. I have this little guy to thank for that." She looks up at Julia and smiles. "That wasn't my husband at book club. That was my friend, Truman."

Saying his name out loud for the first time in weeks, she feels her throat closing in on her.

Julia lifts an eyebrow. "Really? I must've been off my game that night. I got the distinct impression you two were married."

"Off your game?" Libby asks, puzzled.

"Love is my specialty," she says, and laughs. "I'm like *Dear Abby*...when I'm back in Italy."

"Oh my God, I remember now. You answer letters to Juliet. You give people advice about love."

"Been doing it for years, since before Liam was born! I've gotten pretty good at reading people."

"That's my new hobby," Libby says.

Julia's forehead creases, curiosity in her eyes.

"Explain, please," she says.

"Oh, that would take days! Let's just say I've had a tough year and was blindsided by some unpleasant realities. Since then, I've been on a quest for the truth and studying people to see behind the metaphorical curtain. I don't want to live a lie anymore. For too long I took things at face value, was too trusting. Now I know better."

Julia nods her head slowly, her eyes sympathetic.

"I've been watching you and your family," Libby confesses.

Julia's eyebrows shoot up, the corner of her mouth lifting, amused.

"And what do you see?" she asks, smiling.

"A very happy family. Good kids. Two people very much in love. I'm totally jealous," she admits. "How long have you been married?"

"Ah, let's see…" Julia pauses, "Since 2002. So eleven years?"

Libby frowns. Liam's sixteen. And he's definitely Will's son. Julia laughs at her obvious confusion.

"You're right, Libby, we are very happy, but it wasn't always like this. What we have now, we went through a lot to get here. I assure you, it hasn't been easy."

"Explain, please," Libby says, and leans forward in her seat, genuinely curious about their relationship.

"Like you, it's a long story. I've known Will for over twenty years. We were still in college when we met. The first two years were wonderful and horrible, both of us too young and stupid to get out of the way of our own happiness. Then we broke up and he was with someone else. One night, while he was engaged to this other woman, fate stepped in. We bumped into each other in Italy and I became pregnant with Liam. But I didn't tell Will."

Julia pauses to take a sip of coffee. Libby's eyes are wide with curiosity. *What happened?*

"Will was married to his first wife for over five years," she continues. "And I didn't see him in all that time. I stayed with Liam in Italy and tried to put Will out of my mind, which was difficult with his mini-me by my side every day! Eventually, I moved back to the States and we saw each other again, and that was it. We knew we were meant to be together. He got divorced, we got married, and the rest is history," she sighs.

Libby sits back in her chair, her mouth slack. Wow. She did not expect that!

"My husband was unfaithful and I found out when I was pregnant with George. I almost left him for Truman," Libby says then gasps, covering her mouth with her hand. She can't believe she said those words out loud to a stranger!

"It's okay, Libby, I've heard it all," Julia pauses. "So you stayed with your husband?"

"Yes," she whispers. "We're starting over. We love each other...but I've realized we don't have much of a foundation. Love isn't enough."

"Very true. Building the foundation is key. You know, an affair doesn't have to mean the end of a relationship, Libby. Sometimes it's the beginning. Sometimes you have to lose everything to appreciate what you have and stop taking each other for granted. You become the phoenix rising up from the ashes."

"I think that's what's happened for Ted. But while we were separated I fell in love with Truman, my best friend. I've loved him for years, depended on him. We were always there for each other." She can't believe she saying these things to

Julia, but how often do you have one of Juliet's secretaries sitting across from you dispensing advice? "I miss him, Julia. I love him, and I miss him. But I love my husband too. How can I love two men at the same time?"

"I think it's possible when you love them for different reasons," she pauses. "May I ask you a personal question?"

Libby nods and laughs. That's all they've done is share personal experiences!

"Why did you decide to stay with your husband instead of Truman?"

"For my children. To see if there's any chance of being happy together for their sake."

"Do you think there's a chance?" Julia asks. "Rebuilding trust is not easy."

"I think so…" she says, nodding her head. "We've been making a real effort and I'm hopeful. It feels like the right thing to do."

"There's a world of difference between what is right and what makes people happy. My husband tried to do what he thought was 'right' for a long time, staying in a loveless marriage out of a false sense of responsibility. It took a devastating tragedy to open Will's eyes, for him to realize life is too short." Julia takes Libby's hand in hers and gives it a squeeze. "Our time here is fleeting. We don't get to hit rewind when we realize we've made a bad choice. You have to do what makes you happy, Libby. Only you know what that is."

CHAPTER TWENTY-ONE

T ruman's been on autopilot since Libby left for Nantucket. There's so much to do over the summer. Sell this house, find another one, get everyone settled in before school starts. The girls have stayed with his parents in Vermont while he scrambles to get it all done. The house was on the market three days after Libby left town and within two weeks he had a full-price offer. He purposely priced it on the lower end of the spectrum with that very hope. Sell quickly. Get out of Dodge. He'll be gone by the time Libby returns from vacation.

If he actually gave himself a moment to sit and think, he'd be overwhelmed with grief...so he doesn't stop. He always has something to do or somewhere to go. And when he does go home at night? He falls asleep on the couch watching television, distracted by the lives of these insane people on reality shows. He never watched much television, but the last he remembered, there were programs with actors and plots. When did television get taken over by regular people doing stupid things for all the world to see? And why is it so addicting?

For him, reality television is a competition to see who can out-humiliate each other, and watching these strangers embarrass themselves in front of a national audience makes him feel a little less pathetic about his own life. When Libby does pop into his head, he feels like a total fool, believing she'd choose him. For six years he watched Libby with Ted and she adored her husband. The man had a four-year affair with her neighbor and she still let him in the house every day. Why would he ever think she'd leave him?

Because I was always there for her. Because we're a family. They were more married in the true sense of the word than he and Caroline or Libby and Ted. It was real. She loved him…she needed him. Maybe she confused needing with love?

Early this morning, Truman drove to Vermont for the weekend and to bring the girls down to Connecticut to stay with their other grandparents. He didn't tell them he was selling the house until today, when he sat them down to share the news. They're moving to Bayside.

He knew it would be a difficult conversation. The house in Littleton is the only home they've ever known and it's breaking his heart to see their anguish. His parents are consoling Bette, his mother shooting him hateful looks. She's angry they aren't moving to Vermont. He mentioned the possibility months ago and now he's dashed her hopes. He's sure to catch an earful later.

The decision to move was impulsive and he had a rigid timeframe to work within. Sixty days. That's how long Libby's on Nantucket. Not enough time to fight it out with Caroline in the court system, and that's exactly where it was going to wind up. When he brought up the possibility after Libby left, Caroline was adamantly against the idea, and this is what she does for a living. Even if he had more time, he didn't have the energy for the battle.

Watching Bette clinging to his parents on the couch, Truman reminds himself she will be fine. It's just fear of change, he understands that. Bette's going into fourth grade, she's young and outgoing...she'll adjust. It's Sadie he's worried about. She'll be entering high school and won't know a soul. She's already shy, more so now than ever. The way she looked at him before she ran out of the room... She didn't say a word, but she didn't need to. Her eyes, so like his, spoke volumes.

Entering his boyhood bedroom, where Sadie's been sleeping for the past month, he pulls a chair up to the side of the bed. She's lying on her stomach, her head turned toward the wall, and doesn't acknowledge his presence. So he waits. *I can do this all night, Sadie. I'm not going anywhere until we talk this out.* Together, they sit in silence for ten minutes before she finally rolls over and faces him.

"I don't want to move," she says through clenched teeth.

"I know you don't sweetheart, but we have to."

"Why? Because of Ted?" she asks.

How do I handle that question? He looks around the room at his old posters, searching for answers. Billy Idol is no help at all, just sneers down at him from the yellowing poster on the wall. He's forty-four years old and his parents haven't changed a thing. This room is a time capsule, a throwback to 1985.

"No, because it's time for a change."

"Then I want to stay with Libby," she says. "She's my real mother."

Truman's lips part and he feels the heat spreading to his cheeks.

"That's not going to happen. You realize if you stayed with Libby...you'd be living with Ted," he points out.

She frowns. His daughter clearly hadn't thought that one out.

"He won't stay forever. Libby doesn't love him. She loves you, Dad," she whispers. "Are you blind?"

"Why do you say that?" he asks, feeling a bit like a teenager himself, genuinely curious to know his fourteen-year-old daughter's take on Libby's feelings for him.

Sadie rolls her eyes at him. *Duh!*

"It's so obvious you love each other. We just need Ted to leave so we can be a family again."

He takes her hand in his. She sounds so young and naïve, much younger than fourteen.

"Oh, baby…that's not going to happen. Libby wants to make her marriage work with Ted. They're trying to fix what's broken."

"No!" she shouts, tears filling her eyes. "What happened, Dad? Did you two have a fight? We can't move. Don't you see that? How will you get Libby back if you're not there to stop him?"

What is she talking about? He stares at her, his brows drawn together.

"Back, sweetie? We were never together."

"Dad? How stupid do you think I am? After the marathon…you two were in the bedroom together with the door locked. You had the shower running for almost an hour. When she came out, her mouth was all red…from kissing."

Duh, Dad! I may be fourteen but I'm not an idiot!

"For two months, almost every night she came to the house and asked me to bring my sister to her house…so you two could be alone, obviously. And the night before Libby left for Nantucket, I went into the kitchen to get some water and I saw you two kissing in front of the fire."

Triple duh, Dad! He has no clue what to say! She's not as young and naïve as he thought!

"Get her back, Daddy! Go to Nantucket and get her back!"

✳

What am I doing? Truman stands on the deck of the high-speed ferry to Nantucket, the cool ocean spray whipping against his face as he leans over the railing. This is not a completely pointless trip, but is guaranteed to do some harm along with good, at least to his heart. He needs to say goodbye to Libby. He realized having her come home to strangers living next door would be cruel, childish even. She wasn't trying to hurt him by giving Ted another year.

Over the past few days he's sat with his feelings, letting the emotions he's kept submerged for over a month bubble to the surface, and he understands why she's doing this. Libby's trying to save her family. He can't fault her for that. If there had been any way he could've salvaged his marriage to Caroline, he would have, for the girls' sake if nothing else. But they had nothing to work with. The love was long gone.

That's when he realized Libby was doing this for her children, not Ted. Not because she felt anything less for Truman. That comforted him to an extent and he feels a little less ridiculous. He was so busy licking his wounds he never looked at the big picture.

The situation is what it is, he won't interfere with what she's trying to accomplish with Ted. Sadie would like nothing better than for him to sweep into Ginger's house, and snatch Libby out of Ted's sinister arms, running into the sunset with Libby and George. But that's Sadie's fantasy, not his. He just wants to say goodbye…a proper goodbye. They've been friends for too long and gone through too much together to let it end this way.

The ferry docks and Truman grabs his backpack, letting the crowd draw him off the boat and into the congested streets near the ferry terminal. It's a Wednesday, but the island is still packed with tourists. He doesn't enjoy traveling to the islands in the summer. Tourist season is too busy, too crowded. The few times he's come to Nantucket off season, it's been for rest and relaxation, peace and quiet.

There is nothing peaceful or quiet about this place today. He waits in a line twenty-deep near the dock for a taxi to take him across the island to Siasconset, his stomach turning over, twisting in knots.

Again he questions the wisdom of this voyage. He has no idea how Libby is doing, what she's thinking or feeling. He's prepared for a variety of possible reactions to him showing up on her doorstep. Shock, anger, sadness, pity, (dare he say it?) joy. But she's had no warning, no chance to prepare herself for their discussion.

"Truman?" he hears Libby's voice, then feels a hand on his arm. *Holy shit!* He turns around and meets Libby's eyes. She's smiling but her eyes are sad.

"Hi Libby," he says, his voice catching in his throat.

Now he's the one taken by surprise! He steps out of the taxi line and she takes his hands in hers. They stand on the crowded sidewalk looking into each other's eyes for what feels like an eternity.

The noise of the crowd dissipates as he studies her face. Her skin is golden from spending time in the sun, her nose and cheekbones sprinkled with freckles. Libby's hair is threaded with gold highlights, pulled back from her face in a ponytail. She looks wonderful. Her time on the island has been good for her.

"What are you doing here?" she asks.

"I thought we should talk," he replies and she nods her head in agreement.

"Do you want to go to the house? Or down to the beach?" she asks.

"Someplace quiet," he says.

"I have Ginger's car. It's around the corner. Come with me," she says and he follows her to the black Range Rover parked two blocks from the madness of downtown.

On the drive to Ginger's house, Libby asks about the girls and their time in Vermont. He asks about Nate and Emma at sleep away camp, whether they're enjoying it. So normal...as if the status quo hasn't changed.

"They're having a blast," she says. "They've been bursting with excitement every time we talk. It was good for them to get away."

He nods his head and smiles, can picture Nate jumping up and down enthusiastically while he tells Libby about his adventures, and Emma, more subdued, gossiping in a hushed voice about what this bunkmate did or describing the boy she has a crush on. He misses them. And he's in serious George withdrawal.

She pulls the SUV into a circular driveway and sits back against the tan leather seat. A moment later she turns her face to his and sighs.

"It's so good to see you, Tru," she whispers and smiles.

He swallows hard, blinking back the tears pushing to the surface, and nods. Opening the car door, he steps out onto the gravel and clears his throat, trying to regain his composure. Truman reminds himself why he's here, the reason he came to see her today. Following her into the house, he steps into the entryway, and gasps.

"Everyone has the exact same reaction," Libby giggles. "It's something, isn't it?"

"Incredible," he murmurs, walking toward the picture windows overlooking the ocean. Sconset Beach is about a quarter mile down on the right and it's dotted with hundreds of people, despite the cloudy skies. He was going to suggest they walk there, but there's no privacy.

"Are you thirsty? Hungry?" she asks, stepping into Ginger's new state of the art kitchen, and opens the subzero refrigerator. It's lunchtime, almost one-thirty, and his stomach is grumbling.

"Sure," he says. "Where's George?"

"He's with Cadence, my built in babysitter. Ginger has spoiled me rotten this vacation," she says, pulling out provisions for lunch.

Sliced turkey, Swiss cheese, lettuce, multigrain bread. He watches her take the mayonnaise, then pause and grab the brown mustard. He smiles. She remembers he likes mustard on his turkey.

"Why don't you go upstairs and see him while I finish up here? We can eat on the porch."

Standing in the doorway to the nursery, he finds a teenage girl sitting on the floor in front of George, stacking blocks. His mouth drops open. George is five months old now and can sit up on his own. *I missed it*, he thinks with sadness. He wasn't there when George learned to sit up.

The girl turns around and is startled to find a stranger in the doorway.

"Oh! Hello. I'm Cady," she rises and shakes his hand.

"Hello, Cady, I'm Truman, a friend of the family," he says.

He can't take his eyes off George. Truman takes a seat on the rug beside George and the baby gurgles and smiles, two teeth popping through his bottom gums. *I'm missing everything...*

"Hey little man," he lifts George into his arms and holds him close. George leans back and places his chubby little hands on Truman's cheeks and laughs. *A real laugh!*

"How's my boy today?" he asks and Cadence answers for him.

"Oh, Georgie Porgie here is doing fine. We've been reading and stacking blocks. It's almost time for his walk. He's such a good baby," she says with a smile.

Propping George up against his bent legs, they play patty cake. It still makes him giggle. *Oh my God...I love this child!* And he's overcome with sadness, knowing he's going to miss his life, all of the milestones. After today, he probably won't see him again.

He holds George close again and Libby enters the room. Their eyes meet and hers are glossed over with tears. This is not going to be easy. He never thought it would be, but sitting here with George, his heart is breaking all over again. *I don't know if I can do this*, he thinks, then remembers, *I don't have a choice.*

♀

Her heart stopped beating when she spotted Truman standing in line for a taxi. She was in town to pick up a new book, and it looked like it might rain so she took the car. The sky is overcast and the air is thick and muggy. She was walking down Main Street, about to turn onto Water Street to have lunch at the café when she saw him and froze in her tracks and held her breath.

Her trembling legs carried her across the street to where he was standing and she resisted the urge to hold him. That's all she wanted to do...hold him in her arms again.

While he's upstairs with George, she's been thinking about what she wants to say to Truman. At the top of the list, to apologize, but also to explain why she's doing this. To explain what it means to keep her family together and the sacrifices she has to make to do so.

If there was any way they could go back to the way things were before the marathon, she'd do it in a heartbeat. *I'd be Elinor, not Marianne.* But Julia was right the other day. There's no rewind button. She has to live with the consequences of her impulsive behavior. Libby has to tell Truman to stay away so she has a shot of making her marriage work.

Standing in the doorway to George's nursery, watching Truman holding her son, she's reminded of the day he was born. Truman was there by her side through it all, and he's grown so close to George. How can she break that bond? Does she even have the right? *No*, her heart answers. She can't tell him he can never see the children again. Just as he can't keep her away from the girls.

Sadie's been texting her all summer, sending her photos of her artwork and poetry. She's an exceptionally talented artist, but what has become very apparent to Libby is how much Sadie is hurting. In the past, she would have sat with Truman and discussed her concerns, and together, they would've come up with solutions. Exactly what parents do when their child has a problem.

"Lunch is ready, Tru," she says, trying to sound upbeat.

He kisses George and hands him back to Cadence, but the baby cries and reaches for Truman. The look on Truman's face and her son's grief being taken away from him…it's too much.

Libby turns away and runs down the hallway into a guest bedroom, presses her face into a pillow, and screams. Moments later, Truman is beside her and she reaches for him, desperate to feel his arms around her. He holds her close, stroking her back, his own shaking with sorrow.

Libby clings to him, can't hold him close enough, and clutches his t-shirt. *Why? Why do I have to do this?* She thinks about Ted…the little boy wanting to have his cake and eat it too. She finally understands. Her husband's addicted to the high of risky behavior. She's addicted to Truman, his stability and strength, his encouragement and devotion. She wants to have her cake and eat it too.

Truman holds her face in his hands, his questioning eyes meeting hers, and they are overflowing with love and uncertainty. *Yes or no*, they ask. She tries to fight against her desire for him, but is physically unable to stop herself. Eagerly, before either of them has the opportunity to waver, her mouth finds his and Truman returns her kiss with consuming passion, the fire within her burning bright.

In his arms, she spirals into another world, surrendering to the feelings she's suppressed for months. Pulling Truman down beside her, she forgets the promise she made to her husband…to herself…to her family. Right now she doesn't care about anyone but Truman, the feel of his skin, his soft lips pressed against hers. Lying in his embrace and exploring his body, she's found her way home.

Libby slides her hands beneath Truman's t-shirt, her fingertips grazing the lean muscles of his stomach, the soft hair on his chest, the goose bumps that have arisen all over his torso. There is no hiding his desire for her as she slides down the zipper of his shorts, carefully removing them and his boxers in one swift movement. Drowning in his kiss, she reaches for him, feels him throbbing with desire in her hand.

"Libby…" Truman murmurs, his hands roaming her body. "Are you sure about this? We can stop now…" his says against her lips. "Before it's too late."

She stops and looks into his eyes. He's giving her an out. As always, Truman is the voice of reason, putting her needs above his own. A flicker of doubt registers in her mind (*fuck you, Elinor!*) but it floats away almost instantly. Catching her breath, she runs her fingers over his lips and nods.

"I'm sure," she sighs, pressing her body against his.

Truman groans and reaches beneath her skirt, impatiently tugs off her panties, then sits up and removes his t-shirt and the remainder of her clothing. His mouth comes down on hers again and she sighs with pleasure, her legs parting as he settles between them, his body pressed against the length of hers. Her head is swimming, her breathing labored. She wants nothing more than to feel him inside of her, they've waited long enough. Truman's hard against her thigh and she wraps her legs around him, guiding him in, her muscles contracting around him, every nerve alive, sensitized.

She takes a deep breath in, treasuring this heavenly moment, and Truman looks deep into her eyes, then slowly begins to move inside her, his gaze never leaving hers. With each movement, she feels herself slipping further away from the life she chose, letting go of rhyme and reason in favor of the absolute bliss she's experiencing in his arms.

"Truman…" she whispers. *I'm yours…please take me away.*

He slides his hands beneath her hips and plunges deep inside her, and she throws her head back and moans. *This can't be wrong,* she thinks, meeting him with each thrust, her pleasure bordering on pain. Back arching, arms clasped around him tightly, Libby loses herself in Truman, her body shuddering as she cries out and he collapses against her, his breathing labored.

Trembling in each other's arms, they lay in silence, Libby trying to wipe her mind clear of all thought, wanting desperately to hold reality at bay. At least for a little while. *Just give us an hour or two,* she thinks, squeezing her eyes shut and burying her face in his neck. *Please, just enough to get me through this year.*

Truman tilts her head up and kisses her gently. She's afraid to open her eyes, doesn't want him to read her thoughts. Not yet. She wraps her legs around him, pulling him as close as possible. *Don't make me say those awful words just yet.*

"Mrs. Fitzgerald?" Cadence calls from down hall.

Libby sits up and gasps. *Oh Jesus! What if she heard us?* She feels her face turning red and Truman pulls her back down.

"She was taking George for a walk, Libby," he whispers. "They must've just gotten home."

"What time is it?" she asks, searching for a clock in the guestroom.

Truman fishes his phone out of his shorts and holds it out for her. It's 3:55, time for Cady to leave. Quickly she throws on her clothes and opens the door to the guestroom, poking her head out into the hallway.

"Yes Cady?" she calls out, her voice unnaturally cheerful.

Cadence closes the door to George's nursery and holds her finger to her lips.

"He's sleeping," the girl whispers. "I'm heading out. See you tomorrow."

"Thank you," Libby says, closing the door behind her.

Leaning against it, she looks down at her feet, pangs of guilt tearing at her heart, echoing in her head. She could have stopped at any time, but she didn't want to. Truman gave her the opportunity and she said no.

Making love to him was a conscious decision…and she doesn't regret it. What she regrets is making the commitment to stay with Ted for another eleven months. She can't back out of their agreement as much as she wants to. There's too much at stake.

Maybe we can have it all? Ted can keep doing what he was doing and I can keep Truman!

As soon as the thought crosses her mind she realizes how ridiculous and irrational it is, how unfair it would be to everyone involved. Especially Truman. He deserves so much more than this.

When she finally raises her eyes to meet his, Truman is sitting on the edge of the bed, fully clothed. He smiles, extending his hand to her and Libby joins him on the bed filled with sadness, tears spilling onto her cheeks.

"Libby...I understand," he murmurs against her hair.

Confused, she looks into his eyes. He takes her hand in his and lifts it to his mouth. He nods his head and exhales, "I understand what you need to do, Libby. I didn't come here today to confuse you or ask you to leave Ted...." his voice trails off and he turns away from her, running his hands through his hair. "I didn't mean for this to happen," he says, his voice thick with emotion.

"I love you, Tru," she whispers. "Please, never doubt that."

He turns to her and his pain is etched in the creases in his brow, distress reflected in his eyes. Libby wraps her arms around him, and they lie in bed holding each other until their tears run dry.

Then Truman relaxes his hold on her and hands her a tissue from the nightstand, grabbing one for himself. Together, they wipe their tears and blow their noses, trying to clean up after the storm. *This is the divorce right here*, she thinks. Truman and Libby are getting divorced and now they need to finalize the agreement.

"Let's go outside," she says and climbs off the bed.

Checking herself in the mirror above the bureau, she straightens her ponytail and takes a deep breath in. Standing beside her, Truman runs his fingers through his sandy hair, then turns to her. She touches his face, then presses her lips against his, her heart aching in her chest.

These past few weeks with Ted, Libby felt she was doing the right thing. When they made love for the first time last weekend she was certain she'd made the right decision. She's not sure of anything anymore. It took three hours with Truman to knock down the fragile foundation she and Ted have started to build and flood her with doubt. Two hours in his arms to fully understand the sacrifice she's making by staying. If she stays in this room with Truman for one more minute she'll never be able to say goodbye. And she has to.

While George naps, they sit on the porch and Libby clasps Truman's hand tightly in hers, staring out at the ocean. There are no words to describe the sorrow she feels, knowing he'll be leaving her shortly.

"Libby, I need to tell you something," he pauses. "I sold the house. That's why I came here today."

Her heart skips a beat. *Did I hear him right?* Puzzled, she turns to him.

"We're moving in two weeks," he says, his voice soft. "I didn't want you to come home and find new neighbors in the house without warning. It didn't seem right."

She stares out at the ocean, speechless. *He's leaving me? He's taking my girls away from me?* She's having a hard time catching her breath and Truman grabs her hand.

"Libby, look at me." She does as he asks, her eyes wide with shock. "It's for the best. Better for me to not have a daily reminder of what I can't have. And better for you. I meant what I said earlier. I understand why you're staying with Ted. You don't want your children to grow up in a broken home like you did. I may not agree with your decision, but I do understand it. I just can't be there to watch. It would be too hard."

"Truman, I am so sorry. I've wanted to say that every day since I last saw you."

"There's no need for apologies. I knew what I was getting into, Lib. I always knew there was a chance you'd stay with him. It hurts, but I don't want you to feel guilty for what happened between us. And please don't beat yourself up over what happened today. I love you, Libby, and I want you to be happy...whether it's with me or another man."

She turns to him and tries to memorize his face. It's not possible this is the last time she'll ever see him. *This can't be happening.*

"I don't want to lose you, Tru…" her voice tapers off.

She's being completely selfish. Truman needs to move on and she has to give him the space to do that. She nods her head and squeezes his hand, her heart breaking again. She has to let him go…but she'll always wonder what might have been.

PART THREE

AWAKENING

"I wish, as well as everybody else, to be
perfectly happy; but, like everybody else,
it must be in my own way."
~ Jane Austen

CHAPTER TWENTY-TWO

T*he list, the list! Where is my planner?* Libby's going to New York later this afternoon and has to make sure everything is in place before she leaves. Nina will be staying with the family while she's away. This trip couldn't have happened at a worse time! She'll be gone for four days and Ted is in the middle of a huge project and is frantically busy with work. Autumn is chaotic for him every year. His calendar is jam packed, but he's kept his promise to be home for dinner, even if it means working in the den until two in the morning.

They've been home from Nantucket for two months and things are going well between Libby and Ted, but it's been a constant struggle to focus on their marriage since she last saw Truman. She fights against her longing for him every day and Ted's not an idiot. He senses something has shifted, has caught her staring into space on numerous occasions and asked if everything's all right.

She answers him as truthfully as she can. Everything is fine between them. Ted has given her absolutely no reason to complain. He's been wonderful the past few months and has kept his side of the bargain. She can't say the same.

After Truman left Nantucket, she didn't know if she'd be able to move forward with Ted. She was in a daze after he left and if Ginger hadn't arrived on the island the following day, accompanied by Julia and her sister-in-law, Ellie, she doesn't know what she would have done. In their company, she was able to put Truman out of her mind for a few hours, and with the aid of a few drinks, relax and escape her memories.

Ted arrived the following evening and she did her best to focus on him, but she was distracted. *How did Ted do it?* she wondered. *How did he manage to have sex with Caro, then come home and behave completely relaxed and normal with me?*

While Ted slept, she took a walk on the beach to clear her head and figure out a way to move forward with this monkey on her back. She sat on a rock and using her finger, Libby wrote a confessional in the sand, admitting her guilt to the universe and made a vow to never violate Ted's trust again. As the tide came in, it washed away her sin, carrying her words and shame to the ocean's floor for safekeeping.

She considered confessing to Ted what happened with Truman, but what would be the point? It would only serve to relieve her conscience and cause her husband pain. What happened with Truman on Nantucket will never happen again, that's how she rationalizes keeping this from him now. It was a moment of weakness, a lapse in reason, and she begins each day with a renewal of her vow to try her best with Ted. Some days are better than others. Some days, she believes they'll succeed in making their marriage work, and that makes it possible for her to live with her secret.

Ted's taken several overnight business trips over the past couple of months, and she needs these breaks from him. In the past, she would anxiously await his return, but now she finds she breathes a little easier while he's away. He checks in with her several times a day when he's gone, Skyping with the family every night, and calling her before bed. He's trying to assure her of his fidelity by staying connected during his absences. She's told him repeatedly the constant contact is not necessary. She has to learn to trust him and these trips are a part of his livelihood. What she hasn't told him is how little time she spends wondering what he's doing or who he's with while he's away.

Her husband talks openly about the position he frequently finds himself in and how it feels when temptation is flung at him. As it's been since the beginning of their relationship, women are ready and willing to take him to bed. He said every time a woman comes on to him, he thinks of the first time they made love on Nantucket, that feeling of being truly connected to her, and it's enough for him to resist temptation. If the woman sticks around, he pulls out a picture of his family and bores her to tears with stories about them.

Libby cringed when he mentioned making love on Nantucket. It was a beautiful experience, but she'll forever associate the island with Truman. And while she appreciates Ted's candor on the topic of temptation, she's wondered on more than one occasion if she'd feel better about her indiscretion if Ted fell off the proverbial wagon just once.

Then she remembers his four-year affair with Caroline and his numerous one-night-stands and feels better about her own lapse in judgment. What she did with Truman, while morally wrong, doesn't come close to the level of Ted's betrayal...*does it?*

Returning home from vacation and having to dive head first into real life was a difficult transition for all of them, but they've adjusted. Ted is learning to delegate at the office, releasing his vice grip on the reins and allowing the senior associates to take the lead on important campaigns. It's freed up his weekends and they spend a lot of quality time strengthening their family bonds.

Since leaving Nantucket, that's become Libby's true focus, to create a solid family unit. This is where their success lies at this point. Working on their family helps distract her from mourning the family she lost when Truman and the girls moved away.

*

The weekend after Truman's visit to Nantucket, Ginger found a stack of Libby's photographs on her desk in the study. Libby had brought her camera into town to have the images blown up into 8x10 inch prints, her up close and personal studies of people in everyday situations, a glimpse into the real lives of others. Ginger was awestruck.

"Libby, these are phenomenal. I had no idea you were this good. I mean, I know you take beautiful portraits, but you've taken your work to an entirely different level! This is art!"

She shrugged in response. She loves taking photographs and despite the obsessive nature of her hobby and fixation on some of her subjects, is happy to have a creative distraction, something to occupy her time and help her process her feelings.

"You have to do something with these," Ginger exclaimed. "Ted! Have you seen her photos?"

Ted joined them at the table where Ginger had spread out the photographs and picked up several pictures of Will and Julia's family.

"Who are these people?" he asked, holding a picture of Will and Liam standing near the bluffs, his arm wrapped around his son's shoulders with their backs to the camera.

"Ted, you're missing the point," Ginger snapped. "These pictures tell a story...can't you see? Look at this one...and this!" She points to the images of Will and Julia. "This set here is a love story. And look at these candid shots on the beach! Libby these are fantastic! Ted, you're married to an artist!"

"They are really good, Libby," he smiled and squeezed her hand.

"Oh my God!" Ginger cried in frustration. "Am I the only one who sees how special these are? I have loads of friends in the art world. I'm going to show them these prints. Do you have more?"

She's serious? Libby thought, her eyes narrowing. *Are they really good enough for a gallery?*

"Ginger...I have thousands."

Together, she and Ginger sat for days, going through stacks of Libby's prints, selecting what they agreed were the most interesting and dramatic shots from "Love Story" as she dubbed the contractor's family shots, and "Sconset" her candid beach photos.

It was the perfect distraction. Focusing on this task left almost no time to think about Truman, and gave her an excuse to spend less time with Ted that weekend.

The next time Julia brought Will his lunch, Libby gave them a set of her photographs and asked permission to use their images. Julia and Will sorted through the prints and had tears in their eyes when they thanked her for capturing their feelings for one another and their family on 'film.' She was very moved by their reaction, and pleased they gave their permission.

Later that week, Ginger emailed a few contact sheets to some friends of hers in New York, Providence and Boston and the response was immediate. All of a sudden, Libby had appointments set up to meet with different gallery owners in all three cities and her new career as a photographer was born, quite by accident.

"We've never seen anything like these!"

"You're looking at the average American from a completely new perspective!"

"What is your inspiration? Amazing, just amazing!"

She doesn't understand what everyone is so excited about. She takes pictures of average, everyday people, doing nothing special. Just being themselves. Nothing posed, nothing fake. Just real life.

Apparently, truth is fresh, new, and exciting! *Has it really come to this?* How very sad.

❄

Libby's first gallery opening is tomorrow night and she and Ginger are driving to New York City later today, staying at her friend's townhouse in Murray Hill. Ted can't come to her big opening, between his clients and the children. Libby asked Ginger to come for moral support. "I wouldn't miss it if you paid me!" Ginger cried. "You'll be the toast of New York!"

Their lives are about to get more complicated with these new demands on Libby's time. Ted has already expressed his concern that she's spreading herself too thin. Since they returned from Nantucket, she's been out of the house more than ever before, preparing for her opening and giving interviews.

A few weeks ago, Libby rented a small studio around the corner from Ted's office so she could work without distraction while the kids are in school. Once she's home from work, her focus shifts entirely to their family. Those few hours together at night are sacred and the foundation on which Libby and Ted are rebuilding their relationship. The kids come first. That's the golden rule in their house. Projects, deadlines be damned.

Libby runs out to her car to find her planner and watches as her new neighbors pull into Truman's driveway. She will never get used to the sight of strangers living in his house. The first time she laid eyes on them, she stopped in her tracks and felt the wind knocked out of her. She stood immobile as a pretty, young, twenty-something woman climbed out of her shiny new Audi and bounced over to introduce herself.

That's when it hit her. *Truman and the girls are really gone.*

She doesn't keep in touch with Truman directly. Ginger has become the conduit of any important news. She knows he's teaching night classes at the community college in web development, and volunteering at the prison to teach non-violent offenders a new and useful skill. She's proud of him. He's doing good works in the community and there aren't too many people she can say that about, herself included. Truman has inspired her to find a way to instill this value in her children.

Social media has proven to be a blessing. Not only did it spark her interest in taking honest pictures, but it's her only remaining connection to Truman. They became Facebook 'friends' when he joined last year and since Ted has no interest in social media, she hasn't changed the status quo. Neither has Tru.

Since she last saw him, he's been posting pictures of the girls regularly. He hadn't posted a single picture before then, so she knows he's doing it for her. She misses them so much and is grateful to catch glimpses into their new lives. Libby does the same for him, posting pictures of George, Nate and Emma, leaving herself and Ted completely out of her newsfeed.

She's been tempted on more than one occasion to 'like' or comment on one of his posts, to send him an instant message when she sees he's online. She's typed the words, her pinky hovering over the enter key countless times, her heart pounding against her ribcage. *I miss you Truman.* But she stops herself, slamming her laptop shut. Nothing good can come of sharing her feelings with him. It would only confuse the situation.

According to Ginger, Truman started dating a nice woman a few weeks ago. They were having coffee when she shared this news and Libby froze mid-sip and turned to Ginger. Swallowing hard, she felt her ears grow hot and excused herself. Sitting in the bathroom stall, she took deep breaths in and out, getting control of her emotions before rejoining Ginger. Her friend didn't say a word, just patted her hand sympathetically when she returned to the table. Libby knew Truman wouldn't wait for her, nor did she ask him to. But it hurt all the same. He's moving on…just as he should be.

There's no escaping her memories in Littleton. Truman is always with her, but she's had to lock the memory of their day on Nantucket away in the farthest corner of her mind. It's the only way she's been able to move forward with Ted.

But that afternoon, after Ginger told Libby about Truman dating, she took a walk down to the water and unlocked the door to the forbidden memory. She laid in the sand, staring up at the clouds and remembered every touch, every feeling, every sound…and cried. Her resolve to rebuild her marriage was dangerously brittle, and as she walked home, Libby longed to break her commitment to stay.

When she entered the house, she found her family in the kitchen. Ted was alternating between feeding the baby, helping Nate and Emma with their homework and preparing dinner, and she couldn't fail to acknowledge how far they'd come in such a short period of time.

Ted smiled when he saw her standing in the doorway and Libby knew in her heart she wasn't going anywhere. She needs to throw away the key to the memory of her last day with Truman, and never reopen it again. It was too beautiful and too painful.

CHAPTER TWENTY-THREE

O ver Thanksgiving weekend, Libby and Ted bring the children to the Christmas tree farm to cut down the tree they tagged a while back. This is the first time Ted has ever been part of this experience. For the past six years, Truman and the girls came on this excursion and it's odd to be here without them. She has mixed feelings about Ted's presence. She's thrilled for the children; they're so excited their father is here, but she feels like she's somehow betraying Truman. This was their tradition, not Ted's. *It's time for new traditions*, she thinks, and forces a smile on her face.

Once the tree is chopped and bagged, Ted and a farm worker struggle to tie it to the roof of her car and Libby takes the kids inside the little shop next door for hot chocolate.

George is getting so big. He's eight months old and crawling up a storm, getting into everything. This shop is filled with knickknacks. Glass ornaments hang on low branches of the Christmas tree in the corner of the small store and a train chugs along the tracks below it. She can't let him out of her arms, it would be a disaster!

What's taking him so long? she wonders as they wait for Ted to join them. Her patience is wearing thin today and she's dying to get home and hopefully squeeze in a nap with George.

Yesterday was particularly trying for her. They spent Thanksgiving at Maureen's house with the rest of Ted's siblings and their spouses and kids. In the past, Libby enjoyed Fitzgerald family gatherings, felt loved and accepted by the clan...but that lovin' feeling is fading fast.

With the exception of Doris, Libby hadn't seen any of the Fitzgerald's for months, until Ted moved back into the house. And while Maureen had plenty to say when Libby kicked Ted out, her sister-in-law has been surprisingly mute on the subject of their reconciliation.

Libby is dreading going back to Maureen's on Christmas Day. Ted's siblings drew the line in the sand the moment Libby filed divorce papers back in February. Their brother can do no wrong in their eyes and they brushed Ted's bad behavior under the rug, expecting her to roll with the punches.

"He's human, Lib," his brother Matt said to her yesterday. "People make mistakes, right?" Matt rested his hands on her shoulders and looked into her eyes. "We're family, Libby, and family sticks together. Good times and bad."

In other words, the next time Ted sleeps with someone else, look the other way. If it weren't for Doris, Libby would have lost it. Her mother-in-law smacked Matt upside the head and admonished the group at large.

"Mind your own fuckin' business, Matty," Doris hissed. "That's the last I want to hear out of any of you, do you hear me? This is between Libby and Ted. Period."

She's grateful for Doris' support but is so angry at her other in-laws for drawing ranks around Ted, and for somehow making her the villain in this scenario!

In the space of one year, Libby has become an outsider in her neighborhood and her family, and has lost her best friend and surrogate daughters. If it weren't for her new career and the people she's met as a result, she'd feel completely isolated. This holiday season can't end soon enough for her.

Five minutes later Ted walks into the Christmas shop, his face drawn...angry even.

"What's the matter?" she whispers in his ear.

He lifts George from her arms and sets him down on his lap.

"I just saw Tru and the girls. They're outside now," he grumbles.

Her heart jumps in her chest. *They're right outside!* She hasn't laid eyes on Truman since they said goodbye on Nantucket. It's been even longer since she's seen the girls. She bites her lip and looks toward the exit. She misses Sadie and Bette. She misses Truman. *Just go, Libby, before Ted can stop you!* the voice in her head shouts, but she silences it and closes her eyes.

"Did something happen?" she asks.

"No, it's fine. Tru said 'hi' and turned away, Sadie gave me the stink eye, and Bette asked for you and the kids."

She swallows hard, her body twitching, ready to sprint out the door.

"I want to see them," she whispers, and he shoots her a fierce look. "The girls, Ted. I want to see the girls."

"We need to leave," he says, his eyes cold. "Now."

She touches his arm, squeezing it through his thick Irish woolen sweater and considers arguing the point, but who would it serve? The kids would love to see the Whitakers, but this would be for her. And what if Truman is outside with his girlfriend? She couldn't handle seeing him with another woman.

She holds her husband's hand in hers and sighs. Ted's gruff behavior is his way of masking pain; she's learned that over the past few months. The only thing she would achieve by insisting they go outside to see them, is spoil this family outing. She won't be responsible for ruining their day, this is so important to the children.

"Okay," she says and kisses his cheek. "Let's go."

He turns to her, his face flooding with relief.

"Really?" he asks, his eyes softening, meeting hers.

"Yes," she smiles weakly. "Let's leave."

❄

Later that evening, Libby and Ted sit in front of the fireplace in the living room, enjoying the fruits of their labor. She loves the smell of a freshly cut Christmas tree and takes in deep breaths of its rich aroma. The tree is decorated, strung with little white lights and ornaments they've collected throughout the years, many of them made by the children.

Thankfully, Ted was able to put his collision with Truman's family aside and enjoy the night, and she's done her best to put them out of her mind. When they pulled out of the tree farm, Libby caught sight of Truman with the girls lugging their tree to his car. She tried not to stare, aware Ted's eyes were on her, and forced herself to look away.

"I love you, Libby," Ted said as they waited at the stop sign at the tree farm.

"I love you too," she replied and leaned in for a kiss.

Her children have thrived having their father around. Ted's been attending their school performances, soccer games, and even made it to Emma's piano recital last week. They spend a lot of time together discussing school and friends at the dinner table.

If she'd left Ted last summer, none of this would've been possible. Watching Nate and Emma interact with their father, seeing the warmth and growth of their relationship, makes everything she's sacrificed worthwhile.

The kids went to bed a little while ago, and they've taken the opportunity to snuggle up under a blanket on the couch and simply relax together. They never made the time to do this before last summer. Ted was either working or at some event and she was focused on household responsibilities. She's come to enjoy their quiet time together.

Yawning, Libby sets her book down on the coffee table and wraps her arm around Ted's waist, and as she's closing her eyes, catches a glimpse of someone or something outside their living room window. With a start, she sits upright, startling Ted.

"What's the matter, honey," he asks.

"I think someone's outside the window," she says, her heart racing.

"Stay here," he commands, and grabs the baseball bat he keeps handy in the coat closet, then walks out the back door.

She holds the phone close to her, ready to dial 911 at any sign of distress. A few minutes later, as she's on the verge of panic, Ted walks in with Sadie, her eyes downcast, his face resigned. Libby's mouth drops and she runs over to them, wrapping her arms around Sadie. The girl is frozen through!

"Sadie, what are you doing here? It's after ten o'clock!"

"I had to get out of there," she says, her voice soft.

"Your mom's?" Libby asks. It's Friday night and she's supposed to be at Caroline's.

"I can't stand her. She wants me to act like her and be like her. I can't do anything right! Why would I want to be like her?" Sadie turns to Ted, her eyes narrowing. "She's not exactly a positive role model. All she thinks about is herself and her new boyfriend."

Libby raises an eyebrow and shoots her husband a look. *You know how to pick them, Ted!*

"Why didn't you call your dad? He would have come to get you."

"I hate Bayside. I don't have any friends there, it's awful! I just want to come home. Why can't I come home?" she cries.

"I'm so sorry you're unhappy, sweetheart, but you can't run away from your parents. Your mother must be sick with worry. Wait! How did you get here?"

"I took the bus from Kennedy Plaza to the center of town...then I walked."

Libby takes a deep breath in, then leads Sadie to the couch. She walked three miles from the bus route in the freezing cold to come back home. But there's no home to come back to. Her heart aches for this child. Of all the children, Truman's and hers, Sadie is the most like her; sensitive, artistic, quiet, and reserved.

She wraps Sadie up in a blanket and holds her close, while Ted stands over them, his eyebrow raised. He lifts his palms up, his face questioning, *what are you doing?*

I'll tell you what I'm doing, Ted, I'm comforting my daughter! But she can't say that, he wouldn't understand. She's never discussed the special relationship she has with Truman's daughters with him. Libby's longed to see them over the past few months, but hasn't wanted to bring up such a sensitive subject during this critical period in their marriage. But Sadie's here now, and she's not going to turn her away.

"Ted, can you get us some hot chocolate, please?" she asks. "With a few marshmallows in Miss Sadie's."

He stands in front of them for another moment, then shakes his head and walks into the kitchen.

"Sadie, I have to call your mom."

"She hasn't even noticed I'm gone. Look."

Libby takes Sadie's phone and scrolls through her recent calls. She's right. Caroline hasn't called once. Was Sadie hoping her mother would notice? Is this a cry for attention? Plea for attention or no plea, what kind of mother doesn't realize her daughter is missing from home for hours?

Sadie must have left her house between seven and eight to get here at this time. She's fourteen! Is Caroline that clueless? What if some psycho caught sight of this lovely girl on the bus and followed her through the dark streets, forcing her into the woods? The thought makes her nauseous.

"Sadie, that was so dangerous. You could have been kidnapped, assaulted, hit by a drunk driver. Anything! Promise me you'll never do anything like this again!" she pulls her closer and Sadie rests her head against her chest, snuggling against her, just like she used to when she was Nate's age. "You can always call your dad, and if he's not around, then you call me. Do you understand?"

Ted enters the room with the hot chocolate and sets it down on the coffee table.

"Libby, can you come here for a moment?"

"I'll be right back, Sade."

"What's the plan?" Ted asks once they're in the dining room. "Are we calling Caro or Truman? She can't stay here, Libby."

"I think we should call Tru. He can deal with Caroline."

"And when he gets here?" Ted asks, his eyes narrowing.

"Well..." she hesitates. "Then I sit with them and we talk it out."

"Without me?" he asks.

"Yes, Ted...without you. That would be a bit much, don't you agree?" Ted lowers himself onto a chair and runs his fingers through his hair. "Look, Ted...I love those children as much as my own. I've kept my distance from them for you, for our marriage, but I miss them so much. You can't ask me to stop caring about them."

"You miss the girls? Or is it Truman you miss?" he snaps. "Truman you care about?"

"Are you that insecure?" she asks, her voice incredulous. "It's over with Truman. I haven't spoken to him in months. You have to trust me just as I trust you when you're away from home."

"Do you miss him?" he asks, his voice soft.

"Do you want the truth?" she asks, eyebrows raised. He nods, his face softening. "Of course I miss him. We were friends for years, Ted. I've made sacrifices to make this marriage work. Don't ask me to sacrifice my relationship with the girls. I can't do it. I won't do it. They need me and I need them."

"How can that possibly work without you spending time with Truman?" he asks.

"I don't know, but we're grown ups. I'm sure we can figure something out. I'm not leaving you out of this, Ted. Whatever scenario we come up with, I'll run it by you before I agree, but you have to trust me."

"Fine," he says, pouting.

♂

Sadie! What were you thinking? Truman bears right onto the highway, driving toward Littleton. He was finishing dinner with a fellow professor, a woman he's been dating for a couple of months. He knows it's rude, but he keeps his phone on the table in case of emergencies. When his phone lit up, he saw the caller was Libby and his heart stopped for an instant. Something must be horribly wrong for her to call him this late on a Friday night, to call him at all for that matter! He mumbled an excuse and went outdoors for privacy.

"Sadie's here," she said. "She ran away from Caroline's and showed up at my house about a half hour ago. She's fine. Cold, but fine."

"She ran away?" he asked, in shock. *She's in Littleton? How?* He knows Sadie's unhappy, and she hates staying with her mother...but to run away and go to Libby's? "Let me talk to her."

"Before I put her on the phone...I thought you should know Caroline doesn't realize she's missing. Sadie said she left at seven when Bette went into the den to watch a movie. That was over three hours ago."

His anger rose quickly, the heat spreading from his stomach up to his neck and face. *Fucking Caro! How could she not notice our daughter's missing?* Sadie has complained all Caro does is hang out with her new boyfriend, sticking them in front of the television while she does *who knows what* with his daughters in the next room!

"I'll be there as soon as possible," he said and hung up before he could talk to Sadie, dialing Caro immediately.

His call went directly to voicemail. She has her daughters two nights a week! Can't she save date night for one of the other five?

Unfuckingbelievable, he muttered under his breath and headed back inside to explain the situation to his date. Barbara was very understanding, having two teenage daughters herself. Truman paid the bill and offered to bring her home, but she shooed him out.

"I'll grab a cab," she said, smiling sympathetically. "Just go. I'll talk to you soon."

Barbara is the first woman he's met in a long time who's sparked any interest in him, and she came along at just the right time. He needed a distraction, someone to help get his mind off Libby.

Barbara's smart, funny, attractive and has been divorced for five years. She has a stable career, one that doesn't consume her every waking moment, and her life is uncomplicated. Truman likes that most of all. No feelings to sort through, no animosity left between she and her ex-husband. Her daughters are typical teenagers, but she appears to have a close relationship with them. How refreshing!

They're having a good time, but no matter what he's doing, Libby lurks in the back of his mind. He doesn't know how to stop the invasion of memories. Maybe he shouldn't have made love to her? But holding her in his arms, feeling her body pressed against his, he didn't want to stop. He wanted to make love to the woman he loves. Maybe that was selfish of him, but no matter how many times he questions his actions, he can't bring himself to regret it, nor does he feel one ounce of guilt. Saying goodbye to her that night at the ferry terminal was poignant; an ending and a beginning.

Moving to Bayside was the best thing he could have done...for himself, and Bette is adjusting to her new school and making friends, just as he knew she would. But Sadie...he knows how much she misses Littleton, how angry she is with him for not working things out with Libby.

She needs a mother figure now more than ever and Caroline is a disaster. He's in constant damage control mode, trying to repair whatever psychological trauma his ex-wife is causing. He can't count the number of arguments they've had about accepting Sadie for who she is, but Caro doesn't get it. She just doesn't understand how to love her daughter unconditionally. Sadie has given up trying to please her mother, seeing Caro for the shallow, self-absorbed woman she is. At this point, he thinks it's a good thing his daughter has released herself from Caroline's impossible standards. Unfortunately, that hasn't been enough to turn things around for his sweet Sadie.

Truman's doing what he can to help his daughter, but it's not enough. He's trying to be both mother and father to her, and failing miserably. It's Libby she misses, Libby who mothered her, Libby she wants to be with during this difficult time in her life. And that's the one thing he can't do for her. He can't wave a magic wand and turn Libby into her mother. *What a mess!* he thinks as he pulls into the Fitzgerald's driveway.

Shifting the car into park, he tries Caroline one more time, and when it goes to voicemail again, he sends her a text message. **Sadie is with me. Great job, Caro.** He presses send and throws the phone onto the passenger seat before opening the car door.

He hasn't been to Littleton since he moved in mid-August. Turning in a slow circle, he looks around the neighborhood he called home for so long and shakes his head. He feels so disconnected from this place and the fourteen years he lived here. Except for this house…he looks up at Libby's home, and sighs. *There's no disconnect here*, he thinks.

Libby opens the door before he can knock and for just a moment they stand in the doorway, their eyes locked. A wave of sadness washes over him, but he takes another deep breath in and smiles.

"Hi," she says and kisses him lightly on the cheek. "She's in the den."

His heart pounds against his ribcage as he follows Libby through the living room, wondering where Ted is, and how he reacted when his daughter showed up on their doorstep.

Sadie is curled up on the couch, a blanket wrapped around her, sipping hot chocolate. She looks down into her mug, her demeanor guilty, then up through her long eyelashes, trying to gauge his reaction. Truman shakes his head then sits beside her, and hugs his daughter tightly. *I'm so sorry, baby...I wish things were different.* Sadie clings to him for a minute then pulls away.

"Are you mad at me?" she asks.

"I'm furious!" he exclaims, then holds her against him again. A moment later, he sits back against the couch, holding her hand in his. "And relieved, sweetheart. I'm so relieved you're safe. I don't know what I'd do if anything happened to you. You could have called me! I'm always a phone call away, remember?"

"I didn't want to go back to Bayside. I wanted to come home."

Truman inhales sharply, her words, a kick in the stomach. *Oh, Jesus.* He turns to Libby, who has taken a seat in the armchair across from them, and her eyes are sympathetic.

"I've explained to Sadie she's welcome here anytime. I'm just a phone call away as well."

His brow furrows and he tilts his head, staring into Libby's eyes.

"Sade, could you give me and Libby a minute, please?"

She looks at both of them and he catches the faintest glimmer of a smile before she nods and leaves the den. His eyes narrow, following her out of the room. *Did she do this on purpose? Was this an attempt to bring us back together?* That's a conversation for another time.

"Libby, thank you for offering...but you don't have to do this. I know what an awkward position Sadie has put you in, and I apologize if this has caused any tension between you and Ted."

"I've already spoken to Ted about this. I miss my girls, Truman," she whispers. "I want to see them."

He sits back against the cushions and studies her face.

"Ted's agreed to this?" he asks, more than a little surprised.

She nods. "The girls are important to me. I'm hoping we can figure something out, an arrangement that works for us all. I get to see the girls and you can spend time with my kids."

Leaning forward, he blinks back his tears and runs his fingers through his hair. *What's the catch?*

"His only request...is that I don't spend time with you," she says, looking down into her lap.

He nods his head. *That's the catch.* But it's better than nothing. At least he'll be part of the children's lives. He'll be able to spend time with George. Resting his head in his hands, he considers how incredibly odd this is, agreeing to create a visitation schedule for their children.

"As for Sadie...I'd like her to help me out at my studio after school when she can. She's a wonderful artist, Tru. Really gifted. I want to encourage her, expose her to other artists. A girl like Sadie sticks out like a sore thumb at a preppy school like Bayside. Even here in Littleton, with kids she's known forever, the past few years in middle school have been difficult on her. She doesn't fit in, and she thinks that's a bad thing."

He sighs, nodding his head. Libby's right.

"Tru, I know what it's like to be the outcast at school, but she needs to know she's not alone. There are lots of kids like her in other schools. I've done a little research and there are alternative high schools for a creative person like Sadie. I want to see her grow and thrive, not shrink and fade into the background, biding her time until she can escape. Please let me help her do that."

Why didn't I consider this option? He's never had to do this alone before. He had Libby to bounce ideas off of...until he didn't. He misses being able to talk things out with her more than anything.

"I love her, Tru. It's killing me to know she's suffering. We've stayed in touch since you moved. She's so unhappy and I want to be here for her."

"She wants that too. She misses you," he pauses, looking down at his hands. *I miss you.* "Thank you, Libby."

"And Truman...Sadie is old enough to decide whether she wants to spend weekends with Caroline. Bette, too, for that matter. If Caro's not up to the task of being a mother to the girls...fight for them. I'm not saying they shouldn't see her at all, but this is unacceptable. Our girls deserve better."

♀

Truman and Sadie pull out of the driveway and Libby waves, flooded with relief. That went much better than she expected. She's been dying to have this discussion with Truman, and at last she's had the opportunity. It was difficult to sit so close to him, yet feel so far away. Ted may not have been in the room physically, but his presence occupied every corner of the space.

Sighing, she closes the door to find Ted standing behind her, his face red with anger.

"Libby, what the fuck are you doing? I felt like an idiot, standing outside the door listening to you two discussing Sadie's future. 'Our girls deserve better'...You...talking like you're her mother, making important life decisions for that child with Truman. Jesus Christ, Libby! She's not your daughter! Is this how it's been all of these years? You and Truman parenting our children? His children?"

She can't believe her ears. He's tumbling over his words, hardly making sense...but she caught the last few sentences, and she's pissed. *How dare he?*

"Yes, Ted. That's exactly how it was for many years. You weren't around, neither was Caroline. Hmmm...maybe you two were somewhere having sex while we had the 'oh so fun job' of raising our children! I can't believe you! All those years you were hardly home, Truman was here having dinner with us and carpooling our kids to practices. Where were you?"

Ted turns away from her, but she grabs his arm.

"No, Ted. You need to hear this. Truman and I were a team. We parented together. It was either that or do it alone. If the kids were having problems, we discussed them. He was involved in our lives and the children were our focus, every single day. We talked about how they were doing in school, if they were having issues with other kids. Truman and I were in the trenches together. Do you have any idea how much I depended on him? Do I need to remind you *why* I depended on him? That man was always there when I needed him. I wish I could say the same about you."

"So...what you're saying is Truman was more of a husband to you and father to our children than I was," he says.

"Ummm...yeah!" she nods her head in agreement. "Absolutely...for many years he was."

"Well, fuck it, Libby! If I was such a shitty husband and father, why'd you stay? You know what? Sounds to me like you two were the ones having the affair! Why didn't you leave me for Mr. Wonderful years ago?"

"There was no need, Ted. Why do that when I could have my cake and eat it too?" she sneers, and storms out of the den.

CHAPTER TWENTY-FOUR

S he never thought Ted was an insecure person. His confidence was borderline arrogant, but in the five months since their fight Thanksgiving weekend, she's seen another side of her husband. She said some hurtful things that night after Truman and Sadie left...but they were also true. Was he really so shocked to discover Truman had been a surrogate father and husband while he was away? Ted was worse than away...he was absent.

Now, Ted questions everything. *Where is she? Who is she with? When will she be home? What is she doing?* She's being held accountable for her every waking breath and is suffocating under his blanket of insecurity. She's not sure if it's because she's having indirect contact with Truman and spending time with Sadie and Bette, or because her career has taken off. Maybe it's a combination of everything? She doesn't know what exactly sparked these feelings in him, but she's had enough!

Since her first small show in New York in October, the art community has warmly received her work, showering her with accolades and attention, and none of it would've been possible without Ginger. Her friend has pulled every string imaginable, using her influence to get Libby into the best galleries, meetings with the right people and interviews with the big magazines. She's not used to this attention but she's watched 'the master' in action for years and has learned a thing or two about working a room.

Ted's never had any reason to be jealous of anyone before Truman. At every business function he's dragged her to over the past fifteen years, she's practically hid in the corner once introductions were made. But now, Libby's in the limelight and men are paying attention to her. She doesn't read anything into their flirtations. She's turning forty-two in six months, has crows feet, grey hairs and a baby pouch she doesn't care enough about to get rid of. Being flirted with at her age is an ego boost, nothing more.

While she's being fêted, Ted's star has dimmed. He doesn't like being the spare wheel, he doesn't appreciate being talked over by people who have no interest in politics. She tries to include him in conversation at these events, but in this world, Ted's out of his depth and he's never been there before. Libby has lived there her entire life, and is relieved to find she can comfortably navigate these new surroundings.

She wants her husband to be part of the exciting things happening in her life, but can't force him to take an interest in her work or the people she's met along the way. It's discouraging. She's proud of her work and appreciates the recognition its received, but she doesn't need stroking the way Ted does.

The other night, Ted accompanied Libby to a dinner party consisting of people she's become friendly with in the art world and their significant others. Her husband sat across the table from her and for once, seemed to be enjoying himself. Libby's new agent monopolized her conversation most of the evening. Max Vandermark is an old friend of Ginger's who has taken over the publicity and arrangements for her shows, quickly proving himself to be a godsend.

On the drive home, Ted was quiet, but when they pulled into the driveway, he accused Max of coming on to her and demanded she look for another (female) agent. She burst out laughing at the absurdity of his request. Max is a very handsome man, but if Ted had taken the time to talk to him, he would have realized rather quickly Max is gay.

That news silenced his griping and they ended up having a good laugh. But in retrospect…it's not funny. If Max was straight, Ted would have insisted she find a new agent, she would have refused and it would've gotten ugly. He needs to get a grip on his jealousy.

"Why don't you trust me?" she asked the following evening.

"I trust you, Libby. It's these men I don't trust," he answered.

"You know, Ted, it is possible for a man and woman to converse and not have ulterior motives," she countered.

"Baby," Ted chuckled. "You don't know men very well at all, do you?"

She shook her head and sighed. *Not all men are like you, Ted.*

❋

George turned one last month, and this weekend marks one year since the marathon bombing. The experience was horrifying and surreal, and she still has difficulty processing what happened that day. It was a life changing event and also the turning point in her relationship with Truman. She knew when she stepped into the bathroom in that hotel nothing would ever be the same, and she was right. Her entire world has changed in the space of a year; both good and bad.

Time is passing too quickly. Emma and Bette are almost twelve, Nate just turned eight, Sadie turns fifteen next month.

They're growing up so fast. Sadie transferred to an alternative school in Providence a few months ago and joins Libby at the studio often. Sadie's found her tribe and takes the bus across town to Libby's studio regularly with her new friends. She loves having them there while she works. They're good kids and are staying out of trouble. That's all she could hope for.

The girls now have a more flexible schedule with Caroline. Bette spends every other weekend with her mother, and both girls have dinner with Caroline mid-week. Truman didn't have to fight too hard for this new arrangement. Caroline felt horrible after Sadie ran away and capitulated at the mere mention of a custody battle. She knew she would lose.

Her 'trial year' with Ted is up in two months. The first five months they made so much progress, but they flat lined around the holidays, and are still not where she'd like them to be. Dr. Bradford was right about the deadline. It's putting too much pressure on them both and the timeframe isn't as important to her as it once was, but she needs to see some more progress soon.

Libby feels partly responsible for their stagnation. She's been so busy with work she hasn't made as much of an effort to move their relationship forward. Again, she finds they get wrapped up in the details of their lives. It's a never ending cycle. Work and children, work and children. Ted's more involved in the children's lives than he's ever been. That's something. It's another building block. She'll take all she can get.

＊

This evening, Libby attended an artist's opening with Ginger in Newport for a painter she's become friendly with over the past few months. Wendela creates miniature portraits with brilliant jewel colored oil paints, reminiscent of Renaissance artists. Libby loves her work and even though it's a school night, agreed to attend this opening as a show of support, leaving Ted in charge of the nighttime routine. She hopes the kids are actually in bed by the time she gets home, that would be progress. Bedtime routines are not Ted's forté.

Around eleven o'clock, Ginger drops Libby off at home, and she walks into a blessedly quiet house. Not a creature was stirring, not even a mouse. She is pleasantly surprised and smiles as she shrugs off her coat, hanging it in the closet, then heads toward the kitchen for a glass of water. Flicking on the island lights, she jumps back, stifling a scream when she finds Ted sitting at the counter.

"Jesus, Ted!" she cries. "Why are you sitting in the dark?"

He looks down into his glass and shakes his head.

"Ted, what's the matter? Are the kids okay?"

"They're fine, Libby. We're all fine. Did you have fun tonight?" he asks, his voice tense.

"Yes, I did. How were the troops?" she asks, grabbing a glass out of the cupboard and pouring herself some water. "Did they give you any problems at bedtime?"

"Nope, I'm getting pretty good at the bedtime routine, been doing it a lot lately."

She raises an eyebrow. *What is that supposed to mean?* Unless she has a show of her own, she doesn't go out more than one night a week. Is he trying to start something? *Forget it, Ted, I'm not taking the bait.* She walks up behind him and wraps her arms around his waist, pressing her body against his back.

"Why don't we go to bed," she murmurs, kissing his neck.

"Libby...we need to talk about your schedule. This whole photography thing has gotten out of control."

She steps back, dropping her hands by her sides. *This whole photography thing?*

"I'm sorry? 'This photography thing' is my career, Ted. Every bit as much as being a political consultant is yours."

"I understand you're having fun and everything, but what about working on our marriage? I thought that was our number one priority? These past few months, I feel like you've forgotten that. You're so wrapped up in this new world...you're putting me and the kids last."

She stands frozen in place, trying to process his words. *Fun? Priorities? Last? Last!*

"Are you saying I'm neglecting my family?" she asks, incredulous. "Because I go out occasionally for work?"

"Yes, I am," he says. "We said we'd be honest with each other and I'm telling you how I feel."

"That's interesting, Ted. Does that mean when you go out for work at night you're neglecting us?" she asks. Ted raises an eyebrow in response. "By your definition then, you've neglected us for years. How can you even question where my priorities lie or my commitment to this marriage?"

"I think you enjoy all the attention you're getting. Can't you just stay home and be with us? Why do you have to go to galleries and give interviews? Aren't we enough for you?"

Is he kidding?

"What more do I have to do to prove I'm committed to our marriage, Ted? I gave up my first career and sacrificed years of my life helping you grow your business. Now you want me to give up something that fulfills me and brings me immense pleasure?" she asks, outraged. "That's not going to happen!"

"It was a hobby Libby. You enjoyed it as a hobby...why does it have to be more? I make more than enough money to support us. We don't need another income."

She stares at him, her eyes blank. *I don't fucking believe this.* It's okay for him to have a successful career, but not her? That's precisely what he's saying. What decade is this?

"Can't you just be happy for me? Do you think just because I'm out in the world enjoying a tiny bit of success that

I'm less of a wife and mother? We need to be able to balance work and family life, and I think we've been doing a pretty good job. I've never tried to hold you back professionally. How could you even suggest I give up my career?"

"Because we need you here, Libby! The kids need you, I need you."

"I am here, Ted! I've been here all along! You're as bad as every other man on this street! You want a 1950's housewife, someone who stays home all day, whose life revolves around her husband and children. That's not who I am, Ted. I never was. I just pretended to be so I could fit into this lifestyle. Well…not anymore! I hate living here and I don't want to be a stay at home wife and mother. When you met me I was none of those things and you loved me as I was. Well, I'm back. I'm more myself now than I've been in years. I feel alive, like I have purpose, something that's just for me. Don't I deserve that? Doesn't everyone?"

"So you admit what you're doing is selfish? Something just for you?" he asks.

She steps back, her mouth open, her brow furrowed in confusion.

"That's what you got from that whole speech? That I'm selfish?" she shakes her head and sighs. "I'm going to bed."

She turns and walks away, her head swimming with his accusations. *Have I been neglecting him? Or the children? Am I being selfish? NO! No, no, no.* He's the one being selfish, not to mention jealous. He can't stand that she's getting even a speck of attention. Ted hates fading into the background for even an hour. Well, tough shit! He either gets used to it or…*she can't go there.* Whenever she does, she fantasizes about leaving Ted. Every time they have an argument she can't help but wonder what her life would look like without him in it.

It's irrational. Married people argue occasionally, it's totally normal. Admittedly, they don't have a lot of experience in this department. In the past, she went along with whatever Ted wanted, what was there to fight about? Her husband needs to learn how to compromise and adapt. She's not the same person she was before George was born.

She checks in on the children, tucking them in, then gathers the dirty clothes off the floor and sticks it all down the laundry chute. Opening the door to the nursery, Libby picks up the toys scattered around the room and puts them away, then stands over George's crib, longing to pick him up and snuggle with him on the rocking chair.

My beautiful boy. He looks more like her brother, Charlie, every day. The same chestnut brown hair, the same blue eyes. She's hit by a wave of sadness, a sudden desire to talk to her brother. It's been so long. When she met Ted, she felt alone in the world and craved a sense of belonging to a family, but never tried to keep the one she had intact after her mother died. *Tomorrow...I'll call him tomorrow.* She lowers the railing on the crib and leans down to kiss her son.

Standing in the bathroom, she removes her dress, underwear and bra and stares at herself in the mirror. She hasn't worked out in so long...she turns side to side. Not too bad for a middle-aged mother of three. But she's under no illusions, her desirability rating has plummeted over the past five years. She's past her peak physically and is fine with that.

Maybe I'll take up yoga, she thinks. Something relaxing. She cares about her health, but she'll never feel the pressure of being inspected like a piece of meat again. There will always be a twenty or thirty something beauty in the room to outshine her, and that thought fills her with relief.

As she climbs into bed, she holds onto her pillow, trying to forget what Ted said in the kitchen, hoping he'll realize how ridiculous he's being. This is just an adjustment. He'll get used to her having a career of her own. She can be a wife and a mother and still pursue her own interests. He's feeling threatened right now. Instead of fearing Truman luring her away, he's afraid her career will. She can make the effort to stroke his ego a little more because a man like Ted needs to feel important. She is committed to their family. He would have to be blind not to see that.

♂

Truman has been dating Barbara for almost ten months. He cares about her and enjoys her company, but when she used the 'L' word last weekend, he couldn't bring himself to say it back. *Why?* She's smart, funny, and attractive. They have a great time when they're together, and a healthy sex life. What more could he ask for?

Maybe this is what grown up love looks like? He hasn't been in an actual relationship with anyone but Caroline in over twenty years. He's not a kid anymore. Expecting the intense rush of emotions, the tingling sensation, the longing to see that person whenever they aren't around, those are leftover expectations from his early twenties.

When he thinks long-term, he wants companionship and friendship. Sex is important too, but when he's eighty, he hardly thinks his sex life is going to be high on the priority list! He's not saying Barbara is the one he's going to spend the rest of his life with, but he isn't ready to cross her off the list, at least not until he figures out what's missing and if it's something he can live without.

Sitting in Libby's den that night back in November was difficult. He misses her friendship more than anything, misses having someone who loves and understands his children to bounce ideas off of. He took that for granted while they were living next door to one another. Whenever he had a problem with one of the girls he could depend on Libby to be there as a sounding board and knew she had their best interests at heart. As Ginger pointed out last spring, Libby was his surrogate wife. Caroline wasn't there, but Libby was.

It didn't happen overnight, their connection, but over time it grew. Her kids played with his kids, running from house to house. The family dinners began a month or two after Libby and Ted moved in. Backyard barbeques and clam boils evolved into sit down dinners alternating between the two houses year round, not every night, but a few nights each week, once they realized neither of their spouses was around at dinnertime. *Why not share the work and camaraderie? Why not form a hodgepodge family?*

And that bond only grew stronger in time. There was no one there to protest their growing friendship. Caro and Ted were doing their own thing, so he and Libby did theirs. It worked. Truman's heard it said that men and women can only be friends in large groups. Their group wasn't large, but Ginger's membership served as a buffer from most gossip. Other than lack of sex, his situation with Libby was ideal... while it lasted.

Maybe his marriage lasted as long as it did because of Libby and Ted? He and Caro were getting what they needed from their neighbors. Or maybe their marriage would have ended years earlier when his wife realized she married an average guy who put family above career.

Since his divorce, he's thought about trying to get back on the career path he abandoned two decades ago. But, it's too late in the game and he's been away from the field of oceanography for too long to get back into it now. He'd have to go back to school for his master's degree just to catch up with the whippersnappers finishing school and he'd be competing for jobs with kids half his age. No, that boat has sailed, and he's happy teaching computer science and volunteering at the women's prison.

Although Bayside is a lot like Littleton, he's stayed out of the social scene. He's renting a house in the downtown district and enjoys living near the shops and restaurants. Every morning after his run, he heads to the bagel shop and grabs coffee and a newspaper, sits for an hour or so, then prepares for his day. He moors his boat in town and has become friendly with the people who work at the marina, but other than that, he keeps to himself.

He's so grateful to Libby for opening his eyes to the root of Sadie's unhappiness and for suggesting alternate solutions for her education. When considering places to live, he always thought the reputation of the school system was most important, but he had blinders on, never considering what else was out there for his daughter. Schools are not one size fits all. He feels stupid not having realized it sooner. His square peg could never fit in a round hole, nor would he want her to. Now that he understands, he's done the research and is helping her find environments where she can thrive.

He has as little contact with Libby as possible, just what's necessary, per Ted's request. They make arrangements about pick up and drop off via text message, and communicate about Sadie via email. He picks George up on Mondays at Libby's studio and they spend five minutes together, transferring George's stuff from one car to the other. A few hours later, he brings the baby back to Littleton and leaves him with Nina. It's the way it has to be for now.

Maybe that's what's missing with Barbara? *History.* Truman and Libby have years of memories they've created together. That's not something he can snap his fingers and make magically appear with Barbara. It takes time. He didn't fall in love with Libby overnight. Maybe it's the same with Barbara? He just needs some time to get used to the idea.

CHAPTER TWENTY-FIVE

One year. She's trying not to keep the date in her head but it's stuck there. She held onto it for so long it's embedded in her brain. The day has crept up on them and tomorrow is the 'anniversary' of the day she chose Ted. Dr. Bradford was right, the year may be up, but she's not ready to make a decision about the future of her marriage. However, the deadline is looming, messing with her head.

A year ago she was ready to leave her husband, to make a future with Truman. All she had left to do was say the words. Just four little words kept her from a new life. *I want a divorce.* Maybe it was fate Ted decided to drive home from his conference the night before she left for Nantucket? She hadn't been able to say those words up until that point. Every time she tried, she panicked. But when he came home that night, she didn't have to say anything, he saw for himself how she felt about Truman. That was her opportunity to make the break, and Ted was still able to convince her to stay.

This year has been far from easy. For every two steps forward, she and Ted have taken another step back. The advent of her 'accidental career' ushered in a host of new issues for them to adjust and adapt to and has put a great deal of strain on their marriage.

Her husband resents her career. It's as simple as that. He resents every minute she spends in her studio, every interview she gives, every opening she attends, every second she is focused on anything other than him or their family. Ted doesn't want Libby's life to change at all. He wants her to remain exactly as she's been for the past sixteen years. And that's never going to happen.

She loves what she does. She loves being good at something and getting acknowledged for her work. She loves making money that's completely unrelated to Ted's business and she's not giving it up, no matter how uncomfortable it makes him. She's made enough sacrifices for him. Enough is enough!

Last night they had another argument about her schedule, the third this week. Marriage is about compromise, but Ted isn't willing to compromise when it comes to her career. She was in New York for two nights this week and oh, how he resents being home with the children while she's away! The hypocrisy! She's dealt with his absences for years. She spends a couple of nights away from home and you'd think she'd abandoned her family by his reaction.

There's nothing to do but laugh, which makes him angrier, but she's not afraid of pissing Ted off anymore. Maybe that's what he doesn't like? He doesn't have control over her. She's always been aware of how controlling he is in the office, but never thought it extended to their home life. She realizes now that his control was on the subconscious level. He didn't need to exert any energy or force to maintain it, they did his bidding without question. Until now.

She lost herself in her relationship with him once. It won't happen again. She's come too far and despite his claims to the contrary…she's not doing anything wrong. Dr. Bradford said it takes time for a man like Ted to accept change. It's been a battle for the past two months, but she perseveres with the hope her doctor is right. She's still committed to her marriage and family, but things aren't going as well as she'd hoped and her patience is wearing very thin.

It's getting late and she's just finishing up at the studio. Sadie left with Truman a little while ago and Libby picks up the project Sadie's been working on. She's created a collage of the city using different mediums to bring it to life. It's incredible. She's in awe of Sadie's talent.

Usually Truman sends Sadie a text and she meets him across the street. Today, Libby told her to invite him up to view her progress. It's the first time they've spent more than five minutes together since November, and she's glad he came upstairs. He was very interested to see her work and when she unveiled Sadie's piece…the look on his face was priceless. He was bursting with love and pride, hugging Sadie to him. He turned to Libby and mouthed the words, 'thank you,' and she got a bit teary and smiled.

Before Truman left, he studied the photographs hanging on the wall and those propped up on the floor around the room. Sadie showed him some of her favorite prints and he glowed with genuine pride over Libby's accomplishments, the polar opposite of Ted's indifference to her work.

"Libby, you're an amazing photographer. These are incredible," he said.

"Thanks, Tru. I have quite a few of you and the girls. I'll have to show you sometime."

The words tumbled from her lips and he seemed surprised by her offer, but she doesn't regret making it. *Do you remember what tomorrow is, Truman?* she wondered. *One year. One year ago I was lying in your arms. One year ago I made the decision to let you go.* His eyes locked with hers for a long moment and she knew he was thinking the same thing. He didn't forget. Truman broke eye contact before she did and cleared his throat.

"I'd like that. We'd better get going. Thank you, Libby."

She sat at her desk, looking out the window after they left, wondering what her life would be like now if she were with Truman, not Ted. Would she have embarked on this new career? Or would she have been so wrapped up in her new relationship, her latent aspirations would have fallen to the wayside?

More questions left unanswered. In her mind, she keeps traveling down the road not taken, but always winds up in the same place.

This room.

Looking around her little studio, at the prints hanging on the brick wall, the light coming in through the large windows, she feels satisfaction. This is hers. She created this business with her own talent (and Ginger's backing). It's not much. Five hundred square feet to call her own. She's kept the room sparse but comfortable, creating a hang out space for Sadie and her friends. A plush chocolate brown couch, a simple coffee table, two red upholstered chairs, a small refrigerator stocked with bottled water, seltzer and juice. A cupboard stocked with snacks. All Libby needs is her art table and stool, another desk for her computer, and a storage cabinet.

Smiling, she locks up the studio, then decides to walk over and see Ted, hoping they can smooth things over before going home. Libby wants to make peace with him. She hasn't changed her stance on traveling occasionally for work, but given the significance of tomorrow, she's willing to swallow her pride and apologize for her tone last night. *Compromise.* She won't apologize for the content, but she can apologize for the tone.

It's a Thursday night and the office is dark and quiet. The space seems empty, but Ted's car is still in the parking lot. Maybe they can grab something to eat before heading home? She hasn't eaten a thing since lunch and is ravenous. They dropped the kids off at summer camp last weekend and Nina is home with George so they have time for quick bite.

Heading down the hallway toward Ted's office, she hesitates, knowing in her gut something is off… Frowning, she tries to shake off the uneasy feeling and as she approaches his office, Libby finds Ted sitting in his chair with his head back, eyes closed.

And kneeling in front of him is Heather, his assistant, her mouth wrapped around him.

He didn't even close the blinds, she thinks leaning against his assistant's desk, watching her husband being serviced by this eager young woman. Libby takes a deep breath in and waits for them to finish, comfortably numb outside his office. *Yup, his back is arching, he'll be done soon.* She knows her husband well.

Libby lifts her camera from its case and points it toward them. *Ready. Aim. Fire.* She snaps a few shots of Ted's hands tangled in Heather's hair, his face as his breath quickens.

Just then Ted opens his eyes, looks directly at Libby and jumps, pushing Heather away from him, leaving her sprawled on his rug, his erection fading with each passing moment. Libby smiles and Ted struggles to pull himself together, while Heather rises, red-faced and humiliated. Libby hands Heather her purse and the young woman rushes out of the office, lowering her gaze as she exits.

She doesn't feel anything. Not depressed or angry. Neutral. She could have been watching a stranger for her lack of emotion. Why isn't she shocked or outraged? Why? Because she fully expected him to fall off the wagon one day. Ted needs to feel adored, and that ship sailed last year when she saw him having sex with Caroline. No matter what they've done to try and salvage their marriage, that blind adoration will never return, nor does she want it to. It caused her to live in a fantasy world for years, blind to his faults. She never wants to live in the dark, ignorant of the truth about anyone again.

One year. She honored her word and gave their marriage her best shot, for her children, for Ted, for herself. She did what she could to keep their family intact, but she can't sacrifice herself or her happiness for him. Libby will never be the doting wife who lived and breathed for her husband again. She's changed. Learning the truth about her marriage turned her into a stronger person, a more independent person and Ted wants the old Libby back.

She's never coming back. And Ted will never be the man she thought he was.

Libby walks down the hall to the small conference room and waits, staring out the window at the city skyline. A few minutes later, Ted enters the room, his jaw set, his posture defensive. She shakes her head and closes her eyes for a moment. *Is he really going to try and justify his behavior?*

"We never had sex," he says, sitting down in a huff, his arms folded across his chest.

"Please, Ted, don't go all 'Bill Clinton' on me. If you have any doubt in your mind what I think constitutes 'sexual relations' let me clarify. They include anything involving your penis and or someone's vagina. Blowjobs definitely fall in that category," she pauses and looks down at her hands, twisting her wedding band. "But this isn't about you and Heather."

"It didn't mean anything, Libby."

Seems she's heard that one before. The first seed of anger sprouts in her stomach. One year! She gave up an entire year of her life and sacrificed Truman...for what? For Ted? For a man who betrayed her for years? What possessed her to stay? What the fuck was she thinking?

"It never does, Ted," she pauses. "New rules. You're free to fuck whoever you want, whenever you want. How does that sound? You need to feed your ego to feel like a real man? Go ahead. You can take Heather right here on this conference table. I don't care."

"Libby, you're insane," Ted chuckles and settles back into his chair. He thinks she's kidding? He actually believes he can talk his way out of this one?

"Wait, Ted, I'm not done. While you're fucking other women, let me tell you what I'm going to do. I'm going to pick up where I left off last summer. What do you think about that?"

Ted's face clouds over, his jaw clenching, and he sits forward in his chair.

"You slept with Truman, didn't you?" he hisses. "I knew you were fucking lying."

Libby raises an eyebrow.

"Yes I fucking did," she smiles. "And it was the best sex I've had in my life."

Ted's jaw drops open, his face turning red, and he trembles with rage. That was definitely below the belt and he's feeling it.

"Feels pretty shitty, doesn't it?" she sneers.

He takes deep breaths in and out, his nostrils flared.

"I'm going to fucking kill him," he mutters under his breath.

"You appear to have forgotten that you fucked his wife for years," she laughs. "It's only fair he got a little action from me in return."

"Jesus, Libby!" he shouts, slamming his fists onto the conference room table. "Are you just messing with me now?"

"You'll never know," she says, rising. "You know what today is?"

He frowns in response, his brow furrowing.

"Today is the end of our little experiment. I gave you one year and it's up. It didn't work out like we'd hoped, but we gave it our best shot."

Ted sits up with a start, his face pained. With both palms pressed against the table, Libby rises and leans toward Ted, looking him directly in the eye.

"I want a divorce," she says, slowly, deliberately, leaving no room for interpretation.

At long last she's able to say those four little words and feels shockingly calm. She thought she'd feel more something…anger, pain, disgust, sadness? But no…what is this feeling?

This is relief.

"Come say goodnight to the baby, pack a bag and leave. I'm done."

She grabs her bag and walks toward the door, but Ted rushes forward, blocking her exit.

"Get out of my way, Ted," she says firmly. "I'm leaving now."

She couldn't be clearer, but he remains frozen in the doorway.

"Tell me the truth, Libby. Did you have sex with him?"

"I just told you our marriage is over and all you're worried about is whether I slept with Truman?" she asks, incredulous. "You're pathetic. Now get the hell out of my way."

He's too big a man for her to push aside. She picks up her phone and says, "You have till I count to three, then I'm calling the police."

His face transforms into an icy mask and she feels a knot of fear growing in her stomach.

"One," she says, her eyes locking with his.

If she's going down, she's going down fighting. Ted stands over her, trying to intimidate her, but Libby isn't budging.

"Two…" she begins to dial, and he reaches for her phone. "Don't you dare," she hisses, her heart racing. "I'll have you locked up if you lay one finger on me."

Still he doesn't move, but his face is softening, the first hints of regret registering.

"Three," she whispers, her eyes narrowing.

Just as she's dialing 911, Ted steps aside.

"Smart decision," she says. "You were bound to make one eventually."

Libby leaves the office with her head up, her back straight, and doesn't look back.

CHAPTER TWENTY-SIX

A year has passed since she caught Ted and Heather in flagrante and today their divorce is final at long last. Libby and Ginger are celebrating 'D' Day in style with a day at the spa and dinner at Al Forno in Providence, then... nothing. Because when you're almost forty-three years old, and the mother of three, doing nothing is the biggest luxury of all.

Ted has the children this weekend and Libby has to admit she loves having a couple of days to herself every other week. Her plan after dinner is to curl up on the couch with a good book and a cup of tea. Perfect.

Last summer, they sold the house in Littleton and she bought a bungalow on the East Side of Providence. Libby couldn't stand the idea of maintaining another huge home and took the opportunity to downsize.

"A cottage!" Ginger cried when she pulled up to inspect the house. "A cottage is always very snug," she smiled, quoting a line from *Sense and Sensibility*.

It's perfect for them, and not as small as it appears from the outside, with four bedrooms and two baths upstairs and a nice sized living room, dining room, eat-in-kitchen, half bath and a small den on the first floor. The yard is small, but lovely and private with an English garden, trees and shrubs.

"I can picture you here, Lib" Ginger said after the walk through. "I absolutely love it!"

So does she! Libby loves everything about her new surroundings. She loves the culture and diversity of the neighborhood, taking walks down Benefit Street and weaving through the little tree-lined side streets with beautifully restored colonial homes. She loves the bustle of Thayer Street, zigzagging between the Brown and RISD students crowding the sidewalks, and the quaint shops in Wayland Square and on Wickenden Street. She's finally found a place to call home.

The lawyer Ginger retained for her a year and a half earlier did his job admirably. Ted didn't fight her for custody of the children, but when it came to money, he was ready to draw blood.

Fortunately, the first phone call she made when she left Ted's office that night, was to Ginger, who had the lawyers freeze all of Ted's accounts the following morning. Instinctively, Libby knew Ted would try to screw her out of her fair share of their assets. When he attempted to move money around a few days later, he was caught red handed, and the judge came down hard on him.

Judge Reynolds, a recent divorcée herself, sat on her platform up high, listing the grievances against Ted for everyone in the courtroom to hear. Rhode Island is a no fault state, whether he had an affair or not was of no consequence, but the judge wanted to humiliate him for trying to keep money from his children, and Libby sat back and smiled. What can she say? She's human! She loved watching him squirm. She outsmarted Ted, got the right lawyer and lucked out with the right judge.

Her settlement is significant as are her child support payments and alimony. He also had to buy her out of the business and hand over half his 401K. It's going to take him some time to recover from that blow. She thought he was going to keel over and have a heart attack when he sat at that big boardroom table and heard the terms of their divorce read to him. And if he had dropped dead, she would have gotten a hefty life insurance payment (he had to keep that in her name too).

She doesn't wish him dead...herpes maybe, but no bodily harm. He's the father of her children, and she loved him once upon a time. They have to co-parent for many, many years to come, so she's trying to get along with him for everyone's sake.

As content as she is now, telling the children was as awful as she suspected it would be. Emma was particularly distraught, flinging herself into Ted's arms and crying, begging him not to go. It was heartbreaking. She had to excuse herself for a moment to regain her composure. Nate joined her in the dining room and wrapped his arms around her waist.

"Are you okay, Mommy?" he asked.

She knelt down and gathered him into her arms holding him tight.

"I'm going to be fine, Nate. We're all going to be fine, I promise."

And she believed her own words. And she was right.

She is fine. The kids are fine.

The children had grown very close to Ted in the time he made the effort to be a part of their lives. Thankfully, for their sake, that didn't end when he moved out. She's happy he's stayed close with the children. She'd never stand in the way of that, but she wasn't about to let him do it in her home. Ted moved into a spacious luxury apartment building in downtown Providence and is as active in their lives as he chooses to be.

Libby wants to be a positive role model for her daughter, for her sons too, but particularly for Emma. One day, her daughter will learn the truth about her father, and she'll see her mother was strong enough to leave and build her own life. She's leading by example. *If someone isn't treating you the way you deserve…walk away.* It's important Emma learns that now.

Ginger has been pressuring her to start dating, but Libby's not interested. After she left Ted's office that night, and hung up the phone with Ginger, she sat in her car for a few moments to collect her thoughts. She wasn't ready to go home. Sorting through the events of the past year in her head, she could think of only one place she wanted to be. One person she needed to see.

Truman.

She had to know if they had a chance, if he would allow her back into his life. She knew about Barbara, but as she drove toward Bayside, was hopeful it wasn't serious yet. Maybe he was subconsciously waiting out this year for her? It was a longshot, but possible.

Her heart was racing as she pulled into his driveway and before she could talk herself out of it, quickly approached the front door. The sun was setting and the lights in the dining room were on. Just as Libby was about to ring the bell, she heard the girls' voices coming from inside and peered into the window. What she saw knocked the wind right out of her. Truman and Barbara were standing near the sideboard, their arms around each other. As she watched, he threw his head back and laughed, then leaned into Barbara for a kiss. Wide-eyed, Libby stumbled a few steps back.

Then she saw them, the girls sitting around the table with Barbara's daughters, talking and smiling, eating their dinner. *They're a family*, she thought, her throat closing on her. *I've been replaced.* Watching the two families dining together and enjoying each others company was far more painful than the sight of Heather kneeling before her husband. She was too late. Truman wasn't subconsciously doing anything for her after all. He had moved on.

Libby made a choice the previous summer, the wrong choice clearly, but there was nothing she could do about it. She couldn't hit rewind and undo her mistake, as much as she wished that were possible. She lost her opportunity with Truman. Libby didn't listen to her heart or follow her instincts when it came to Truman, and as a result, lost her best friend and the possibility of a future with the man she loves.

Truman and the girls are still part of her life, but their arrangement hasn't changed significantly since she left Ted. Ginger hoped Libby and Truman would be able to resume their friendship, that the three of them would be together once again, but after a few awkward coffee shop gatherings, Libby stopped going. Last fall, she sat in the parking lot during a rain storm and decided she couldn't do it anymore. As long as he's dating Barbara, she has to limit their interactions for her own sanity. It's too painful.

He's been dating Barbara for quite some time and she can't interfere with his relationship, not after all she's put him through. His girlfriend lives a few streets away from her on the East Side and Libby bumps into them occasionally at the local Starbucks. The first time she saw them there, her heart sank as she stood in line and watched Truman and Barbara sitting at a table, talking, smiling, holding hands and looking into each other's eyes. *That should be me*, she thought, tears blinding her. But Barbara is a genuinely nice woman and Truman seems happy. That's all Libby wants for him, that's what he deserves.

She doesn't know what Truman's told Barbara about their relationship, though she suspects he's told her the truth. She can't imagine Truman keeping that a secret. They were a big part of each other's lives for a very long time. Their shared experiences have forged a bond between them that can never be broken...but it's better for everyone concerned if she keeps her distance.

♂

Are his expectations completely unrealistic? Truman's been dating Barbara for almost two years, and she's perfect for him in so many ways. She's kind and caring, sweet and generous, a great mother and wonderful with his girls. Their sex life is good...a solid seven. What's stopping him from taking the next, most logical step?

Barbara has been dropping hints about moving in together, and whenever she does, his stomach twists into knots. Is it fear? Is he hoping something within him will ignite and he'll wake up ready to take the leap? That's kind of what happened with Libby. One day, years after they became friends, he realized he felt more for her. Is that his modes operandi? He has to be with someone for years before he feels those pangs?

He's simply not ready to take their relationship to the next level. If he was, he'd know in his gut it was the right thing to do. His gut is ambivalent at best, staying disturbingly quiet when he needs to hear it roar.

Ginger has her own theory regarding his hesitance to move in with Barbara. Of course she does! He knew mentioning it to her would open up a whole new can of worms. They were having lunch the other day and she was chock full of opinions!

"I think you're full of shit, Truman. You're not in love with Babs. Face it. After two years you either shit or get off the pot! It's obvious what you're doing."

"Really? What's that? I'd love to know because I'm completely in the dark."

"Are you in the dark?" she asked, eyebrows raised. "Come on, Tru. Think about it. About a year ago, you mentioned the possibility of moving in with Barbara. Don't you remember?"

Did I? He remembers having a discussion with Ginger about where their relationship was going, but did he actually say those words?

"Then what happened? Almost exactly one year ago?" she paused, sitting back in her chair.

Truman remained silent. He knew where she was going with that one and considers it a miracle she managed to keep the words in for so long.

"I'll answer for you, since you are mute on the subject. A year ago, Libby left Ted."

"That had nothing to do with me, Ginger."

"No, it didn't. You are correct on that count. Ted and Lolita sealed the deal for her," she laughed. "Oh, for Christ's sake, Truman. Am I the only person who sees this? You're biding your time until Libby is ready to reenter the world of dating."

"Please," he scoffed, shaking his head. "Don't be ridiculous!"

When he found out Libby and Ted were getting divorced, he was happy for her. He knew Ted wouldn't remain faithful and was relieved Libby wasn't heartbroken. She broke free of Ted's web on her own and has built a life for herself and the children. A part of him was tempted, but he stayed away from Libby for two reasons. *One?* He didn't want to be the rebound man. *Two?* He wasn't going to blow what he had with Barbara for a possibility.

That's all it was, after all. A possibility. Libby loved him, he's sure of that. But he's a reminder of her past. The few times they went for coffee with Ginger last fall, it was painfully obvious how uncomfortable she was in his company. And that day in November…he stood in the rain waiting for her, but when she waved, he knew she was leaving and wouldn't be back.

Ginger sat in her chair by the water, tapping her fingers against the tabletop, waiting for him to continue.

"Has she said anything to you?" he asked, his voice soft, and Ginger smiled.

"Wouldn't you like to know," she teased him.

"Ginger, really. I'm not in the mood for games. Has Libby said anything about her feelings for me to you at any point over the past year?"

"Hmmm…she said she knew you wouldn't wait for her. And she's happy if you're happy."

What does that mean? he wondered. *Was she hoping I'd wait for her?*

"She's happy if I'm happy?" he repeated.

"Uh huh. You know what that means, don't you?"

He shook his head. He had no fucking clue!

"God! Men are totally oblivious!" Ginger sighed, rolling her eyes. "It means she'd be happier if you were with her."

"I'm sorry…what am I missing? She never said she wanted to be with me."

"She doesn't need to. It's implied. Why else would she stay away from you? She doesn't want to interfere with your relationship with Babs, just like you didn't want to interfere with her relationship with Ted. Because she loves you enough to stay away, just as you loved her enough to do the same."

"But I'm not married to Barbara…" his voice trailed off.

"Yet, Truman, you're not married to Babs yet. Keep traveling down this path and that's exactly where you'll end up."

"Would that be the worst thing in the world?" he asked, defensive on Barbara's behalf.

"You tell me?"

"When did you become a frigging shrink? You know what, Ginger? It's been two years since we said goodbye. I'm not the same person I was back then, and neither is Libby. And this isn't just about me anymore."

"Was it ever?" she cut him off. "It was always about you and the girls and Libby and her kids. Package deal, always."

"Sadie and Bette have grown close to Barbara and her girls," he continued. "Any decision I make affects my daughters. I don't want to hurt them."

"Do you honestly believe your girls would be upset if you ended up with Libby? That they'd grieve the loss of Barbara and her daughters? They might miss them a little bit, but they'd be thrilled, Truman, and you know they would. Sadie wants nothing more than for you and Libby to be together."

He sat back in his chair, looking out at the harbor. It's true. As much as she likes Barbara, Sadie's been urging him to ask Libby out since she filed for divorce.

"Tru, when you're a divorced parent and you begin dating someone exclusively, there's always the chance it's not going to work out. Does that mean you never introduce your children to that person? No. It means you carefully consider whether that person is worthy of their time. After that, it's a crapshoot. There's no guarantee you'll end up together, and the girls understand that. Are you seriously going to continue dating someone because you don't want your daughters to get hurt? I promise you, they'd be more upset seeing their father unhappy."

That's just it! He's not unhappy. He's not happy either. He has a lot to think about...

✳

Tonight is Barbara's birthday and they're going to her favorite restaurant to celebrate. He has spent the afternoon struggling with the selection of her gift. Jewelry is the obvious choice. Every time they walk by the jewelers in Wayland Square, she admires the diamond stud earrings in the window…and the engagement rings on display. He wants to buy her the earrings, but is afraid of sending the wrong message. Diamonds make a pretty strong statement in his opinion. They scream commitment.

The saleswoman has pointed out all sorts of gemstone earrings, but he keeps returning to the diamonds because he knows how much she loves them. Eventually he caves, but as the saleswoman places the earrings in a little black velvet box, his heart stops and he interrupts her. *I cannot hand Barbara a little black box!* She will automatically assume it's an engagement ring.

"Do you have anything bigger to put them in?" he asks, biting his lip.

The saleswoman shakes her head and frowns.

"The next size up is way too big for earrings," she explains.

"How about another color?" he persists. "Something less…black?"

"Ah," she smiles. "You want an un-engagement-like box?"

"Precisely," he exhales.

"I've got green or red. Christmas colors. Red says 'passion,' green…'friendship'."

Truman raises an eyebrow as he deliberates his choices.

"I'll take the green, please," he murmurs.

✳

The restaurant is very crowded and despite having reservations, their table isn't ready when they arrive. That's not unusual here, but the food is delicious and well worth the wait. Truman and Barbara make their way through the crowded bar area and order a cocktail, waiting to be called. Barbara looks beautiful tonight. She had her normally wavy hair blown out at the salon this afternoon, and is wearing her favorite red sheath dress. It's a night for celebration and her cheeks are flushed with excitement. The little green box is burning a hole in his coat pocket. He's not sure he made the right choice. Maybe he should have bought the ruby earrings? They would look perfect with her dress...

"Isn't that your friend Libby over there?" Barbara asks, pointing across the bar.

Surprised, he follows the direction of her finger and spots Libby seated at the far end of the bar...and she's not alone. *Who is the man she's with?* He watches their interaction and frowns. Whoever he is, she seems very comfortable with him. Her hand is on his arm and she leans in to listen, then smiles into his eyes. Ginger never said Libby's dating someone!

"Yes, it is," he replies and takes a sip of his drink.

"Why don't we ask them over?" Barbara says.

"No, this is your night," he insists, shaking his head. "Another time."

Just then, Libby makes eye contact with them and Barbara waves.

"One drink," she replies, waving Libby and her date over. "Come on. It'll be fun."

"Okay..." he says, forcing a smile.

He does not want to have a drink with Libby and her date, but it's too late. They're already making their way through the crowd toward them. His conversation with Ginger the other day was confusing and he's tried to put it out of his head. She has no evidence. What Ginger said boils down to speculation. That hasn't stopped his subconscious from taking over and Libby usurping his dreams once again. He thought that phase had passed, but he was wrong. His nighttime fantasies are exceptionally vivid and when he opens his eyes in the morning, it's jarring to find Barbara beside him instead.

"Hello!" Barbara greets them and kisses Libby on the cheek. "What a surprise! It's so great to see you."

"Yes," Libby smiles. "It's nice to see you both. Truman, Barbara, this is my friend and super-agent Max."

They shake hands and Truman sighs with relief. *Her agent! This must be a business dinner.*

"It's my birthday," Barbara smiles. "The big four-five!"

"Happy birthday!" Libby exclaims.

"You don't look a day over thirty-five!" Max says.

"Oh, I like him, Libby!" Barbara laughs and wraps her arm through Truman's, pressing against him. This is normally when his arm would wind around her back, but he looks at Libby and hesitates. This is so awkward!

"Why don't you join us?" Barbara suggests.

Libby's eyes grow wide and her lips part, but before she can say a word, Max chimes in.

"That would be fabulous! Let me tell the hostess," he says, and takes off before anyone can stop him.

This occasion calls for alcohol, he decided about five minutes after Libby and Max joined them. Just enough to take off the edge. Thankfully, Max and Barbara hit it off and have been chatting without much help from either he or Libby. The first layer of awkwardness wore off for Truman when he realized Max is gay. The man has unabashedly flirted with him all night long and while most straight men would be uncomfortable with this attention, Truman finds it amusing. So does Barbara.

The final layer is lifted by the time he finishes his third drink. He has a slight buzz on and while Max is entertaining Barbara, he and Libby have been catching up on the children and before he knows it, they're reminiscing about old times. They've steered clear of the painful memories, but it feels so good to talk with her again, to discuss their shared history without sadness or regret. It's a relief to him. Maybe they can be real friends again one day? This evening has given him hope.

The waiter carries out a small chocolate cake with a dozen candles ablaze, and the restaurant employees and patrons break into song, wishing Barbara a happy birthday. She looks so happy as she blows out the candles and makes a wish, then leans in for a kiss.

"Happy birthday, Barbara," he whispers.

♀

If she could crawl under the table and die right now, she would. This evening has been torture! The calm, relaxing effect of her spa day with Ginger was replaced with massive anxiety the moment she laid eyes on Barbara and Truman across the bar. *It's 'D Day' for Christ's sake!* This is her moment, not Barbara's! Libby was supposed to be celebrating with Ginger, but Alex had a fever and Max stepped in at the last second, and thank God he's here to keep the jokes and conversation rolling!

Libby's been drinking steadily since they sat down and during appetizers she reached a state of moderate inebriation, just enough to help her relax and forget Barbara's presence. Once she and Truman started their journey down memory lane, it was just the two of them at the table, the energy and attraction between them undeniable. Then, just as Truman rested his hand on hers, the cake arrived, jolting her back to reality.

It takes Libby a moment to get her bearings, to remember exactly where she is and who else is present. Everyone is singing and as Barbara blows out her birthday candles, Truman leans in to kiss his girlfriend. *His girlfriend!* Libby closes her eyes, digging her fingers into Max's thigh. This is unbearable! Is Truman trying to punish her? Watching them so affectionate with one another…it's too much.

She downs what's left of her third glass of wine and decides it's time to switch to vodka. Dulling the pain isn't enough at this point. She wants to be completely numb!

Max scowls and slaps her hand away.

"What is wrong with you?" he whispers, taking in her stricken expression. "Are you going to be sick?"

That's a real possibility! She turns to him with tears in her eyes.

"Oh Mother Mary!" Max whispers in her ear. "I didn't realize. He's the one!"

"Shhh!" she warns him, swatting his leg. "I need vodka."

"Immediately," he reassures her and flags down their waiter. "Two double vodka gimlets on the rocks, please. And there's a big tip if you bring it ASAP!"

Libby takes a big gulp of her double gimlet and sighs. This is exactly what she needed. She can feel the alcohol absorbing into her bloodstream, soothing out her frayed nerves. One more gulp and she'll be all set for the evening.

Max keeps Barbara busy so Libby can spend time with Truman…at least she thinks that is what's happening. She is having trouble focusing on anything at this point. The vodka has taken control of her senses and she surrenders to it.

"Lib, do you remember that night in my backyard…" Truman whispers.

"Tru, you gotta be more specific. We've spent hundreds of nights in your backyard."

"We were in front of the fire pit…" his eyes meet hers.

"You know it's final today," she whispers.

"What is?" he asks.

"My divorce. I'm legally free from Ted."

Truman leans in and takes her hand again.

"I'm so happy for you, Lib. Congratulations."

They stare into each other's eyes and she wants to kiss him so badly. She's made such a mess of things. This is why she stays away from him! It hurts too much to know she turned him away.

"I made a mistake, Tru," she whispers, then rests her head in her hands. Her eyelids feel heavy and the room begins to spin.

"One mistake. Sixteen years of mistakes," she murmurs. "I miss you Tru."

"Are you okay, Lib?" Max asks.

"Yup, Fine," she whispers and closes her eyes.

"Libby…" Truman's voice sounds far away. "Libby…"

♂

Well, that was one for the books! The whole night was unreal. How could he have been so inconsiderate to Barbara? It was her birthday and he spent the majority of the evening with Libby. Not just talking to her, he was with her in mind and spirit. Was it the alcohol or his true feelings surfacing? He was so engrossed in their conversation, he's ashamed to admit this…he forgot Barbara was there. Not for just a moment, for minutes at a time. What kind of person is he? He held hands with Libby in front of his girlfriend! If the alcohol hadn't gotten the better of Libby when it did, he would have kissed her. *He wanted to kiss her.*

Truman dropped Barbara off fifteen minutes ago and she's distraught. She didn't realize he was involved with Libby once upon a time. He never told her about their brief romance, didn't see the point. When they left the restaurant, she was confused and upset, asking him questions about their relationship. She believed they were just old friends who used to live next door to one another and couldn't understand why he kept this information from her.

The truth is, he didn't share it sooner because he wanted to leave it in the past, but he was left with no choice when they left the restaurant. He had to tell Barbara what happened between them on the drive home and she was crying by the time they reached her house.

"You still love her, don't you?" Barbara asked through her tears.

"Barb...come on," he said, avoiding her question.

"Just admit it Truman! We've been together for almost two years and I've never seen you look at me the way you looked at her!" she cried.

He didn't know how to respond to that, so he didn't.

"Tell me you love me, Tru," she whispered, lowering herself down into an armchair.

"Barbara..." he kneeled in front of her, his hands on her knees. "Of course I love you."

"Then let's move in together. If you love me, what's stopping you?"

He shook his head and sighed. How could he say the words? They sound so cruel in his own head. *I love you, but I'm not in love with you.*

"I'm just not ready," he finally said.

She stared at him, eyes wide.

"I want to be alone tonight," she said, rising. "Really, Tru. Please go."

With a heavy heart, he placed the little green box on the kitchen table and left her crying, alone and rejected on her birthday.

Now he's sitting in front of Libby's house, wondering what the fuck he's doing. He's worried about Libby. He's also furious with her. She made a mistake? *Damned right she did!* And it's too late to undo it!

Then what am I doing sitting in front of her house at midnight?

Max drove Libby home after they forced her to drink a few glasses of water. She was far from sober when they left, and she shouldn't be alone. He foresees a long night of vomiting ahead of her.

While he's sitting in his car, conflicted, Max walks out of Libby's and heads straight for him.

"Hey, handsome. I saw you from the window."

"How is she?" Truman asks.

"A mess, my friend. An absolute mess. I've never seen her like this before."

Truman shakes his head and sighs. He has. He's seen Libby at her absolute worst.

"Why don't you head out Max? I'll take care of her. It won't be the first time."

"Aren't you a doll," Max says. "You know, Tru. You two make a lovely couple."

"I'm not sure we're still a couple. Barbara is pretty upset right now."

"Oh, honey. I wasn't talking about Barbara," Max laughs and winks, then pats Truman's arm. "Good lord, you're gorgeous! Take good care of our girl."

CHAPTER TWENTY-SEVEN

I *can't believe she's making me do this*...Libby lies across her bed, scowling. Ginger is rummaging through her closet, trying to find 'the perfect dress' for Libby's big date this evening. For the past week, Ginger has been gushing about this guy she met, claiming he's just perfect for Libby. He's tall, he's handsome, he's sweet. He's so wonderful...why isn't Ginger going out with him? Which is exactly what she said the first time Ginger brought him up.

"Oh, I would, Libby, trust me. If I weren't dating Simon, I'd be all over him. Like white on rice! Remember what I told you about the dating scene at our age? The good ones are snatched up and what's left are the creeps, weirdoes and homely men. Look what happened to your old neighbors! And mine! Their lives will never be the same."

A few months back, Littleton was rocked by scandal when someone hacked into the database of Ashley Madison, a website for married people looking to cheat on their spouses. Four thousand men from Littleton were registered users, most of them concentrated in Libby and Ginger's neighborhoods. On Garland Drive alone, six marriages were affected.

Half of those women filed for divorce, her book club friends, Greta and Sarah included. Of the six core club members, only Anabelle's marriage is standing. The other unsuspecting victims? They're trying to hold their marriages together, but their painstakingly crafted images are shattered. There's nothing to hide behind now, the truth is out there for the entire world to see. She feels for them and wishes them luck piecing their lives back together. It's not easy.

Out of a morbid sense of curiosity, Libby perused the list and was relieved Ted and Truman weren't on it. At least Ted didn't stoop that low! Then again, he never had to seek out women. Women always gravitated to him, and still do. He didn't waste any time returning to the dating scene once he understood it was truly over between them. Ted doesn't dip his toe into anything, he dives in headfirst. As long as he keeps the women away from her children she doesn't care who he's sleeping with. He is free to do as he pleases.

Life in Littleton will never be the same and Libby is glad she escaped before the earthquake struck. She wouldn't have been able to tolerate the drama and intrigue, to bear witness to the destruction of so many lives. She had uncovered some of their secrets when she scoured through social media after George was born and wasn't surprised by many of the names on the list.

Now, the women of Littleton are bound by something so much worse than Lilly Pulitzer and country club memberships. The vast majority have Ashley Madison in common, too. That's a club they'd rather not belong to.

"Snatch him, Libby!" Ginger persisted. "Before one of the scores of other single divorcées sink their teeth into him. It's dog eat dog, my dear! I've told him all about you and he's very interested. Come on, for me? Just one date? I'll call you an hour in and if it's awful you can say there's an emergency and you need to leave."

After three days of badgering, Libby agreed to go on the blind date. One hour. *What's one hour?* She gave Ted sixteen years of her life. She can give this guy sixty minutes.

"Fine, I'll meet him at the bar at Café Nuovo, Friday at seven."

"You won't regret it sweetie! I have a feeling about you two!"

Maybe Ginger's right? Maybe it's time for her to get out there and move on? She's still reeling with embarrassment over her drunken behavior two weeks ago at dinner, and humiliation over what happened early the following morning. *Divorce decrees, alcohol, and repressed feelings of love should never mix!*

Truman stayed with her that night and did what he's always done, take care of her. He held her hair away from her face as she vomited, rubbed her back and helped her to bed. There, he made her take a couple of Tylenol and drink more water.

When she woke up, Truman was lying beside her in bed, on top of the covers and fully dressed. For a moment she thought she was dreaming, and touched his face to see if he was real. Truman shifted toward her, still sleeping and she took his hand, clasping it gently in hers, afraid to wake him. She watched him sleep for close to an hour and when he woke, he smiled into her eyes for a moment, before confusion settled in. Then, he sat up and ran his fingers through his hair.

"How are you feeling?" he asked, turning to her warily.

"I'm okay," she whispered. "I'm sorry for ruining Barbara's birthday."

"Yeah, so am I," he sighed. "Look, Libby…"

"Don't," she interrupted him. "I was drunk last night. I understand you're in a relationship and I was inappropriate."

"Did you mean it?" he asked.

She struggled to remember exactly what she said before she virtually passed out at the table. *Did I tell him I love him? I miss him? I regret turning him away?* It was definitely something along those lines, in which case it was true. She nodded her head and Truman closed his eyes.

"You can't do this to me, Libby," he muttered. "Too much has happened."

Her eyes filled with tears and she nodded.

"I understand."

"Do you?" he asked. "Do you have any idea what it was like for me? What we had was so special, Libby, and you threw it away. Now I'm with a woman who loves me and wants to live with me. Barbara wants to spend her life with me," he paused. "And now you tell me you made a mistake and miss me? What am I supposed to do with that information? What do you want from me?"

Her heart stopped beating in her chest and tears slid down her cheeks. What is he saying? He's moving in with Barbara? He's going to marry her? *No! Please, God! Don't let that happen.*

"Truman. I want you to be happy, that's all. I wish I could turn back the clock and change what happened, you have no idea how much."

When he turned to her a few minutes later, his eyes were so sad. Truman wiped away her tears, his hand lingering on her cheek, and for a moment she thought he was going to kiss her.

"I can't do this…" his murmured, then turned abruptly and got off the bed. "I've got to go. I'm sorry Libby."

❋

It's the night before the Fourth of July and she didn't realize there was a special lighting on the river tonight. Waterfire is a fire sculpture installation in downtown Providence. Wood stacks crackle and burn in elevated pits above the river, reflecting on the water below. Gondolas filled with couples drift along the river and the most eclectic mix of mystical, romantic and eerie music resounds through hidden speakers, echoing off the buildings and filling the city streets.

The restaurant she picked is right on the river, smack dab in the middle of all the action. The streets are incredibly crowded, but it can be a beautiful experience when you're with someone special. She hopes this guy doesn't think she picked this restaurant because of Waterfire! It's obnoxiously romantic!

Because of the traffic she's running a few minutes late. She could've walked, but she spent the half hour she would have been on foot, vacillating. *Do I stay or do I go?* In the end she thought it was wrong to stand the guy up…so here she is, pulling into valet parking, and wondering yet again, *Why did I agree to do this?*

She hasn't been on a date in over sixteen years! How will she know who this TJ is? Ginger said she showed him a picture and he'll find her.

When she enters the restaurant, Libby ducks into the ladies' room and checks her hair and makeup, patting her face with a paper towel to remove the little beads of sweat that have appeared. She's not sure if it's nervousness or the heat causing her to perspire. Maybe both? Except for the excess perspiration, she looks fine. Better than fine.

After much deliberation, she and Ginger decided on a sleeveless, navy blue dress that shows just a hint of cleavage, is fitted through the bodice and flares slightly at the waist. Her hair is pulled back away from her face and secured with a clip. The only jewelry she's wearing are her diamond stud earrings, and a cut crystal bracelet. Simple, yet elegant.

Whatever! She just wants to get this blind date over with so she can go home and relax.

Within moments of taking a seat at the bar, she feels a hand on her shoulder. Libby takes a deep breath and closes her eyes, then turns to find Truman seated beside her.

"Truman," she says, swallowing hard.

If Truman's here, Barbara can't be far behind. She's mortified. She owes Barbara an apology, but doesn't think she'll be able to look her in the eye.

"How are you?" she asks, her voice strained.

"I'm fine, Libby," Truman smiles and kisses her cheek. "I saw you come in and thought I'd say hello. It's good to see you."

Really? She would have thought he'd feel just the opposite. Maybe he's just being polite?

"I wasn't sure you'd want to see me at all. Where's Barbara? It was a nightmare driving here from the East Side because of Waterfire," she rambles, nervously.

"I'm alone," he says. "What are you doing here?"

"Honestly? I have no idea," she mutters, looking around the bar.

"Are you meeting someone?" he asks.

"Yes...no...I don't know..." her voice trails off.

What should she tell him? After a moments deliberation, she decides to tell him the truth.

"Truman, Ginger set me up on a blind date and I don't want to go through with it. I know this is a lot to ask, but could you stay with me for a little bit? He's looking for a single woman. If he sees me with you, he may leave."

"Sure, I'll stay with you. What are you drinking?"

"I honestly don't care," she sighs with relief.

He smiles and calls the bartender over.

"The lady will have a vodka gimlet on the rocks and I'll have a Manhattan," Truman says. "Are you hungry? Do you want to get a table?"

"Okay," she says.

Why is he being so nice to me? The last time she saw him, he was so upset with her but you'd never know it by his behavior tonight. They take their drinks to the table Truman had reserved by the windows overlooking the basin. Settling into her chair, she looks out at the fires burning along the river, takes a deep breath in and sighs. It really is a spectacular sight.

"So, what are you doing here alone?" she asks.

"Well…" Truman pauses, leaning in toward her. "Barbara and I decided to go our separate ways."

Her heart skips a beat and her lips part.

"You broke up?" she asks, her heart racing.

"Yes, Libby…we did. She's a wonderful person, but something was missing."

She's positively giddy with relief and looks down into her drink to mask her smile. He's not marrying Barbara! They are not moving in together! Over the past two weeks, she convinced herself he was lost to her forever. That's the only reason she agreed to go on this blind date. What does this mean for them now? *He's single. I'm single. At last!*

"What was missing?" she asks, feeling the flush of excitement rise to her cheeks.

Truman takes her hand in his and looks into her eyes.

"You, Libby."

Her eyes fill with tears.

"Me?" she whispers.

Truman nods his head then guides her to her feet. Libby's floating on air as Truman wraps his arms around her, holding her close, and brushes his lips against hers. A delicious tingling spreads throughout her body and she eagerly returns his kiss. She must be dreaming. For two years she's yearned for his touch, longed to feel his lips against hers, and now he's here.

When they come up for air, his eyes are burning with love and desire…for her.

"You, Libby. It's always been you," he whispers.

"I love you, Truman," she says with a sigh.

His face breaks into a radiant smile and he holds her tight.

"I love you, Libby," he murmurs into her hair.

She takes a deep breath in.

"Wait a second," she looks up at him. "You're TJ. Truman Jacob Whitaker. Ginger set me up on a blind date with you?"

Truman throws his head back and laughs.

Two Years Later...

"I come here with no expectations, only to profess,
now that I am at liberty to do so, that my heart is
and always will be yours."
~Jane Austen

EPILOGUE

Today is the big day. Truman closes his eyes and leans back against his chair, enjoying this moment of peace and quiet after his late morning run on the beach. The roar of the waves crashing to shore calms his slightly frayed nerves. They've been on Nantucket for a few days with all five kids, enough to frazzle anyone's nerves.

He can't believe how quickly time has flown by, how big they're all getting. It's rare to have all of the children together now, they're so busy with their own lives, doing things teenagers do. So far, they've all managed to stay out of trouble, though Emma, with her fixation on the opposite sex, has given them a few grey hairs. Sadie is graduating high school next month and attending the Rhode Island School of Design in the fall. Bette and Emma are freshmen in high school, and Nate's in fourth grade. Even George will be starting all-day pre-school!

Everyone is inside getting ready for the ceremony, but he's not ready to leave the calm of the beach and re-enter the whirlwind of activity just yet.

"Hey you," Libby says, standing over him with her camera in hand. He smiles and she snaps a few shots, then lowers herself onto the blanket they set down earlier for breakfast.

"I thought you'd be getting ready by now," he says, watching her lie back and close her eyes.

"The kids have taken over the bathrooms," she sighs. "We have plenty of time."

He raises an eyebrow, checking his watch.

"Lib, we have an hour before the ceremony. Maximum."

"Plenty of time," she opens one eye and motions for him to join her.

He lowers himself onto the blanket beside her and she turns to him, resting her head against his chest.

"I'm all sweaty, sweetheart," he whispers, kissing the top of her head.

Libby props herself up and looks him up and down, smiling, a glimmer in her eye.

"I like when you're all sweaty," she murmurs climbing on top of him. She leans forward and brushes the hair away from his damp brow and kisses him, gently at first, the intensity building quickly. Truman sits up and pulls her close, her legs wrapping around him and he loses himself in their kiss, forgetting where they are. He reaches beneath her shirt, his palm cupping her bare breast.

"I want you right now," she whispers in his ear.

Those words are music to his ears. He smiles, raising an eyebrow.

"The guest house is occupied and there's absolutely no privacy in the main house..." she says, surveying their surroundings. "How about the loft above the garage?"

She smiles a mischievous grin, and rises, impatiently pulling him to his feet and grabbing the blanket. It wouldn't be the first time they've used the loft for these purposes.

Together, they run to the detached garage and climb the ladder to the loft, hastily removing their clothes. She pulls him down onto the sandy blanket and he closes his eyes, feeling her soft skin pressed against the length of his body. Truman traces a path with his lips from her stomach to her mouth and looks into her crystal blue eyes, spilling with desire for him. Libby wraps her legs around him guiding him deeper and deeper inside of her, and he groans with pleasure. He moves slowly, his hands clasping hers, until he feels her tightening around him, her back arching in anticipation, their bodies trembling as they lose themselves in a moment of pure bliss.

It's been almost two years since their 'blind date' and he's never regretted his decision to take a chance on love. Before he left Libby's house the morning after Barbara's birthday dinner fiasco, Truman wanted to kiss away her tears, lose himself in her touch, but he stopped himself. It wouldn't have been right. Closing Libby's door behind him, he was confused for about thirty seconds, then he knew without a doubt what he had to do. He had to end his relationship with Barbara.

It was a risk and he hasn't taken too many of those in his life. He was sure of Barbara's feelings for him, knew he could have a pleasant future with her, and she'd never break his heart. But he wanted love in his life, he wanted to feel the surge of passion and intensity he felt with Libby again. As much as he wanted it to be there with Barbara, it wasn't. Knowing how Libby felt about him, that she still loved him, there was no denying his own feelings for her.

The night Libby walked into the bar in her blue dress, he knew he'd made the right decision. When he kissed her, he saw his feelings mirrored in her eyes, the love and longing. *She's ready for me*, he thought. *She's ready for us.*

They've never looked back.

Their relationship has only gotten stronger and better with time. The first year, they lived apart, but when they decided to get married, they bought a house together on the East Side, and merged the two households at last. It's chaos having five children living under one roof, but happy chaos. Every day, he thanks the powers that be for bringing Libby into his life, and for the happy family unit they have created. It's a house filled with love. What more could he ask for?

He and Libby are the closest of friends, true partners in life, and passionately in love with one another. Maybe that passion will fade in time, but as with everything else in life, it takes commitment and effort to keep the flame burning. They're fully committed to one another, and they're fully committed to their family. He has no doubt in his mind about their level of devotion to one another.

Loving someone completely, caring about their needs, respecting what's important to them…those are some of the key ingredients to a lasting relationship. With Libby, those ingredients were in place long before they became physically involved. It's what binds them to one another and sustains them through trying times.

"Mom!"

"Dad?"

The kids are calling for them outside the house and it won't be long before they're discovered. Truman collapses against Libby and sighs as the children's voices grow louder, inching closer to the garage.

"Thank God we're staying at a B&B tonight," he murmurs into her neck.

"Amen to that," she groans, and sits up, pulling on her shirt.

"Oh shit!" he cries, looking at his watch. "Libby, we're getting married in twenty minutes!"

"Oh my God!" she jumps up, pulling on her skirt.

The wedding is small, just twenty-five guests, including the children, Ginger and Alex, Julia and Will, Ellie and her husband, Max and his boyfriend, Truman's parents, and his sister, Gwen, and her family. Libby's brother and his family flew to the island yesterday. She's been in frequent touch with Charlie over the past two years. It means a lot to her that they've become close again, and has added another dimension to her life, one that brings her joy.

Ginger promised she'd throw them a wedding if they ended up tying the knot, and she was true to her word. They are getting married at her house on Nantucket, on the bluffs overlooking the Atlantic Ocean. It's early May, so the summer crowds haven't yet arrived, but the weather is perfect today. They didn't want anything fancy; a justice of the peace for a simple ceremony, their families and close friends, and afterwards a delicious meal. And that's exactly what Ginger has arranged for them, along with a string quartet, more flowers than he's ever seen in one place, and a two-week all expense paid honeymoon in Italy.

Truman pulls Libby into his arms for a slow, lingering kiss.

"I'll see you at the altar," he whispers.

♀

Wearing a simple ivory dress, Libby looks into the mirror and runs her hands through her semi-damp hair. *This will have to do*, she thinks, pulling her hair away from her face and twisting it into a knot, securing it with a few hairpins. They're running about thirty minutes behind schedule...*but it was so worth it*, she smiles, her cheeks turning pink.

Today she is marrying her best friend. Their hearts are already joined, their lives forever entwined. This ceremony is merely a formality. She didn't care if they ever made their relationship legally binding, she wasn't going anywhere. But when Truman asked her to marry him she knew in her heart she wanted to pledge her life to him...to their family. She wants to say the words out loud, to make a vow to stand by him in good times and bad...always.

As she stands on the porch overlooking the ocean, Truman waits for her down the aisle, surrounded by their five children. Never in her wildest dreams did she imagine she'd be the mother of five! When Ted said he wanted as many children all those years ago, she could think of nothing worse. She was wrong. Being a mother to these five children and raising them with Truman by her side brings her such happiness, along with heartache, irritation, and fatigue, but she can't imagine her life without them.

Stepping onto the grass, George runs to her and everyone laughs as he tugs at her free hand, the other clasped around a simple bouquet of daisies.

"C'mon, Mama! Pop is waiting," he shouts, jumping up and down.

"I'm coming sweetie. Can you go wait with Pop?"

He nods his head and runs back down the aisle, and Truman lifts him into his arms for a squeeze, then hands him to Ginger.

"Are you ready, Lib?" her brother Charlie asks.

"I'm definitely ready," she smiles.

They walk the few yards to where Truman is waiting, so handsome in his beige suit and light blue shirt, his warm hazel eyes overflowing with love as he watches her walk toward him with her brother by her side. Libby hands her flowers to Sadie, kisses her daughter's cheek, then turns to the man she loves and takes his hands in hers.

In her life, she's experienced the depths of darkness and pulled herself into the light to find a brighter future than she imagined possible. She used to believe two halves made a whole, but she learned no other person could make her whole, she had to do that on her own. She's worked hard to put the pieces together and create a fulfilling life. It hasn't always been easy, but she's stayed true to herself and is fortunate to have met a man who loves her just as she is. Truman is the icing on the cake.

She is a mother, an artist, a friend, a sister, and in a few moments, she will become a wife again. Libby smiles into Truman's eyes, her heart bursting with joy. Today she's pledging her undying love and devotion to her dearest friend, promising to stand by him for better or worse, in sickness and in health, all the days of her life.

Their family and friends applaud as Libby and Truman seal their vows with a kiss, and the children encircle them, sharing in their parents' happiness. Wrapped in the warmth of her family's love, she smiles up at her husband and Truman shakes his head, tears in his eyes.

"What more could we ask for?" he whispers in her ear.

"Absolutely nothing," she smiles.

She's almost forty-five years old. This is her second act.

And it's so much better than the first.

ABOUT THE AUTHOR

As it Seems is Jayne Conway's second novel. Her first book, *What if I Fly?,* was published in June, 2015. Jayne is a graduate student of life and resides in Rhode Island with her three beautiful children. She's currently writing her third novel.